5—

The History of My Body

The Fleur Trilogy, Book 1

by

Sharon Heath

D0043718

The History of My Body
The Fleur Trilogy, Book 1

Copyright © 2016 Sharon Heath

All rights reserved. No part of this book may be reproduced or transmitted in any form or by any means without written permission from the publisher, with the exception of brief quotations in a review.

This book is a work of fiction. While some of the place names may be real, characters and incidents are the product of the author's imagination and are used fictitiously. Any resemblance to events or persons living or dead is purely coincidental.

The author gratefully acknowledges permission to reprint excerpts from:

"Anthem" Words and Music by Leonard Cohen. ©1992 Stranger Copyright © 1992 Sony/ATV Music Publishing LLC and Stranger Music Inc. All Rights Administered by Sony/ATV Music Publishing LLC, 424 Church Street, Suite 1200, Nashville, TN 32719. International Copyright Secured. All Rights Reserved. Reprinted by Permission of Hal Leonard LLC.

"When the Red, Red, Robin (Comes Bob, Bob Bobbin' Along)" by Harry Woods. Copyright © 1926 by Bourne Co. (Copyright Renewed). Rights for extended renewal term in USA controlled by Songwriters Guild of America on behalf of Callicoon Music. All rights outside the USA controlled by Bourne Co. All rights reserved. International copyright secured.

Harold Pinter's Nobel Lecture. © The Nobel Foundation 2005.

Author photograph by Marcella Kerwin.

Library of Congress Control Number: 2016961931
1. Contemporary fiction   2. Literary fiction   3. Coming of age
ISBN 10: 0-9979517-0-2
ISBN-13: 978-0-9979517-0-7

Second printing December 2016 by Thomas-Jacob Publishing, LLC

Thomas-Jacob Publishing, LLC, Deltona, Florida USA

Contact the publisher at TJPub@thomas-jacobpublishing.com.

"Ring the bells that still can ring
Forget your perfect offering
There is a crack, a crack in everything
That's how the light gets in."

Leonard Cohen, *Anthem*

The History of My Body

The Fleur Trilogy, Book 1

by

Sharon Heath

Chapter 1

THE BIBLE SAYS that in the beginning was the void, and it hasn't escaped me how fast the Lord moved to take care of His own particular vacuum—dividing day from night, spitting out vast oceans, carving out competing continents that could one day have the power to blow each other up. What an inspired series of creations to keep the devil of boredom at bay. No wonder God kept seeing that it *was* good.

Maybe it all would have happened differently if the bird on the front lawn hadn't given me my idea about my grandfather's balls. Or maybe not. You never know in this life; there are too many variables. In ancient times they might have called it Fate, more recently the Butterfly Effect, but I like to think of it as the human race's chronic aversion to boredom. I figure any species lacking fangs and claws had a powerful incentive to evolve an active sort of mind.

I suppose I'm not the only one who likes to hear about her own beginnings. Luckily for me, Nana loves to reminisce about the period in her life that coincides with my first eleven years, when we all lived together on what *Time Magazine* once described as "Senator Robins' conspicuously spacious Tudor estate in the Main Line suburb of Gladwyne." While the rest of us spent virtually all our time on that property, Father often spared us his presence, commuting to an apartment in D.C., where, as he liked to put it, he served as the only senator from Pennsylvania defending the sanctity of human life.

I had my hands full defending my own. Looking back from the perspective of my fifteen years, I have to appreciate my infant ingenuity in keeping me just this side of the lurking pit of nothingness. Nana says I made more of a racket than all the saved babies combined, directing frantic tom-toms at my mother, who'd cry back at me from the foot of my crib, a drowning woman clutching her wine glass like a life raft. The crib still exists. I saw it a few years ago, its slats bearing the imprints I made with my bullet-shaped head.

I saw Mother defend me against Father only three times in my life. The first was on my tenth Easter. I remember because I was wearing the dreamy pale blue dress and matching strappy shoes Nana had bought me for just that occasion. Having talked Cook out of one of her yummy lemon squares after returning from church, I was humming and chewing my way toward the den until I realized Mother and Father had gotten there first. Father had already begun one of his rants against the devil abortionists. This time he added an extra twist. "Who knows," he taunted Mother, "how much you wanting to get rid of her made our only child autistic?"

Usually, when Father got mean, Mother ran up to her room, but this time she stood her ground, though her voice quivered noticeably. "That's not what Dr. Sand said!"

Father made a sound that was more like a bark than a laugh. "Oh, what's the difference? Doesn't matter a hell of a lot when everyone can see she's a freak. Spinning like a maniac her first day of Sunday school just because some kid made a dumb crack about the crucifix. Kids are like animals. They know. No wonder none of them would go near her after that."

"Don't!" Mother stepped back as if she'd been hit. "That's not fair! It was an awful thing for that boy to say. Dr. Sand isn't convinced she's even on the spectrum. You can't shove her into some category just because you don't know what to do with her." I watched her face turn a particular shade of pig-pink. "Besides," she added breathlessly, "if someone's getting punished, maybe it's the senator who had to marry the child he took out for a burger and a good screw after a pro-life rally."

Transfixed, I watched spit fly out of Father's mouth as he shouted, "Child? Hardly! But you're right about one thing. You may stink as a wife, but you were a hell of a good screw. As for the kid, maybe you're right about that, too. Maybe she's just a born space cadet. Or maybe it all comes down to maternal neglect. Maybe if you hadn't been at the bottle all these years, she'd be cured by now."

2

Just then, Sister Flatulencia had rushed into the room and was steering me out of it and down the stairs toward the kitchen, one hand on my shoulder and the other frantically fingering her rosary beads. I had barely been able to follow my parents' argument—I had never heard the name *Autistic* before, and the part about screws was more than a little confusing—but I always felt sorry for Mother when Father blamed her for not wanting to have me. Why *would* she have wanted a child like me, who was always driving people away with her words and her whirling and flapping?

When Sister Flatulencia and I entered the kitchen, it was apparent we'd walked in on the beginning of a game of Hearts, the three-handed variety they occasionally had to resort to when they couldn't scramble up a fourth. Nana and Fayga and Cook each held a clumsy spread of seventeen cards, and a one-card kitty interrupted the pattern of the washable Stars and Stripes tablecloth covering the small kitchen table.

Sister Flatulencia answered their upturned questioning faces with a curt, "They're at it again," but that didn't stop me from loosening myself from her grip and approaching Nana, asking, "What's *autistic* mean?"

Nana snorted and replied with a dismissive, "Shhh, don't be silly," cuffing me on the ear with her handful of cards more forcefully than she probably intended. That was the odd thing about Nana. For a nanny with an addiction to a game called Hearts, she had all the gentleness of a Mack truck. Just like the angel in the Bible who wrestled with Jacob and made his thigh go out of joint before blessing him, one minute she was treating me like a side of beef, the next she'd be showering me with little chicken-peck kisses that sent waves of pleasurable goose bumps over my oddly shaped head.

As Nana's eyes veered back to her hand, Fayga chipped in with a nasal, "I can't believe he actually said that in front of the child," her wriggling worm of an upper lip stretched tight and wide, like it was getting fried to a crisp by the sun. I'd often reflected that it was too bad about her face, which was so nondescript that it looked dangerously like a void punctuated by the teensiest salvation of a wormy lip.

Cook chimed in predictably, "I can't believe it either," looking around the table as if she'd actually contributed something. Cook was a weakling when it came to having her own opinions. When Fayga was mean, Cook thought she had to be, too, which made me worry that perhaps Cook wasn't real at all, just a little trick of the void to personify itself. Sometimes I had to remind myself that Cook was really one of my angels, the only one in our house who could bake angel food cake, which is my favorite food. Luckily for me, she'd baked a nice round loaf the night before, so when she set down her cards and pushed up from the table, her round body sailing past me toward one of the long kitchen counters, I held my breath, and not just because I'd gotten a whiff of her hands and breath, which smelled eternally of garlic and onion.

Suddenly Fayga threw down her cards and flew out of her chair to the corner of the kitchen, stomping her Comfort Flex shoe on the floor several times. "Got you!" she cried. She hated roaches. Short of burning down the house, she did everything she could to kill them. Her mission in life was to keep dirt under control, which was pretty clever of her, because the earth is made of dirt, so her particular method of keeping the void at bay had a pretty good shelf life. But when she was overworked she tended to get mean and complain a lot, particularly about the washing she had to do for Father's saved babies: dirty diapers, pukey crib sheets, soiled terry cloth infant sacks constructed with arms but no feet as if we were host to mutant Martian babies with only one set of limbs apiece—all of it purchased in lots of a hundred from Leland DuRay, an infant clothing wholesaler who was one of Father's frequent contributors.

I tried to keep my eyes averted from the squished roach Fayga was scraping up from the floor as Cook motioned me to sit down at the table, setting my second dessert for the day in front of me. I was still licking my lips fifteen minutes later as I took the stairs two at a time up to my room to look up my new word.

I'd been using the dictionary and encyclopedia to battle boredom ever since teaching myself to read, my little bottom planted comfortably on a potty stool painted a pastel yellow that put my amber pee, stinking of vitamin drops and creamed asparagus, to shame. I created something of a household brouhaha back then by graduating so quickly from *Goodnight Moon* and *Green Eggs and Ham* to increasingly hefty dictionaries, Sister Flatulencia's *World English Bible*, and an assortment of dog-eared *Vogue* and *Elle* magazines Mother kept in the pretty pink basket in the corner of her bedroom. As you might imagine, sounding out words at the age of four was a lot easier than comprehending their meanings, but a couple of phrases have stayed with me to this day, like "an honest answer is like a kiss on the lips" (*Proverbs 24:26*) and "pearlescent pink and robin's egg blue are all the rage for spring" (*Vogue Magazine*).

Autistic sounded a teensy bit like me, but mostly it didn't. It wasn't that I hadn't been called names before. Sweetie Pie was one. I stopped liking it after dreaming of lying curled into a ball on a giant pie tin at the center of our massive, burled wood dining table—shined up so often by Fayga that every piece of food I ever ate there smelled like Ye Olde English Furniture Paste. On one side of me sat a slightly burnt apple pie with sickly-green crescent moons decorating the top and on the other a lemon meringue, one of my favorites ever since I discovered I could make Jillily sneeze if I put a dollop of meringue on the tip of her pink triangle of a nose. But here's the worst part: everyone but Grandfather was salivating and aiming giant forks in my direction.

Fortunately my second name, Angel Face, didn't disrupt my sleep. Since my potty stool was convertible, with a lid that could be flipped over to stand on, I could slide it across the marble floor to the flower-and-butterfly-painted sink that Nana never failed to remind me was much nicer than the plain white ones in the big, bare bathroom father built for the children he'd saved from the devil abortionists. Standing on tippy-toes, I'd spend hours staring at my angel face in the mirror, hoping I'd see wings start to sprout from the curved handles of my ears so I could fly out of the house and up to heaven.

I entered Father's new name for me in my diary. I liked to keep lists of words I looked up, taking particular pleasure in words with more than one meaning. But the reference to the major characteristic of the name *Autistic*—poor eye contact —made me nervous. I scrambled off my bed and stood in front of my dresser mirror, staring straight into my watery blue eyes and counting out a full sixty seconds without blinking, until I got distracted by the shape of my head, deciding it really was pretty pointy at the top.

Nana once told me that my bullet-shaped head is living evidence of my mother's distaste for anything too painful. She said that when it came time to push me out of her body, Mother gave one heave that allowed the tip of my head to squeeze through the swollen opening at her bottom, then decided it hurt too much and waited around until Father yelled bad words at her before reluctantly releasing me into the world. The other problem is that my bullet of a head is covered with funny-looking bumps and indentations. I saw them for the first time on the afternoon of my fifth birthday, when Nana said, "Oh, for heaven's sake, I'm not going to watch you scratch yourself like a monkey one minute longer," and drove me off to the doctor.

Only days before, I'd wandered over to the wing of our house Father had converted for the children he'd saved from the devil abortionists. Climbing into one of the new toddler's cots, I'd put my body right up next to hers so I could pretend we were Siamese twins. With her peach-fuzz cheeks and round blue eyes, she looked so much prettier than pale-eyebrowed, crooked-grinned, stringy-blond-haired me. Who knew she was going to infect me with a nasty case of ringworm and make me get my head shaved?

My rash prompted Father to permanently ban me from the saved babies' wing of the house, so I mostly struggled in secret with my insatiable curiosity about those other children. It wasn't as though I had a bunch of friends to distract me. Thanks to my banging and flapping, none of the local private schools were willing to accept me, and Mother wasn't exactly rushing to organize play dates.

I suppose I should give Nana credit for the bumps and indentations on my head. It probably took her flinging me into hundreds of hard landings onto my old rock of an infant changing table for me to realize I could actively give myself pain. Nana still cringes when she describes the first time she caught me squirming around my crib, rhythmically banging my head against its slats as if I were consciously aiming at slightly varying angles each time. I personally count it my earliest achievement, a terrific means of dispelling the void. Because as sure as my grandfather's balls could qualify for the Guinness record of the world's most gargantuan testicles, conquering the feeling of emptiness was the chief challenge of my young life. After all, Nana couldn't spend all her time slathering my little butt with Johnson and Johnson's. There were all those other butts, that revolving door of children my father kept rescuing.

But it wasn't just pain and reading and making lists that kept me going. Ever since turning four, I've had Jillily. As long as I can remember, Sister Flatulencia liked to call Jillily a tuxedo cat, which set the stage for some awful confusion when Fayga remarked offhandedly sometime after my sixth birthday that tuxedos were how Father dressed when he went off to rake in the dough. On the next Saturday that Father stayed out late, I tried to keep myself awake as best I could, pinching and banging until he got in, so I could sneak into his bedroom when he was showering and try to find his cat suit and where he kept his dough. I didn't find either one, not even a streak of flour on his wide-lapelled jacket, although I detected some unfamiliar perfume mixed in with the sharp jolt of bitterness in the jacket's armpits.

I vowed to try again, so the next time Father didn't come home for dinner, I kept myself awake by busily pinching my belly fat in a room that was pitch dark except for a little circle of light around my nightlight in the shape of a duck with a chip at the edge of its bill. My belly started hurting so badly that I opened my eyes and saw the silhouette of my mother at my doorway. She was craning her head in my direction, as if she couldn't quite see me, and she was holding her arms with her hands, as if she had to hold herself in one piece, and she was crying softly, just like Jillily after Cook shut the kitchen door on her paw. My room started smelling like the rubbing alcohol Nana dabbed on my knee whenever I fell, and I found myself hating Father, though I couldn't have explained why.

Under normal circumstances, when there was something confusing going on that I was trying to figure out, I felt good, because it filled up the you-know-what. But when my mother slipped away and took with her that disturbing smell, I had to pinch my tummy a lot harder to keep myself out of a pitch-black pit.

Nana yelled at me the next morning, "What's your doctor going to say when you go for your tests this afternoon?" I asked her why I had to go to so many doctors, anyway, if I wasn't even sick, but she turned away and muttered under her breath, "I have to see to the babies," and left the room without answering.

Needless to say, none of this resolved my confusion about Father's pits and the mysterious perfume he used to bring home with him instead of dough. The fact was, except on his late nights, Father had no smell to him at all. Which should have been a clue right there. Most people have the common courtesy to give off a little whiff of something to help other folks with their voids.

Nana, for instance, was pretty generous in that department, walking around the house with the perpetual stink of baby puke on her left shoulder and the faint perfume of Johnson's Baby Oil on her hands, and underneath them both, a hint of strong dirt somewhere under her skirt, like a body that lived mostly in caves, without much air circulating around. Every once in awhile, all of those smells, the puke, the oil, the cave dirt, were overtaken by the sharp punch of chocolate, which was Nana's favorite food. She liked every kind of it—from bittersweet to creamy white. One time, I heard her whisper to Fayga and Cook that chocolate was better than sex, and they all giggled, but then Fayga slapped my arm for listening, and Cook got all flush-faced and nervous and sent me out of the kitchen, and I had to bang my head against the Laura Ashley floral wallpaper on my bedroom wall a couple of times to make myself feel better.

Of course, the most aromatic member of our household was Sister Flatulencia, who, by the way, was never called that name to her face. Nana made it clear to me early on that she was to be addressed simply as Sister. For all I knew, Sister Flatulencia had never been given a proper name at all, but she was anything but anonymous. She was the tallest person in our household, taller even than Father, and though most of the time she kept her hair wrapped inside a royal blue bandana, she couldn't seem to fasten the scarf tightly enough to stop little grizzled curls from peeking out of it. She might have looked a little prettier if, besides her bandana, she didn't dress exactly like a man, with a white shirt tucked so tightly into her tailored black trousers that even her meager little breasts didn't show. As it is, with no makeup on her face, she looked just like a very tall man playing at being a woman by sticking a bandana on his head.

Speaking of whiffs, when I tried to ask Sister Flatulencia why I had to go for so many tests, she just passed some of her famous fruity wind and batted her eyelashes over her flying saucer eyes and kept muttering her name for me over and over again, "You Poor Child, You Poor Child, You Poor Child." I didn't particularly like that name, either; it made my tummy feel like those balloons they tie up at the county fair to look like animals, but they never do. What kind of animal had no eyes, or nose, or even a mouth? An animal without a mouth would die in a couple of days from starvation. I shuddered to think of it, imagining what it would be like to float in the void with that bored-as-hell God, who wouldn't even let you get born so you could do things like give yourself pain to save yourself.

Not that Sister Flatulencia would have seen it that way. Before she became Mother's companion she was a nun, or at least she had been until she had a nervous breakdown. Nana told me that the nervous breakdown came from taking care of all those babies my father saved and feeling bad that she never had one of her own. I guess that's why Nana could do it, since she had her very own baby, even though he died serving his country. One time I tried asking her, "Was your son a waiter or a cook like Cook, and how do you serve a whole country? It sounds like such a lot of work to do. Did he die of working too hard to make his whole country fat and happy?"

But Nana just said, "Shhh," and got up and acted like she had a lot of things to do, even though she'd seemed quite content the minute before to sink with me into the softest of our chintz sofas to watch re-runs of *I Dream of Jeannie*.

I used to wonder why they don't let nuns have babies. Maybe it was because nuns are married to Jesus. This is how my thinking went:

1. Father says that Jesus is God, so maybe God needs nuns to send every single bit of their love His way because it helps fill His void.

2. God is pretty big, so it figures He has a bigger void than any of us to fill.

3. Come to think of it, a country's pretty big, too, so it makes sense that a son who's trying to serve it could end up dying from over-work.

4. Maybe Sister Flatulencia's nervous breakdown saved *her* from dying of over-work.

Sometimes I passed the time by wondering, what is a nervous breakdown, anyway? Is it a constant state of gas? That is what Sister Flatulencia had, which worked to our advantage when it came to sitting by ourselves in the middle of the Majestic, with lots of space between us and little groups of teenagers making disgusting slurp sounds to force the Coke up their straws from the bottoms of their paper cups. Myself, I didn't really mind Sister Flatulencia's farts. They were much sweeter than a lot of people's smells, definitely sweeter than Father's pits and Nana's pukey shoulder and Mother's medicine odor whenever she stood in my doorway. I'd take them any day over Jillily's vomit, when she ate grass and it came out the same shape as it went in, but surrounded by stinky brownish goop, murky tide pools all over the carpet. Sweeter, too, than the sickly pee smell of Grandfather when his balls started to swell from congestive heart failure.

And just so you know, I haven't said much about Grandfather so far, but not because he wasn't important. On the contrary, he was my favorite person in the whole world.

I used to find it confusing that the name Grandfather could belong to more than one person in a family. Nana used to call my two grandfathers Grandfather Phillips and Grandfather Robins, which was pretty strange, because it was Grandfather *Phillips* who used to watch the birds with me. Grandfather Robins didn't watch anything but his pennies; at least that's what Cook used to say. Come to think of it, I'm not sure anyone had to tell Cook about that, so maybe she wasn't so opinionless after all.

Nana said that Cook didn't like anyone who pinched pennies because it took a lot of money to buy the freshest meats and vegetables. That comment of hers was extremely helpful in the void-management department. I used to spend hours trying to imagine how you could pinch a penny. Belly fat, yes. The little bit of flesh hanging from the underside of your arm, easy. Really, anything that has a little plumpness to it is pretty pinchable. Not Jillily, though. I learned that the hard way. Before I learned that not everybody likes pain the way I do, I made Jillily cry.

I tried to tell myself that it would never have happened if she hadn't gotten taken to the vet to get fixed. Personally, I had no idea why she had to get fixed. I never noticed anything about Jillily that looked broken. To me, she was perfect in every way. But in the weeks after coming back from the vet, she walked funny, her white furry belly all loose and hangy and swaying from side to side. I figured anything that pouchy-looking was fair game for a pinch, so one day, when I came into my bedroom and she was lying on her back on a little patch of sun on the carpet the way she likes to do, with her legs spread open and her paws flapped up in the air, I felt the itching for a pinch come over me, the way it can. Everybody laughed at Jillily when she struck that particular pose of hers. Fayga would call her Charlotte the Harlot, but then Sister Flatulencia would make a mean squint of her flying saucer eyes and Nana would say, "Hush!"

Anyway, there was Jillily, my favorite person in the whole world besides my grandfather, even though Nana has always insisted that Jillily isn't really a person. Sometimes Nana's mind is just a little limited, if you know what I mean. But Nana wasn't there when I reached down and gave that empty-looking belly a nice, squeezy pinch. In one quick second, the world went black as the blankest void. Jillily yowled and gave me a look like I'd sold her to the devil abortionists, then she ran away from me and squatted under my four-poster, with her body clenched up all tight and the muscles in her back twitching like she was being bitten by fleas. I flattened myself like a crocodile to slither under the bed and coax her back out, and I had to give her a thousand chicken-peck kisses all over her back and ears and belly before she let her motor whirr again, and when she finally let me kiss her little pink triangle of a nose, I could see the wet gook in the corners of her yellow eyes and I knew that I'd made Jillily cry.

That was my first time realizing there are some things worse than boredom. My whole body felt like something ugly and stinky and I kept wishing that my skin was a pair of pajamas I could just take off and fling into Fayga's dirty clothes bin, along with all those Martian infant sacks. A part of me wanted to bite off my ugly, stinking fingers, but Jillily's whirring told me she needed me to keep patting her, so I kept my fingers out of my mouth and stroked Jillily with them, instead.

That afternoon, I told Grandfather what I'd done. We were sitting together facing the big lead-paned front window of Grandfather's bedroom, Grandfather in his recliner and me in my giant-sized, cushiony rocking chair that I'd inherited from my mother. We were watching our tree like we always did, and I kept opening my mouth to say what was on my mind and then closing it again. It was only after the last mockingbird had flown away and the branches looked as desolate as a motherless baby that I finally turned to Grandfather and told him. For a long time, he looked at me, his eyes brimming over with kindness, and then he stretched out his big, twisty hand and put it over my evil, Jillily-pinching one and he made his sounds.

Nana said that the sounds Grandfather made sounded like "ugga umph ugga," but what if they did? Grandfather's infirmity didn't stop Nana from inviting him up to her bedroom at the end of the day if she needed him to make a foursome. If you're not a cards player you might not know that it takes four people to play a proper game of Hearts. Grandfather wasn't so good at Hearts. He hardly ever won.

But when Grandfather put his Hearts-losing hand on mine and looked so tenderly into my eyes, my hatred at myself for making Jillily cry flowed right out of me. After a while, Grandfather let go of my hand, and we both turned back to watch our tree. A pair of sparrows was hopping from branch to branch in a complicated zigzag pattern. They like to keep busy to fend off the void. I snuck a quick look at Grandfather. The edges of his lips were turned up in a peaceful grin.

I suppose I should explain about Grandfather's inability to make language. Nana said that Grandfather had suffered a stroke. I already knew that stroke is one of those double-meaning words, so I asked her. "Did somebody pat Grandfather the wrong way, like somebody rubbing Jillily's fur from her backside to her head instead of the right way around? Or did he go swimming one day and do the butterfly stroke so fast that his words dissolved like butterfly wings in the swimming pool?"

But she just laughed and said, "No, Angel Face, nothing so fancy. A stroke is just an infirmity—a sickness like a bad cold, only it doesn't go away." She added, "It's a good thing his stroke didn't affect anything but his ability to make words." I knew from personal experience she was right. He could read just fine. If anything, he understood way more than most. But he couldn't write anymore, let alone speak comprehensibly.

Grandfather didn't seem to mind that he couldn't talk like the rest of us. It didn't stop him from taking his bulldog-headed cane for a slow walk around the grounds every day, it didn't stop him from poring over the pile of newspapers beside his place-setting at our Ye Old English Furniture Paste-smelling dining room table each morning, and it didn't stop him from sitting by my side in his room, stroking my hair and sneaking me red jelly candies and listening to me copying all the bird calls as we watched our tree.

Grandfather and I had a lot in common. We both knew what it was like to not be understood. I could say words better than Grandfather, but that didn't guarantee that people wouldn't look at me as if I'd just said "ugga umph ugga" when I talked to them.

Grandfather and I both liked to watch birds. Birds have a couple of very good ways of dealing with the void—they can fly and they can sing. They also provided Jillily with an antidote to boredom. When birds flew past the window, she made deep noises in her throat that sounded friendly, but they weren't, they were about wanting to kill, which made me have second thoughts about Jillily until I remembered how much I liked to tear hunks of chicken off the bone with my teeth and forgave her.

Speaking of eating, another thing that Grandfather and I had in common was a taste for red jelly candies, which were hard and shiny and sweet. The only trouble was, when I went to brush my teeth at night, if I'd sucked a red jelly candy that day my tongue would still be bright red at bedtime. No amount of brushing would make the redness go away. When I get an idea into my head, it's not so easy to get rid of. Plus, there's something about the nighttime that's just an invitation to the void, so once I got the idea into my head that red was the color of blood, I started to worry I was dying. After that, whenever Grandfather would slip me a piece of red jelly candy, I'd pretend to put it in my mouth, but really I'd stick it in my pocket. But then I worried I might be saving myself, but what about Grandfather? What if those candies had given him his stroke?

That was when I decided to sneak into Grandfather's bedroom while he was taking one of his walks and steal his candies from him. I found the drawer where he kept his crinkly plastic bags of red jelly candies. Right next to them, though, was something even more interesting: a photograph of my mother when she was a teenager and marrying Father, who wasn't a teenager at all. I could tell that Mother was getting married because of what she wore. I thought she looked very pretty, her long white dress bulging at her middle as if she'd eaten a couple of Cook's biggest angel food cakes.

I knew Grandfather still had an hour to go before he'd finish circling the grounds, so I settled into my mother's rocking chair and studied the photo. There was a much younger version of my grandfather peeking into it from the uppermost left corner. The top of Grandfather's head was chopped off by the white border, but he didn't seem to mind; he was smiling a big fat smile at his only daughter. My father was there, too, tall and skinny, with his hair pale yellow and fluffy, like one of Fayga's mops. I almost laughed, but when I noticed the way my father was looking down at my mother in the photo, goose bumps started marching up and down my arms. Father had the same exact look in his eyes as a dog I'd encountered in front of the doctor's office when I was little, all sharpy-tooth lunging at me with a volcano growl coming out of his throat and Nana yelling, "Hey, buddy, that dog needs to be put down!" before wrapping her thick arms around my body and chicken-peck-kissing me.

That photo took my bad feeling about my father from the Saturday night I'd heard Mother cry and turned it into a rock in the middle of my chest. I just couldn't understand why my beautiful young girl of a mother in her white dress wasn't running from my father as fast as her feet could take her. And, worse still, why my grandfather was smiling. Shouldn't he have been shielding Mother with his body, yelling, "That man needs to be put down?"

I realize this doesn't begin to explain about the bird on the lawn and my grandfather's balls, but I hope I've given you enough of a preview of coming attractions to help keep your void at bay. As for me, I'm afraid I've worked myself up a little. But don't worry—give me a moment to recover, maybe a pinch or two, and, as Nana likes to put it, "Bob's your uncle, I'll be as right as rain."

Chapter 2 🦋

I FEAR I may have given you the impression that I thought you had an uncle named Bob. Maybe you do, and maybe you don't, but I certainly don't, at least not that anyone else ever knew about. I don't even have an aunt.

The fact is, *Bob's your uncle* is just an expression—which is different from the look someone gives you when they're trying to tell you something but they're too stingy to put it in words. It wasn't unusual for me, back in the early days, to manage the void by wondering what kind of expression my Uncle Bob would wear. First of all, he would look nothing like Father or Mother. He would, however—at least in the quizzical, pale-eyed department—look just a little like me.

The best Uncle Bob I ever thought up—and the one who managed to stick around, developing a life of his own—had an ability to expand and shrink that was quite amazing. Sometimes, he was exactly the same height as me and he liked to skip. The two of us would skip in unison all the way to the first fountain, counting the number of trees we passed, even though we both knew there were exactly fifteen. And sometimes, if Nana came running out of the house, yelling, "How many times do I have to tell you you're not to play on the grounds without me. Do you want me to get fired," he'd shrink to the size of the palm of my hand, so I could shove him into my pocket to hide him from her, his curlicue moustache tickling my fingers as I tucked him in.

With or without my expandable Uncle Bob, it was always a treat to roam the grounds of the house I was born in, even before I found out that most people never got to see so much grass and so many flowers except in a public park. Nana used to say that the one thing my mother was good for was caring for her beds of David Austin roses. I never could find the beds, but you couldn't miss the roses. When springtime came, you could close your eyes and follow their noisy scent right out of the house and straight to where Mother had planted them. They budded, blossomed, and dropped their petals in void-filling patterns along a sunny stretch of grass beyond the second fountain, where the glowering giant fish at the corner spewed mossy spitballs at the floating water lilies.

I hated that fish. It figured in some of my worst nightmares and even swallowed Uncle Bob in one of his miniature phases. But I liked the roses a lot, even though I learned early on to try not to get too attached to them. The first time I found the stem of an Abraham Darby hanging limp and beaten over his sad loss of apricot petals, I could have watered a dozen of his brothers with my tears.

Though none of the other trees meant as much to me as the sycamore that Grandfather and I kept watch over, they all had their ways. The weeping willow by the first fountain kept its void at bay by constantly sweeping its longest limb across baby Eros' peeing member. "Member" was Sister Flatulencia's word for it. Nana called it a penis, but said I should never say that word out loud, so I never mentioned it to my skipping uncle and I certainly never uttered it around Father.

The fact was, I was less likely to see Father at home than on TV, talking about how we owed it to Jesus to take care of the helpless. I, personally, didn't think his television appearances did him much good, given the fact that the screen made him look like a lizard. He was extremely tall and unusually skinny, and his greenish-tinged skin looked tough and rubbery—just the opposite of Mother, whose arms were so white and delicate that you knew they should never be touched.

I can't tell you how many times I dreamed of leaning my head against Mother's waist and going right through her body to her other side. It was just like the chutes in Chutes and Ladders. One minute you'd be on her left side, staring up at the beauty mark beside her left nostril, wondering whether it really was shaped like a teensy-weensy

Uncle Bob, and leaning in toward her body to get a better view, and the next thing you knew you'd be on her other side, looking up at the right side of her nose, unmarked and lonely for an Uncle-Bob-ish kind of friend.

You wouldn't have wanted to touch Father, either, but for an altogether different set of reasons. For one thing, in spite of saving so many children, he didn't like them under his feet. At least that's what he always said, which made no sense at all. To my knowledge, not one of those saved children had the gift of shrinking like my private Uncle Bob, so I didn't see how they could fit under my father's size thirteen shoes. Whenever I had to walk past him, I pretended I was balancing a vase full of roses on my head. That gave me an excuse to keep my eyes focused forward, so I didn't have to see him purse his lips at me and squint his eyes, as if he were trying to decide whether he should have saved me from the devil abortionists after all.

The advantage of having Father captured on TV was that it shrunk him nearly as small as miniature Uncle Bob, which made it a lot safer to scream at him while he made one of his speeches about caring for unwanted children and unwanted senior citizens—actually using Grandfather as an example—and making his voice lower than it ever was at home. The truth was, Father's real voice had a little squeak to it, and not too long after I started keeping track of double-meaning words, I made a separate section in one of my diaries for listing the number of squeaks I heard coming out of Father's mouth. I had to ask Nana to buy me a whole new leather-bound notebook just for that purpose after I got up to two thousand and three.

I never screamed at Father when he was his regular-sized self, not even when he made Mother cry. That was because of those mean eyes of his and his habit of pinching my arm when he got mad at me. His pinches belonged to an entirely different category from the ones I gave myself to break the spell of boredom. When Father twisted and turned my flesh with his powerful grip, it gave me an uh-oh-I'm-about-to-faint feeling and made Nana curse so much after chicken-peck-kissing my bruises that Sister Flatulencia had to cross herself and leave the room.

You could keep the boredom at bay for hours just thinking about all the ways my father's eyes could look mean. Strangely enough, the worst shape I ever saw them in had nothing to do with children underfoot. I was eleven then, and we were enjoying a break in what had been an unusually severe Pennsylvania winter. Cook had made a particularly yummy bouillabaisse to celebrate. Afterwards, Mother retired, as usual, to her bedroom, while Nana and Sister Flatulencia and I went into the den with Father to watch TV.

I sat pleasurably squeezed between the two women on our cozy chintz couch. Father was perched on the very edge of his leather ottoman. To our dismay, were just in time to see the 76ers lose to the Celtics. The buzzer went off, the crowd roared, and Father angrily whipped the remote from a side table, changing the channel to a preview of upcoming *60 Minutes* segments. I instantly wished he hadn't. Mitchell Manus, the other senator from our state, was telling an interested-looking Ed Bradley about "the hypocrisy of Senator Robins' so-called support for the value of human life." I already knew about the feud between Senator Manus and Father, thanks to Grandfather sliding me the front section of the *Philadelphia Inquirer* each morning after he'd read it from cover to cover. When I read the newspaper, I felt even closer to Grandfather, since it gave me some idea what he was thinking about.

Anyway, there was Senator Manus, speaking quietly but confidently on TV, and there was Father, sitting a few feet away from me, looking like his eyeballs were going to pop out of his head. Senator Manus added to the overall tension in the room when he continued, "It's so typical of the far-right—trying to marginalize universal health care by calling it socialism, when Canada and virtually all our European allies offer it. You have to admit it's pretty hypocritical, denying the most basic of rights to all those children they insist should be born." Father threw down the remote so violently it came perilously close to cracking the glass-topped coffee table. Without a word, he stormed out of the room.

As soon as he was gone, Nana heaved a sigh of relief, her ample breasts resettling themselves on her belly. But then she said rather ominously, "We haven't heard the last of this." And she was right.

I don't know if I've mentioned this, but I don't like change, particularly when it comes to people I know. And having them disappear all of a sudden is particularly nasty in the void department. I learned the next morning that I wasn't the only one. Feeling that predictable waking-up urge for a pee, I shuffled down the hall in my fuzzy polar bear slippers, coming out of the bathroom again just in time to see Nana at the top of the stairs, saying to a particularly dried-worm-mouthed Fayga, "None of us is safe around here anymore, not with the media giving Senator Manus so much air time. Talk about scapegoating. The asshole fired Cook because he says she was ripping him off."

I tiptoed back down the hall to Grandfather's room. Grandfather lit up as soon as he saw me, but once he registered my expression, his own face dropped and he scooted over to the side of his bed to make room for me. This was hardly the first time I'd curled on top of his duvet while he lay under it, his left arm stretched over the covers and around my shoulder and his milky breath warming my cheek.

I told Grandfather about Father saying Cook was ripping him off. I knew Cook would never steal. "She's not a taker-awayer, Grandpa. She's a putter-inner. She tells anyone who'll listen to her that Father could use a little more meat on his bones. She's always spooning extra servings of that Irish stew he likes onto his plate before she lets Fayga take it out to him." The more I talked, the more indignant I felt. "Grandpa, she always says her angel food cake tastes so good because of the extra egg white she adds to the thirteen eggs in her mother's recipe to take her cake out of the unlucky thirteen category, but that didn't make her lucky enough to keep herself from getting fired. That's what Father did to her." Grandfather looked just as outraged as I was.

Settling my head more securely into the crook of his arm, I added, "I don't know about you, but I love Cook's cooking. I feel sorry for her that everyone in our family is so skinny, since she's always trying to make us fat." Grandfather laughed then—not so much with his voice as his belly. It jiggled under the covers. Before I knew it, I was laughing, too, partly because of Grandfather's bouncing belly and partly with relief that someone understood exactly how I felt.

Things got a lot more complicated in our house after Cook left. For one thing, Dhani was hired to take her place, but not until Fayga nearly poisoned us with her cooking. The day Cook left, Fayga got it into her head that she could replace her. She failed on her very first attempt at Cook's recipe for cumin-and-lime-marinated chicken. I had something of a history with that particular dish. It had given me a terrible fright the first time I saw it in its pre-cooked state when I snuck down to the kitchen after bedtime for some soy milk and cookies, only to discover a Pyrex dish full of helpless little bird wings in the refrigerator, drowning in what looked suspiciously like baby poop.

It wasn't that Fayga's cooking was all that bad. Her presentation was certainly impressive. She marched her sizzling platter into the dining room with the expression of Jillily springing onto my bed with a giant roach in her mouth. But when Mother and Father and Grandfather and I lifted our first forkfuls of chicken to our lips, we were nearly overcome by the metallic tang of silver polish. Mother carefully replaced her fork onto her plate, avoiding Father's eyes. Grandfather held his own fork up to the light, turning it around and around to see if Fayga had forgotten to wipe the silver after polishing it. As for me, I knew that Fayga tended to over-wipe the silver, if anything, but I did wonder if she'd immersed her hands in cleansers and polish for so many years that she was doomed to contaminate anything she touched.

There I sat, taking advantage of this priceless opportunity to fill the void by trying to figure out how I could avoid eating my chicken without mortally wounding Fayga's feelings, when Father piped up, his eyes all lizard-slitty, "What? One of them schemes to rob me blind, and now this one is trying to kill us?" I had to bite my upper lip until it bled, which wasn't very pleasant, I can tell you, because my tongue had to suffer a sickening slurry of salty blood, a little lime, a lot of cumin, and more silver polish than I'd ever wanted to know the taste of.

Luckily for us, Fayga didn't take it too personally. I think she was secretly relieved to get back to her mounting piles of dirty Martian infant sacks. As for me, I was relieved to discover, when Dhani Srivastava was sent out by the housekeeping agency the next day, that she was a proper cook, just like Cook. It turned out she liked to spice things up with cumin, too. The similarity between the two of them ended right there. If Cook was round and heavy and given to turning red in her opinion-less mode, Dhani had lots to say about nearly everything, all of it spoken in what Nana called the King's English, though I never figured out which king. Small and dark and filled with a lively energy, she moved from stove to sink to cutting board with the easy fluidity of Jillily chasing a fly.

But her exotic Indian beauty proved to be a bit of a problem. Toward the end of her first week with us, I went down to the kitchen for my before-bed cookie, only to find Father leaning against the refrigerator, saying, "You're a lovely woman, you know." It was Dhani he was talking to. She wasn't looking at him. She was sweeping a dishcloth in graceful arcs across the granite counter. Father was so intent on watching her he didn't even notice I was there.

I was in shock. Father never showed his face in the kitchen. And I'd never heard him speak in such a gentle tone. But watching Dhani rhythmically wiping the counter, the lace at the hem of her white apron twisting coyly at her calf, I had to agree with him. I made a little cough, and Father looked up, his expression instantly changing. He carelessly knocked my shoulder with his elbow as he pushed past me out the door.

The room felt lighter as soon as he was gone. When I told her what I wanted, Dhani's dark eyes crinkled with pleasure. She sat me down at the kitchen table with a glass of soymilk and the last of Cook's peanut butter cookies. Sliding into the chair opposite me, she asked what I'd done that day, frowning just a little as I listed all the Austins I'd managed to visit. The grandfather clock in the hall chimed ten times while Dhani absent-mindedly ferried an errant peanut butter chip around the saltcellar. Finally aware of what she was doing, she laughed at herself and scraped back her chair. "It's a bit late, don't you think?" she asked, rising. "School day tomorrow for you, my girl."

Licking the last crumb from the corner of my lip, I corrected her. "I don't go to school."

Dhani cocked her head. "Why ever not?"

A hot, prickly feeling came over me, but I resisted the urge to pinch. "Nana calls it home schooling. She says it's the schools' fault and who needs them anyway, but I think if I'd only been able to…"

Dhani sat down again, favoring me with a look that seemed to say, "Well?"

I didn't really want to continue, but Dhani's gaze was so warm and unwavering, so obviously *interested*, that I did. I told her how all the private schools in our neighborhood claimed they were full as soon as they met me. How Father swore that, until I shaped up, he wouldn't dream of sending me to our local public school. How Mother had driven me herself all the way to Radnor to enroll in the new Willow Tree Montessori—putting on her best linen suit and cream silk blouse the morning of our appointment before finishing off her ensemble with a generous spritz of Chanel. How I'd made a complete hash of Mother's efforts, screaming so piercingly when the Principal asked Mother to leave us alone in the office for my interview that Mother had no choice but to drag me back to the car. What I didn't tell her, feeling it would be some kind of betrayal, was that Mother had cried like a sick baby all the way home.

By the time I finished, my face was on fire and Dhani's black eyebrows had inched together into one long caterpillar. But her voice was so calm I couldn't help but relax. "I see," she said slowly. "So, your mum teaches you your lessons?"

I hastened to explain that it wasn't really like that. "Ever since I taught myself to read, I've pretty much been learning on my own. Nana helps, of course, and, when I need to have something explained that she doesn't understand, she takes me to the Gladwyne Free Public Library. Mrs. Perle, the head librarian, is terrifically helpful. Sometimes I think she's read every single book on the shelves. Actually, we go there once a week, no matter what. I get to bring home all the books I want, as long as they cover the basics."

Dhani's eyebrows lifted like butterfly wings. "The basics?" she prompted.

"Mm hmm. You know, math, history, nature studies, literature, essay writing. And I study the Bible with Sister Flatulencia on Sundays."

"But what about mates?"

"Mates?" I asked, confused.

"Friends. Girlfriends. I haven't seen any other children around, except for the…"

"Oh," I replied airily, fighting a feeling of pressure at the back of my throat. "I've got Nana and Jillily and Sister Flatulencia and Fayga. And I used to have Cook."

Dhani fell silent. She seemed to be turning what I'd been saying over in her mind. Then she looked up, smiling faintly. "Well, I hope you'll come to include me in your list." She pressed her hand lightly against my cheek before reaching to clear my plate from the table, using my soiled napkin to sweep my crumbs onto the dish. "I'm afraid that's the last of the batch. You'll have to tell me all your favorite desserts."

And I did, right there and then. But all the while, I had to dig my nails into my palm to remind myself to stop staring at her naturally-red-jelly-candy-colored lips and her dainty chin with a tiny Uncle-

Bob-sized pinch taken out of it. I was all too aware of my own boring blue eyes and dead-grass-colored hair and pale white skin that turned a little yellowish every winter.

As the days wore on, we all grew quite fond of Dhani. Except for Mother, that is. I'm sure Mother would have liked her, too, if only Father had kept his hands to himself. As it turned out, there was something about Dhani that kept more than one man's hands out of his pockets. That other man was our new gardener Ignacio, whom Father hired just a few weeks after Dhani came to us.

It occurred to me later that Father fired our old gardener Franklin because scapegoating Cook hadn't been enough. But he claimed at the time it was because Franklin was letting the garden get out of control. I didn't know gardens needed controlling and I didn't know much about Franklin, only that his face was red and criss-crossed with wrinkles and whenever I skipped past he acted too busy to speak to me.

It was different with Ignacio, who was a talkative sort of man. He told me the first time I met him that he'd only lived in Pennsylvania for a year, Texas having been ruined for him after his wife Rosa was murdered while sneaking back across the border to Mexico to help her cousin Hilda with her new baby.

Anyone hearing that would have to feel pretty bad about Ignacio, but when you learn about our first meeting, you might feel just a teensy bit sorry for *me*.

That's because of the weeds. I don't know about you, but I have never met a weed I didn't like. Whether they are thick or thin, dull or shiny, the bright green of rye grass or pale yellow, like wheat, they all seem to be propelled by a void-vanquishing knowledge of where they want to go, and that's closer to the sun. They make themselves at home in well-watered plots of earth, right next to flowers that someone has planted, or else they force themselves up through little cracks in the sidewalk, edging and pushing and sidling through, just so they can signal, "Here I am, sun!" and breathe.

I'd discovered all this only a month before, having fled the house after Mother and Nana started yelling at each other about Father's idea that I should be sent away to some school for children like me. Needless to say, I was more than a little curious about what children like me were *like*. I'd known for years that I was different from most kids. Whenever Nana took me to the doctor or we went shopping for clothes at Born Yesterday or made our weekly trips to the library, I'd make a beeline for anyone close to my size, trying to help them with their voids by filling them in about Nana and Cook and Fayga and Grandfather and Mother and Jillily and Sister Flatulencia. They would usually do one of two things: laugh with their mouths but not their eyes (always a bad sign) or slowly back away with their fronts facing me, which sent me straight to the mirror when we got home again, worried that I'd turned into a dangerous dog that Nana would have to put down.

Actually, it was when I was trying to put down one particularly determined weed that I discovered weeds' true nature. It was the shiny kind, and I guess that was what first caught my eye as I ran toward Mother's invisible flowerbed. The weed was sparkling with dew and trying to get the sun's attention by sticking up straight and tall from a jagged crack in the path just beyond the first fountain. But then I noticed that it was trailing a second, ground-hugging shoot that seemed to be aiming itself in the same direction I was heading. I stopped and studied it until I was overcome by the inky pit-ish conviction that this might be some kind of alien Martian plant with a particular appetite for David Austin roses. With a pounding heart, I tried to squish the weed back into the crack with the heel of my shoe. When that didn't work—my shoe was too clunky—I got down on my hands and knees and sort of shmooshed it back in.

But every day after that it managed to pop right up again. I know because I kept checking. As I may have mentioned, I was terribly fond of those roses. Worse still, each day the weed got thicker and stronger and harder to stuff back down. After a particularly bad flu kept me inside for a whole week, I bolted out to the garden as soon as I was better, only to discover that the weed, like one of Father's unwanted babies, had undergone a sudden growth spurt, sending shoots way across the path and lacing itself into coarse knotty clumps that even the strongest of Uncle Bobs couldn't yank out.

I stood in the sun and considered my predicament. I pretended to look away, then whirled back around and eyed it suspiciously, but the weed didn't move; if anything, it looked like it was hunkering down, spooked, under the cloud of my long spiky shadow. I thought a little harder. Any Martian weed in its right mind would never have used up all of its rose-eating energy tying itself into knots.

I knew about knots; sometimes in the middle of the night when I woke from a nightmare and Nana was snoring too heavily to hear my screams, I would try to curl my legs and arms into knots so that not one of the monsters hiding under the bed could grab hold of a finger or toe to yank me into the hole of everlasting emptiness. It occurred to me that maybe I had everything backwards. What if I was supposed to be that weed's friend and not its enemy? After all, it had given me no end of respite from the void.

After that, I made sure that my weed got plenty of attention. I took no end of trouble sneaking little plastic bags of water out to it when the weather was hot and dry, even though Uncle Bob complained the whole time that no pocket was meant to hold both an uncle and a water-balloon of a plastic bag.

You can imagine how I felt on the day I was doing my fastest skipping past the ugly fish in the first fountain, only to see a dark-skinned man up ahead of me, wearing an olive green uniform and an Uncle-Bob-ishly thick mustache (but without the curlicues) and holding a clear plastic bottle with something attached to it that looked suspiciously like a gun. And what do you think he was aiming his gun at but my weed!

I skipped even faster and yowled in my best imitation of Jillily when someone accidentally catches her swishy question mark of a tail in the swinging kitchen door. The man stopped what he was doing and stared at me. As I got closer, I saw a second plastic bottle, smaller and brown and gunless, sitting on the ground by his feet and giving off the most putrid smell—nothing that you'd ever want to fill *your* void with.

By this time, I was upset enough to disobey Nana's rule never to speak to a stranger. Eleven years old, and three-quarters as tall as Grandfather's doorjamb, I felt entitled to speak out against injustice. "What are you doing to my weed?"

The man looked very surprised and didn't answer right away, and I worried that in my distress I'd actually said something like "Ugga umph ugga." But then he grinned, and I must confess there was something about the apostrophe mark dimples on each side of his smile that made me relax a teensy bit in spite of the sickening smell that enveloped us. Then he did something that surprised me—he knelt on one knee, setting his gun down on the path, and put the cap on the little brown bottle. The air got better right away. Pushing himself up, he said, "You must be Senator Robins' daughter. My name's Ignacio. Ignacio Hertado. I'm your new gardener." He started to reach out his hand, then seemed to think better of it and stuck it into his pocket.

I was still pretty worried about my weed, so I repeated my question.

He shrugged. "What do I do with any weed? I kill it. Your father has spent a lot of money to make a perfect garden. He wants me to keep it that way. No more weeds."

The enormity of what he was saying hit me like a blast of one of Sister Flatulencia's more sulphuric farts. So that was why Father was so determined to send me away to school. I wasn't perfect enough for his perfect house and his perfect garden. I looked around for something to bang my head on, but then I remembered my weed. "How can you even think of killing this weed? Do you have any idea how hard it's working to get where it needs to go?"

Ignacio's smile turned upside down and his face paled. He looked like he was going to fall over. Instead, he sat down, pulling his knees up to his chest. And then he cried. I had never seen a man cry. Mother, yes. Me, absolutely—there is nothing more satisfying than watching yourself cry. The uneven pattern of red splotching alone is well worth the price of admission.

I settled onto the grass next to Ignacio and asked why he was crying. It was then that he explained about the death of his wife Rosa. I explained about my weed. We came to a pretty good understanding, particularly when I assured him that Father never set foot on the grounds, except for photo-opportunities in front of the house.

"So." Ignacio brushed some dirt off his pant leg and shot me an appraising look. "The *muchacha* knows more than her years. But she also has a good heart and wants to help living things stay alive. That reminds me of something that happened to me when I was young myself—not so young as you, but still young. Want to hear a story?"

Was he kidding? Hadn't stories been invented expressly to fill the void? I nodded, and he began. "Everybody wants to come to this great country, but it's not easy for some of us. I came here knowing just a couple words of English, but I studied three nights a week for eight years at San Antonio College and got my papers, thanks to the *amnistia*. I wanted to get Rosa her papers, too, but we only had enough money for a lawyer for one of us, and Rosa said it would be worse for us if I were sent back, since I was the one who made more money." Ignacio looked like he was going to cry again, but forced himself to go on. "I was sixteen when I came to this country. I came in secret and on foot with three others from my village near San Luis Potosi. Our walk was hard and long, but we still managed to have a laugh or two." He shook his head. "We didn't laugh when we saw a skeleton a couple of miles inside the Mexican side of the border. We knew it had been left there by *La Migra* to discourage people like us."

I was careful not to flinch. I wanted him to keep talking.

"We were crossing the desert in the middle of summer. We'd planned to come in May, but my cousin Francisco promised his wife Catalina that he would be there for the birth of their first child." Ignacio frowned. "It was bad. The child came out quiet and yellow. He didn't even live long enough for Catalina's milk to come down."

"It was hot as a griddle by the time we came to the border. I didn't like to complain, but my feet were bleeding from walking too far in shoes that were too tight. Only the devil himself knows how something like that can get the best of you. We knew we had to wait for night to make our crossing. I walked a little away from my *companeros*. That was when I saw *el coyote*." Ignacio scratched his nose with his thumbnail and looked off into the distance. "He wasn't the kind of coyote who takes your money and leaves you to find your own way across the desert, but an animal, a wild dog. This one was young, not much bigger than my two hands."

Ignacio showed me how small his coyote had been, putting one flat, open hand next to the other, and I couldn't help but notice the lines and calluses on his palms.

"I knew *el coyote* was there because of the sounds he made, like my little brother Pablocito, only louder. As I approached him, he growled, but I could tell from the iron smell that there was blood, and since he didn't move I knew he was caught in a trap. A trap meant for people like me."

Ignacio stood abruptly and started to pace back and forth. "I went back to our camp. Took my jacket and wrapped it around my arm." He pointed a finger at me. "Here's something you should know, *muchacha*. Never try to save a trapped animal with your own skin exposed. In its fear it will try to kill you." Ignacio was so intent on his story he didn't notice me shuddering. This was like a suspense movie, the music driving you nearly to the edge of the void, but there's no way you're going to stop watching.

He went on. "I could tell he was a survivor. He'd been chewing at his leg to work himself free. It wasn't easy to loosen the wire that bit into his flesh. He snarled and tried to sink his teeth into me. But it was *his* blood that covered my jacket, not mine. I wondered if he'd be able to walk, with only three good legs and a fourth heavy with pain." Ignacio shook his head. "I didn't need to worry. Once I worked the wire off, that coyote ran like the wind."

All this time, I had been sitting very still, cross-legged, averting my eyes from the poison gun on the grass. As if he could read my mind, Ignacio grabbed the gun and the brown bottle. "What's the matter with me?" he scolded himself angrily. The he shot me a sideways look. "I don't know what it is about you, *muchacha*. Easy to forget you're a kid. Forget what I said. I'd hate to think I gave you bad dreams."

But I told him I liked his story, especially the part about the coyote running free. Ignacio asked me then if I'd like him to walk with me back to the house. We took a brief detour to the garden shed, which I'd never been inside before. There were so many bottles labeled *danger* and *poison* in there that I worried about their easy accessibility to my father, given how he felt about growing things that are flawed.

When we got back to the house, Ignacio insisted on going inside the back way. He gestured for me to go first, and when I did I saw Dhani at the sink, her rounded forehead shiny with sweat and rainbow colored soap bubbles popping in the air around her. She looked up at me and her face crinkled her welcome, but then her eyes went right over my head and I could see her dark lashes flutter like hummingbird wings. If I knew then what I know now, nearly four years later, I would have understood that those wingy eyelashes were a sign that Dhani felt a special feeling for Ignacio in her tweeter.

But at the time, all I wanted to do was run upstairs to Grandfather. It had finally dawned on me that, if I was sent away to school because of my imperfection, there would be no one left at home to watch over Grandfather, whose *ugga umph uggas* and increased tendency to pee in his bed might make some people think he was very flawed himself.

Grandfather was already stationed by the window when I reached his room. I figured he'd seen me and Ignacio through the window because he shot me an unusual number of *ugga umph uggas*, so I explained about saving my weed and the death of Ignacio's Rosa and *el coyote* running like the wind and how important it was not to try to save a trapped animal without protecting your own skin. I knew that Grandfather appreciated Ignacio's warning, because he nodded vehemently and took my hand and looked so pointedly into my eyes that I had to look away. It was then that I noticed that, compared to Ignacio's hands, Grandfather's were white and small and covered with twisty pop-up veins, but in their favor they were as soft as the silk on Jillily's belly.

Luckily for me, the school idea died as surely as Ignacio's skeleton in the desert. It seemed that none of the schools Father visited accepted new students in the middle of the school year. So we continued our current arrangement, with me using the books Mrs. Perle gave me to learn as much as I could on my own.

But there are some things you'd rather not know. I may have been minus a whole host of ghostly grandmothers and unshrinkable uncles, but I'd never lost a Rosa. For several weeks, I tried going back in time and reinventing Ignacio's fate by imagining that Rosa had played a trick on everyone and purchased a round trip ticket for herself and flown safely down to Mexico and was so busy helping take care of Hilda's new baby that she'd forgotten to write. But inside I could feel myself joined like a Siamese twin with the real Rosa, for whom poverty and bad luck had purchased a one way ticket to one of the deepest layers of the void, where it's all black, but sticky, too, like flypaper, and no matter what you do you can't escape.

Chapter 3 🦋

A FEW MONTHS after Dhani arrived, Nana said it seemed like she'd come to our house just to open Pandora's box, which was pretty confusing, since no one in our household was named Pandora. Unless it was one of the children Father saved. They came and went with such frequency that I'd given up trying to keep track of their names.

It was only after sneaking into Nana's smallest closet one night when she was torturing Grandfather and Fayga and Dhani with Hearts that I concluded that Pandora must live in somebody else's house and not ours. Which left my mind scrabbling over why Dhani would come to our house to open some other family's box, and what was in that box, anyway? Maybe it was a giant crate of delicious candies, in which case it wouldn't hurt to know which family that was.

Nana had two closets in her bedroom. One was lined floor to ceiling with ancient cedar paneling that smelled so strong that I sneezed whenever I felt compelled to take refuge there, nestled in tightly between the wall and Nana's furry green bathrobe that slumped unevenly from a hanger overhead. Butting my backbone satisfyingly hard against the nail heads in the wall, I'd stick a fistful of robe right up against my nostrils to give myself deep whiffs of her cave-scent, which would pretty much hold me until she Mack-trucked from the saved babies back into our wing of the house again.

Nana's other closet was much smaller and lined with smooth rose-papered shelving, where she stored piles of receipts for deliveries of formula and diapers and footless Martian pajamas and rows of tattered yellow pads containing the names of every child Father had saved from the devil abortionists, most of them with big red checkmarks beside them signifying they'd come and gone to somebody who actually wanted them running underfoot. Searching for a Pandora, I went through every name I could before I heard Nana scrape her old wooden chair back from the card table and cackle, "Thought you had me that time, didn't you?" By then, I'd found no end of Emilys and Jakes and a predictable number of Marys and Matthews from the days when Sister Flatulencia was still in charge of the children, but not a Pandora in sight. I was beginning to get a little frantic. Mysteries that go on too long are a magnet for the void. But since Pandora was such an unfamiliar name, I decided to stretch onto tippy toes and snatched down Nana's *Book of Names* from the second topmost shelf. While Nana was still bragging about how cleverly she'd played her cards, I slipped past the four of them and ran down the hall to my room, tightly clutching the book that Nana used to call her Bible, though you can well imagine she never said that when Sister Flatulencia was around.

I guess I was more scared about stealing the book than I realized, because when I settled myself onto my bed and opened the *Book of Names*, I had to keep my tongue out to catch little drops of sweat pouring down my face before they hit the P page. I found Pandora all right, just after Pamela, which means *sweetness*, and before Pansy, which you might be as surprised as I was to learn means *thought*. You can't imagine how relieved I was to learn that, after all her self-inflicted troubles, Pandora ended up with Hope. Anyone who has had as hard a time as I have holding off the void knows the miracle and practical necessity of hope, like your body's memory of the exact path from your bed to the bathroom when it's the middle of the night and the little bulb in your duck-shaped night-light has burnt out.

Which brings me back to Dhani, who told me a few months after coming to us, "I'm fairly certain that if I'd had a night-light shaped like a duck like yours when I was a girl in India, everything would have turned out quite differently." Except when she said *girl*, it came out sounding like *gull*, and when she said *India*, it sounded like *Eenja*. Dhani was the first person I ever met who came from another country. Once I found a way to wrap my mind around that one, I got pretty excited. I mean, the existence of whole continents' worth of people creating millions of boredom-battering customs (not to mention languages, laws, and expressions) meant that if you ever ran out of things to do, you could always fly to another country and have to learn to speak a whole new language in order to buy butter, find the toilet, and figure out when people were joking and when they were not.

Dhani liked to say, "I came to your family from New Delhi via Islington and ignorance." I understood that the Islington part had to do with where she'd lived in England in between leaving India and coming to America, but the ignorance part only became clear later.

When I first heard Nana whispering to Fayga about Dhani's bun in the oven, it was very confusing. Dhani didn't cook buns, but she did make the most amazing *chapatis* and *naan* and *papadums*. Once she'd fully settled in, I liked to hitch myself up to the kitchen stool, latching my ankles against its wooden support bars, and watch her knead and pat and pinch her dough, feeling happy as a lazy monkey as the air got fat with spice and smoke. Dhani was like a busy bird, but I could tell that she actually listened to me as I talked, her eyes brimming over with wetness as if my words were like one of those sad movies that has the odd effect of sweetening your own void.

But I did have some misgivings over what got into her when she put her mind to cooking a main dish. The first time I tried her curry, it made my poo smell loud and angry and burnt my butt like the devil on the way out. When Nana saw what kind of state I was in, she shook her head and fetched me a tube of A and D Ointment before marching downstairs to instruct Dhani to make my meals separately and put a lot more cream in.

Fayga always used to say that cream made you fat, so I assumed it was the adjustment of my diet that was making my chest go all lumpy. But I had no explanation for why little hairs began to sprout up from my tweeter—by the way, that was Nana's word for it; Mother called it *gyna*, which sounded so wrong I was convinced she'd made it up. I worried that the fuzz on my tweeter was because I hadn't wiped carefully enough, front to back like Nana had taught me, and my loose pee was watering a budding bed of hairs on my skin. I tried to keep the hairs a secret, but Nana saw them one time when I forgot and changed into my non-Martian two-legged pajamas—the ones with little upside-down and turning-around puppies and kittens—in front of her. She cried a little, which got me pinching myself, but then she grabbed hold of my hand and sat us down on the side of the bed, muttering under her breath, "In a normal household, your mother'd be the one to tell you, but never mind." She proceeded to explain about breasts and tweeters and pubic hairs and periods, which, I don't need to tell you, got me very anxious, indeed.

I never did have the heart to tell Nana how she'd caused me a month's worth of nightmares with that one, all of them variations on the theme of me leaking melted red jelly candies out of my tweeter and red-hot curry out of my butt. I solved that one by inventing a nightly ritual of falling asleep holding the plump little folds of my tweeter kissing-close with one hand and the other cupped over my butt. My sleep wasn't exactly comfortable, and I woke up each morning with a terrible crick in my neck from all that awkward stretching, but at least when I examined my bed sheets each morning they were as unspoiled and white as Cook's perfect meringue, and I felt pretty sure I was still alive.

By the way, Nana's cutting reference to my mother didn't exactly surprise me. During our final year in Gladwyne, it wasn't at all unusual to find the two of them arguing. Well, to be fair, Nana would be the one arguing; Mother barely said anything at all. I tried to avoid passing Mother's bedroom as much as I could. I dreaded hearing Nana say things like, "For God's sake, Margaret, you can't stay in bed all day," and "Can't you make some kind of effort, at least for the child?"

I knew Nana was wrong about one thing. Mother didn't spend all her time in bed. One morning, feeling the need for a tight space and not being able to take refuge in Nana's closet—it was being treated for rotting cedar—I snuck into Mother's bedroom while she was in the bathroom and hid in *her* closet. When Mother came back, I peeked through a crack in the door. I saw her take off her robe and stand naked, staring at herself balefully in her mirror. Unlike my straight-up fur, my mother had wild, every-which-way pubic hair. I couldn't help but wish that she acted more like those hairs looked.

I was getting more and more worried about Mother. Each day, she was becoming less of a presence, as if you wouldn't even have to lean against her body to go right through her. You could just look and shoot through to the other side. The more times Father came down to the kitchen to tell Dhani how beautiful she was, the more Mother seemed to shrink. I began to form a disaster plan to whisk her safely into my pocket in case she showed signs of getting too small to withstand Father's baby-saving rages. The thought of Father trampling a shrunken Mother underfoot was too terrifying for words.

But it wasn't just Mother I was worried about. Grandfather was peeing his bed almost nightly now. Nana kept saying, "Don't worry. Your father is interviewing nurses for him. You'll see. He'll do much better when he has someone taking care of him full time." She didn't even bother to reply when I proposed myself for the job.

Grandfather's nurse arrived on a seemingly normal day. I was keeping busy stroking the flappy sack of Jillily's belly, making my breathing match the rhythm of her whirring motor, and noticing, not for the first time, that the bottoms of her paws smelled just like toe jam. When the doorbell rang, Jillily shot away as if she sensed a dog that needed putting down. I don't know if you've noticed, but animals can smell danger much faster than humans, which is hard to understand since their noses are so small.

Once Jillily ran off, I skipped down the stairs two at a time and skidded toward the front door just as Fayga was opening it to the scariest-looking person I had ever seen.

The first thing I noticed about her was her mouth. Do you remember the story called *Little Red Riding Hood?* Actually, I always thought of it as *Red Riding Hood and Her Granny*, since Red Riding Hood seemed to have very similar feelings about her Granny that I had for Grandfather. You can imagine how sick I felt in my tummy when that sneaky wolf tried to pretend he was Granny instead of the mean devil he actually was. Anyway, when Fayga opened the door, the nurse was already wearing one of those wide, tooth-showing smiles that you're only supposed to make when you are particularly fond of the person you are smiling at. I'd already had enough experiences in my brief time on this planet to know that anybody who has her biggest smile on before she even knows who will be opening the door is like that big bad wolf. She is pretending.

Now, I like pretending as much as the next person. But pretending you're happy to see someone when you don't even know who they'll be is just plain wrong. It would be like Jillily whirring her motor for just anyone, rather than saving it for me. The nurse kept smiling her fake smile as her black eyes shifted toward me. My skin felt hot and itchy. Not caring about breaking Father's rule, I ran as fast as I could across the long upstairs hall to the other wing of the house, skipping around several crawling babies as I yelled to Nana to come quick, the wolf was here and we had to save Grandfather.

But it was no use. Nana shouted in her harshest Mack truck voice that she had a sick baby on her hands and it was just plain selfish of me to lie to get attention. I could see she was right about the sobbing baby, but she was as wrong as could be about me. I had never lied about anything but pretending to eat Grandfather's red jelly candies. But I couldn't waste a minute being angry at Nana. I had to get to Grandfather, and fast. I turned around to head back to our wing of the house, nearly stepping on one of the crawling babies. In order to avoid crushing its pudgy little hand, I made a quick but unfortunately awkward jump, which landed me flat on my back so hard it knocked the breath right out of me.

Nana yelled, "Shit! Are you okay?" Sister Flatulencia came running, her face all wiggly as if she were unable to decide whether to be mad at Nana for saying a bad word or worried for me that I couldn't catch my breath enough to sit up. She let her hand solve the dilemma, crossing herself two times, once for anger and once for worry, and knelt down beside me, telling me not to move. I think she was afraid I'd broken my back. As luck would have it, though, as she knelt down, she let free one of her silent but deadlies, and I scrambled to my feet quicker than a cockroach. That night, when I explained to Nana what had gotten me moving, she laughed and said maybe that was really meant by the expression, "getting a second wind."

Sadly, though, from that day forward, Nana remained deaf and blind to what I had to tell her about Grandfather's new nurse. Everyone in our household seemed more than willing to notice little things like the sink getting blocked up or Leland DuRay overcharging for Martian pajamas, but were perfectly content to ignore true evil.

By the end of her first week in our house, Nurse managed to do these things:

1. Have Fayga get Ignacio to move a bed for her into Grandfather's room;

2. Move Mother's rocker away from the window so that she could sit in it while Grandfather slept, waking him every couple of hours to take him to pee so she wouldn't have to change his sheets all the time;

3. Smile at everybody like she was particularly fond of them, but make mean faces at Grandfather and grit her teeth when he *ugga umph uggà ed* at her; I know this because I climbed our tree and spied on her;

4. Talk to Grandfather like he was a baby;

5. Say I could only visit Grandfather once a day, since my visits agitated him.

This was not good. It took me a while to figure out how to get her away from Grandfather's room long enough to find out how he was managing. It finally occurred to me that, with Grandfather stuck in bed most of the time these days, Nana was missing a fourth for Hearts. Luckily, I was able to persuade her to invite Nurse to be their fourth, and Nurse turned out to be good enough at the game that she would drop everything to be able to gloat at besting Nana and Fayga and Sister Flatulencia.

That was how I got my chance to see the bruises on Grandfather's shoulders and back that I was in a particularly good position to know came from pinching. It was also how I got my first look at Grandfather's woefully swollen balls. I knew they were way too big because Mrs. Perle had slipped a book called *Changing Bodies, Changing Lives* underneath *Wuthering Heights* in a pile of books I'd checked out from the library a few months earlier. Needless to say, I'd been tremendously relieved to discover I wasn't the only girl my age beset by curiosity about the male member, which I'd nursed in secret ever since seeing Michelangelo's David on the cover of a book on Renaissance art.

Anyway, there we were, Grandfather and I—watching our tree, me having dragged Mother's rocking chair back to the window and then helping Grandfather to his own chair, which I hated to see took us three whole minutes to get him to. It was hard to believe he'd still been completing the circuit of our grounds only a month ago.

Once we got settled, though, we were doing fine. I was pointing out a hummingbird with particularly shiny green feathers, and Grandfather grinned and *ugga umphed* like I hadn't heard him do for ages. But then a strange look came over his face and he stood up abruptly, trying to simultaneously shuffle in the direction of the bathroom and

undo the tie of his pajama bottoms. The pajamas fell down to his ankles, putting a stop to his efforts to move his feet.

I managed to push aside my horror at the thickly blue-veined
balloons suspended on either side of his pinkish member. I yanked
up his pj's and retied them. Taking Grandfather by the hand, I led
him to the bathroom, whispering, "Hold on, Grandpa, just hold on a
little longer, we're nearly there." The good news is that we made it in
time. The bad news was that I realized something was terribly wrong
with my grandfather.

Chapter 4 🦋

NANA USED TO say that seven and eleven were lucky numbers, but being eleven wasn't breaking any records in the happiness department, especially given Grandfather's failing health. One particularly crisp spring morning, Uncle Bob and I were just beginning to pick up steam when I saw Ignacio approaching from the direction of the invisible flowerbeds, shaking his head and sporting an ominous red and black bottle. Hurriedly stuffing Uncle Bob into my pocket, I ran to my friend. Ignacio wasn't a man to mince words. He told me that Mother's Anne Boleyn rose had gotten bug-ridden and sickly, despite his resorting to a potent series of ministrations of insecticides and fungicides. I insisted on taking a look myself. There was no denying it. Anne Boleyn was nothing but a criss-cross of dry, gray sticks. I turned away to spare Anne my shock.

Despite his objections, I insisted that Ignacio come with me to tell Mother. I simply couldn't bear doing it by myself. She'd planted each one of those Austins—every single Anne Boleyn, Abraham Darby, and Jude the Obscure herself. We found her in the dining room, pushing a scrambled egg around her plate. She looked up from her dish, and I saw that the circles under her eyes were darker than ever. Ignacio explained apologetically that he'd tried everything he could think of. He told Mother it was very mysterious, since that particular variety of rose is known for its disease resistance, but he was certain Anne would never flower again.

Mother merely brushed her hand in the air and forced a laugh that was more like a nervous dog barking than a real laugh, saying,

"Well, then, Anne Boleyn and I have a lot more in common than anyone knew."

She pushed herself up from her chair and proceeded to waft up the stairs like a ghost. After that, no one could persuade her to come out. Even when I tiptoed into her room the following Friday, whispering, "Mother, won't you come out to the garden with me for Anne's burial?" she merely trailed her fingers over the top of my head before turning her back to me, mumbling, "Sorry, Flurry. I'm just so tired."

The name *Flurry* was one I was rarely called. I tended to associate it with disappointment. As I've mentioned, the staff called me things like Sweetie Pie, Angel Face, Muchacha, You Poor Child, and The Unluckiest Child. But never Flurry. That one seemed to be reserved for my parents. And since Father tended to be pretty oblivious to my existence, it was mostly used by Mother.

The first time I recall hearing it, I was quite young. It was a spring evening, and the night blooming jasmine was sending its heavenly perfume through my bedroom window. Mother had returned to the house from tucking the roses into their invisible beds and came into my room as I was putting on my pajamas. Placing a vase with three Eglantynes onto my night table, she helped me on with my pajama top even though I had recently learned to do it myself. She sat me on my bed and put her face right up to mine, tilting my head up to hers with a finger under my chin and kissing me quickly on each cheek, whispering, "My dear little Flurry." But when I decided, a couple of hours later, that it would be much nicer to sleep in Mother's bed than my own, Nana had to come and put a hand over my mouth and force her body between me and Mother's door, which I was trying my best to kick in, telling me, "Hush, child, your mother isn't well. You have to let her sleep." Even then, Mother seemed to need a lot more sleep than I did.

As for the name itself, I assumed it came from my flurrying habit of spinning around and around and flapping my arms *fla fla fla* whenever I was particularly anxious. Jillily often joined in by chasing her tail in excited little circles, which would help, because it would make me laugh.

But I wasn't flurrying and I wasn't laughing when Ignacio and I returned Anne Boleyn to the earth in a small grave beyond the first fountain. Instead, I stood shivering as Ignacio shoveled dirt over her woody stems, which looked unbearably voidish without their pink rosettes and soft green foliage. Ignacio threw down his shovel when he was done and wiped his hands carefully before taking my hand in his calloused one and promising me, "Now it's nature's turn. That bush will fertilize many beautiful things in your garden, *muchacha*."

His kind words *did* comfort me some, but I'd been doing some research. Mother's allusion to a special connection between her and Anne Boleyn was definitely not a good sign—Anne Boleyn's husband had cut off her head. I tried comforting myself that it would have pleased Mother to see me place my diary containing lists of weed names on Anne's little burial mound as a mark of respect. But when she finally emerged from her bedroom, I never got around to telling her. I was on my way to look in on Grandfather at the time and was just about to pass Mother's door when it opened quite suddenly. Mother stepped into the hall and caught hold of my elbow, her kimono flying open to reveal her pale breasts. Her hands were clutching at me like desperate little animal claws, and she wasn't even looking at me, but staring down the hall at something I couldn't see. Hearing Nana's heavy footfalls on the stairs, I wrested free and ran to my room, pinching my arms and thighs with a vengeance until they went numb.

The next day, I was sitting cross-legged and sore on the lawn near the invisible rose beds when I heard someone whistling a song I didn't recognize in a voice that I did. I looked up, shielding my eyes with my hand from the noonday sun. Ignacio's smile was particularly cheerful. He threw something down onto my lap.

"What's this?"

"Why don't you look, and you'll see?"

So I did. It was a David Austin brochure. It pictured hundreds of climbers and ramblers, double-blooms and tea roses, cabbage-shaped flowers and clustered ones. The written descriptions were so vivid, I imagined I could actually smell each one.

Ignacio sat down beside me, folding his long legs, and said softly, "Since your mother's not well, I think you should pick the new rose to replace the one that's gone."

I couldn't decide between A Shropshire Lad and Brother Cadfael, so Ignacio said, "I'll take you to the nursery. Easier to make up your mind when you see them there."

We arranged to meet at 11:00 the next morning, but Ignacio was late. Ignacio was never late. By 11:15, I had to deal with the voidish possibility that he'd forgotten. I was so anxious that I started skipping around the grounds, searching for any new weed that might have sprouted since my last visit there. That was when I saw the bird. It was right under the first tree. It was lying on its side without moving, which no bird in its right mind would do near a house with a Jillily in it, so I ran up to see what was what.

I could see that the bird was what Nana liked to call a common sparrow, which was pretty disrespectful, given that sparrows can fly as fast as fifty miles an hour. But this particular bird didn't even move as I skipped toward it. I don't need to tell you that this was not a good sign. And when I slid down to the ground as slowly and un-threateningly as I could, I could see it was a baby, its little heart beating clippity-clip clippity-clip, faster than mine or Jillily's ever did, and its little eyes were blinking and its little beak opening and shutting, but it still didn't move its little wings or its little feet.

I looked up at the tree, hoping to see a mother bird up there who'd swoop down and regurgitate a piece of worm into its open beak to strengthen it so it could fly. But after all the tree watching Grandfather and I had done, I was pretty good at discerning hidden birds in trees, and there was no mama hovering over this baby.

Panicked, I ran to the house, racing up the stairs to my bedroom. I scrabbled for a shoe box in my closet, flung my powder-blue sneakers out of the box, hurried into my bathroom, grabbed a washcloth, nearly flew down the stairs and sped to the baby bird, who looked about the same, only its chest was beating a little more faintly and when it blinked it took longer to open its eyes again. Its belly did not look as round as it had just minutes ago. The baby bird was shrink-ing. It needed plumping up, and fast.

I don't need to tell you how scary it was to pick up the bird and lay it on the washcloth that I'd folded into the box. I tried pretending it was a layer of Cook's phyllo dough that I knew I must not drop. I held my breath the whole time.

Holding the box as still as I could, I took the steps to the second floor, one at a time and very slowly. I have to confess that I shoved Jillily away from my bedroom door with my foot when she tried to follow me and that I actually hated her a little when she meowed and meowed on the other side of my closed bedroom door for me to let her in.

Okay, I kept saying to myself. Okay. It will be okay. Just go down to the kitchen, get a saucer of milk. Remember the eyedropper that you used when Jillily had itchy eyes? Find it and rinse it out a lot to get the old medicine out of it. Drop a teensy drop of milk into the baby bird's beak. Do it near an open window. Maybe the bird will rouse itself and fly.

Do it now. Down to the kitchen. Nobody here. Good. Get the milk. Up the stairs with it. Jillily's gone. Must be in some other part of the house, pouting. Fine for her. Open the window. Put the saucer of milk in the shaft of sunlight coming through; that will warm it a little. Check the bird. Chest still moving up and down? Good. Now into the bathroom. Find the eyedropper. Wash it with shampoo. Rinse it. Rinse it again. Dry it. But wait—maybe there's still medicine in it; wash it and rinse it some more. Dry it again. Hurry now, back to the baby bird. Stroke its belly with your little finger to let it know you won't hurt it. Suck the milk into the eyedropper; hold it close to the little beak.

No, wait! Practice emptying it a few times into the saucer. Now—carefully, one teensy drop into the open beak. Oh no. Too much. Wipe the beak with the tip of your fingernail. Try again. Careful now, straight in.

But by now the baby bird's head was drenched with milk, and it was shivering and a blue film was coming over its eyes like a translucent screen. My heart was beating in the same fast and slow pattern as the baby bird's. I lifted it up as gently as I could and held it close to my heart, covering its trembling little body with chicken peck kisses.

But it stopped breathing and never started back up again. Its little head flopped to the side loosely, as if it had no neck.

There are times when you have to face facts, when the thing you least want stares you in the face and you just have to stare back.

The baby bird was dead.

I had not meant to put it down.

I could feel a pulsing, evil shape forming at the pit of my belly, moaning like a coyote caught in the tightest trap of all. I didn't want to hold the baby bird anymore. I dropped it back into the shoebox and flopped onto the floor, positioning my back against the familiar sharp edge of the dresser. I thought and thought about what I needed to do, which wasn't so easy, because of the evil thing in my belly wanting my attention, instead.

This was my dilemma: when a living creature dies, its ability to chirp or breathe or fly may fall into the void, but its body does not. The thing about that baby bird was, as much as I knew it was dead and that its body should be given at least as much respect as Mother's Anne Boleyn, I couldn't bring myself to consider sticking it in the ground. It's one thing to put a mildew-eaten rose bush into the earth. All its life the dirt has been its home. But birds are another thing altogether. When they're not keeping their voids at bay by flitting around in trees, they like to fly.

But how can you send a bird back to *its* home in the sky when the lack of flapping wings will pretty much guarantee it'll end up right back on the ground again? I briefly considered the possibility of inventing a giant slingshot to fling it farther than our planet's atmosphere so it could escape the pull of gravity, but the thought of the baby bird floating in space like one of the upside down cats and dogs on my pajamas almost stopped my heart beating. Far too much void.

What complicated matters even further was that, as I pondered my dilemma, I became aware of Nana's heavy feet Mack-trucking up the stairs, most likely aiming for my bedroom with a question about why I wasn't on my way to the nursery with Ignacio. That was when I made my second mistake. I lifted the bird from my shoebox, only slightly aware of how cooled down its soggy body had become, and yanked open my middle dresser drawer, stuffing the bird behind a pile of winter wool sweaters.

When Nana flung open my bedroom door, I was already standing with my back to the dresser. I'm ashamed to say I had a pretend smile on my face. Nana didn't seem to notice, though. She merely told me that Ignacio wouldn't be taking me to the nursery that day. She said that Grandfather was feeling especially poorly, and Mother didn't fancy Ignacio going off the grounds when she was waiting for Grandfather's doctor to make a house call. She might need him to get some medicine.

When I heard that piece of news I forgot about the bird. I raced to Grandfather's bedroom, but Nurse was barring the way as if she'd known I was coming, claiming that Grandfather was too sick to be bothered by children and that I should go and play. Since I wasn't children, but me, and I knew Grandfather would want me by his side if he weren't feeling well, I started screaming. But then Nana came and said how could I disturb my grandfather at a time like this and dragged me away to her room and tried chicken-pecking me. I made my throat be silent because maybe she was right. I didn't want to disturb Grandfather, but I didn't want her chicken peck kisses, either. I wanted only to close my eyes and invisibly glide down the hall, right around that mean old nurse, under the crack in Grandfather's bedroom door, up onto Grandfather's bed, where I could snuggle tightly at his side and stay with him until he felt better. So I closed my eyes tightly and wished as hard as I could. Nobody could make me open my eyes, not Nana, not Mother, not Fayga nor Dhani nor even Sister Flatulencia, who had entered Nana's room trailing one of the worst farts ever known to mankind.

You can imagine my relief when I learned that Grandfather's bad feeling turned out to be what Nana called a false alarm. At her insistence I was allowed to visit him before dinner, so I opened my eyes to walk to his room. Everything looked especially bright and clear after all that eye-squishing, and when I curled into bed with Grandfather and he brushed my hair tenderly with his blue-veined hand, I studied every single wrinkle and funny-shaped brown spot on his face so that I could be sure to remember them for a new diary I decided right then and there to start keeping. I called that diary, "List of the Wrinkles and Brown Spots on Grandfather's Face," and, sure enough, more wrinkles and spots seemed to bloom on grandfather with every passing day, so it was good that somebody was keeping track of them.

As for the bruises on Grandfather's arms, I'd already started keeping a list of those in another diary, but Nana refused to believe me when I told her about them, and when I tried to explain to Fayga, she insisted on washing my mouth out with soap. I decided to keep my Book of Bruises somewhere safe and secret for the day when somebody came into our house who wasn't nervous about losing another Hearts partner and actually wanted to hear the truth.

Long before, when I was five and had just found out I wasn't going to be starting school after all, I'd discovered there was a loose brick in my bedroom fireplace. I hadn't yet discovered the comforts of Nana's second smallest closet. In some ways, the fireplace was even better. It provided a tight enough fit to stop me from shattering into a million pieces over the disappointment of not being able to play with other children at school. But it had the disadvantage of leaving me frightfully ashy when I came out again.

Sure enough, though, there was just enough room for my diary right behind that loose brick in the fireplace, and if the brick stuck out just a little now with the diary stuck behind it, it didn't really matter. It was mid-April, and with any luck some truth-liker would show up before the weather turned cold again.

My biggest concern at that time was to sneak enough time with Grandfather to be able to keep track of his wrinkles and spots and the bruises on his arms. I pushed the baby bird to the back of my mind, as if my mind had its own dresser with color-coded winter sweaters to block the bird from view.

But despite the troubles in our home, Ignacio and I finally did make it to the nursery that week. It turned out Ignacio liked to sing Mexican folk songs while he drove his big white truck, but, while the ride there was quite entertaining, I felt a pang seeing children riding their bikes and walking together as if it were the most natural thing in the world.

Once we got to Somerset Nursery, we were disappointed to learn they were out of stock of Shropshire Lads *and* Brother Cadfaels. I ended up picking a Mary Magdalene. It was in its bare root state, so my nose had to imagine its "tea rose scent with a hint of myrrh." I knew from reading Sister Flatulencia's Bible that myrrh was one of the Wise Mens' gifts to Baby Jesus, so I figured it had to be fine for Mother and me. As Ignacio and I rode home, he assured me that I had made a fine choice and that it was good I was willing to take a risk based on my keen imagination.

I ran into the kitchen, shouting excitedly, "We've got our Mary Magdalene!" Sister Flatulencia crossed herself and left the room. Fayga's eyes started wandering everywhere except toward the part of the kitchen where Dhani was standing. Dhani shot a quick look at Ignacio while curling a protective hand over her newly rounding belly.

My first thought was that maybe I shouldn't have relied on my keen imagination, after all. Maybe I should have brought home a third Sweet Juliet, instead. I started to feel hot and pit-ish, so I ran to my room and flopped onto the bed. Even pinching felt like too much work. Luckily, Jillily jumped up beside me and curled into a ball with

46

her back against my face. I breathed into her fur, my breath spreading a hot little circle on her back, and I could think of nothing for a nice long while but her.

But within a few days, my room starting reeking something awful. At first, we all assumed it was Sister Flatulencia, who'd being coming for years to my room at bedtime to make sure I said enough Hail Marys to save all the unwanted babies in the world. But eventually it became clear that not even Sister Flatulencia's infamous farts could account for the sickly-sweet smell pervading my room.

The smell got so putrid that even I had to acknowledge that something was terribly wrong. But it took me overhearing Fayga tell Nana that she was convinced the smell was something dead trapped in the fireplace, and that she had called a chimney sweep to take care of it, for me to remember the baby bird. It was as if I'd put a padlock on the dresser drawer in my mind. It was pretty scary to realize that someone with as much of a dread of voidishness as me would have her own personal black pit to fling things into that she didn't want to think about.

That was when I made another one of my ill-conceived plans. I decided I would pinch myself into staying awake that night until the whole household was asleep, and then I would take the bird out to the grounds and spoon out a little place for it in Anne Boleyn's grave, praying that Anne would take pity on the poor creature and keep it company, since it would be stuck so far from its home in the sky, feeding the worms in the ground rather than the other way around.

Staying awake that late wasn't half as hard as I'd imagined. I'd gotten a jagged fingernail from trying to push the Book of Bruises further back into its hidey-hole, so my pinching packed an extra punch of pain, which proved quite helpful.

The house was as dark as it could be when I cautiously slid open my middle drawer. I nearly fell over from the smell.

I had to concentrate on swallowing to keep myself from puking. I could sense Jillily rousing at the foot of the bed, stretching and curling her tail into a question mark as I opened the drawer. My fingers found the bird, which was so loose-skinned that it threatened to fall apart in my hands. I hurriedly wrapped it inside a sweater and stuffed the whole thing under my pajama top, breathing heavily through my mouth to spare my nose the realization of what lurked right below.

Suddenly, light filled the room. A nightgown-clad Nana stood at the door, one hand on the light switch and one over her mouth. The decomposing baby bird tumbled out from my pajama top, scattering feathers everywhere. Jillily leapt down from the bed faster than a flying roach, fastening her sharp little teeth around the dead bird's head.

I don't even want to tell you what came next. There are some layers of hell one wouldn't wish on one's worst enemy.

Needless to say, Fayga cancelled the chimney sweep, so the Book of Bruises was safe, but I soon discovered I'd been given a new name. You can imagine how surprised I was, coming down for breakfast the next morning, to see that Mother was awake at a normal hour and was actually sitting at the table with Father. But then Father started describing in shaming detail the antics of someone called That Creepy Child. He continued, "You know, they say people who become serial killers usually start out torturing animals. What kind of person hides a stinking dead bird in her bedroom?" It didn't take more than a few seconds to sort out that that person was *me*.

I waited for Mother to leap to my defense, but she didn't. She merely gazed intently at her eggs Benedict as if the olive circles on top were staring back at her. She stabbed the tines of her fork into one of the eggs, dragging Hollandaise like an infected sore across her plate. I altered my path and headed for the kitchen. The fact that Mother hadn't uttered a word on my behalf wasn't lost on me. It felt terribly unfair that someone I constantly worried about didn't seem very worried about me.

Chapter 5 🦋

LUCKILY, THERE WERE a couple of people in the house who chose not to subscribe to my new name. One of them was my increasingly frail Grandfather, whose recognition never took the form of words, anyway, but announced itself in the lift of his walrus moustache when I climbed onto his bed and the meltiness of his eyes when I snuggled next to him, his veiny hand gently untangling my hair. The other person was Dhani, whose visibly rising bun in the oven seemed to make everyone else in our household want to avoid her like one of Sister Flatulencia's silent but deadlies.

It became a kind of ritual that whenever Nurse would shut me out of Grandfather's room, I'd wander down to the kitchen. There—with my feet tucked under the rail of the kitchen stool—I'd listen for hours to Dhani's King's English and watch with great interest as she ground coriander and cardamom and cumin seeds for *garam masala*, browned lamb with onions and garlic for lamb korma, and soaked raisins in water to make them plump and soft for chicken curry.

I couldn't help but notice that the more Dhani's bun stuck out in front of her, the more her mind seemed to stretch behind her to her years in Islington and to Delhi, where she was born. Listening to Dhani's soft voice made pleasurable goose bumps all over my head, as if her words were stretching my mind in every direction with thoughts and pictures I could store for the relief of future boredom.

These are some of the things I entered in my diary about what I'd learned in Dhani's kitchen:

1. Islington is the home of the football team, which isn't what you might think, because the players are not encouraged to crash into each other on purpose like football players on our television sets, but to bounce balls on their heads, instead.

2. Dhani's mother has a red dot on her forehead, right between her eyes, and Dhani once did, herself, until her job interview with Father, who told her he wouldn't tolerate any hocus-pocus in his household.

3. In Delhi there is a holiday named Holi where everyone throws colored water and colored powder called *gulal* at each other.

4. Father likes Dhani in ways that don't bear thinking about. I did not learn this by hearing him say so. I learned it when Dhani and I were doing our own version of Holi right outside the kitchen door.

This is what happened: Dhani's back was hurting from being thrown out of balance by her bun, so she decided to heat up some leftover *biryani* for dinner that night, which I thought was a terrific idea, since *biryani* is even tastier the next day.

We sat awhile on our kitchen stools, pretty quietly for Dhani, and pretty quietly for me, until Dhani's void got the best of her. She said, "I'll tell you what, let's pretend it's Holi." Then she asked me if I had any leftover dye from Easter eggs. I went looking in Nana's smallest closet—fortunately, Nana was busy on the saved children's wing—and, sure enough, there was enough dye to make colored water for our pretend Holi.

It was while I was gathering together packets of dye that it occurred to me that coloring eggs is our way of showing how happy we are that Jesus came back from the grave. According to Sister Flatulencia, Christ rose from the dead after three days, which is how everybody knew that Jesus is Lord. I still didn't get the connection between colored eggs and an alive Jesus followed by a dead Jesus followed by an alive Jesus, except that if you leave your Easter eggs out in the sun long enough they smell a lot like what happened to the baby bird on the lawn, so maybe Jesus' grave was as cold as a refrigerator, and that was how He kept from getting spoiled and why we can still eat His body and drink His blood in Church without getting as sick as Jillily when she steals rancid food from the garbage bin out back.

Anyway, those were some of the thoughts that helped me fill my void before I got back down to the kitchen. By that time, Dhani had decided that, since we had no *gulal*, powdered cardamom would do. She insisted I go back upstairs one more time to put on a pair of white shorts and a white T-shirt that Fayga could bleach when we were through, but she didn't bother to change clothes herself, saying she was so sick of the wide yellow smock and stretchy-waistband denim pants she was wearing that she'd just as soon burn them when we were done.

It was a warm day, so the buckets of cold colored water Dhani flung onto my limbs while we stood outside the kitchen door made me screech like one of the wild parrots that riot over our grounds every spring. Dhani passed me the bucket and twirled in careful circles, arms curled protectively over her bun in the oven, while I tossed enough water at her for her burnable clothes to be covered all over in pleasing pastel patterns.

Dhani had second thoughts about using cardamom for our *gulal*, worrying that my pale skin might get a rash from being covered in gritty spice, but she did make a paste of some cardamom and water and put a dot of it onto my forehead right between my two eyes, which gave me no end of stimulation trying to cross my eyes sufficiently to see it.

Then she sat on the ground and cried a little, and when I sat down beside her, rocking with nervousness, she said not to worry, it was just that a woman wanted her own mother at a time like this.

"You mean a time like Holi?"

She shook her head. "No, love. When you're having a baby."

You can imagine the questions I wanted to ask right then, but we both heard a sound and looked up in unison. I am sorry to say that it was not Dhani's mother who emerged from the kitchen door, but Father.

I guess we'd been making more noise than we'd realized. Father came out of the house with his I-hate-children-under-my-feet expression, which quickly grew even more ferocious as he took in my soaking state and the cardamom dot between my eyes. He gave me that impatient wave of his that meant he wanted me to go away.

I was torn. I couldn't wait to get away from Father, but I was worried what he'd do to Dhani. What if he fired her for showing me how to celebrate Holi? So I went inside, but left the kitchen door open a crack.

I watched Father walk right up to Dhani and say, "Well, who's a fat little ball of cotton candy? If I don't say so myself, you look good enough to eat."

The thought of Dhani being gobbled up by Father sent me reeling dangerously close to an especially large and vacuumy void, but Dhani just blushed a matching color to the pink Easter dye on her arms.

Father didn't seem to realize that the color on Dhani's cheeks wasn't dye. He rubbed her face, softly, with just his thumb, and put his other hand over her bun in the oven as if he owned it, saying, "Is that a nice little cotton candy baby you're growing for me? Shall I eat it, too?"

To my surprise, Dhani didn't get angry. Instead, she flitted her butterfly eyelashes the very same way she flitted them at Ignacio, and she didn't even flinch when Father slid his hand down her belly like a sneaky skier till he stopped at the V of her tweeter.

I dropped to my knees, but kept my eyes on the two of them. Father began to nibble at Dhani's lips. I knelt there in a blank and terrible place until I managed to catch my breath and tiptoe away.

Even though my belly felt queasy every time I thought about Dhani letting Father chew on her lips, and even though I knew Ignacio would be very unhappy if he'd seen it, I continued to be fond of Dhani. The truth is, though, it was hard to tell the difference between feeling affection for Dhani and wanting to *be* her. Think about it. Who would you rather look like—a flat-butted, flat-chested, too-skinny girl starting to shoot Alice-in-Wonderlandishly up towards the ceiling or a nut-brown woman with cushiony red lips and a dimply chin and mysterious dark eyes and black hair that shines blue in the sun and a body with all kinds of interesting curves even before she got her bun in the oven?

Which is why, just a week or so after our pretend Holi, I stuck a black cardigan over my hair for a wig and painted my lips with a stolen tube of Mother's Chanel Infrarouge lipstick and stuffed a pillow under my dress, fastening it to my middle with the tie to Nana's cave-ish robe, so I could strike poses and admire myself from several angles in my bedroom mirror.

How was I to know that Mother would choose that moment to pay me one of her increasingly rare visits?

I saw her first in the mirror. She was wearing a pink satin robe and one of those crooked smiles that seemed to accompany her heaviest medicinal smell, but once she took in my black-sweater hair and poofed-out belly and bright red lips and bright red dot between my eyes, she started shouting bad words, and all I could utter in my own defense was *fla fla fla!* and flap my hands as if they were the missing wings of my bodyless-duck night-light, and then Mother whooshed out of the room to turn her screechiest voice onto Father, yelling, "Now my own daughter is strutting around imitating your latest whore!" and Father squeaked back, "I don't know what you're talking about!" and then Nana rushed into my room and slammed the door and gave me a withering look before flopping onto the bed and saying in a decidedly un-Mack-truck voice, "Oh, my dear, you *are* the unluckiest child."

Which is the one thing you do not want to hear when you live in a household full of unwanted children.

That night, I had a particularly scary variation of my old nightmare, with Cook returning to our house from Senator Manus' and forcing me into a big round pan, slathering with me with heaps of heavy winter apples before sliding me into the oven, then fetching me out afterwards, all hot and shriveled and crispy, and delivering me to the middle of the dinner table, where Grandfather lay trussed on a companion platter.

I shuddered awake with the certainty that something was wrong with Grandfather.

I ran to his room, but the door was locked. I pounded for Nurse to let me in, but she didn't even bother to yell at me to go away. I sped down the long hallway to Fayga's room, only to discover a heavy Hearts session in progress, with Nurse making a fourth. I shouted that we needed to check on Grandfather, but Nurse kept saying there was no need to check on him, that Grandfather was fast asleep with a sleeping pill she'd given him, and couldn't I just keep quiet a minute, it was her play. The rest of them didn't seem inclined to challenge her, though Sister Flatulencia did let a silent fart and guiltily shifted her eyes between me and her fan of cards.

They should have listened to me. Grandfather never fully came to from his sleeping pill, and Mother had to call the doctor back out the next morning. After his examination, I managed to sneak inside Grandfather's room as Mother and Nurse and Father spoke with the doctor downstairs.

Grandfather's eyes were closed and he seemed to be asleep. His breathing was heavy and snorey, but that wasn't what grabbed my attention.

Nobody had bothered to cover Grandfather's naked body. He lay there, looking strangely vulnerable for such a large person. His skin was as white as mine, and big spidery veins crawling up and down his legs. But what really worried me was that his previously humongous balls were shriveled and purple and sore-looking, hanging like wrinkled sacks beneath a sad little member that curled toward his thigh as if it wished it could just disappear.

I didn't want to disturb Grandfather, so I tiptoed to the window. It didn't seem right that our tree was in full bloom. I had to keep pinching my arm as I watched scores of sparrows hop from branch to branch in intricate patterns.

You should have heard the ruckus when Nurse came back into the room.

From the way she acted, you would have thought that me seeing Grandfather naked was the worst part of what was going on, rather than it having been months since Grandfather had felt well enough to sit side by side with me to watch over our tree.

I am going to say the next thing very fast, because you are not going to want to hear it any more than I want to tell it. My grandfather died that very same day. I never even got the chance to say goodbye. Which was why, I suppose, I simply did not believe he was gone forever. I couldn't imagine he would let himself slip away without some kind of signal to me, his very best friend.

While the rest of the household was full of activity, I lay flat on my back in my darkened bedroom, with Jillily motoring sympathetically beside me as I pondered long and hard over everything Sister Flatulencia had told me about Jesus. This is what I finally concluded: if Jesus had managed to come back from the dead in three days, could there be any doubt that an angel like Grandfather would find his way back to me in a similar amount of time? It was going to take a lot of pinching and banging, but I could probably manage to hold out for three days without Grandfather's *ugga umphs* in my life.

Once I'd gotten that one sorted out, I was able to fall asleep, my hands encircling Jillily's vibrating body and my nose pressed nice and tight against her back.

When I woke the next morning, the first thing I noticed was how hungry I was. The prospect of waiting three whole days for Grandfather's resurrection made my tummy feel especially empty, so I slid down the banister toward the kitchen, determined to eat extra large portions to keep myself going until his return. But when I skipped into the kitchen I got an uncomfortable surprise. It was Fayga, not Dhani, making the oatmeal, stirring popping yellow-gray lumps of it with slapping motions of her big spoon. I asked anxiously, "Where's Dhani?"

Fayga's worm of an upper lip stretched straight as a ruler. She said, "Dhani's no longer with us, missy. Your little fashion show yesterday wasn't exactly a hit with your mother. Didn't you stop to think you might be rubbing it in that your father's bastard was about to be raised under the very same roof as her own child?"

As I struggled to understand what she was talking about, Sister Flatulencia came clumping down the stairs and into the kitchen, her eyes as red as a rabbit's. She flung a hand to her forehead. "How on earth can Senator Robins be so heartless as to invite the whole press corps to Mister Phillips' funeral tomorrow? Not just to the memorial service, but the burial itself? Can't he give the family a little privacy?"

Burial? Tomorrow? I nearly fainted on the spot. I grabbed hold of Sister Flatulencia's trouser leg and shook it. I had to stop this dangerous rush to stick my Grandfather in the ground before he could find his way back to life again. "No!" I cried. "You said Jesus needed three whole days to arrange his resurrection. You have to tell Father that Grandfather must not be put under the ground. He'll listen to you. You're the expert on these things. You're a nun."

She eyed me strangely, and I worried that in my agitation I'd inadvertently *ugga umph ugga'ed.* Making the sign of the cross, she said, "Dear girl, I can't be hearing this. You're not putting your *grandfather* on a par with our Savior?" The way she pronounced the word *grandfather* warned me not to speak the truth.

Of course Grandfather was on a par with our Savior—every day he saved me from Father's cruelty, Mother's helplessness, Nana's Mack-trucking, Nurse's meanness, my bad feelings about putting down the baby bird, and every other major life-threatening void. Grandfather offered daily salvation with his devotion to our tree and his milky breath and untangling my hair with his old man's hands and our secret language of melty eyes and the two of us beaming invisible messages back and forth from our hearts.

It suddenly became clear to me why Sister Flatulencia could no longer serve as a nun. She had no idea what a true savior was.

That was when I formed a plan inspired by what I'd learned from the baby bird on the lawn. The plan was simple, but the pressure to get the resuscitation right this time was so intense that I had to postpone indefinitely the self-punishing head-banging I owed Dhani for having brought misery down upon her.

Instead, I turned myself into a soldier. I dutifully shoved extra servings of Fayga's gloppy oatmeal into my mouth for breakfast and slurped a bowlful of Cheerios for lunch. In between, I took care not to get under Father's feet while he strode around the house firing off orders of how he wanted "this funeral to go over without a hitch, and for Christ's sake keep the bitch away from the booze," and tried not to be bothered by the pitiful sobbing emanating from my mother's bedroom.

When Father was in this kind of mood, the rest of the household tended to scatter, so I didn't see Nana until bedtime. Her face was flushed when she burst into my room. She said, "Forgive me, poor child. I've had you at the back of my mind all day, but we've got three sick children, and, with Fayga stuck in the kitchen, I've been working my fanny off." She dropped onto my bed, mopped her forehead with a handkerchief that had suspicious greeny-yellow stains on it, and muttered, "I think it's shameful, pushing forward the date of the funeral just so he can glad-hand with the Governor at some bill-signing. He's driving us all nuts." She shot me a wry look. "Little does he know that, on such short notice, I've got to leave the children with Dhani. Fayga's going to sneak her in through the kitchen once everybody takes off." For the briefest of moments, Dhani's kind brown eyes flashed before me, and my eyes pooled with tears. Nana's voice went all chicken-pecky. "Aw, you poor thing, we've all been so busy, and you probably don't feel so good. I know how much your grandfather meant to you."

A part of me longed to lean into those thick arms of hers and to let myself fall asleep to her tuneless singing. But sleep was one thing I couldn't afford that night. Instead, I had to pretend. I had to pretend long enough to get Nana out of my room, so I could concentrate all my attention on the details of my upcoming mission.

I went through the necessary motions the next morning in a fog. Somehow, I managed to get Jillily fed and to step like a zombie in and out of the shower, climbing afterwards into the itchy black dress with three-quarter sleeves and a satin bow at the collar that someone had laid onto my sweat-drenched sheets while I was in the bathroom. It was probably Mother; Nana knew all about my sensitive skin.

When I peeked out my bedroom door, I could tell that the household was in chaos. Mother was wandering around like an ant separated from its line, her dark glasses a poor disguise for all her crying. Nurse and Fayga and Sister Flatulencia and Nana kept to themselves in a corner, undoubtedly wishing they could escape their own itchy black suits.

The front door was wide open, and startling explosions from the camera crews outside periodically brightened the walls of our rather dim entrance hall. I saw my mother jump with every flash. Father's fake senatorial voice managed to slither back into the house from out front. But then I heard the sound of tires crunching the gravel of our winding driveway. The cars were arriving to pick us up. That was my signal.

I rushed to Grandfather's room. I knew he wouldn't be there. Sister Flatulencia had explained to me the day before how he'd been taken to a funeral home, where they were making him look nice for the viewing. I thought that was one of the stupidest things I'd ever heard. You didn't have to *do anything* to make Grandfather look nice.

I hadn't gone up to Grandfather's room under the delusion that he was still there, but merely to sit for a few moments in his chair and take a last look at our tree for the both of us. I didn't want anything happening to it while I was working on Grandfather's resurrection. If anything, there seemed to be more birds than usual, as if every sparrow and mockingbird and parrot we'd ever gazed upon had returned to wish me luck. It made sense. Being seen does no end of good in vanquishing the void.

I didn't really wake up until I was inserted between Mother and Father in the back seat of a limousine. The tension between the two of them was so sharp, it pierced the fog and stabbed me in my heart. Remembering my mission, I sat up a little straighter and placed a soldierly hand over each knee. Father smiled one of his uglier smiles and said, "Well, at least this one's behaving herself." Then, when Mother didn't even look in his direction, he actually said something to *me*. "I hope you keep it up. This is a very serious event, and there are going to be a lot of extremely important people here."

Right. *Like Grandfather.*

Father's interest in me dropped into the void just as soon as we pulled in front of the funeral home. I scrambled out behind him. Mother slid out of the car and stood there with her hands floating around as if she didn't know what to do with them; I could see that her fingers were shaking. Father just grabbed hold of her and pulled her toward a small cluster of men on the lawn wearing identical black suits, all of them with the same carefully waved haircuts. A gaggle of press people ran toward them like it was a race, which had to be hard, as they were lugging all kinds of equipment.

But now Nana had appeared at my side, fussing over my skin, which had broken out in little red bumps from the black wool dress I wore. She said, "Let's at least get you out of the sun. Do you want to see your grandfather?" She flicked a nasty look in the direction of Father and his friends. "Better go now before the Mongol hordes descend."

I didn't know anything about Mongol hordes, but her offer was the answer to my prayers. We approached a glaring white room where a long bronze box with an open lid dominated a cream-carpeted stage. Awful music spewed from a couple of speakers mounted on the ceiling. I asked Nana if I could be alone with Grandfather. I spoke in my best pitiful voice, the soldier in me not even worrying how good I was getting at lying and pretending. I was pretty confident she'd accommodate my wishes, and she did.

There he was. There was Grandfather. The fact that he didn't move and that he didn't really look like Grandfather didn't much bother me. Once I got him back home again, I could wipe that powder off his face and uncover every age spot and wrinkle I'd documented in my diary, removing, as well, the ridiculous black eyebrow pencil obscuring his sparse silver eyebrows. Then he'd open his eyes and see our tree and I'd tell him how I'd washed him to life again and he'd *ugga umph ugga* and I'd lean against his chair and he'd comb his fingers through my hair and we wouldn't have to worry about him dying again, ever, for now he would be eternal.

My mission was to plump up Grandfather's balls, just like Dhani had plumped up the raisins for her yummy chicken curry. The idea had come to me during those unspeakably dark hours following his death. While Grandfather's balls might have looked a little scary in their swollen state, it was their shrinking that had signaled his death. What I hadn't understood until then was that a grandfather's balls are his living treasure, a key to whether he lives and whether he dies. I needed to return that precious pair to its pre-shrunken state, and for that I needed water.

When I'd rehearsed my mission in my mind the previous night, I had planned on getting water from a bathroom at the funeral home. That's why I'd brought along a plastic bag with me, tucked into the handy little side pocket of my itchy black dress. I can tell you right now that Uncle Bob hadn't been thrilled with the arrangement. But now I sniffed. And then I sniffed again. When I'd entered this room, I'd had one thing on my mind, and one thing only, and that was Grandfather. Now I looked around me and saw that there were flowers everywhere.

Most of them were arranged dramatically in over-sized vases, testimony to the barbaric notion that a flower that has been ripped from its invisible bed is as beautiful as a live flower, rooted in its own earthy home. With a quick apology, I reached toward the closest vase, a tall white one, and chicken-pecked its assortment of stargazers and gerbers before removing them, all goopy and dripping, from their ceramic container and stuffing them under a sage velvet upholstered chair near the foot of Grandfather's coffin.

Now was the tricky part. With the fiasco of the baby bird very much in my mind, I hefted up the vase and carefully poured its greenish water over the zippered line where my Grandfather's shriveled testicles must be. It took seven pourings to empty the vase. I wanted my Grandfather's balls as thoroughly soaked as possible, figuring that resurrection—unlike chicken curry raisins—takes a significant amount of liquid for the plumping. Then I set down the vase and studied my handiwork.

I was pleased to see I'd poured perfectly. The watermark made a greenish-brown diamond bisected by the zippered crotch of Grandfather's tan trousers. I'd come a long way since clumsily drowning the baby bird. I turned from the coffin with a feeling of satisfaction, just in time to see the first wave of mourners approaching the doorway. I nearly saluted when they entered the room. Instead, the room became stuffy with people, many of whom came forward to shake my hand and make sad faces and mutter awkward words of sympathy. I favored each one with a triumphant smile, but I couldn't help but sneak quick looks every once in awhile in my grandfather's direction. Even though I'd pushed forward the date of his resurrection, I was already getting a little pit-ish with the need to have him alive again.

The rest of the crowd seemed oblivious to my grandfather's lying in state. They were all scuttling after Father, who was shaking hands and grinning one of those Red-Riding-Hood's-phony-granny grins and speaking in his fake-lowered voice. He gave a little squeak when someone I recognized from TV burst into the room. Senator Manus had his own entourage, which included a young man who looked to be in his late teens or early twenties, with owlish eyes and a robust body, despite an oddly corkscrewed left leg that made him limp. The room went silent for a few seconds, and then everything became even noisier and hotter with the pops and flashes of multiple cameras. I saw Father break from his circle and stride toward Senator Manus with a hand outstretched and an expression on his face that looked as if he couldn't decided if he wanted to smile or puke. The news photographers flew after him like flies after a garbage truck.

For the first time, I saw Nana and Fayga and Sister Flatulencia and Nurse and Mother, who'd evidently been avoiding the crowd just outside the doorway. Now they shuffled toward Grandfather's casket along with the rest of the guests, following the lead of Senator Manus, who had given my Father a plain gentleman's handshake, introduced the limping young man to him as his son Adam, then proceeded in the direction of the opened bronze box, declaring loudly enough for the whole room to hear, "Time to pay my respects to the old man. I always liked him, you know. Who wouldn't? You never heard anything but God's truth from the lips of Sylvester Phillips." His words immediately endeared me to Senator Manus, no matter what Father had said about his allegiance to the devil abortionists. But as my eyes tracked his progress toward my grandfather's casket, I caught sight of the stems of the gerber daisies and stargazer lilies I'd stashed beneath the velvet chair, poking out like gloppy pick-up sticks. A hot, uncomfortable wave broke over me, starting with my scalp and leaking past my itchy-wool-covered chest. Something told me I really needed to get over there and shove those flowers out of sight. At the same time, I became aware of Nana's beady eyes on me and a suspicious expression coming over her face. She began moving toward me, fast.

I was aware of two simultaneous races. Would Senator Manus beat Father to the side of Grandfather's casket and be the first one to get his picture taken saying goodbye to Grandfather? Would Nana get to me before I reached those dying flowers?

I just barely beat out Nana, managing to nudge the flower stems further back under the chair with the tip of my shiny patent leather shoes before anyone else noticed them, but that didn't stop her from giving me a look that said, "I know you've been up to no good." And Father got to the casket just a nose before Senator Manus, but not soon enough to stop his counterpart from looking down at my grandfather and exclaiming: "Good God, man, he's peed himself. Is it possible this man is still alive?"

Which, I don't need to tell you, lifted my spirits like a thousand Christmases and birthdays and Holis and the second coming of our Lord Himself. I rushed to greet my Grandfather, but was blocked by the imposing wall of my father's body and by his hands, which gripped my arm with such force it was like being caught between a couple of branding irons. This was the most important moment of my life. I let out a shriek and screamed, "Let go of me, damn you! Can't you even let me see my own grandfather's resurrection?" There was a collective gasp. I saw Sister Flatulencia slump to the floor just before the pain in my arm made the room go black.

I opened my eyes again to one of the kindest voices I'd ever heard. I wondered if I'd died in Grandfather's stead and landed in heaven and this was God himself, which made me pretty nervous as soon as I remembered that I'd sworn at Father. But the voice just murmured, without the slightest hint of punishment, "Why, Frank, this child must be pretty upset. Let's see, little lady. Let me help you up." And then, quite a bit louder, "For God's sake, what's this on your hand?" You might think he was referring to my itchy-wool hives, but no. Flash bulbs popped like the Fourth of July as Senator Manus held my arm in the air so everyone could see my wrist, bearing finger-shaped welts rising up in the exact shape of my father's hot pincer of a hand.

Chapter 6 🦋

IT WAS DHANI who introduced to me the notion of reincarnation. It sounded such a handy relief from the void that I checked in the dictionary to make sure she wasn't making it up. Sure enough, there it was, sandwiched between *incarnadine*, which sounds exotic enough to be the name of a David Austin but actually refers to the color of flesh and blood, and *incase*, which means to close something up. Which makes sense, since *incarnation* means sealing up spirit in flesh and blood form.

In my experience, people do a fair amount of re-incarnating in a single lifetime, getting fatter or thinner or even modifying their spirits before their bodies give up the ghost once and for all. Little did I know, as I came to in the shocked silence of the Eden Rest Mortuary viewing room, that I was about to embark on my own second incarnation.

There we all were, Senator Manus holding up my wrist for everyone to see, and flash bulbs popping, and Father turning a particularly unsavory shade of gray, and all I could think was that I had to get to Grandfather, who would probably need a little help navigating his way out of his velvet-lined casket.

My father pushed through the crowd and out of the room, and, in the chaos generated by the sharp shift of events, I broke free from Senator Manus' grip and made for the coffin. When I got there, I saw that Grandfather had not moved, nor had he opened his eyes or cracked enough of an expression to shift the powder and rouge on his face. The zippery place on his pants where I'd poured the water was still flat, and, if anything, a little sunken and wrinkly at the edges where it was starting to dry.

I realized then that I'd failed at the one thing that mattered most in the world. I hadn't managed to plump up my grandfather's life-giving balls one solitary little bulge. Something picked me up and flung me into a cold dark space where everything was empty and I was *screaming screaming screaming*, not even *fla fla* but just one long, ear-drum-piercing cry.

When I'd used up all my screaming, I opened my eyes, surprised to find myself outside the funeral home, sitting on its rolling lawn, which was punctuated by the occasional white oak and row upon row of carved humps of gray concrete and shiny black stone. A few inches from my nose, a pair of big green eyes stared straight into mine. Tears streamed down either side of this stranger's nose like two winding rivers. The two of us sat knee to knee, Indian style, and there were hands resting lightly on my shoulders that belonged to the out-stretched arms of the young man who'd been introduced to Father as Adam Manus in the room where my grandfather had…I tried to scream again, but my throat was too raw.

My soldierly spine gave way. I tipped forward so that my fore-head came to a stop at this stranger's chest, which smelled comfort-ingly of Campbell's Chicken Soup and B.O. He clasped me tightly with his sturdy arms, the arms that must have carried me out here, and we rocked awhile just like Mother's rocking chair, until the sound of birdsong got me cranking my head toward a nearby oak. A pair of mockingbirds was hopping from branch to branch in a particularly interesting pattern.

The ache started up all over again and a fit of hiccupping came over me, the loud kind that comes with an air-filled burp at the end. Without any warning, Adam yelled *Boo!* scaring me so much I could scarcely catch my breath, but then I realized he'd scared away my hic-cups. I guess I must have given him a pretty accusatory look, for he made a sorry face, pooching out his lower lip and accentuating the long groove between his thick black eyebrows like he'd been frown-ing ever since he'd been born. His sad eyes sucked me downward. I fell and fell, down the everlasting pit of eternal emptiness.

And while I fell this is what I thought: *Grandfather*.

The rivers were on the sides of *my* nose this time and my wet snot was on Adam's sleeves and all over his fingers, which kept brushing my face in tender swipes, and it occurred to me I was just like one of Nana's pukey little babies.

But here's the strange thing: seeing my snot streaking this stranger's clothes and registering how he didn't even notice it himself but just kept whispering, "I know, I know," gave me an unfamiliar sense of peace. My tears kept coming, but they were quiet now, as if they'd been around forever, a natural phenomenon like roses and dirt, the water from my eyes making a pool for me to float in, lying on my back looking up at the sky and for one brief moment catching sight of a fledging sparrow flying west. In that moment I had the most unusual thought that perhaps the void wasn't always monstrous, that there was actually such a thing as rest, like sleep without nightmares, only better, because you are awake enough to enjoy it.

But then I heard someone shouting. I looked around and saw Nana and Fayga and Nurse and Senator Manus and a phalanx of photographers coming up the hill. Nana got to us first and yanked me down the lawn in the direction of the parked limousines. I stumbled and tripped past photographers and men with walkie-talkies and Nurse, who just stood there with her phony-Granny mouth making a giant confused-looking O, and Senator Manus, who seemed to have eyes only for Adam as he hurtled unrecognizing past me, trailed by several black-suited, wavy-haired men, and shaking a finger at his son.

Nana crammed me into the closest car, which started moving as soon as she slammed the door. Mother was the only one in the car besides our driver. She sat stuffed into the corner of the back seat, and she sobbed more pitifully than a saved baby, moaning things like, "Oh, Dad, I let you down, I let you down," and, "God forgive me for what I've done to my little girl." Needless to say, her words didn't do too much for my own spirits, which had sunk lower than the deepest pit of hell.

I would learn later that Grandfather's burial went ahead without us. It was probably at the very moment he was being lowered into the ground that I watched my father and mother fight over my failed attempt to resurrect him. The arena was our entrance hall, with the front door gaping open from everyone being too tired to close it after piling dispiritedly out of our limousines. Mother and Father flung awful words at each other, while Nana huddled next to me on the fourth stair and Fayga scrunched down right behind us on the fifth, her knee jutting satisfyingly sharply into the small of my back. Sister

Flatulencia sat with her back against the wall and her tree trunk legs stretched along the bottom stair, her hands in her lap worrying at her rosary.

Father started it, shouting at Mother in his screechiest register, his eyes roach-like and mean. "Where is she? Is that her up there? God dammnit, get out of my way. She won't know whether she's coming or going once I get hold of her."

Mother stepped around him to block the stairway, crying and yelling at the same time, snot drizzling onto her upper lip. "Oh, no you don't! You wouldn't dare. Jesus, I think that's just about enough, don't you? For God's sake, the whole world is going to see what you did to her."

"What *I* did to *her*? You saw that water on his crotch. What about what she did to your father? The kid's sick. She's some kind of pervert."

Mother cried even harder, but she held her ground. "Whatever Flurry thought she was doing, you know as well as I do how much she adored him. At least she didn't kill him. If anyone sped him on his way it was you." She blew her nose before adding mournfully, "I can't imagine what it was like for him to have to watch how you treated the two of us all these years, without even having the words to tell you what a bastard you are."

Father looked as though it was all he could do to restrain himself. His hands were balled into fists, and the veins in his neck were bulging. "Oh, but it's not me who's the bastard, is it? It's that weird kid of yours who's the bastard. Or she would be if I hadn't had the kindness to marry you."

Mother stepped back as if she *had* been struck. "Oh, really? I think the word *bastard* applies best to that Hindu baby your little whore is carrying. Kindness? Give me a break. This marriage was simply to protect your ambition—oh, excuse me, did I say *that*? It's all for the *cause*." She laughed without sounding at all happy. "Face it, Frank, it was my father who talked me out of the abortion, not you. As for turning our house into a warehouse for the unwanted—what a joke. Forget Flurry, you know you've never given a shit about those kids."

Thinking about Dhani holding the fort on the other wing, I darted an anxious glance at Nana. Mother was right about the babies.

Neither she nor Father seemed at all concerned about who had been watching them during the funeral—who was watching them *now*, as they fought.

But Nana didn't catch my look. She and Fayga and Sister Flatulencia were busy making eyes at one another, but they didn't move off the stairs. It was as if someone had glued the four of us into our positions.

Father poked his finger frighteningly close to Mother's face. "*You're* lecturing *me* about parenting? Don't make me laugh. The lush who retreats to her bedroom every afternoon? You're right. Maybe the kid isn't autistic. Maybe she's just a classic case of maternal neglect."

But now Mother was screaming that she was going to leave this house forever, and a trapdoor opened in the pit I thought I'd already reached the bottom of.

Father's response shoved me in. "Oh, fucking Jesus, Mary and Joseph. When have I heard that one before? Why don't you just bypass the drama and pour yourself a drink? Come on, bitch—what are you waiting for? You know you want it."

That was when Sister Flatulencia wrestled her angular body from the bottom step and literally threw herself between Father and Mother, shouting, "Stop! Just stop it!" Father fell back a few steps as Sister Flatulencia said, "Margaret's going to stop drinking and make a real life without you, aren't you, Margaret?" The look Mother shot her showed that it was news to *her*. But Sister Flatulencia was not about to be deterred. She gave Mother a little shove in the direction of the stairs and followed her, stopping only to throw back over her shoulder, "Don't you dare interfere, or you will be punished by the Lord Himself."

Father scowled and his chest heaved up and down and I could tell he wanted to yell something very bad, but he just tightened his lips and stalked out the front door.

Chapter 7

AS IT TURNED out, and much to everyone's surprise, Sister Flatulencia proved to be right. Mother allowed herself to be driven to an AA meeting the very next morning, and she became a friend of a man named Bill W. within the week. I never met up with Bill W. myself, but—now that Father was spending virtually all his time in D.C.—some of his friends started coming to our house on Saturday nights, filling the house with the smell of freshly-brewed coffee and, much to Fayga's dismay, acrid hints of nicotine. I grew rather attached to the sounds of their laughter traveling up the stairs as I lay in bed with Jillily pressed against my chest. Just knowing that Mother was making new friends sent little beams of light through the dense fog that enveloped me ever since my grandfather was gone.

On the seventh Monday following Grandfather's burial, I woke to the surprising sight of Mother flinging open my curtains, singing, "Wake up, wake up, wake up, you sleepyhead. Get up, get up, get out of bed!" I recognized the song. Mother had sung it to me a time or two when I was little. It began with the words, "When the red, red robin comes bob bob bobbin along," and I assumed Mother had made it up herself until Nana bought me a *Jazz for Kids* CD that had Carmen McRae singing the song. I hadn't heard it in ages, nor had I seen much of Mother in the past month and a half. She'd gone straight from spending most of her time in her bedroom to spending most of her time at AA meetings, so my own situation, company-wise, hadn't much changed.

But here was my mother, chicken-pecking my forehead and cheeks, saying brightly, "Get up, get up, we're off for an adventure!"

And we were. Right after breakfast, she and Nana and I set off on a two-hour chauffeured ride to Manhattan, where a real estate agent with enormous purple lips and an impossible amount of black hair piled on top of her head showed us a series of properties for sale, the last one a penthouse apartment overlooking a series of city streets that were filled with smoke-spewing trucks and big buses plastered with ads and noisy fire engines weaving in and out of traffic in fascinating void-killing patterns. I never got past the living room, where I stood glued to a spot in front of an enormous plate glass window, while Mother's high heels clacked through the apartment and the voices of Mother, Nana, and the purple-lipped agent echoed through its empty rooms.

I heard the agent say rather forcefully, "You won't find this kind of value anywhere else on the Upper East Side," and then, "Take your time. I'll just step out to make a call or two. Give a shout if you've got any questions." I heard the front door open behind me, and I had to resist the impulse to turn around for one more glimpse of that teetering tent of black hair.

After I observed seven buses and twenty-six cars pass through the closest intersection, Mother and Nana's voices became louder, with Mother saying a lot of what-do-you-thinks and Nana saying more than a few this-place-goes-on-forevers, until, a few seconds later, they were back in the living room and Mother was by my side and a pigeon flew past the window, as if looking for somewhere to land. Mother stole a sideways look at me. She must have seen something in my face.

She said, "Well, I can see Flurry likes the view." As if she had X-ray vision, Purple Lips was instantly back in the room, and before I knew it Mother was shaking hands in turn with the grinning agent, Nana, and me, announcing, "Well, that's that, then. Say hello, Flurry, to your new home." But I didn't get much time to say that hello. Instead, I was whisked down the extraordinary see-through elevator to our waiting town car, which deposited us at a restaurant called Chat Noir, which Mother—giggling giddily—told me meant black cat. I already knew that, since Dhani had a poster of Toulouse Lautrec's painting in her bedroom. The food at Chat Noir was yummy, but I felt pit-ish that there was no Jillily under the table to savor a few bites of my pignoli-crusted salmon steak. I made Mother promise that Jillily would come with us when we moved.

But Mother and Nana and I didn't get to our new incarnations as smoothly as that preview of coming attractions might suggest. First we had to deal with our losses, and there were many of them to mark in the month before our departure from Father's estate.

It was a month of goodbyes to Fayga and her furniture paste, to Sister Flatulencia and her farts. The sorriest of goodbyes had to be said to Uncle Bob, who deliberated long and hard before deciding that a miniature man like himself would skip along crowded city streets only at great peril to life and limb. But he did relieve me of a great load, promising to keep on eye on the Austins in my absence. You can imagine what it took to say goodbye to each of *them*. As for Mary Magdalene, let's just say that I assured her that I would always remember her, and she in turn vowed to keep me in her prayers. I'd been pretty much avoiding Baby Eros and his peeing member ever since the advent of my hairy tweeter, but I forced myself to send him a little wave on one of my last tours of the grounds, turning away quickly in case he decided to wave back.

I kept putting off saying a final goodbye to Ignacio. The fact was, he'd been making himself so scarce he was easy to avoid. I heard Nana comment to Fayga that he'd turned into a shadow of his former self ever since Dhani had left. I knew what she meant. I missed her terribly myself.

The fact was, my life felt like nothing but loss. I spent whole days hunkered down in Nana's second smallest closet, tickling my nose with the edge of her cave-scented robe. It was there that I worked on a hymn to commemorate the joint burial mound of Anne Boleyn and the baby bird on the lawn. In the end I decided to keep it simple. I ran outside and sang in a trembling voice, "Rest in peace, Anne Boleyn, rest in peace, baby bird, help each other with your boredom, goodbye."

But, over time, loss began to blossom into gratitude. It was a thank you for learned lessons to my first shiny weed, which had repaid my conversion from hatred to affection by producing as many descendants as the biblical Abraham. And on the morning of our actual departure, I said a heartfelt Godspeed to the saved babies. In spite of all their peeing and pooping and depositing pukey smells on

71

Nana's shoulder, I figured we were almost related, so it was particularly painful saying goodbye.

And speaking of peeing, before leaving the house for good I paced a final fond farewell—fourteen steps exactly—to the familiar path between my bed and the bathroom, with a tip of the proverbial hat to my duck-billed night-light, which I had decided to leave behind as a parting gift for Uncle Bob.

In the course of all those goodbyes, I discovered something surprising. It was almost as difficult saying goodbye to the bad memories as the good ones. Pinching Jillily's belly, staring at my lumpy shaven head in the bathroom mirror, sneaking past the mean-faced fish at the corner of the second fountain, even the remembered smell of Father's armpits made me moody; there is no accounting for the mystery of the human mind. It was as if there were pieces of me floating around that house of my first incarnation, like armless, legless ghosts with nowhere to land.

In the end, I had to find places in my mind for all those memories, which is when I learned another important lesson about loss: if there were no loss, there would be no memories, and memories are what you use to begin filling up your void.

As for Grandfather, it wasn't my mind that I filled up with him. His home would always be inside my heart. Saving his ghost from aimlessly wandering the rooms of my father's home was the least I could do to repay him for being my very best friend in all the world.

There was another thing I ended up saying goodbye to: pinching my butt and tweeter closed while I slept. Biology made my efforts in that department pointless. Three days before we moved into our new apartment, I lay on my bed doubled over with stomach cramps, my belly as bloated as Sister Flatulencia's on one of her gassier days.

When Nana came into my room with more boxes for packing, I told her I couldn't possibly unfold from my fetal position.

She scooted a box filled with sweaters and hoodies out of the way and approached my bed, looking annoyed. "What's wrong?" I told her, and then she asked me the oddest question. "How old are you?"

A little insulted that she'd forgotten, I reminded her that I'd turned eleven the previous December.

She sniffed, "A bit early, but there you go. It's the hormones in the chicken, mark my words. I'll have to send Sister Flatulencia out for some pads." Clearly agitated by all the packing she wasn't getting done, she hastily explained about periods, predicting I'd be getting mine any minute now and offering one ominous piece of advice: "Don't worry about the blood. It's only Mother Nature."

I hadn't realized Mother Nature could be so mean. Writhing like a slithery eel on my bed, I decided that physical agonies visited by Mother Nature were in a different category entirely from self-inflicted pain. I tried making a deal with that mysterious Mother, hoping she'd go lighter on me in the 480 or so months to come if I stopped my pinching and banging. And I tried, I really did.

As for multiple incarnations, I couldn't get over the fact that just a week or so earlier I'd been just a girl—with a few errant hairs sprouting down below and a trainer bra covering my pointy little nipples up above—and now I was a woman with breasts overflowing their AA cup, compelled to drench my panties with Mother's Chanel No. 5 to mask the fishlike smell rising up from my tweeter.

As if that weren't enough, packing produced its own dramas. As you might imagine, it was taking forever to gather up my leather-bound books of lists. Nana, overstressed by her role of coordinating our move, was very angry with me that I'd accumulated so many, but she got even angrier when she came into my room just as I was climbing out of the fireplace, my Book of Bruises in my hand and most of me covered in soot.

Grabbing the journal from me, she cried out loudly, "What are you doing? Is there no end to the mischief this child gets up to?" Sister Flatulencia and Fayga must have heard her, for they burst into my room. While Fayga threw a fit over my ash-streaked clothing, Nana flipped through the entries in my book, until she said, "Oh my God. Wait a minute." She sat abruptly onto my bed and motioned to Sister Flatulencia and Fayga. As the three of them inspected my carefully compiled lists of Nurse's cruelties to Grandfather, Sister Flatulencia sighed heavily, Nana clucked, and Fayga's upper lip stiffened like a sun-fried worm.

Seeing their three heads bent forward all in a row—Nana's tangled and yellowy-white mop, Fayga's silver waterfall spilling from her crown, Sister Flatulencia's pubic-style coils bursting exuberantly from her bandana—I felt a pit-ish pang, wondering if I would ever see those three heads bobbing at some card table again, giggling and swearing over a heated game of Hearts.

The pain of sensing that I might not was worse than pinching. I ran out of the house and didn't stop running until I came across Ignacio, dead-heading a Graham Thomas and muttering "*come mierda, come mierda*," an expression I later learned referred to eating shit. I could tell how angry he was by his brisk snips at the rose with his orange-handled shears.

He looked up at me and sighed. "*Ai, muchacha*, what a terrible time." Tossing his shears onto the grass, he stood up and rubbed the small of his back. "Little one, both our hearts are breaking. What are we going to do?"

I knew my own heart was broken; the tear in it was how I'd managed to insert Grandfather's ghost inside me.

Just then Ignacio cried out plaintively, "*Linda paloma*! She has flown from me. What am I going to do?"

The thought of Dhani winging off into the sky made my belly stir in that diarrhea's-coming sort of way, especially with the grave of my dead baby bird so close by. I piped up anxiously, "Do?"

Words tumbled chaotically out of Ignacio's lips. "Your father wants Dhani to give up our baby. He says it's his. He wants *la monja que es como un arbol* to care for it like those other *povrecitos*. Everything he says is wrong." I could see that Ignacio's hands were shaking. "I swear to you, *muchacha*, I know in my bones that child is mine! But Dhani is blinded by guilt. She says she'll never forgive herself for betraying me. She wants to punish herself by signing up with the Indian Matrimonial Society."

He stopped for a moment and took his handkerchief from his pocket, passing it across his sun burnt forehead before shoving it back in. Just then, a hummingbird zipped between us and disappeared just as quickly. As we turned back to each other, Ignacio's voice was calmer. "You know, before Rosa was killed I was a jealous man." He shrugged. "But now? Dhani is…she's young and far from home. I believe what she said. She was lonely and her loneliness made her give in to the devil a time or two." He knelt down and ran his thumb repetitively over one of Graham Thomas' yellow petals. I wanted to tell him to stop, but I didn't have the heart. His dark eyes were wet as he looked up at me. "Muchacha, if she gives up her baby—our baby—it will kill her spirit." He looked up to the sky, whispering, "*Dios*, do not cheat me a second time."

I found Ignacio's words confusing. I'd been picking up a word of Spanish here and there, so I already knew that *povrecito* meant poor and that Ignacio had his own name for Sister Flatulencia, referring to her laughingly as *the nun who is like a tree*. I had a pretty good idea, too, of what he meant by Dhani succumbing to the devil; I hadn't forgotten our Holi, with Dhani letting Father paw her tweeter and chew her lips. But the Indian Matrimonial Society? I had to ask Ignacio to explain. He told me it was not uncommon for a Hindu immigrant to be matched for life with some stranger by a Society in faraway Delhi, which seemed as foolish as purposely inserting a weed at the base of an Eglantyne.

I must have looked preoccupied, because Ignacio paused, then said, "Ai, *muchacha*, how selfish of me, complaining like a woman, while your own grandfather is barely settled in his grave."

His characterization of women slipped right past me (though it would occur to me later that night that—in my own family, anyway—it was Father who'd complained the most). Instead, I was more gripped by Ignacio's words about Grandfather. But I resisted the temptation to respond. Even someone as kind as Ignacio couldn't be expected to know what it cost to have my grandfather sewn carefully inside my heart instead of softly *ugga umphing* and stroking my hair while we watched over our tree. Instead, I turned my mind to Ignacio's predicament. I hadn't been able to save my grandfather any better than I'd saved the baby bird on the lawn, but perhaps I could do something helpful about Ignacio's lost dove.

I said abruptly, "I have to go now," skipping back to the house so fast Uncle Bob could barely keep up with me. It took awhile before I found Nana. She was in the other wing of the house, holding one of the saved babies and sniffling over its bald little head. When Nana finally registered I was there, she said, "Aren't you supposed to be packing, missy?" Then, clearly recalling what she'd read just a half an hour before in my Book of Bruises, she sweetened her tone, bending with her baby to chicken peck the top of my head. "Never mind. What is it, Deer?"

That was a new name and a surprising one. I had to physically restrain myself from running back to my bathroom mirror to see if I'd sprouted a pointy black nose and stick-out ears. Instead, I said, "Do you know where Dhani is?"

"Dhani? You know she's been fired. She doesn't live here anymore."

"Yes," I said, "but where is she?"

Nana just stared at me, then shuffled back toward one of the cribs and let the baby down with a sigh. She turned to me with a decidedly Mack truck expression. "You're not cooking up another one of your *plans*, are you?"

My turn as a soldier had improved my capacity for deception. "Of course not," I said, fingers crossed behind my back. "I just wondered if she's okay and everything. If she and her bun in the oven have enough food to eat and all." Nana's eyes still looked suspicious, so I left the room in search of a new strategy.

An hour or two later, with Nana safely distracted packing up the contents of her smallest closet and stifling sobs as she pored through her book of babies' names, I tiptoed downstairs to ask Dhani's whereabouts from Sister Flatulencia and Fayga. They chimed in, nearly in unison, that they had no idea where Dhani was, but Sister Flatulencia's eyes flicked around guiltily and I doubted it was because of the silent but deadly that forced me and Fayga to shuffle back a few steps.

I nodded politely and made a great show of retrieving a can of cat food and a clean dish for Jillily before marching out of the kitchen. As soon as I turned the corner, I marched in place for a while, and then aimed my right ear toward the kitchen, fanning my hand behind it like Grandfather when he couldn't hear what you were saying.

His method was surprisingly effective. I could hear Sister Flatulencia's words quite distinctly. She was saying, "That reminds me. I promised Cook I'd take over some infant sacks and diapers this afternoon. She thought washing and folding them would help Dhani snap out of her depression. Can you sling some in a bag for me?"

"Well, it'll take me a while to get them washed and ready," Fayga replied, a little nervously.

Sister Flatulencia snorted and farted at the same time. "What's the use of that, if the whole point is to get her distracted with washing them herself?"

Fayga didn't say a thing. Instead, she kept folding her apron skirt into little accordion pleats.

Sister Flatulencia broke the silence. "Just make sure Senator Robins doesn't find out. He'll kill us if he hears she's up at Manus' place."

So that was where she was. I couldn't help but think that Senator Manus was going to end up becoming one fat senator if he had both Cook and Dhani running his kitchen.

Fayga said, "How are you going to get out there?"

"Ignacio said he'd take me over in his truck. Poor man, even though she refuses to see him, he can't resist an excuse to be in her vicinity. If you fling a bunch of pj's into one of those big plastic bags for me, you can leave it by the back door. Ignacio said he'd be free about four o'clock."

I carefully set down Jillily's dish and knelt to untie my shoes. Fishy food dish in one hand and stinky tennis shoes in the other, I breathed as shallowly as I could as I tiptoed upstairs toward my bedroom. I figured Fayga would have the layette washed and dried and perfectly pressed and folded by 3:45 at the latest. If I do say so myself, my timing was excellent. She was just setting a tall Saks bag tied with a graceful yellow bow onto the kitchen counter when I returned to the kitchen at 3:43. I ran to her and tugged at her sleeve. I said, "Fayga, Fayga! Jillily just ate a mouse and is making noises like she's going to throw up on my carpet." I added one of my finely tuned renditions of a cat throwing up to drive home my point. Fayga grabbed some carpet cleaner and a rag and dashed out of the kitchen, her shiny hair swinging from side to side like an out-of-control pendulum.

As soon as she was gone, I hurried to push aside the bow and insert the letter I'd composed under the second topmost pair of footless Martian pajamas inside the Sak's bag. I had to hurry back to the guest bathroom and let Jillily out, or else she'd yowl so loud that Fayga would know she'd been tricked.

This is what my letter said:

Dear Dhani,
Everyone here is sad. Nana has to leave her babies. Mother has to leave Sister Flatulencia, who I worry will have another nervous breakdown caring for all those babies. And Fayga and Sister Flatulencia are losing a third and fourth for Hearts. You must not give Father your bun in the oven. He might eat it and then you will

be sad, too. Even if Ignacio is not the father, you should let him
take care of you and your baby dove. Please do not fly into the
hands of the Indian Matrimonial Society. You might get lost on the
way and end up back in Islington or Ignorance.
Your friend,

And then I stopped. I had been called so many names, but I only called myself *I* or *me*. Finally, I settled on:

The possible sister of your bastard child.

Uncle Bob and I kept an eye on Ignacio for three days, knowing that if Dhani took my message to heart, she would not show her face inside the house and risk my baby-eating father. It worked rather well for me, since I still had a lot of goodbyes to say on the grounds. Here are the David Austins I visited with during that time:

1. Charlotte;

2. Constance Spry;

3. Country Living;

4. Eglantyne;

5. Evelyn;

6. Fair Bianca;

7. Geoff Hamilton;

8. Gertrude Jekyll;

9. Jude the Obscure;

10. Mayor of Casterbridge;

11. Othello;

12. Prospero;

13. St. Swithum;

14. Sweet Juliet;

15. The Prince;

16. William Shakespeare.

It took the whole three days to say my goodbyes. I wouldn't dream of paying my respects to such perfect beings with a quick "See you later, alligator." Instead, I sat silently beside each one for an hour or two before putting nose to petal, sniffing, blinking several times in quick succession, repeating its name, then adding, "Oh, how beautiful you are! You are my very favorite member of the David Austin family," before scooting along to the next bush in the bed. And in case you are worried that Charlotte or Fair Bianca might take offense at hearing Gertrude Jekyll being called "My Very Favorite," never fear. Any flower as naturally exquisite as a David Austin feels quite certain that you are telling *her* the truth and lying politely to all the others. I say *her* merely to avoid the awkwardness of the English language. Believe me, William Shakespeare and Jude the Obscure are every bit as vain as their female counterparts.

On the third day after sneaking my note in among the Martian pajamas, I was working my way toward the Mayor of Casterbridge and keeping Ignacio in my sights as he solemnly rode his mower across the lawn, when I spied Dhani's familiar black head coming round the second fountain. Actually, Uncle Bob saw her first and alerted me by jumping up and down and congratulating me on the success of my letter.

As Dhani neared, I could see her bun was pushing her pink smock to near-bursting point. It seemed Ignacio had sighted her, too, for he'd jumped off his mower and was running to his dove at breathtaking speed. I turned away and kept my eyes pinned on the Mayor of Casterbridge. For one thing, I did not want to insult him by giving his goodbye shorter shrift than I'd given the others. For another, I had learned from painful experience that there are some things that are meant to be private, and people chewing Dhani's lips was one of them.

Chapter 8 🦋

AS I MAY have mentioned, ever since the funeral Father had been spending almost all his time in D.C., but he happened to come home that weekend. When he found out how I'd contacted Dhani, he called me Sneaky Little Monster. As names go, I guess you could say it was a nasty one. Though I didn't much like the monster part, the reference to sneakiness was fairly accurate. I was working hard to give up pinching and flapping, but my soldierly proclivity for deception was threatening to become a habit.

Nonetheless, the whole household intervened when Father—accosting me when I came downstairs for breakfast—looked liable to escalate from flinging sticks and stones into breaking my bones. Sister Flatulencia said, "Senator Robins, if you lay one hand on her, I will walk out this door and tell Social Services to come and get the children." Nana chimed in, "Don't you even think about it, buster," so Mack-truckishly that Father seemed to shrink a little, as if he really were related to Uncle Bob.

Fayga, a bowl of oatmeal in each hand, just stared at him like he was a flying roach, and Mother…Mother put her body between me and Father and said, in the firmest tone I'd ever heard from her, "Frank." It may not seem like much, but I had never heard a name used in such a way that its object simply froze. For one brief moment, I felt I could lean against Mother's body and it would hold me forever, without letting me slip through to the other side.

Mother pushed forward our moving date to the next day. As we prepared to leave, Father was nowhere to be found. That was all right by me. It made it easier to sneak into his wall-length closet, sliding my nose along his color-sorted stand of dress suits and fortifying myself with lungfuls of stale armpit and cheap perfume, without having to risk getting underfoot of the man himself. Nana caught me coming out of his bedroom and rolled her eyes as if I'd been up to something awful, but I just gave her a nod—she wouldn't understand my sadness any more than I did.

I went to fetch Jillily's baby blue cat carrier and brought her down the stairs with me. Sister Flatulencia watched our progress from a corner of the entryway, fiddling frantically with her rosary beads. Fayga's empty hands mimicked Sister Flatulencia's, twisting her fingers together instead.

When it came to actually leaving the house, Nana went first, face flushed and feet full of hesitance like she was trudging through dog poop, but Mother nearly danced out the door. I had to wriggle pretty carefully onto the seat next to her so I could solidly balance Jillily's carrier on my lap. The limo driver angled our car away from the curb. I looked back, and am I ever glad that I did. Our tree was chock-full of mockingbirds, rearranging themselves in a myriad of designs; I hurriedly rolled down my window to hear them weave their songs through the void one last time.

The ride to our new home took an eternity. I skirted a whirling pit of loss by staring out the limo's bug-slimed window, struck by how the constantly changing vista of city streets was such a sharp contrast to Father's grounds. Of course, I knew there was lots of movement in the natural world. Wind fussed at tree limbs, dying leaves leapt to earth, birds busied themselves in the sky. But most of Nature's changes were slow and mysterious, like my first weed, knotting and stretching in the night when everyone else was sleeping, or imperceptibly shifting, like a flower. I had never, for instance, actually *seen* a rosebud uncurl.

It occurred to me then that, when people cover the earth with concrete, they close off its secret workings, making everyone so vulnerable to the void that they have to keep moving quickly. They hurtle around in cars and trucks and buses, making as much noise as possible, as if they could drown out the silence with motors and radios and honkety-honk horns.

We arrived at our penthouse in the early afternoon, and the temperature seemed to have climbed twenty degrees between Main

Line and Manhattan. As we ascended to our new tenth-floor home—the see-through elevator just big enough to hold me and Mother and Nana and Jillily and our new friend Doorman and three bulging Louis Vuitton suitcases—I felt pretty floaty. At least in my first incarnation, I'd had recourse to Father's grounds to give me a sense of connection to the earth.

As soon as I set foot in my new bedroom—third door down the hall on the right, pale yellow carpet spread like butter on the floor, not a single sycamore visible outside—I set Jillily down. She was moaning and hissing to beat the band. (Just an expression—no need to worry about the health of any excellent trombonists you might know.) I hurried to pinch open the hinge of her cat carrier, having a pretty good idea what she was going through. I was feeling pretty trapped myself. She took awhile oozing through the opening, black fur electrified every which way, body slung low to the ground. She moved her head from side to side, nostrils flared suspiciously like she didn't know what she was smelling, but it just might be skunk.

Taking my cue, I got down on all fours beside her, though my bulgy new breasts made it hard to get my belly as close to the carpet as hers. When she moved, I moved, and when she stopped, I stopped, all the time sniffing and listening, pausing only for the occasional reassuring rub against one another, nose to nose. Then we'd inch and sniff some more.

Overall, I counted fifteen rooms:

1. Living room, not as big as Father's but filled with more light;

2. Den (ditto);

3. Kitchen (way more modern than we were used to. Jillily and I licked our icy reflections in the stainless steel mirror of a fridge);

4. Dining room (long and narrow, as opposed to Father's nearly square affair);

5. Breakfast nook (big enough for all of us to sit in, with a built-in wooden bench and chairs with little blue and white striped cushions, one of which Jillily immediately puked on);

6. Four bedrooms (a dozen less than the house of my previous incarnation, if you count the saved babies' wing);

7. Three bathrooms (not one with a floral-painted sink);

8. Laundry room (*much* smaller than Father's house; guess why);

9. Pantry (with shelves big enough to fit Jillily; I know, since she sniffed her way in and out of each one);

10. The hall (what can I say? A hall is just a hall, the most dangerously voidish room in any house).

All but the bedrooms and bathrooms had bare floors. The floors of the laundry and kitchen and pantry were styled with oversized black and white checks like a giant chessboard; the rest were just wood.

Occasionally, Jillily would stop and twitch her nose, then lift her face with that odd wrinkling of upper lip that is a cat's way of indicating, "P.U." I myself could smell very little, but the wood floors, polished with something all-too-reminiscent of Fayga's Ye Olde Furniture Polish, were pungent enough to guarantee a week's worth of Sweetie Pie nightmares.

As you can imagine, it took us a fair amount of time to feel at home in our new apartment. For several weeks, we were totally un-settled—Jillily creating curdles of cat puke all over the pale-colored carpet; me cleaning the curdles up; Nana at what she called sixes and sevenses, walking around sniffling and bumping into boxes, with no saved baby puke on her left shoulder to comfort her; Mother shyly trailing deputations of admiring Bill W.'s back home from meetings. I had mixed feelings about that crew. After one of them caught me attempting to crawl into the kitchen one night to sneak myself an oatmeal raisin cookie, he conferred on me the new name *Odd Duck*, which may or may not have had something to do with my fuzzy duck slippers.

What ultimately settled Mother and Nana and me into our new digs, besides deciding which pieces of furniture went where, was the household emergency of Dhani spitting Angelina from her gyna ear-lier than expected (and a good ten minutes before the paramedics arrived), right in the middle of the big bed in the fourth bedroom—fifth door down the hall on the right—which was linked to my own room by a bathroom with a door of its own enclosing a pit-ishly silent toilet.

I suppose I should explain how the same woman whom Mother had characterized most recently as Father's "little whore" came to be living with Mother and Nana and Jillily and me in the home of my second incarnation.

It all started with Sister Flatulencia and Fayga's visit to our home a few days after we moved in. They did a lot of oohing and ahing over the spaciousness of the apartment and the vastness of our view, but the best part of the visit was when we all sat together in the dining room, munching peanut butter cookies they'd brought along from Cook. I sensed that both Sister Flatulencia and Fayga were being tactfully circumspect about what was occurring back at Father's house, more out of deference to Nana, who was inconsolable with grief over leaving the saved babies, than for any concern about Mother, who flounced around our new digs in one of her new Juicy Couture tracksuits like a woman released from a breathtakingly binding girdle. They probably would have avoided mention of the Manus household as well; it was too much of a reminder of my misadventure at the mortuary. But something had to be done about Dhani.

I knew by then, of course, that Dhani had been working with Cook at Senator Manus' house ever since Father had fired her. But only a few days before leaving Main Line, I'd been playing Sneaky Soldiers outside Mother's bedroom keyhole just as Nana told Mother, "The only reason Senator Manus was willing to take Dhani into his household in the first place was that it was a big F.U. to Senator Robins."

Never having heard the expression "F.U." before, I'd tiptoed away to look it up in the dictionary. By all rights, it should have been right after *ft.*, (which, as I hope you know, is an abbreviation of the word *foot*) and before *fubsy*, which refers to a fat person or plump child. But there was nothing between those two entries, so I assumed *F.U.* was an invisible bridge between them, a kind of secret code for taking a fat person or plump child underfoot. In the case of Dhani and her bulging bun, I guess you could say that both meanings would have applied.

But now Sister Flatulencia was sitting in our new dining room, telling Mother how Senator Manus was getting tired of paying two cooks when the only ones who were ever home to eat what they made were him and Adam. She said that something had changed for Dhani, too: she had agreed to move in with Ignacio. But not until they got married. And that could not take place until Ignacio got a death certificate for his Rosa from Mexico.

This was not good. Dhani's baby was going to get itself born no matter what, it needed a name so it would not be a bastard, and she needed a place to stay until Ignacio could drive to Mexico and liberate his Rosa's death certificate from what Sister Flatulencia called "Mexico's tight-fisted bureaucracy."

Sister Flatulencia twirled an errant coil of gray hair escaping from her bandana. "Cook managed to guilt Senator Manus into giving Dhani a going-away gift by paying for a rental car for Ignacio to drive to Mexico, but that doesn't exactly help Dhani find a place to stay. So," Sister Flatulencia concluded, "I thought I'd have a word with you."

Mother was listening to her intently. We had all shifted to the living room, Sister Flatulencia stretching her tree trunk legs out in front of her, me on the couch scratching the silky white patch under Jillily's pointy chin, Mother poised at the edge of her chair. Nana stood with arms crossed behind Mother.

As usual, Mother seemed oblivious to my presence. She may have learned to abstain from alcohol, but she still tended to overlook me most of the time. I tried telling myself that meetings with a bunch of enthusiastic Bill W.'s had to fill a lot more void than one still-pretty-skinny, if increasingly breasty, nearly-twelve-year-old girl, but it still hurt.

Anyway, I have to say that Sister Flatulencia was pretty persuasive as she made the argument to Mother that, even if Dhani's baby were Father's, it would be her own daughter's half-sister. In other words, family.

Mother snorted. "Well, I must say that one never occurred to me." But then she started fiddling with a tassel on one of the side cushions. "Are you suggesting that Flurry... I don't know... Nana's a fine companion, but Flurry *does* play on her own quite a bit." I wondered whether Mother was still stinging from Father's suggestion that my oddness derived from maternal neglect.

As if she could read my mind, Mother shot me a penetrating look. "You always *did* like Dhani, didn't you?" I waited to see if she was going to swear and throw things the way she had when she caught me preening before my mirror with my black-sweater wig and her Chanel Infrarouge dotting my forehead like a red-jelly third eye, but she turned back to Sister Flatulencia. "It's crazy, but I've had a yen for Indian cooking ever since we got here. Ever since I sobered up, it's as if my taste buds have come back from the dead."

You can imagine what it cost to hear her speak of things coming back from the dead. What a mess I'd made of Grandfather's resurrection!

But just then Mother threw her hands in the air, crying, "What the hell," causing Sister Flatulencia to cross herself and Jillily to tear out of the room, leaving a runway of scratch marks on the back of my hand. "May as well let bygones be bygones. Really, she did me a big favor. I should have left the bastard a long time ago. Tell her she's welcome to come, as long as she doesn't mention the S.O.B.'s name."

Sister Flatulencia brought Dhani to us the next morning, followed close behind by Doorman, who had to take several trips to cart up the suitcases and grocery bags the two had brought with them in their taxi. Dhani was wearing a purple and gold sari and looked fatter than I would ever have believed such a petite woman could get. As soon as she arrived, Nana shushed me into my room so Dhani and Mother could talk, saying she was going out for groceries herself. I didn't mind too much. Thanks to the urgings of my favorite librarian back in Gladwyne, Mrs. Perle, I had finally begun tackling world literature; my current challenge was *Anna Karenina,* and I wanted to chart all the names and nicknames so I could make sense of who was who.

I never knew what Mother and Dhani said to each other, only that by the time I ventured out to see what we were having for dinner, the two of them were yattering away and laughing in our shiny stainless steel kitchen as if they'd been friends forever. As soon as Dhani saw me, her round cheeks dimpled into a smile. I could see she was preparing lamb biryani. There were floured pieces of lamb on the counter, and she had a couple of onions spread out on the cutting board. "It's wonderful to see you, child. I do think you're going to be as tall as that old sycamore by the time you're fully grown." Her hand flew to her lips, and she shot a pained glance at Mother. "I forgot.

Did Sister Flatulencia tell you *he* hired a crew to chop that beautiful tree down the day after you left? He asked Ignacio to do it, but he refused. Who would want to get rid of such a healthy, old tree?" She sliced into an onion so fiercely that a glob of juice flew into my eye. Everyone assumed my crying was because of the onion, rather than the ghost of my grandfather nearly spilling into formlessness through the sudden rip in my heart.

For the next week or so, I was forced to go about my daily routine with the handicap of keeping at least one hand covering my chest (which is not so easy to do when you need to eat, drink, pet Jillily, and wipe your poo and pee) just to make sure Grandfather's ghost didn't leak out and float over to Father's house to haunt him forever for killing our tree—in some respects not such an unsatisfying prospect but for the fact that it would leave me with a chasm in my heart I could never hope to fill.

I had read some time before about the philosophical problem of the tree falling in the forest. I for one had no doubt that our favorite tree was sufficiently substantial to make plenty of sound, no matter who did or did not hear it go down. I can't tell you how many times I replayed the image of it hitting the ground, limb by severed limb, until its massive trunk collapsed in one achingly reluctant finale. As for the seasonal ranks of migrating birds discovering a stump in place of their favorite void-filling playground, it simply didn't bear thinking about.

But it was good to have Dhani with us. She brought a warmth into our home that made it feel, somehow, rounder. I wasn't the only one drawn to her kindness. A few weeks into her stay, on a rainy afternoon when Nana was out doing errands, I was blissfully folding newspaper cones and Dhani was dicing onions for a spicy snack called *bhel puri* when the buzzing of the intercom interrupted us. The two of us exchanged a quick look. Hardly anyone came to call when Mother was at one of her meetings. I ran to push the button and asked Doorman why he'd rung.

"Young man here says he's Adam Manus, miss. You know him?"

It took a moment for the name to register.

The intercom crackled. "Miss?"

"Yes, yes. It's okay." I was aware that my voice sounded strangely high-pitched. "Please send him up."

In the minutes before he arrived, Dhani and I wiped our hands and removed our aprons. I knew Dhani had made a friend of Adam in the brief time she'd worked for his father, but she'd looked surprised herself when I'd dashed into the kitchen to tell her who was wanting to come upstairs.

I stood back a bit as she let Adam in. Despite the fact that he was obviously soaking from the rain, she pulled him into as much of a hug as her bulging belly would allow. He shot me a questioning look over her head that reminded me that the only other time I'd seen him I'd been howling like a baby and drizzling snot onto his shoulder.

"Hey," he said.

I felt my face go red. I didn't know whether to smile or cry.

Dhani let Adam go. Looking back and forth between us, she said unnecessarily, "I think you two have met before." We stood there awkwardly for a second until Dhani broke into the silence with her infectious laugh. "Here. Let me take your coat."

Adam shrugged free of his hooded jacket, and I could see he'd cut his hair quite close to his head. A few drops of water fell into his intense green eyes and he blinked. While Dhani went to hang his jacket in the hall closet, he looked at me as if he wanted to say something, but before either of us could speak, Dhani was back, motioning Adam to follow her into the living room. "Come in, please. Don't be shy." She let herself down cautiously onto the couch and patted the place beside her. "Sit, sit. I want to hear everything. How is Cook? I see she hasn't managed to make you fat yet."

Adam limped to the couch and sat down. He certainly wasn't fat, but I couldn't help but notice the contrast between his slightly skewed foot and his muscular chest and arms. He was laughing, shaking his head. "She tries, she tries."

Dhani put a hand to his cheek. "It's so good to see you. But, Adam, why are you in Manhattan?"

He shrugged. "Schools. I have to be practical. I've got an appointment with the Admissions Dean at NYU. I've got this great research assistantship there this summer, and I guess it'd be the best backup in case I don't get into Caltech in the fall." I didn't know what Caltech was, but I could tell he wanted badly to get into it.

Dhani turned to me. "He's a physics whiz, this boy. Did I tell you?" She sighed. "I barely managed to get an O level in it myself. Only geniuses can fathom it."

Adam broke in, seeking my eyes as he laughed, "Hey, don't let her spook you. With a good teacher, it's a piece of cake. Well, maybe not a piece of cake, but fun. *Really* fun." I realized he'd mistaken my expression for intimidation. The fact was, I didn't actually know what physics was and had to stifle the impulse to excuse myself to look it up. He sat back and eyed me appraisingly. "Let's see, you must be in seventh or eighth grade. Biology, right? I didn't get into science myself until chemistry."

I had no idea what he was talking about.

Dhani looked uncomfortable. "Actually, Flurry isn't in school."

"What do you mean?"

"She's home schooled." From the sound of her voice, I could tell Dhani didn't approve, and my belly went all queasy.

But the conversation was moving on, mostly with Adam asking Dhani about what her plans were once Ignacio returned. I could see he was surprised when she told him his father had leased the car that Ignacio was driving to Mexico.

Too soon, Adam said he had to go or he'd be late for his appointment with the Admissions Dean at NYU. While Dhani went to get his jacket, he said quickly, "Are you okay?"

This time I knew what he was talking about. "Sort of," I said.

"It'll get better, I promise you." Somehow, the way he said it made me almost believe him.

Dhani came back in and Adam shrugged into his still-damp jacket. As he walked out the front door, he looked back at me over his shoulder. "I really want to talk to you. I'll try to get back here soon." Something unfamiliar was stirring inside me, a kind of breathlessness, and I found myself hoping he really meant it.

But I didn't end up seeing him again until after Dhani had her baby—which was much sooner than everyone expected. Several weeks before her due date, she woke the whole household in the middle of the night, crying, "It's coming, it's coming." Before anyone could think of dialing 911, she screamed, "I mean it. It's coming now!"

Nana commented later that Dhani's labor was shockingly hasty for a first-time affair, but it went on long enough to offer me a once-in-a-lifetime opportunity to observe Mother Nature do her mysterious work. I felt like I was actually *seeing* a rosebud uncurl.

I had already discovered my natural gifts as a soldier; now I found that others' tendency to treat me as invisible stood me in equally good stead to be a spy. While the rest of the household screamed and cursed (mostly Dhani) or sought refuge from the racket by crawling under the bed (Jillily) or rifled desperately through Dhani's suitcase for diapers and Martian infant sacks (Nana) or held Dhani's hand, urging, "Now, take another nice deep breath and push" (Mother), I myself stood just inside the threshold between the bathroom and the bedroom, mouthing in unison with Mother, "One, two, three—push!" Whenever Mother reached the point of the ritual where she'd step away from Dhani's body, saying, "Now you can take a little rest," I'd pull my head back from the doorway and do some extra breathing myself.

This went on just long enough to convince me that Dhani knew at least as many swear words as Mother and Father, that Nana was now back in her element (face set in Mack-truckish determination, wiping little poop-noodles from Dhani's butt that slithered out every time she pushed), and that Mother made a much nicer nurse than the one at my doctor's who never bothered to gentle her voice when she took my blood.

As for the baby actually emerging from Dhani's tweeter, I had never seen anything like it. Dhani's bun burst from her oven head-first, landing in Mother's waiting hands streaked with blood and mucous and looking like she wasn't cooked nearly enough. Once Nana had cleaned her up, her diminutive dark face poking out prune-like from her new Martian pajamas, I personally thought she cried out for a little plumping. As far as I could tell, she didn't look like either Father or Ignacio, or even Dhani for that matter, but her size bore a definite resemblance to Uncle Bob.

When the paramedics finally arrived to take Dhani and her baby to the hospital, I found myself praying that the little girl wouldn't prove to be Father's child. It was enough that Father had contributed fifty percent to my own existence.

Just a few months later, I would read about the subtleties of genetics and the theory that we all share one common matrilineal ancestor, an African female called by researchers the Mitochondrial Eve. I loved imagining the unbroken line of sturdy mothers passing along

Mitochondrial Eve's original DNA to each generation and felt grateful to be able to think of sharing my genetic goop with that Eve, rather than her Biblical namesake, who I tended to associate with Father's television tirades against Satan and what he liked to call "the sins of man born of woman."

But getting back to Dhani's baby, worrying about her father's identity soon gave way to worrying about Ignacio. In the weeks following Angelina's birth, Dhani breastfed her wrinkly-faced newborn into reassuringly fat-cheeked plumpness, but her smiles at her baby were interspersed with bouts of heavy sighing. No one had to ask why. She hadn't heard from Ignacio since the day before the baby's delivery.

Up until then, he'd been calling each evening from a series of motels along the way to Mexico. And then his calls just stopped.

Of course, he couldn't have known that Dhani's bun would be born early, and we couldn't have known that his rented Chevy Malibu would break down on the outskirts of Manuel Benavides, that he'd be plied with too many tequilas by a sympathetic barman, that he'd insult the policeman on the barstool next to him for failing to prevent Rosa's murder, that he'd be thrown into a roach-infested jail minus his cell phone and cash, and that someone named Maria Quintero—the sympathetic cousin of his equally drunken cellmate—would kindly bail him out. Nor could we have predicted how much money Ignacio would have to borrow from Senorita Quintero to bribe a series of low-level officials to provide written proof of Rosa's death.

When Ignacio finally called Dhani from the sole working payphone at a bus station in Ciudad Juarez, Mother and Nana and I huddled around her while she held the kitchen phone. We flooded her with so many questions as they talked that she ended up shouting, "You need to shut up, the sodding lot of you!" Shocked, we all did, in fact, shut up, having to make do with her side of the phone conversation, which went something like this: "What do you mean you just got out of jail?" (angry tone). "Who is this Maria woman?" (definitely suspicious). And "Oh, Ignacio, are you sure you're all right?" (an unusual worry line bisecting her forehead like a sideways third eye). Then, "Well, thank God for that, anyway."

With an expression mixed with mischief and delight, she took Angelina from Nana's shoulder and held the receiver close to her baby's burbling lips. Once Angelina commenced her delicate *ugga umph uggas*, we no longer needed Dhani to translate for us. We could hear Ignacio whoop at the other end of the line.

I was already familiar with the magic of Angelina's sound effects. But my fondness for the baby made Jillily terribly jealous, especially since she and Angelina were pretty much the same size. The first time I sat next to Dhani while she was breastfeeding, Jillily hissed and moaned and stalked out of the room with a couple of nasty backward glances to make sure I'd gotten the message. I ran after her, trying to explain that no one could replace her question mark tail, her Charlotte the Harlot pose, her sleek back inserted into the cleave of my bulbous breasts while we slept. Thankfully, Jillily's memory was short, and as soon as we were off on our own, she seemed to bear me no grudge, trusting I would gently rub her white belly for several minutes with the tip of my forefinger, just the way she liked.

I, personally, thought Jillily could have been more generous, especially since she'd been puking excessively ever since we moved and it was now up to me to clean it up. There was no Fayga in the home of my second incarnation, just some weekly house cleaning by Ruby, a young woman with a stud in her nose and hair as black as a crow's wings, who "did the heavy work," as Nana liked to call it, though I didn't get what was so heavy about scouring toilet bowls and vacuuming dust-bunnies from under the bed.

As for Jillily's amped-up puking, it took me awhile to recognize that the problem was the lack of a yard for her to roam. She'd always counted on eating grass to help her throw up when her tummy was upset and, as much as she'd left a fair share of puke pools inside Father's house, she'd undoubtedly deposited a great deal more on his grounds. Once I figured that one out, I lobbied Nana to install little boxes of kitty grass along one side of the living room balcony to help Jillily empty her unwanted contents onto the mosaic-tiled floor. I discovered that the trick was to let it dry completely before you swept it up.

Anyway, it was on the day before Ignacio flew back to the U.S.—and just as I was feeling rather sorry myself for having to dump a third load of dried puke into the waste basket—that Dhani rushed into the kitchen to tell me that Adam had phoned. "Oh, Flurry! He got in. He got into Caltech!" Before I knew it, I found myself dancing through the apartment behind her, Dhani still holding the carrot she'd been peeling and me dragging my broom.

But later that night, as I was tiptoeing toward the kitchen to liberate a leftover *chipati* from the fridge, I overheard Dhani say to Mother and Nana, "I didn't find out until the second time he called. Poor boy. First he loses his mother, then he's sent off to live with his grandparents. After that, boarding school, and now he hasn't got a penny for room and board while he's at Caltech. Senator Manus said it was enough that he was paying twenty-one thousand in tuition. Meanwhile, the bastard's house is probably worth millions."

My heart dropped pit-ishly into my stomach and I rushed into the living room. "Adam? Adam lost his mother? And now he doesn't even have a penny?" Dhani turned her head toward me, startled, then she shot Mother a questioning look.

Mother leaned her head against the sofa back and laughed, "Oh, why not? Has anyone ever been able to keep anything from this child?" So Dhani filled me in on what she'd been talking about.

I don't know if you have noticed, but Fate is far from fair. Not only had Adam emerged from his mother's belly with a left leg twisted like a corkscrew, but his mother was buried a week after his birth.

"Why was that?" I asked apprehensively.

"Because, when she was pregnant, she fell from a ladder while changing a light bulb." Dhani looked like she was trying to find a nice way to say it, but then she just gave up. She told me that Adam's mother had lapsed into a coma from which she'd never recovered. "They had to do an emergency C-Section."

Whatever that was, I didn't like the emergency part. I asked her to explain.

It was then that I learned that Adam wasn't born like most people, spat like misshapen seeds from their mother's swollen-watermelon tweeters (which, by the way, makes about as much sense to me as monthly menstrual cramps linking a celestial body 239,000 miles away with red jelly blood coming out of your tweeter). Instead, the doctors made a cut in his mother's belly and scooped him right out.

But then Nana chimed in, throwing a meaningful look at Mother. "Fell or jumped? Elise Manus was vainer than a peacock. Rumor had it she couldn't bear the thought of ugly stretch marks and saggy breasts."

That explanation wasn't just unbelievably voidish. It made no sense at all. How could a woman about to have a baby want to die? Or, for that matter, think she's ugly? I looked at Dhani, who'd started out slender, if curvy, then plumped up from her ankles to her cheeks in a way that would have done wonders for my hapless baby bird. Whenever she bounced little Angelina in her lap—the baby leaking drool from her lips like tree sap—Dhani's apple-fat-cheeked smiles rainbowed the room like a giant, generous Holi.

Dhani looked over at Mother. "When I was living there, Senator Manus never seemed to take much of an interest in Adam. I'll bet you the only reason he brought Adam with him to your father's funeral was that it would impress his constituents."

It wasn't so easy to fall asleep that night. The cruelties of Adam's life were too much to absorb. But all thoughts of him were momentarily forgotten when Ignacio arrived at our apartment the next day. Mother had been generous enough to invite him to stay with Dhani and Baby Angelina in our fourth bedroom until they could sort themselves out, and Ignacio couldn't stop saying things to Mother like, "Thank you, you're too good to me, I will pay you back for the airfare as soon as I can, I swear it," until Mother told him she'd kick the three of them onto the street if he didn't stop.

Sometimes I didn't know when Mother was joking. That particular threat of hers earned the flap of skin under my arm more pinches than you can imagine. Needless to say, I was more than a little reassured when I came out for dinner several hours later to see Mother and Nana and Dhani and Ignacio all seated at our dining table, just waiting for me to join them so they could chow down on Dhani's celebratory vegetable pakora.

Despite Mother's hospitality, Ignacio was a proud man. He was anxious to provide his new family with a proper home. Within days of his return, he did two things. He filled out an application for a gardener's job at the Central Park Conservancy, and he went to explain to Senator Manus how he'd had no choice but to leave the leased Chevy Malibu as collateral with the police of Manuel Benavides.

Poor Ignacio. Who could have predicted that some fledgling freelance reporter, eager to get a permanent perch on the staff of the *Philadelphia Inquirer*, would end up tailing him as he left Senator Manus' house? Or that the same reporter would unearth the dismaying detail that Ignacio had been bailed out of a Mexican prison by the daughter-in-law of the boss of a major drug cartel?

And poor Senator Manus, so consumed with suing the *Inquirer* for its nasty insinuations that he had no time to muster an effective re-election campaign.

I'd kept up the habit of reading the morning papers in honor of Grandfather, so I knew all about the elections—how Senator Manus' first term was nearly up, and how Father, who wasn't even supposed to be up for re-election this year, had been forced into a recall battle by a group of scandalized constituents.

On the Wednesday after the elections, I sat down in the breakfast nook with some Indian rice pudding and slid the *Inquirer* toward me. Unfolding the front page, I nearly gagged on my pudding. There was Father's face right next to a photo of Senator Manus. Just above them were two larger photographs of Pennsylvania's new senators-elect: a bow-tied African-American sporting narrow black glasses and a woman with a witchlike pickle nose and similarly scary ink-blot eyes. The voters of our state seemed to have gotten into the habit of splitting their preferences quite evenly; it was the witch who'd taken Father's place in the fight to save babies, leaving it to the bow-tied Senator to favor the devil abortionists.

I was beginning to feel unsettled around that time about the designations "pro-life" and "pro-choice," as if life and choice somehow precluded one another. The more I read in the papers and watched the news, the more it struck me that pro-choice politicians seemed comfortable with unborn babies being put to death, but were often fervent advocates of peace. And that pro-lifers seemed surprisingly comfortable sending young people to die in wars. Whenever I dwelt on those contradictions, I found myself dangling precariously close to the chasm of everlasting confusion.

But getting back to the paired pictures of Senators Robins and Manus, as soon as I scraped the last of the pudding from my bowl, I ran to my room and clipped out Father's photo to paste into one of my journals. It was the closest I'd gotten to him since we'd moved. I'm sorry to report he wasn't interested in visitation rights.

But I didn't quite know what to think about Father losing his recall campaign. Examining his grainy photo, I couldn't help but notice that he was surrounded by the usual gaggle of phony-granny-grinners, but from his expression he might just as well have been trapped at the bottom of a solitary pit, crumpling in the face of the void. In contrast, Senator Manus looked to be weathering his defeat rather well, making a philosophical shrug above the caption, "Cleared of Mexican Mafia Allegations, but Voters Opt for Clean Sweep Anyway." Father's caption wasn't so kind. It read, "Anti-Abortion Crusader Fathered Five Illegitimate Children—More Single Mothers Break Their Silence."

I can't explain why I kept the photo of Father. It wasn't exactly that I missed him—I hadn't forgotten his treatment of me and Grandfather and our tree. But something about how forlorn he looked reminded me of my own sorry state before loss began moving memories into the vacant rooms of my mind. I couldn't help but hope that, at the bottom of his despair, Father might find the seeds of a more angelic nature.

As Nana liked to say, "Hope springs eternal in the human breast," though I must admit I never actually witnessed it. Milk, yes. Especially Dhani's, which right from the get-go spurted like a geyser at the slightest whimper from Angelina's little lips. I couldn't help but marvel at the delicacy with which Dhani applied the tip of her finger to one side of her ample brown nipple while nursing her baby, sparing Angelina the bother of spluttering and gagging.

I knew that my own human breast leaked neither hope nor milk. Ever since getting my period, what seemed to want to spring from it was merely more breast. Sometimes I woke in the middle of the night convinced I'd grown yet another cup size, worrying that I'd float to the sky, tethered to my two giant balloons, with nothing to stop me but the star Betelgeuse, otherwise known as "the armpit of the great one." Or, just as bad, that the expansion would reverse itself, like Grandfather's balls and the baby bird on the lawn, shriveling my breasts before shrinking the rest of me until I died. As you can imagine, it wasn't so easy to fall back asleep after those kinds of thoughts, or even the ones that had to do with Father looking uncharacteristically frail and Adam Manus not having enough pennies to take to Caltech in the fall.

In such moments, even the most conscientious of creatures might find themselves reverting to a bit of pinching and banging to hold off the voidish tide.

Chapter 9 🦋

DHANI CONTINUED TO cook for us after she and Ignacio moved into an apartment on Amsterdam Avenue, and she fussed just as much over the dinner she made for my twelfth birthday (lamb *dhansak* curry followed by mango soufflé) as she did over the traditional Christmas roast beef and Yorkshire pud she whipped up for nine of us the following week. But working for Mother wasn't just a labor of love. She needed the money. Ignacio's new position as a zone gardener for the Central Park Conservancy was a major step up in the world, but it barely covered the basics for a family of three living in the Morningside Heights neighborhood of Manhattan.

But I'm afraid having Dhani and Angelina around while Mother spent virtually all her days at Bill W. meetings didn't exactly cure my allergy to boredom. After the clamor of saved babies in the home of my first incarnation, I was astonished by how much time a wanted infant could spend snoozing in contentment and how long a sleep-deprived mother could lay curled on a bed beside her while a curry gently simmered on the stove. As for Nana, she seemed to spend as much time traveling back to Gladwyne to help Sister Flatulencia with the saved babies as she did at our home. There is only so much reading that even the readingest twelve year old can do. Used to spending a great deal of time skipping around Father's grounds, I was so antsy being cooped up in the apartment that I was at risk of driving Jillily nuts with my non-stop fussing and stroking.

Which was why I got it into my head that it was about time to explore my new neighborhood. I'd already developed some familiarity with the surrounding streets from what you might call a bird's eye view, which was our tenth story penthouse apartment. (As for calling the floors of a building *stories*, you have to admit it makes perfect sense. I couldn't possibly have been the only one living there with a tale to tell.)

Anyway, I knew how the cars and trucks and buses moved fairly easily through traffic between the hours of 10 a.m. and 2 p.m. and how they stood still for ages, spewing exhaust fumes, in what Nana paradoxically dubbed the rush hour. I knew which dogs were walked by which people and when, at what hours the garbage truck double parked in front of our building, and how many trips it took for the trash man to sink his boots into gobs of dog poop while hauling bulky plastic bags back to his truck. Because of my poor sleeping habits, I knew just what the newspaper delivery van looked like and when the traffic lights went from flashing red to steady green and red and yellow. I knew the tallest building in our vicinity, as well as which ones were being torn down.

I saw where the homeless people liked to shelter from the rain, though I couldn't begin to understand why they weren't directed to pitch tents on Father's grounds, where they could fill their noses with the scent of David Austins and their bellies with the new cook's cooking. As for the latter, I heard all about her during Sister Flatulencia's frequent visits. She said she was very pretty, with long and lustrous hair and long and scarlet fingernails. I later learned she was one of the women written up in the newspaper, the ones whose misfortunes crossed Father's path like weeds to trip him up and bring him down.

In case you're curious about what can be gleaned of the world from a bird's eye view, here is one of the lists I compiled before I had the chance to explore the city from the bottom up, rather than the other way around:

> 1. 5 a.m. Folded newspapers fly from back of dirty white van to gutter, causing Doorman to shake fist at departing vehicle, which fails to slow down, but merely farts dark smoke back at him. (Doorman must be an even lousier sleeper than I am, since he is already dressed up in his costume, while I am still wearing my pajamas.)

2. 5:30 a.m. Dogs pull their owners out of their buildings in interesting staggered patterns. Owners look away politely while they smell each other's butts (the dogs, not the owners). My favorite—the considerate brown-skinned lady with curly white hair, who picks up her miniature poodle when there are puddles and carefully picks up his poop when there aren't, which is more than I can say for the tall man in the tall suit, who looks in both directions, then hurries away, leaving his pooch's poop perfectly positioned for the garbage man.

3. 5:45. Long haired gray cat slinks along side of building into back alley. Though he wears a collar and should therefore belong to someone, his outsized fist of a head suggests that he has fathered kittens while still a kitten himself

4. 6:00. Two skinny people in jeans come out of our building. One has long hair and little bumps that might be breasts, the other short hair and no evidence of breasts at all, so I assume they are a woman and a man. He keeps talking; she keeps nodding her head, but when they separate her steps look much lighter than his.

I felt a pang for the skinny man as I noted the jeans-wearing woman's obvious relief at being rid of him, but my reverie was interrupted by a surprise visit from Uncle Bob. He was in the miniature form he'd favored ever since he'd nearly lost his head to a tree limb on one of his more gigantic days. I dropped my book and ran to him, letting him leap onto my palm so I could lavish him with chicken peck kisses. When he protested he'd had enough of a bath, I sat him down on the top of my dresser, right next to a tiny photo of Grandfather, whose grin stretched agreeably from the white border on the left to the one on the right.

The first thing I noticed about Uncle Bob was that he'd lost a lot of weight. More than a little concerned, I suggested he stick around awhile. I figured Dhani could fatten him up. She was constantly concocting something delicious for us, like *biryani* and *tikka* and exotic sweets of every description, and I knew from seeing how nicely she and Ignacio and baby Angelina had filled out, that she was cooking up a storm at her own home, too. Sometimes I lulled myself back to sleep after a particularly vicious nightmare by imagining the desserts that were doing all that plumping: *gajar ka halwa* (carrot and milk pudding), *ras malai* (cheese dumplings in thick cream sauce), and my own favorite *rasgulla* (*paneer* balls dipped in sugar syrup)—yum yum.

Fortunately, Uncle Bob was agreeable to the plan, especially since things had evidently gotten a bit bare bones over at Father's house. (That piece of news threw me close to the edge of deepest darkness; if the pickings were that slim at the home of my first incarnation, what about the David Austins? Was anyone even bothering to fertilize and water them? Sometimes, with all the Bill W.'s littering our new home and demanding Mother's attention, it was only my memories of Abraham Darby and Charlotte and Constance Spry and Country Living and Eglantyne and Evelyn and Fair Bianca and Geoff Hamilton and Gertrude Jekyll and Jude the Obscure and Mayor of Casterbridge and Othello and Prospero and St. Swithum and The Prince and William Shakespeare and Mary Magdalene, waking each morning in their invisible beds, that made it possible for me to go on.)

Anyway, it was Uncle Bob who actually tipped the scales in favor of my first field trip into the neighborhood by agreeing to a little skip for old time's sake. I still might not have ventured out the particular morning I did—solo forays into the wider world being strictly forbidden—had Dhani not had a well-baby appointment for Baby Angelina and Mother not gone off to one of her many meetings and Nana not been in bed with a particularly bad cold, no doubt picked up from one of her beloved saved babies.

Uncle Bob and I quickly changed into clothes more suitable for skipping, both of us donning matching yellow shorts and white tops with lace collars, which did wonders for Uncle Bob in particular, who I must confess was looking somewhat ancient with his graying pony tail. Before locking the door and slipping the spare key in my pocket, I made sure that Jillily knew she was in charge, warning her not to wake Nana, nor open the door to strangers, though that was probably an unnecessary precaution. It was Doorman's job to prevent unauthorized visits to our building. I knew because I'd had no end of squabbles with Nana over why we couldn't let a few of the homeless sleep in our spare rooms.

Speaking of Doorman, it was fortunate I knew his schedule, especially how he disappeared without fail into the men's room behind his ground floor kiosk, a folded newspaper discretely tucked into his armpit, at precisely 10:15 each morning—which was how I timed our departure. I had worried I might be a bit underdressed for the city, so I'd lathered my lips with Mother's Chanel Infrarouge and lined my lashes with mascara, a little too thickly as it happened, so that I couldn't stop blinking as I skipped. But even so, despite a little nervous flapping somewhere behind my belly button, I was happy to be out and about again with Uncle Bob. I'd explored the neighborhood a bit with Nana already, but had never much bothered to see which direction we were walking. I was glad I'd been inspired by *Hansel and Gretel* to bring along some chocolate chip cookies, throwing crumbs as we turned unfamiliar corners.

People in the city suffer from a certain kind of selective blindness. Uncle Bob and I skipped and sang and chattered and stopped to study storefronts without a single soul saying *howdy-do* or even *hello*. After surveying the length of a particularly busy thoroughfare, Uncle Bob and I each had our favorite store. His sold antique guns and swords, which surprised me for such a peaceable man, but he had such fun slaying invisible flies and mosquitoes with the invisible sword in his hand as he stood outside the store that I had the sense to keep my yap shut, which is something Nana had been encouraging in me for as long as I could remember.

My own favorite shop had calligraphic lettering on the outside that read, "A Bird in the Bush." Putting my nose against the front window, I saw that on the inside it was so stuffed with birdbaths that even a shrunken Uncle Bob would have had to suck in his slender tummy to make his way through. Many of the baths, decorated with floral designs and animals and angels, put me in mind of the grounds of my earlier incarnation. One chubby-limbed angel in particular was a dead ringer for Baby Eros in Father's first fountain.

Inspired by my newfound sense of freedom, I found myself skipping a little wilder and a lot farther than I'd planned. Poor Uncle Bob kept shouting at me to wait up. I covered such a distance that I couldn't even see my ten-story building when my eyes scanned the skyline. I sat a panting Uncle Bob down on a bus bench. Battling a fiercely voidish longing for a St. Swithum to smell, I spun and spun till my face felt hot and red. It was then that I saw the teenaged boy, not much younger than Adam but with legs as straight as pick up sticks, who was watching me with a smile that would have reached the white borders if he were a photograph.

"Hey, Beautiful," he said.

I looked for Uncle Bob, but he was nowhere in sight. So much for the brave warrior he'd been playing at. Later, he confessed he'd dived into some bushes at the boy's first approach.

As you must realize, Beautiful was a new name for me, a definite promotion from the downward spiral of Sweetie Pie, Angel Face, Flurry, The Little Muchacha, You Poor Child, Crybaby, The Unluckiest Child, That Creepy Child, and Sneaky Little Monster. It took me off guard, making me breathe so fast that my bulbous breasts bounced up and down, though that might have been from all the spinning.

So when the boy proposed I meet him later that night at a very special place, just around the corner from where we stood—he still emphatically smiling and me still emphatically breathing—I nodded in agreement. Only then did I catch sight of Uncle Bob, peering nervously out from the bushes as the boy strode swiftly away.

Uncle Bob was so ashamed of his behavior that he kept silent all the way home. When I asked if he thought I was Beautiful, he simply kept skipping, looking, if anything, a bit smaller than usual. I guess that's what embarrassment does to you.

He wasn't much help that night, either. While I wrestled with two opposing inclinations, he pretended to be asleep, leaving me without a referee. Being admired by a male of the species was a novel experience for a girl whose father had treated her as little more than a slug. But still. Sneaking out for a bit of an outing in the middle of the day was a far cry from venturing into the unknown in the darkest night. The part of me that wanted to preen like an Austin before the strange boy's sun of a smile fought with the nervous part that insisted I put the events of the day behind me. In the end, it was only when a third part emerged—the part that Nana liked to call Your Infernal Curiosity—to align itself with this compelling new hunger to hear myself called Beautiful again, that fear slunk like a sore loser to a far corner of my mind.

When the hour arrived to put my soldierly skills to use—this time with the rest of the household at home and Doorman downstairs to contend with—Uncle Bob merely clung more tightly to

Jillily's silky coat, curling like a caterpillar in the cocoon of her half-mooned body as I tippy-toed my way past a snoring Nana (first room on the right) to let myself out of our apartment into the tenth floor hall. Despite my best efforts, the door squeaked as it shut. I froze. Mother, in particular, had a tendency to wake at the slightest sound. But luck was on my side. At least I thought so at the time. I made my escape without a peep from either one of them.

I managed to elude Doorman by taking the elevator to the parking garage, then sliding under its automatic gate to the street. It was a good thing I'd had plenty of practice doing the limbo in the old days, taught by none other than the queen of limbo herself, Sister Flatulencia. To hear her tell it, her double-jointedness had given her a consistent winning edge at her Catholic girls' school, despite her ungainly height. And that, evidently, was not all she'd excelled at. I'm thinking, right now, of a particularly intimate moment—walking home with her hand-in-hand from the Majestic and varying our pace with synchronized precision whenever she let a particularly odious fart fly—when she'd made the satisfyingly void-filling remark that some of the things she and her friends got up to at St. Hubert Catholic High School would make your hair curl.

My own hair was still straight after I emerged from the parking garage. I know because I put my hand to my head before dusting off my clothes. I was slightly disappointed, but even as every muscle in my body trembled at what I was doing, the secretive soldier in me found consolation in having effectively eluded Doorman's eagle eyes.

Escaping the building turned out to be merely the first of many challenges. Reconstructing my earlier journey was considerably more complicated, especially in the dark. The streetlights cast ominously suggestive shadows, and several times I had to fight the impulse to turn back. But when I rounded the corner where the boy who called me Beautiful had promised to show me something wonderful, I found his promise hadn't been empty.

Here, in the midst of a city that roared and clanged and frazzled everyone's nerves in the daytime, was a soothing paradise of the night. The street was shaped like a sinuous snake, and the mansions lining it, accented by artful lighting, bore no relation to the hard brick boxes and modern towers of the surrounding neighborhood. Just opposite me floated a vision suggestive of Sleeping Beauty's castle.

The only thing missing was a moat. I know because I searched for it, prompted by a gentle trickling sound and a faint moistness to the air.

I sniffed my way across the road, and sure enough, discovered a small pond within the wrought iron gates of an Italianate townhouse. With silent dispatch, I let myself into some lucky family's Garden of Eden. Water lapped at the edge of a mossy bank, feeding giant ferns, night blooming jasmine, and tropical-looking flowers the likes of which I'd never seen. Following the contours of the pond, I slipped around the side of the house, only to discover roses—David Austins!—fast asleep in their invisible beds.

You can imagine how I felt.

Just as I took my first step toward what looked in the dim light to be an Eglantyne, the boy who'd asked me to meet him materialized by my side. In the dim light, his long black coat and red ski cap put me in mind of the devil himself, particularly since the evening was so warm that I'd tied my cream sweater round my waist. But then I recalled how many times Nana had complained that I let my imagination get the best of me, especially in the deep of night.

I straightened my shoulders, leaving it to the soldier in me to keep my imagination in check, and forced myself to attend to him, though I ached to turn to the Eglantyne for reassurance. He whispered so softly, I had to lean forward to hear him. "Hey, Beautiful. I wasn't sure you'd come."

He removed his coat and pulled off his cap, leaving his long black hair looking a bit messy and revealing a white T-shirt and blue jeans. Without a word, he turned and sloped back around the corner. Not wishing to be impolite, I followed him and saw that he'd laid his coat on the mossy edge of the pond like a picnic blanket. He made a gesture for me to sit. I did, with my knees up to my chest and my hands clasped around them. The scent of the jasmine was strong, and I pushed my finger above my lip to stifle a sneeze. Despite it being warm enough for the top of my lip to be covered with perspiration, my teeth were chattering.

The boy didn't chatter, nor did he seem to be perspiring. He simply stared at the pond and murmured, "I'll bet you five dollars you don't have the nerve to get in the water." He added, as if it had just occurred to him, "Of course, you'd have to take your clothes off. It wouldn't be good to get them all wet."

I knew all about betting from watching Fayga and Cook and Sister Flatulencia and Dhani and Grandfather—Grandfather!—play Hearts. I knew it was something that people did to prove who'd won. I'd never really understood the need to win, nor the need for money for that matter, but the strangeness of the moment—the sweet-scented night, this enchanted garden, a boy who called me Beautiful—had cast its own particular spell. Despite a little warning light flickering frantically inside me, I proceeded to take off my clothes. One by one, I removed the sweater that was tied around my waist, my pink Capri pants, my white blouse with six buttons (the second one down slightly chipped at the edge), my white cotton underpants with pale pink and yellow flowers, my C-Cup bra (no lace; Nana didn't hold with such sophisticated touches for a girl of twelve).

The boy sat cross-legged, just at the edge of the water. When I untied the sweater from my waist, he reached for it and bunched it in his lap, taking what seemed like an awful lot of trouble tucking it into the triangle of space above his knees. He watched me take off my pants and my blouse and my panties and my bra, each time bunching my discarded garments tightly to his lap. I'd been so preoccupied with removing my clothes that I had not noticed the look in his eyes. I had not realized until then that they were just like Father's before he started chewing Dhani's lips. Not wanting anybody chewing on mine, I turned and quickly submerged myself in the water—first my feet, then my belly, and then my bulbous breasts, finally dunking my whole head before shooting straight up again. The water was much too cold.

I scrambled out awkwardly, my feet slipping on slithery moss. Too late, it occurred to me there was nothing to dry myself with, but the boy had removed his T-shirt and before I knew it was rubbing my goose-bumped body with it. I had never had anyone touch my naked body before except Nana and occasionally Mother and even more occasionally my doctor and his nurse. A t-shirt is nothing like a towel. It did not do much good getting me dry. And when the boy touched the shirt to my tweeter, it felt far wetter than when he'd started. I had the funniest feeling, but not funny ha-ha. It was like fluttering wings at the bottom of my belly. The wetness trickled from my tweeter and I worried I'd gotten my period. I put my hand there to check and the boy moaned and rubbed the zipper covering his member. I felt my lips stretch across my teeth, but it didn't feel like a smile.

And then the garden was illuminated by blinding brilliance, as if God had shrugged off his void to decree, "Let there be light." And there was light. And people on a balcony above us in their pajamas and robes, shouting and pointing. And two policemen in costumes with badges, one aiming a gun at the boy and one aiming a gun at me. From my personal perspective, and contrary to how it might seem to the Lord, this particular intervention of God's was definitely *not* good.

These are the ways in which it wasn't:

1. It was not good facing the black tunnel of a gun barrel.

2. It was not good that the policeman who took my arm had a pincer-grip just like Father's.

3. It was not good that everyone was staring at me like I'd let the filthiest fart in Christendom.

4. It was not good that I was wet and naked and when someone finally thought to put a covering over me, it was a wooly blanket thrown down from the balcony that made my skin break out in a rash.

5. It was not good that my hands were put into handcuffs that aggravated my itching.

6. It was not good that I was pushed into the back seat of a police car with wire mesh separating the boy and me from the policemen. (I would later make strenuous amends to Jillily for having ever cooped her up in that misnomer of a cat carrier, which I realized was actually nothing more than a cage.)

7. It was not good that I was locked in a small room with no windows and no one asking me if I needed to use the bathroom.

8. It was not good that I got even wetter from peeing in the Capri pants they'd finally let me put back on.

9. It was not good that I languished in the bottomless pit of eternal emptiness until Mother and Nana came to get me out.

Needless to say, it was very good that they did.

Chapter 10 🦋

MY BRIEF TIME in jail ended up stretching the scope of my world more satisfactorily than a rolling-pinned slab of pie dough.

Having been fast asleep when I snuck out of the apartment, neither Mother nor Nana even realized I was out until the police phoned with the news that they had me in custody. Mother immediately called Dhani and Sister Flatulencia and Fayga and Cook. By the time she brought me home, there was an anxious greeting party awaiting me, but no one yelled, "Surprise!" Instead, I was met with curious looks—not unsympathetic curious looks, but curious looks nonetheless.

Within an hour, our living room was a disaster zone, cluttered with so many empty coffee cups and used tissues that Fayga looked like she was going to have a fit until Sister Flatulencia shoved her out the door. Once I'd finished my Oreos and soy milk and said my requisite goodbyes to everyone, I was more than a little ready for bed. But Mother and Nana weren't done with me. They insisted on having me repeat every moment of my misadventure until I was fully awake again.

Somewhere in the middle of that trying discussion, it dawned on me that I might be just as much a filler of Mother's and Nana's voids as they'd been of mine.

Adam once said that we learn more about people by the questions they ask than their statements, and looking back I've considered that conversation with Mother and Nana as a case in point.

Nana set the tone. Here are some things she asked:

1. "Who the heck is Uncle Bob?" (Luckily, she went right on to the next questions, so I managed to evade a response. Uncle Bob and I had gotten into the habit of keeping our friendship a secret, and I wasn't about to change things without the two of us having a long talk, which, given his recent cowardly behavior, was certainly called for.)

2. "How could you go out like that in the middle of the night?" (She seemed singularly uninterested in my description of taking the elevator to the parking garage, and she showed no signs of recalling Sister Flatulencia showing us her masterful limbo moves.)

3. "How could you speak to a stranger after all I've taught you?" (Evidently, she couldn't quite grasp that in my two encounters with the boy I hadn't said a thing.)

It hadn't escaped me that not one of her queries was actually a question. Questions are things people want answers to, and her remarks were more like remonstrations that, frankly, left me significantly more pit-ish than when she'd begun.

Mother's questions were more like actual questions, but she seemed to want to answer them herself. Here is what she said:

1. "Was it because you were lonely? Didn't Nana tell you I've hired Adam Manus as a special friend for you? He's going to start tutoring you next week." (My belly instantly became home to a hundred butterflies, and I wanted to ask *her* some questions, but she kept barreling on.)

2. "You say this kid offered you five dollars. Why didn't you tell me you wanted an allowance? It's not as if we're poor. Even your father couldn't get around child support and alimony." (This was going to take a little research. I had no idea what she was talking about.)

3. "Couldn't you have asked me or Nana if you wanted to see the city? I didn't think you cared to get out that

much. Nana says you always seem, well, a little nervous when she takes you to the doctor's or the library. And you seem so preoccupied with your dictionary and your diaries. I thought you were one of those…you know, bookish kinds of girls." (On the whole, I decided I'd rather be called bookish than duckish.)

From that night forward, Mother began the practice of handing me a five-dollar bill every morning before leaving for meetings. At first I didn't know what to do with the money. It took Adam to provide me with a proper place to keep it.

The topic arose during our second week of tutoring, which began just a week after my imprisonment. Adam had been explaining how Dhani's hero Mohandas Gandhi had been jailed four times between 1922 and 1942. He looked up from the book he was quoting from and said, as if it had just occurred to him, "Your nana told me some kid got you into your own brush with the law not too long ago."

I flushed, feeling more than a little betrayed that Nana had confided in him about the boy who'd introduced me to Sleeping Beauty Castle and the Garden of Eden and feelings in my tweeter that I later discovered I could reproduce all on my own. Not that she knew about the latter. That was a confidence I'd been keeping even from Jillily, who I'd push off my bed before slipping my hand into my pajama bottoms and then into the folds of my tweeter. Shame is something that can separate you from even your very best friends. I did tell Grandfather though, whispering down into that hole in my heart where he lives. I figured if he could forgive me after I'd made Jillily cry he wasn't about to quibble about me making explosions in my tweeter that actually melted the void for a few intensely pleasurable minutes.

Anyway, Adam asked me a very different set of questions from Mother's and Nana's. To his credit, each time he waited for an answer.

Tossing Patricia Marcello's biography of Gandhi onto the floor, he ran a hand over his bristly head. "Your Nana tells me he bet you money you wouldn't take your clothes off. Did that really happen?" Then he sat quietly, perched on the corner of my new burled-wood desk, right beside a pile of books that started with *Algebra I: Explorations and Applications* on the bottom and blossomed into *A Wrinkle in Time* at the top. He didn't smile. He didn't frown.

"Yes," I said.

"Were you scared?"

I walked back into that place in my mind. Since at first I couldn't find my answer, I decided to take a page out of Jillily's book and get onto my hands and knees and sniff around. I sniffed into holding my breath while I tiptoed past Nana's bedroom, and I sniffed at the exertion of my lower-than-low limbo that got me out of the parking garage. I sniffed the spooky city shadows on the way to my assigned meeting place. I sniffed into the surprise of the stunning street. I sniffed into the beckoning pond, and I sniffed into wishing I could live in the house with the glorious Garden of Eden. I sniffed into the boy's black coat and his ski cap and his slyness when he made his bet with me. I sniffed into the heart-stopping glare of the lights going on. I sniffed into the terror of a gun pointing straight at the hole in my heart where my grandfather lived. I sniffed into the deadly emptiness of the holding cell. I sniffed into wetness: the air, the pond, my feet, my belly, my bulging breasts, my head, my tweeter, little explosions, the burst dam of pee soaking my pink Capris. I blushed and said, "Yes. No. Sometimes. A little. Sometimes a lot."

He nodded in commiseration. "Makes sense to me. How about now? Are you still scared?"

I shook my head. How could I explain that the strange boy with what Nana called "antisocial antics" had introduced me to a particularly pleasurable method of derailing the darkness? It wasn't until much later, after Adam introduced me to the mysteries of the Butterfly Effect, that I could put words to my discovery that surprisingly good things can come from bad (as well, I'm sad to report, as the other way around).

Speaking of good things, though, I wasn't the only one who ended up profiting from the events leading to my incarceration. Scores of birds benefited, as well. That's because I used most of my allowance money for birdseed once Adam taught me how to manage my money. The day after our Garden of Eden conversation, he brought with him a London-phone-booth piggy bank with a slot at the top wide enough to accommodate my five-dollar bills. Handing it to me, he said, "We can open a bank account for you as soon as you fill it. I realize this is just a step or two up in the dignity department, but really, your old potty stool simply will not do."

He was referring to my initial receptacle of choice for allowance money. I had fought Nana before the move for wanting to throw it away, or worse yet, leaving it for the saved toddlers. As I believe I've mentioned, that particular combination of toilet and library seat and step stool had been one of the mainstays of my early years, and I'd gotten pretty attached to it. Having been persuaded by Sister Flatulencia to let a particularly sick baby have my old crib, and having left my duck-billed night-light behind for Uncle Bob, I needed to draw the line somewhere. My potty stool, with its yellow hue so reminiscent of David Austin's Jude the Obscure, was the ideal item to halt the attrition, though I have to admit that it turned out to be a less than perfect housing for my five-dollar bills, especially once Jillily realized that the folded bills were an excellent substitute for toy mice, causing nearly as many bills to disappear under the bed or dresser— and even one mysterious time on the bathroom counter right behind the toothpaste—as stayed in the stool.

As it happens, the stool proved to be just as much of an attention-getter as Jude the Obscure. It was the first thing Adam noticed on his initial visit to my room. He'd come in carrying a teetery tower of books and said rather frantically, "Hey, Flurry, where's the best place to set these down?" But when he spied the potty in the corner with its little crumpled turds of five dollar bills, he laughed so hard that his whole body shook and I was afraid he was going to drop his books on Jillily, who was weaving in and out of his legs, both the straight one and its corkscrewed partner.

Though a bit stung on behalf of my stool, I was used to people laughing at me, so I simply replied, "Here," as I slid my grandfather's photo a little to the side to make room for the books on my dresser. (I hoped Grandfather wouldn't mind, since books were some of his favorite things in the world.) It was only later that Adam taught me to say things like, "That hurt my feelings," "I'm sorry," "Let me put that another way," and "I'm frightened. I need a little T.L.C." Mother called those parts of my lessons "the acquisition of people skills," but Adam insisted privately, "It isn't that you haven't been skillful at managing people. You've been doing a damn good job of it all your life, but nobody's bothered to ask what you actually feel."

The challenge, he said, was putting those feelings into words. That was after he'd witnessed a few bangings and whirlings and episodes of *fla fla fla* when Nana took Jillily to the vet for painful peeing and when one of his own history lessons catapulted me into a minor meltdown as I tried to fathom the dizzying depths of voidishness that would beget concentration camps and terrorism and giant mushroom clouds vaporizing people and cats and roses.

Unlike the rest of my household, who responded to my void-filling flapping by wringing their hands or yelling or walking out of the room, Adam just wrapped me tightly in his arms, loaning me his own skin and muscles to keep the darkness at bay. But that was Adam all over. As you might recall, he was the one who'd helped me weather the first wave of loss of my favorite person in the world.

Adam once told me that maybe it was because of his leg, but he couldn't bear to see someone in pain. He wondered out loud, "Could it be that you're like that, too?" I knew he wasn't referring to my legs, since neither one is corkscrewed, though I do have a large-ish mole on one knee. He waited, as usual, for my answer—this time, a tentative "maybe"—loosely clasping my right hand while Uncle Bob tightly gripped my left as we walked passed a store selling puppies and kittens. I supposed Adam had sensed me tensing up just as Uncle Bob started trembling with fear that he'd be the next to be stuffed in a cage. Adam was always optimizing opportunities for learning.

That was undoubtedly why he suggested a month later that we make a field trip to the home of my first incarnation. Earlier that week, Dhani had burst into the bedroom, just as Adam was trying to explain the basic principles of Chaos Theory. Her grin had to be a good six inches wide as she chirped excitedly, "This is surely the happiest of days! Your father's lawyers have agreed to sell his estate to a consortium set up by your mother and a few of her AA friends. They're going to turn it into a culinary school." Before dancing out the door again, she threw over her shoulder, "And Cook and I are going to be founding members of the faculty!"

Adam and I exchanged an astonished look, then I burst into tears.

He slid off his chair, and his arms were around me in a second. "What is it, Flurry?"

But the chasm between my feelings at that moment and words was just too deep. No words would come.

Adam just held me, rocking me back and forth, until he began to speak in short little spurts, as if he were thinking out loud. "Okay. I think I get it. That place was your home. What if we...I think this is what we should do. We should pick a nice day. The weather's supposed to brighten up soon. I'll have to make sure your father's gone." I felt soothed by the way his chin fitted perfectly over my head, his lower jaw poking my scalp with every word. But then he skewed around to look me right in the eyes. "What do you think? Might help you vanquish a ghost or two."

What could I say? I was magnetized by his Campbell's Soup B.O. and his earnest green eyes.

As it happens, Dhani's happy news would never have been possible but for Father's nervous breakdown. Just the day before, when I'd shown Nana the *Inquirer* article saying Father had been observed being whisked into Bryn Mawr Hospital's mental unit, Nana had commented, "Locked up the loony bin, is he? It figures. Pride cometh before a fall. A man with that big an ego can't stand coming down in the world." I suppose it didn't occur to her what it cost me to think of my own father locked up in some cell, even with his penchant for shouting and pinching.

That was something I could never quite reconcile about Father—despite all the ways he'd made it clear he didn't care much for me, and despite the fact that I could jump out of my skin just being around him, I couldn't bear the thought of anything bad happening to him. Nana liked to say that blood was thicker than water. Was it the thickness of my blood that made my heart so heavy when I read the article?

As for Mother's role in establishing the culinary school, Dhani said that her newfound business acumen was thanks to her new sponsor, a wealthy recovered alcoholic who'd taken Mother under his wing. I figured that sponsor of hers was one of her angels. I hadn't seen a bird big enough to take anyone's mother under its wing.

Actually, the whole concept of sponsors was pretty interesting, good for filling a fair number of voids if you have any interest in etymology. The way Mother explained it, AA sponsors are people who listen to your secrets and encourage you to make your amends so you won't drink alcohol anymore. Which I found quite confusing once I looked up the word *sponsor* in my etymological dictionary and found that the roots of the word mean *to promise a libation*—which is, in fact,

117

an alcoholic drink. And while libation can refer to actually drinking alcohol, it can also relate to the ritual of pouring wine on the ground as a sacrifice to a god.

I don't think the god referred to is Jesus. Jesus likes us to drink wine, not to spill it, at least in Holy Communion, because He likes us to drink His blood. Which makes Jesus sound a lot more like Count Dracula than the Lord of All Creation, but I am getting way off the point. My question is: which meaning of libation do the friends of Bill W. most embrace—drinking wine or spilling it on the ground? I suppose it depends whether they are on or off the wagon. And if you can't quite determine which wagon that is, then you and I are in the same boat—which is yet another expression guaranteed to keep you busy filling your void. So I guess you can see what I mean about the usefulness of sponsors in filling the void.

Anyway, the time finally came for our field trip to Father's old estate in Gladwyne—weather just this side of chilly but sunny enough; Father long gone; Mother having obtained keys to the new locks on the doors. Just as soon as his car took the curve of that familiar driveway and came to a stop where the press pool once parked, I spilled out of the car without even bothering to close the door behind me, speeding off so quickly in the direction of the first fountain that Adam could barely keep up with me.

There were so many old friends to see.

First stop: the great-great-grandchild of my first weed. It was doing quite well, clumping so heavily across the path that I'm afraid it nearly caught Adam's foot as he struggled to catch up to me at the first fountain.

I stopped dead in my tracks when I reached Baby Eros, trying to puzzle what was wrong. It finally dawned on me that the weeping willow had become so lachrymose that its lagging limbs were clogging the flow from the cherub's peeing member into a muffled gurgle. After breaking the spell of my *fla fla fla* with a reminder to use my words, Adam helped me unbraid the long branches from their stranglehold on Baby Eros' torso, securing them to the ground with an ornamental stone that took both our efforts to push across the lawn. After a brief pause to admire our handiwork, it was off to the second fountain, where I forced myself to greet the glowering fish in the corner, who I'm sorry to report looked no happier to see me than in the old days.

The David Austins were another matter. I heard Adam gasp with delight as we approached them. Pretty choked up myself, I dropped to my knees to caress one of Eglantyne's perfect pink petals with the tip of my forefinger. Thorns notwithstanding, roses appreciate a tender touch. As you can imagine, it took some time to introduce Adam to all my old friends, row after row of them shamelessly flirting with him as they stretched and fluffed in their invisible beds. Needless to say, I was as proud as if I'd birthed them myself, though recalling baby Angelina's entrance into this world, I wouldn't want to consider the cost of pushing a rose bush out of my tweeter.

Just a few skips away stood the joint burial mound of Ann Boleyn and the baby bird who'd given me my bright idea about Grandfather's balls. A particularly fine variety of weed, sprouting clusters of tiny red flowers in interesting patterns, sprawled across it like one of the quilts Sister Flatulencia's old friends sold at Christmas time, which in case you don't know is the celebration of Jesus' first incarnation, when he was still busying himself with accepting gifts and disciples and foot washings. It was only after dying on a cross and coming back to life after three days that He confirmed the Buddhist belief in re-birth.

Anyway, I was experiencing a mush of mixed emotions—sorrow tinged with horror—as I realized both Ann Boleyn and her avian companion would have pretty much decomposed by now. I prayed that they'd kept each other's spirits up as they provided sustenance for worms and weeds. I teetered at the edge of a whirling black pit for having drowned the baby bird in the first place, and worse, having failed to resurrect Grandfather.

It was too painful. I strode back to the living flowers. Adam followed me, but stood back a-ways as I wept. That was one thing about him. He always knew when not to intrude.

"It was prophetic that your mother named you Fleur," he finally said. I had no idea what he was talking about. I guess my expression gave that one away, since he repeated his words. Then he said, "*Fleur*. Well, she said it's actually *Blanche Fleur* on the birth certificate. Fleurie, didn't anyone ever tell you what your name means?"

I dumbly shook my head.

"F-L-E-U-R. It's French. It means flower. And Blanche means white. White Flower: that's your name."

Not Flurry, but Fleurie? Fleurie as in Blanche Fleur? The shift in perception was too vast to stand up to. I flopped onto the ground, right next to Abraham Darby, who promptly dropped a few petals in commiseration. Mother, who'd loved her roses more than almost anything, had named me White Flower. I realized right then that Mother was one of my angels. How could I have missed it before? She might be a bit of a flawed angel, but couldn't the same be said of Nana and Cook and Sister Flatulencia and Fayga and Dhani? (Not Grandfather, of course, but you could hardly expect others to live up to his standards.)

So there it was. The Austins were namesakes, like family. I felt like Alice after she took her first bite of biscuit, outgrowing everything she'd taken for granted.

I suppose it was my increased stature that helped me bear it when, hiking back to the house, Adam and I approached a sizeable plot of scrabble-earthed ground, its slight incline toward the center the only hint that something wide and deep had once inhabited the spot.

Adam saw something in my expression. He said, "Can you put what you're feeling into words?"

I told him then. About the mockingbirds and hummingbirds, the parrots and the doves. About the infinitely interesting patterns. About the branches swaying sweetly in the wind. I told him everything I could about our sycamore, Grandfather's and my tree.

"Oh, Fleurie, " Adam said. "I'm so sorry. That's awful. Would you like a hug?" I would. He did. And I have to say it helped.

I felt ready to take on the house now, but, following Adam over the threshold, I nearly had to step right out again. It was a ghost house, haunted by the faint hint of a baby crying, even though I knew that the last of the saved children had been farmed out to foster homes ages ago. Or at least I thought they had. I crossed over to the other wing, worried that one poor saved child had gotten lost in the shuffle, and not in a game of Hearts, either.

I couldn't help but notice that Fayga had excelled herself. The rooms were empty and immaculate. You'd never have known that hundreds of saved babies had peed, pooped, and puked their guts out here.

But what about those cries?

Adam followed as I returned to our family's wing of the house, but he stood hesitantly at the doorway when I tiptoed into Mother's room. The absence of her Queen-sized bed with the satin sheets was voidishly palpable. This was a room I was been shut out of more than welcomed into, a room of profound mystery, the repository of my deepest longing. In the early days, the pink basket in the corner with its *Vogue* and *Elle* magazines had been a gateway to a whole new world of words, but the door to the room itself could have been a brick wall for all the banging I'd uselessly done to be let in. The fact was, I'd seen more of Mother by sneaking into her walk-in closet. Watching her snore in bed with her right hand cast carelessly across her nightstand, the tiniest of burgundy puddles at the bottom of her wineglass telling its own tale. Seeing her pose in front of her mirror, making angry faces at her naked body with its every-which-way pubic hair.

I inspected that closet now for the source of the sobbing. Nothing.

Every subsequent room was just as empty, waiting patiently for the carpenters and painters who'd been hired to turn the house into a school.

In Nana's nursery, I found evidence of Sister Flatulencia's sentimentality. My old crib stood like a solitary orphan in the center of the room. The cries grew louder. I walked to the foot of the crib and looked inside.

She was a mess. Small as my palm, her munchkin face scarlet with screaming. Worms of snot slithered from her nose, and a pool of poop stained her Martian pajamas. I picked her up, pulling her close to the hole in my heart where my grandfather lived. He reached out his soft old man's hands and, with the faintest *ugga umph ugga*, gently took her from me. The crying stopped, and my unease melted as she disappeared from view. Was this what it was like for soldiers who actually made it home from their war?

It took me a while to realize someone was talking.

"Fleurie," Adam was saying. "Fleurie, are you all right? Do you want to go?"

For some reason I couldn't speak, but I was able to shake my head and gesture with my hand for him to wait for me. I had one more thing I needed to do. I made my way to Grandfather's room. If I hadn't known it was his bedroom already, the wiggly pencil lines on his doorjamb tracing my growth spurts would have been a good enough clue.

The rocker was still there, right beside Grandfather's chair, facing the window—yet more evidence that, despite her defective digestive system, Sister Flatulencia was no fool. I lowered my nose to Grandfather's seat, but not a single whiff of his scent survived. Nonetheless, I chicken pecked every spot his sturdy body had once touched.

A silent Adam led the way out of the house. Before buckling my seat belt, I looked back one last time at Grandfather's window, Pandora-ishly hoping I would see him waving at me. But of course I couldn't.

That visit to the home of my first incarnation turned out to be one of the things I am most grateful to Adam for. The next time I returned was for the opening of the Cookery School, with Mother and Cook and Dhani linking hands out in front, posing for the cameras with giant grins on their faces. By then, there was no trace left of my first eleven years. Every room had been transformed, just like my void, which was filling up with memories as fast as my diaries were filling up with information, impressions, and unanswered questions.

Speaking of diaries, Adam ended up buying me a brand new one—well, actually, it was more like a notebook—in honor of me turning twelve-and-a-half, which coincided with our five-month anniversary of tutoring. He said, "God, Fleur. I never would have dreamed we could cover the kind of territory we have in such a short space of time."

We both glanced at my newest bookshelf, delivered just days ago by Ignacio. On the top row, leaning slightly to the left, stood *Bullfinch's Mythology, The Origin of the Species, Great Expectations, A Swiftly Tilting Planet, The Language of Mathematics,* and *A People's History of the United States.* Talk about void-filling, I had to assume that Darwin and Dickens and Zinn and L'Engle, god-like in their vision, must have had particularly immense voids to fill.

But getting back to my diaries, Adam had learned about them early on. You couldn't exactly miss them. Except for my new books and my bed and desk and dresser, they pretty much took up every inch of space in my bedroom, with Ignacio coming over every couple of months with a new custom-built shelf or two to further blanket the walls.

Anyway, Adam knew what was inside my diaries because he asked for permission to read them. No one had ever asked before. (We can't exactly count Nana and Sister Flatulencia and Fayga groaning over my Book of Bruises, snatched from my hands without one solitary, "Do you mind if I take a peek?" after I retrieved it from the fireplace.) He spent a whole hour with my first diary—the one listing multiple-meaninged words—carefully turning its well-worn pages as he sat on the edge of my bed. I was on one side of him and Jillily had spread herself out Charlotte-the-Harlot-ishly on the other. She'd grown fond enough of Adam to submit to his rather exuberant method of stroking, to the point of actually whirring her motor from time to time. Thanks to Adam's Big Pie Principle, I wasn't even jealous. The way Adam put it, love is like yeast, it likes to stretch and spread. In other words, there's always enough to go around. Anyway, when Adam finally looked up from my Book of Multiple-Meaninged Words, he said, "I have never met anyone more meticulous at making lists." Which puffed me up like a fully baked pie.

But I never did show him the diary that explained how scores of birds indirectly benefited from the affair of the Boy with Antisocial Antics, which was mostly thanks to birdseed and water. The seed part was simple. I brought it home from the vet's after my *fla fla fla* convinced Nana to bring me with her when she went to pick up poor Jillily from the vet's. Nana paid for Jillily's special new dried food for cats suffering from cystitis and I shoveled out a few of my five dollar allowance bills for the birdseed for robins and sparrows who'd never had cystitis at all.

I'd never been to the vet's before. It was my kind of place. The smell itself could have filled several people's voids for a year or two. The waiting room was packed with an intriguing variety of creatures. Here is what I saw:

1. A very small brown dog with very large ears, which put me in mind of angel's wings, so I told his rather sour-faced owner that he was very lucky to have a friend like that, which made every one else in the room smile, but didn't seem to impact the owner, which just goes to show that some people don't even deserve their angels;

2. A scrawny gray cat with a black moustache that looked disconcertingly like Adolf Hitler's, who most assuredly

belongs in the void of everlasting-minus-zero nothingness; not the cat, by the way—she was a charming creature and her owner, a woman with the biggest glasses I have ever seen in my life, let me hold her until she started tapping my chin with her paw every time I stopped petting her, which got rather tiresome after a while, so I gave her back;

3. A snake, which contrary to everything my father had ever said about the Garden of Eden, couldn't possibly be responsible for all the sickness and death in the world; it was just too small and didn't even have a smell.

4. A very lively blue parakeet in a domed cage that was parked in the lap of a young woman who might have been Dhani's twin and who said the bird was called Teddy and liked to play games; he kept picking up a gold hoop earring from the poop-littered bottom of his cage, then hopping to the edge of the cage, where his owner would tug it from his beak and fling it back in;

5. And, finally, Jillily, who was so relieved to see me through the bars of her own confining cage of a cat carrier that she hissed and motored at the very same time.

If there had been two of each of these creatures, I would have been happy to build an ark and start the world all over again, this time without an ounce of emptiness anywhere. But then again, I thought, the consequences might just be a bit claustrophobic, with everyone and everything compressed into a limited space rather than what Adam claimed was an ever-expanding universe, which was certainly worth thinking about. Though I wouldn't advise you to do so in any but a relatively void-free frame of mind.

But, getting back to the animals at the vet's, I did voice the wish to bring them all home, which of course meant including Dhani's near-twin and the skinny boy with the snake and the lady with giant glasses and the sour-faced man, since it wouldn't be fair to kidnap their pets, but Nana said no, our home was too small—which made me wish for a brief moment we lived in the house of my previous incarnation. Then I realized what must have motivated Father all those years, having so much space when there were so many babies to save. Then again, if he cared about them so much, why didn't he like them underfoot?

But I had to be honest with myself. I wouldn't much like a parakeet under my own feet. The thought of squashing it under my tennis shoes didn't bear thinking about. Was it possible that Father didn't like children nearby because he was afraid he'd hurt them? And did that mean that Father was more angelic than I'd ever imagined? These were void-filling thoughts that I carefully shelved inside one of the cupboards in my mind.

Anyway, speaking of void vanquishing, it wasn't just birdseed I put out for the neighborhood birds. I persuaded Nana to take me to The Bird in the Bush, where I paid a small fortune for a smallish fountain. It was an attractive sparkly gray with a pedestal, and the bath itself resembled a broad canyon with gracefully scalloped edges. Ignacio was kind enough to pick it up from The Bird in the Bush and install it on the second, smaller balcony outside the kitchen, the one Jillily was no longer allowed onto since she started using it as a place for left-out-food stealing forays. I figured that was the best place to put the fountain, since you didn't have to be the Lord to figure out what Jillily would do with all those birds. Angel that he was, Ignacio brought me a hut-shaped birdhouse as a bonus, where I could sprinkle little piles of black and tan seed, making a convenient one-stop shop for the birds to satisfy their nutritional needs.

As it happened, Adam had gone on a retreat at that time for new admits to Caltech, so, for a couple of days, I filled the void by stationing myself on one of the kitchen stools, feet pretzeled around its legs, to watch the birds. I could sense Grandfather keeping me company, peering out from the hole in my heart, but, as you can imagine, it wasn't nearly as comforting as the fleshy Grandfather sitting by my side in the old days, the two of us watching our tree.

But getting back to my second incarnation—and Lord knows how many times Adam urged me to stay in the present—the first birds that arrived at my new fountain were a pair of robins. To my surprise, they didn't drink the water. Instead, they jumped into the fountain like it was a bathtub, hopping and flapping and pecking away at the armpits of their wings. Other birds arrived and the robins took off. Throughout the day, more and more birds came along in interestingly-patterned waves. There were sparrows and mockingbirds and pigeons and even a couple of hummingbirds. To a bird, they all became increasingly animated the more they flapped around in that water. While it was quite entertaining, by the end of day two I was pretty depressed. I couldn't get it out of my head that, in the case of water, more is more. I should definitely have put more water on Grandfather's shrunken member.

It wasn't that hard to put my feelings into words at that moment. In fact, it was really quite simple. What I felt right then was *desolate*.

Chapter 11 🦋

HAVE YOU EVER noticed how much of life is about change? And how change rearranges the way you manage your void?

Once Father's grounds turned into The Cookery School, Dhani's fortunes improved immeasurably. She decided it was time to give Baby Angelina her first swimming lessons. She herself had never even seen a swimming pool before coming to the States, and she wanted her child to be able to swim with the best of them.

I whirled with excitement when she invited me to join the two of them for Baby Angelina's first lesson at the Aquarius Club. Sitting with a gaggle of mostly-fair-skinned grannies and mostly-dark-skinned nannies on a damp bench, I watched with some astonishment as the six-month-old who'd once been a bun learned to hold her breath and paw the water and kick with her surprisingly robust little legs. At some point, I realized I was holding my own breath whenever Dhani dunked her baby, only letting it out again once I saw Angelina come up for air again, simultaneously sputtering and giggling with glee.

But it wasn't just Angelina and Dhani that I observed. The pool itself provided more entertainment than the screen at the old Majestic. I used to think watching birds was the best bet to stave off boredom. But water? I decided right then and there that water is one of life's premier consolation prizes for sticking us with the void.

These are some of the things I noticed about the pool at the Aquarius.

1. Even though it had four very defined edges, what happened inside was limitless.

2. The water had a few basic patterns, comprised of concentric circles that proceeded outward from wherever it was touched and white amoebic shapes wiggling all along one side.

3. Thanks to the kinetic hyper-reactivity of water and its relationship with light, the essential patterns were perpetually subject to change; the pool was all movement; from moment to moment nothing stayed the same.

4. Its ripples resembled wrinkles, which put me in mind of *A Wrinkle in Time*, which in turn took me back to Adam's lesson about Einstein's notion of space and time as a fabric, navigable via folds and wrinkles, like a spider making a fast getaway from my flicking finger by taking a short cut on the twists and creases on my blouse.

5. A pool pump is its own kind of miracle, keeping the water fresh by maintaining circulation—another piece of evidence that rigidity is a first cousin to death and the void.

6. The pumped-in air provided a most pleasurable sensation of pressure if you let it push against your cupped hand.

7. Dragonflies appreciate pools at least as much as I do. I enjoyed swimming and knew the forward crawl, the sidestroke, and the breaststroke, but not how to soar like those dragonflies, back and forth over the length of the pool, daring every once in a while to dip close enough to skim a sip of water. I could never decide which I'd rather be: an iridescent turquoise dragonfly or one like a little lick of flame. No matter their color, I was convinced the dragonflies were Angelina's guardian angels, ensuring her

flailing limbs continued to keep her afloat. Stranded at
the bottom of a swimming pool is not a place a baby
would like to be.

And speaking of change, it was on our way back to the apartment from Angelina's lesson that I saw Father for the first time since
my second incarnation. He was coming out of a medical building—I
knew that's what it was because of the black and white sign on its
brick exterior saying *Medical Arts*. I don't know about you, but I'd
never thought of medicine as an art. It confused me terribly until I
realized it must be a kind of cousin to Martial Arts, only hopefully a
little less violent.

I thought Father looked rather peculiar, but it took me a while to
pinpoint the problem. He never once looked up as he crossed the
street to where his car was parked. (Or at least I assumed it was his
car, since, as soon as he got in, it he drove away. It was streaked with
dust and bird poop and sure as heck wasn't the Bentley.)

I'd read in the *Inquirer* several months ago that Father had been
released from his stay at Bryn Mawr Hospital for what they described
as nervous exhaustion, but now something else seemed to be wrong.
His demeanor resembled the red-faced young woman living in the
building next to ours, who shuffled up and down the block each afternoon, wearing nothing but her baby blue robe over a white lace
nightie, scrutinizing the sidewalk as if she'd lost something. The first
time I saw her, I started skipping toward her to ask if I could help,
but Doorman got hold of my arm and whispered in my ear that I
needn't bother—he said that what she'd really lost was her mind.

You can imagine what kind of pit *that* threw me into.

What kind of God would let people lose their minds? And was
there some kind of cosmic Lost and Found where He kept them? I
tell you, it gave me a serious case of the heebie-jeebs, thinking of
God feeling so empty and alone that He needed to steal people's
minds to stuff inside His own unfillably huge one. What kind of discord would *that* create, with one filched mind challenging the next,
getting into disagreements and perhaps even Martial Arts clashes, on
and on to the point of infinity? No wonder weather was so unpre-
dictable, with all of God's stolen minds making a contradictory hash
of things.

I didn't say anything to Dhani—she was too excited about Angelina taking so enthusiastically to the water—but once I'd seen Father cross the street looking for his lost mind, I decided it would be my job to find it. After all, as far as I could tell, Father wasn't exactly rolling in guardian angels.

Since I didn't know where Father lived anymore, this was going to be quite a challenge. I would have to use detective skills to find the two missing items: my newly mindless Father and his admittedly less-than-admirable mind.

Detective skills weren't entirely foreign to me. I'd read enough about *A Wrinkle in Time*'s Charles and Meg Wallace and Harry Potter and his friends to realize that being a detective is a little like being a soldier. Both involved a fair amount of pretending, which I prayed wasn't going to turn me into a perpetual Phony Granny Grinner.

The following day, I took the risk of asking Adam how I could track Father down. Not wishing to shame Father any more than he'd already shamed himself, I didn't mention the bit about the lost mind.

Adam was sprawled across my bed, stroking Jillily in that exuberant way of his, the vigorous petting causing my cat to shed enough thick black fur to make a decent-sized dust cloth. Not bothering to look up, Adam asked, "Why not ask your mother?" He politely refrained from asking why I wanted to know.

I told him that asking Mother might not be the best idea. I added, "Nana's convinced Mother's still sober because she doesn't have to deal with Father anymore."

Adam threw me a sideways glance. "Gotcha. She's probably right." He continued to stroke Jillily until she decided rather dramatically she'd had enough. Licking the dots of blood pearling his forehand, Adam pushed himself up and sat on the edge of the bed, his corkscrew leg tucked discretely behind its partner. "I've got a great idea," he grinned. "Let's ask Fiske." I paused to consider his proposal. I knew that Stanley H. Fiske was Adam's mentor and this summer's visiting distinguished science scholar at NYU, who'd be returning to Pasadena to head Caltech's physics program in the fall. But I didn't see how he could help in the Father-finding department. But Adam was standing now, ineffectually brushing cat hairs from his light khaki chinos. "I've been wanting you to meet him, anyway." He looked at his watch and started moving toward the doorway. "His office hours start in an hour. We can surprise him."

As we hopped a cab for Washington Square, I have to admit I felt a little nervous. Adam had been singing Stanley H. Fiske's praises ever since he'd begun his research assistantship under him at the end of May. He'd explained that his professor was so intelligent he'd been awarded a prize in the name of the man who'd invented dynamite. I shuddered to think of it.

From the way Adam had pronounced the words *Nobel Prize*, I imagined Adam's mentor being a near-relative to God, or at the very least scary and intimidating. But the first thing Stanley H. Fiske did when Adam introduced us was kneel down to tie his shoelace, somehow managing in the process to retrieve a quarter from between the arch of my foot and my flip-flop, tickling my big toe and giggling like a goofy eight year old. This was the world's expert on quantum mechanics? I guess I shouldn't have been surprised. Adam always said that quantum theory was how geniuses got to play.

As Stanley H. Fiske continued to pull coins out of all sorts of improbable places, I couldn't help but laugh myself. It wasn't just the magic tricks. The fact was, Stanley H. Fiske looked a lot like a frog. I don't mean he was short and green, or that he crouched and croaked. No, it was more that, in spite of having an unusually tall frame and particularly long neck that made him look like a normally tall person struggling to see over the heads of some invisible crowd, his wide forehead and wide cheeks and wide nose and wide mouth were so compressed and close together that it made his wide eyes look even bulgier when he stared at you from behind his inordinately thick-framed eyeglasses.

I learned soon enough that Stanley H. Fiske wasn't just smart and funny. He was kind. After demonstrating every magic trick he knew, he insisted on taking me around to introduce me to his other summer research assistants, all of whom—like Adam—would be heading out with him to Caltech in the fall. I was relieved to find that Adam's associates—Amir Gupta, Katrina Kelly, Gunther Anderten, and Tom Haggis—were just as friendly. They decided I just had to be given a tour of the campus, which included a fortifying pit stop at the crowded Downstein cafeteria and a detour for dessert at Dunkin' Donuts.

Loaded up with enough fast food to feed a small town, we continued on until we came upon the school's 25-meter pool. Swallowing the last of my garden burger—which I had to help down with a nice long slurp of Diet Coke—I couldn't help but share my observations about the patterns of water in the pool. Stanley H. Fiske listened intently, and not one of his students treated me as if I were saying *ugga umph ugga*. Instead, they jumped in with their own thoughts, speaking an incomprehensible language all their own, composed of phrases like *double beta decay*, *heavy quark symmetry*, and *anomalous magnetic moments*. Of course, the fact that they were wolfing down powdered sugar-covered jelly donuts while they talked didn't help me make out their words any easier.

By the time we returned to Stanley H. Fiske's office, I was exhausted. But before Adam and I left, Adam remembered why we were there in the first place. Stanley H. Fiske—being a practical man as well as a theoretician—responded to Adam's question about tracking down my father with a suggestion that I look around my house for an alimony check. His students concurred that that was a damned fine idea, and then Stanley H. Fiske surprised me again by jumping up in the air (*really* looking like a frog this time) and doing a little victory strut. I figured if he took that much pride in assisting me in my rather low-level detective work, he must've literally flown over the Caltech campus when he learned about his share of Alfred Nobel's dubious earnings.

It was during our cab ride home—me with a slightly sick tummy from too many jelly donuts and Adam with his own evidence of indulgence on the powder-sugared tip of his nose—that Adam asked how I'd found Stanley H. Fiske.

I said, "I didn't find him at all. You did."

Adam snorted. He was particularly proud of my newfound ability to tell a joke. He thought it would help when I started my first school in September, which Mother was determined to have me do. She'd decided that I needed to make friends my own age, which convinced me she didn't know me at all. I'd learned from my early trips to the Gladwyne Free Public Library that children my own age wanted nothing to do with me. And who needed them, anyway, when I had Adam to talk to about anything that mattered?

"You're lucky," I said. "Stanley H. Fiske seems like a handy angel to have."

Adam looked at me strangely. "Angel? What do you mean *angel?*"

Surprised he had to ask, I said, "You know. Someone sent by God to help you stay out of the giant hole."

"Giant hole?"

"Uh huh."

Our cabbie was honking vigorously at the car ahead of him, but Adam seemed oblivious to the noise. He cocked his head. "I don't know that I'm familiar with that hole, Fleurie. Could you tell me a bit more about it?"

So then I had to explain about the void and Adam had to strain to understand, and I can tell you right now, it wasn't easy. By the time we got back to our apartment building, Adam and I were both sweating. No wonder Grandfather and I had had such rapport. Without words as our primary currency, we could let stroky hands and melty eyes bridge whatever chasms there might have been between how we each managed our voids.

Anyway, my discussion with Adam about angels and the void proved to be quite fruitful. The next time Adam came to tutor me, he brought with him a new book for me to read. It was Jean-Paul Sartre's *Being and Nothingness*, and if you are ever feeling particularly nothingy, I can highly recommend it.

Not that I fully understood all of what Sartre wrote—though I have to confess I took a secret pleasure that someone so brilliant was preoccupied by many of the same things I was. But as much as I admired Sartre's ability to flit around nothingness with his giant microscope of a mind, he struck me as a rather dour man. Though I tried and tried, I simply could not imagine him fishing in my flip-flop for a quarter, or even, for that matter, a French centime. I had to concede that, when it came to geniuses, Stanley H. Fiske was my man.

The following morning, as soon as Mother left for her meeting, I embarked on my detective search. Despite Stanley H. Fiske's suggestion, I couldn't find an alimony check from Father—certainly not on top of Mother's desk, which proved to be a messy hodge-podge of receipts from the conversion of the home of my first incarnation to The Cookery School, a good half-dozen private school brochures, and lengthy letters having to do with Mother's fulfillment of her ninth step. But I did find something significant at the back of the bottom drawer. It was an envelope from Father. My hands trembled as I pulled a piece of stationary out of it and read:

Dear Margaret,

I know you think I'm evil, but I still think I helped you more than I harmed you. You were a wild girl and would have come to no good if you hadn't met me. If you're honest with yourself, I think you will have to grant me that. Your promiscuity began long before we met, and I hate to think where it would have led you but for the child we conceived together, thanks to the grace of God. Certainly, from the reports I hear of her, she is coming along nicely. Do you still wish you'd aborted her? I take some small satisfaction in continuing to work for the salvation of souls like Fleur. Despite my own personal misfortunes, now that I have made my penance, it seems I can still be of some use in the larger cause. I hope someday you can say the same for yourself.
Frank.

I must confess that the first time I read this, tears flowed from my eyes. Fortunately no one in the house was close by, except for Jillily, who butted her forehead against mine and licked my face, which I admit must have tasted as salty as a tube-full of Laxatone, the fishy-smelling tummy-settling paste I gave her to dissolve her hairballs.

I was startled by the creak of the front door and realized Mother must be back from her meeting. Stuffing the letter in my jeans pocket, I scooped up Jillily and sneaked back to my bedroom, where I continued crying a bit, letting Uncle Bob console me. He'd gotten rather fat by then, thanks to Dhani's cooking, so when he lay next to my cheek on the bed, his belly was like a pillow. I comforted myself for a while counting his heartbeats.

The good news was that the envelope from Father had an address on the back. Stanley H. Fiske hadn't known exactly where I'd find my clue to Father's whereabouts, but he'd been wise enough to aim me in the right direction. When I told Adam about it the next day, he laughed and said, "Well, that's science in a nutshell, isn't it?"

I didn't know what branch of science he was referring to, but the effect on my own fate of Stanley H. Fiske's preoccupation with alimony—Adam later divulged that Professor Fiske had recently been divorced by his wife Doris, who got sick of serving scores of research assistants for dinner each night back at their Pasadena home—seemed to hark back to the Butterfly Effect, which I'd learned by then was scientist Edward Lorenz's fanciful name for the *sensitive dependence on initial conditions* in Chaos Theory. Lorenz must have had a rather poetic sensibility. He borrowed a meteorologist's phrase that "one flap of a seagull's wings would be enough to alter the course of the weather forever," changing the word *seagull* to *butterfly*. I'm glad he did. *Butterfly Effect* has a much nicer ring to it than *Seagull Effect* or, for that matter, *sensitive dependence on initial conditions* any day.

But getting back to my detective work, I managed to climb out of the dark pit into which Father's letter had thrown me by fastening onto the lifeline of his words, "*From the reports I hear of her, she is coming along nicely.*" If I needed encouragement to proceed with my plan to help Father, that was certainly it.

I snuck off to Father's the following Saturday. As it happens, he wasn't living that far away, on East 90th Street, in a fourteenth floor penthouse apartment of his own. I couldn't help but ask myself, "What is it with people?" There did seem to be something worth noting that when their old lives fall apart, they had this impulse to locate themselves farther and farther away from the ground.

Father's building had no doorman, so I merely had to walk into his building, study a listing of residents that included Norris Heelcraft, Samantha Aames, Elliot Feldman, Gordon Knoxx, Henry and Pearl Gravenstein, Estelle Dowd, Ferdinand Frateria, and Paul and Bethany Porter, and take the elevator to the fourteenth floor, where I knocked and knocked until Fayga opened the door.

She didn't utter a word. Nor did the other three people seated around a low coffee table in front of a giant television in the living room. Despite their gaping stares, I felt oddly at home. There was a game of Hearts going on. The trio holding their splayed out hands of cards were Father, Sister Flatulencia, and a wrinkled old woman whom I later learned was Father's latest cook, Carmelita. Besides having her jaw hanging open like the rest of them, Sister Flatulencia looked ashamed. Carmelita didn't look ashamed, only a little green. Since she was sitting next to Sister Flatulencia, I figured my old friend had let a fart for old time's sake. Father looked not so much ashamed as smaller. I said a silent thank you to the Lord Jesus. If Father was playing cards, he hadn't lost his whole mind. On the other hand, the fact that he'd deigned to play with his servants was evidence he'd lost a lot of it.

But I suppose I don't need to tell you that Father with half a mind was still Father. He walked toward me without hugging arms opened wide, but with his right hand outstretched, as if I were one of his old constituents. But detectives, like spies and soldiers, know not to take things personally. I gripped Father's hand like a pro, noting that my eye-level now reached his Adam's apple, which I couldn't help but notice was about half the size of Stanley H. Fiske's. Given the respective proportions of their two minds, that figured. What didn't figure was how choky my voice got when I finally forced, "Hello, Father," out of my throat.

Fayga and Sister Flatulencia had the grace to usher Carmelita out of the room with them, leaving Father and me floundering near the coffee table, behaving as if our arms and legs didn't quite belong to our bodies. I couldn't help but notice that Sister Flatulencia had left behind a faint whiff of undigested broccoli along with a spread of cards on the table that looked to be a likely winning hand.

Speaking of grace, Father showed little evidence of possessing any, failing to offer me a seat or a soda or even an insincere, "How have you been?" Was this more evidence of his mindlessness or merely how he'd always treated any but his adoring tribe of true believers? I wasn't sure, but I felt suddenly quite tired, so I flopped onto the sofa and let him borrow my own grace by suggesting he take a seat himself.

It was more than a little awkward. The last time I'd sat next to Father had been in the back of a limousine on the way to my grandfather's funeral. You can well imagine the impact of that particular memory, though it certainly filled up the blank hole of conversationlessness between us. I was tempted to just get up and walk out, but then I saw my father looking down at his feet like my red-faced neighbor in her nightie, and I took pity on him all over again.

"So," I said, "read any good books lately?"

Father looked at me as if I'd proposed to preside over a couple of abortions. So I quickly changed tack. "Father, are you sick? I saw you coming out of the Medical Arts building."

Nana used to say that honesty was always the best policy. Have you noticed something about clichés? They are often quite right. The wariness melted from Father's face and he actually looked nearly human. He said, "Ah. Well, you are getting on, aren't you, Fleur? Twelve years old now, I think?" I nodded, and he continued. "I suppose you should know. I've been told I've got a problem with my ticker. And I'll tell you right now, facing mortality is enough to make a man turn his mind to the bigger picture."

I knew that the big picture had to do with questions like *What is life?* and *What does it all mean?* I also knew questions like that were guaranteed to send anyone into the deepest and darkest of pits.

If that was where events had taken Father, then we might now speak a similar language. Hesitantly at first, then more easily as he appeared to listen with genuine interest, I talked to Father as I never had before, mostly about my first incarnation—about the slats in my crib and the pleasures of head-banging, about my potty stool and my nightmares, about Nana's cave scent and Cook's angel food cakes, about David Austins and my weed. Having become a pretty good soldier, I carefully avoided any reference to Grandfather and our tree, to Senator Manus and his son, or to Dhani and Ignacio and Baby Angelina and Mother. I did, however, raise the topic of loss and my discovery of the usefulness of memories in filling up the void. Given his loss of office and his loss of house and grounds and his loss of Mother and his loss of his mind, I figured he might care to take a leaf out of that particular book. I talked so long that in the end I grew hoarse. And I told him so. I said, "I'm sorry, I'm a little hoarse."

And Father, who hadn't said a thing the whole time, merely staring at me as if he'd never realized I could talk at all, burst into laughter and actually gave me a gentle shove on my shoulder. "You are," he said. "You're a little horse. I'm a slightly bigger one." And with that, he stood up and began galloping around the room, spanking himself on the hip with an invisible whip so convincingly that I half expected him to dump a ripe loaf of horse poop on the living room floor.

Sister Flatulencia must have heard the racket. She rushed into the room, saying, "Senator Robins, have you lost your mind?"

As for me, I was smiling, because I knew she'd gotten it all wrong. He was just beginning to find it.

Chapter 12 🦋

WHEN I ENTERED the elevator to return to ground level after visiting Father's apartment, I was enough of a child of my first incarnation to feel just a little spooked as I noticed that the control buttons skipped from the twelfth floor to the fourteenth—which meant that, in truth, my father lived on the thirteenth floor. If there is one thing Sister Flatulencia and Nana and Fayga and Cook all agreed on, it was that thirteen was a very unlucky number.

For some reason hesitant to reveal that I'd visited Father, I still couldn't stop myself from blurting out to Adam the next morning, "Don't you think people who live on the thirteenth floor are pushing their luck?"

Adam and I were just about to set off for another visit with Stanley H. Fiske, and he paused with one arm thrust into his jacket sleeve and one still out. He shook his head at me, laughing. "Oh that! Like most superstitions, it has quite a history. Did you know there's a name for it? Fear of the number thirteen is called *triskaidekaphobia*."

I tried pronouncing it myself, but I'm afraid I made it sound a little too much like "ugga umph ugga," which made me grateful we were alone in our building's see-through elevator, descending slowly to the ground floor. Looking up at Adam, I had to squint as a blinding sun rose above the tall buildings outside.

Adam continued, "Some people say the number thirteen got its bad reputation because of Judas being the thirteenth guest at the table of the Last Supper, but it actually goes back a lot farther than that. The story of the Last Supper echoes an even older banquet in

Norse mythology, when the god Balder was killed by Loki, the spirit of discord, bringing the number at the table down from fourteen to thirteen."

The god Balder? How many gods were there in this world, anyway? This was definitely a topic I wouldn't dream of raising with Father or Sister Flatulencia. Frankly, I found it quite frightening. With all these gods, did that mean there were just as many voids? And if so, once I suffered a sufficient series of losses to populate my pit of nonbeing with memories, would I continue to be faced with more and more layers of nothingness to contend with?

Luckily, I learned soon enough from Stanley H. Fiske that there is one particularly ingenious method for filling virtually any void, and it's called science. When Adam and I arrived at his mentor's airy classroom in the Meyer physics building, Adam said brightly that we'd just been talking about Balder and Loki and the number thirteen.

His eyes bulging with enthusiasm, Stanley H. Fiske hopped right in. "Well, myths are nice, but science has its own view of thirteen." Turning to me, he said, "It happens to be a Fibonacci number. Has Adam gone into that yet?"

I shook my head, anticipatory goose bumps springing up on my arms.

Stanley H. Fiske smiled like a toad who'd just spotted a fly. "Well, let me tell you something about the genius of the natural world. Fibonacci refers to a sequencing of numbers of which the first two are 1 and 1 and then each succeeding number, or term, is the sum of the two immediately preceding it. What's more," he added— sweeping a pile of papers to one side of his desk so he could sit on it, one long leg crossed froggishly over the other—"thirteen is part of a universally occurring ratio that's been called the Golden Mean or the Golden Spiral, manifesting in such diverse things as the branching patterns of leaves, spirals of a seashell, human bone structure, harmonic intervals, and the Great Pyramid."

Frowning with concentration, I could almost feel my brain expanding. It occurred to me that any number contributing to something as awesome as the Great Pyramid had to trump even the eternally infamous Judas Iscariot. Stanley H. Fiske, taking note of my expression, slid down from his desk and knelt by my side, then slowly rose again, managing along the way to pluck a quarter from the spot where my gym sock folded over my ankle, a dime from one of the belt loops on my jeans, and a penny from the pink rubber band on my ponytail. Flaunting the three coins in his hand with a little dance, he threw Adam a look. "Don't want the child to take it all too seriously, do we?"

At that moment, the classroom door squeaked, and we looked over to see a softly-treading Amir Gupta slipping into the room, holding out a sheaf of papers like a peace offering, his brown face flushed with excitement. Before I knew it, he and Adam and Stanley H. Fiske were engaged in a fast-paced conversation about emergent five-dimensional black holes. I kept myself amused by skipping around the classroom's twenty desks, tracing a different path each time and so intently focused on my task that I didn't realize Stanley H. Fiske had joined me until he bumped into one of the desks and shouted, "Ouch!"

When I looked up at him in surprise, he said, "I like the pattern. Speaking of Fibonacci, do you know we can write your movements down as a mathematical sequence?" But before I could respond (and before he showed me how to numerically describe on the blackboard what my skipping feet had sketched out first), he said, "Skipping is one of my favorite exercises. Bet you wondered how I keep my tiny figure trim." He looked like he was expecting me to laugh, and in fact I snorted just a bit, but I also felt a little unnerved.

As I may have mentioned, Stanley H. Fiske was taller than both Father and Sister Flatulencia, though his head looked as if it had gotten squished by some inconveniently low doorways. I couldn't help but speculate how such a scrunched-up head could contain such a far-reaching brain, wondering if some of his mental activity might have relocated to that elongated neck of his with its protruding Adam's apple. Maybe that was the secret of Stanley H. Fiske's brilliant thoughts. After all, it was Eve's apple that was said to have been plucked from the Tree of Knowledge.

But I couldn't stay with that train of thought long. Stanley H. Fiske had taken a few long strides to the blackboard and, picking up a piece of chalk, was deftly diagramming my movements around the desks before turning them into a formula. After patiently explaining what he'd done, he said, "So, do you think you could spare a little time to skip with me around campus? Say, Monday, Wednesday, and Friday mornings? I think we might teach each other a thing or two."

I was shocked. What in the world could I teach Stanley H. Fiske? But how could I say no?

I looked at Adam, who grinned knowingly and dramatically swept his hand before his chest in a graceful arc before bowing slightly. "Pleased, I'm sure, to be Mademoiselle's chaperone." On the way home he confided, "Hey, any additional tie to Stanley's a bonus for me. Besides, he'll take you farther than I ever could."

Thankfully, Mother went along with the plan, especially once Adam gave it a name they could fasten their minds around. He called it P.E., which I was relieved to find out was a lot different from P.U. While Mother and Nana were aware that Adam was escorting me to the university for my exercise, they didn't quite appreciate that I had an unusually brilliant man for my P.E. partner. The fact was, my intellectual advancement began in earnest the moment Stanley H. Fiske and I each lifted a skip-ready foot.

Stanley H. Fiske was the best void-filler I knew. He had no patience for an empty mind. So, while we skipped, we took turns talking, him trying to sharpen his newest ideas on entropy and tachyons and supergravity by making them explicable to a twelve-year-old girl and me trying to work out my own conundrums—including how to prepare myself for middle school in the fall. Physics came to life for me like the water in the Aquarius swimming pool, especially once I'd devoured a series of books on linear algebra, functional analysis, calculus, and group theory. Adam was astonished that I was managing to absorb so many prerequisites to quantum theory in so short a time, but with Stanley H. Fiske answering my questions three times a week, how could I go wrong?

On one of our skip-fests, my new friend told me he'd bought us tickets to see *Ariadne auf Naxos* at the Met. I'd never seen an opera before, so I couldn't wait to tell Adam. But he just made a sour face when I told him and said that I couldn't possibility submit myself to the oddity of Strauss' opera—he clearly wasn't much of a fan himself—without at least knowing the original story. As soon as we got back to the apartment, he found the section of Frazier's *Golden Bough* describing how Ariadne helped Theseus kill the murderous Minotaur at the center of the labyrinth by giving him a magic sword and a ball of thread to find his way back out after stabbing the monster. I couldn't believe how Theseus repaid her loyalty by dumping her on the island of Naxos. How could the Greeks call a man who abandoned his own helper a hero?

Adam seemed surprisingly unsympathetic to my outrage and tried distracting me by telling me how pleased he was about my sessions with Stanley H. Fiske. I already knew that. While Stanley and I exercised our minds and muscles during our unusual P.E., Adam used the time as an opportunity to consume enough jelly-filled donuts to put a bulge in his usually taut belly as he solidified a connection with his fellow research assistants Amir, Katrina, Gunther, and Tom.

When flattery failed to work, Adam shifted gears, explaining how the term *Ariadne's thread* is used in the areas of logic, algorhythms, and artificial intelligence to describe the process of recording all the available options to solving a problem. But I insisted it was Ariadne herself who grabbed me. She was such a generous soul. Frazier had remarked in the *Golden Bough* that her name actually translated as "Utterly Pure," and I can't tell you how gratified I was to read that, after Theseus had callously abandoned her on the island of Naxos, the God Dionysus fell in love with her and made her his bride.

After Adam left, I found myself thinking how much Ariadne's tale highlighted Father's frugality in his depiction of God. I'd already learned from mythologists like Frazier and Joseph Campbell that our Lord Jesus had had lots of company over the years in the amplitude of His void, not just the denizens of the Greek Pantheon into which Ariadne married, but also odd duck gods like the ancient Egyptian Thoth (depicted as a baboon-headed dog and said to be responsible for sacred geometry) and Amon (presiding over things hidden), as well as the Celtic Dagda, master of magic, and Brigit, ruler of Martial, if not Medical, Arts. Those were but the tip of a worldwide iceberg. There were gods in every culture and nation, from Aztecs to Hindus, the Norse to the Masai.

But if Father had certain limitations in the scope of his mind, playing ponies with him on the day of our reunion had actually contributed to the development of my own imagination. As I raced my imaginary colt to catch up to his shiny steed in his thirteenth floor living room, the moment had wrapped around me in a quiet quilt of space and time. The link between Father and me felt as fine and strong as it was invisible, lacing my scalp in pleasurable goosebumpy waves.

Little did I suspect at the time that the seed of that sensation would secretly plant itself inside me, waiting patiently—as seeds do—until unleashed into action just a few weeks later, as I sat with Amir Gupta at Dunkin' Donuts while Adam graded papers with Stanley H. Fiske. As Amir leaned precariously back in his chair, musing aloud about the possibility of looped strings being a part of the ever-elusive Theory of Everything that physicists everywhere hunger for, something just clicked.

The fact was, Amir had a rather circular mind of his own. His ambulation along a series of alleyways of still-unanswered questions regarding string theory, the space-time continuum, the relative weakness of gravity, and mini-black holes prompted me, with that one casual remark, to see in a whole new light the notions of visibility and invisibility, or—put in another way—matter and its voidish twin, anti-matter.

We ended up spending half the day at Dunkin', where Adam had finally found us and happily joined in, plying us with enough sugary Glazed and Maple Frosteds and Boston Kremes to stimulate an increasingly fast-paced conversation about what sorts of human progress might be plumbed from invisible dimensions. As we pursued each thread of possibility, only to arrive at a series of dead-ends, I found myself thinking of the myth of Ariadne again—how the labyrinth was designed as a kind of void from which no one could return. Ariadne's story was rife with examples of multiple incarnations, which, when I thought about them, were nothing but departures into the void and return. Her thread helped Theseus get out of the maze once he got in, and she herself was abandoned by her sweetheart, only to gain a lover known for inducing a state of abandon—and if you think I was too young, at the age of twelve, to know about ecstatic abandon, you have forgotten what I've shared with you of making little explosions in my tweeter after the events at the Garden of Eden.

It also occurred to me that the story's theme of transforming loss into gain was relevant to science as well as mythology, especially when I discovered that the word maze refers to something *puzzling* or *confusing*, and labyrinth means *to labor into*. I was beginning to appreciate how religion and mythology and science were all attempts to labor into the void at its most confusing.

But before we pursue that particular path, I probably ought to return to the current state of my father's mind. I was pretty preoccupied with it myself, my ambitions having crept forward like a burgeoning weed from helping him find the rather-limited original version to constructing a more expansive one. But it wasn't easy. For one thing, I could only visit Father when Mother and Nana were both out, and even then I had to concoct all sorts of lies to account for why I hadn't answered the phone when they called. My lies ran the gamut from claiming I'd been playing Beethoven's *Fidelio* too loud on WQXR to taking a lengthy bubble bath, and I fear it says a lot about my unworthiness of their trust that they believed me.

But if all that subterfuge guaranteed that I shoulder a certain amount of guilt, helping Father's mind stretch made me even more creatively sneaky. Taking a leaf from Stanley H. Fiske's book and from Father's own surprising imitation of a horse, my technique consisted mostly of finding games to lighten Father's seriousness. We seemed to be making progress, until one day, in the midst of playing Twenty Questions, Father guessed my secret word—*pew*—then promptly burst into a torrent of tears so strong he could barely catch his breath.

I froze, watching a wet worm of a booger slide down from Father's nose.

He said in his squeakiest voice, "My mother. Pregnant with twins. We were at church. It was Easter. The pew was narrow. Couldn't sit still. I was just seven." He held up his palms piteously. "And bored. I was only seven. Did I say that?"

While still in a state of shock myself, I managed to give him an encouraging nod. I could tell more was coming and he needed some help getting it out.

"My foot was wiggling. How could I have known she would rise up so fast and need to cross in front of me? The pew was criminally narrow." He looked at me as if I knew what he was talking about and could actually offer him an answer. "She had to use the ladies. You know—pregnant women."

I did know. Dhani used to say she made more use of the toilet during the months she carried her bun than in all her previous years.

But Father was sobbing so heavily at this point that I had to strain to understand him. It pained me to see how pink and wet and doughy his face looked, like a grotesquely giant baby. "She tripped on my foot. She f-f-fell hard. She was so big. I was knocked down my-self. My head got stuck for a second under the pew in front of us. I didn't know what happened. But not a bruise on *me*." He shook his head in disbelief. "She miscarried. Lost both the babies that same night."

For some reason, the sequence he'd described appeared before my eyes in the form of a cartoon—Mother rushing to pee, tripping on bored boy's wriggling foot, and tumbling down. I don't know if it was nerves or something more sinister, but I had to stifle a laugh. I saw that Father was no longer crying, but staring at me in horror, as if he couldn't believe what he'd just revealed. I sensed it would be a mistake to express sympathy. Instead, I ran to fetch a box of Kleen-ex. He took a tissue from me without a word and honked into it.

I asked, stupidly, "Would you like a game of Chinese Checkers?"

Avoiding eye contact, he replied in a monotone. "Not right now. I think it might be time for a little rest."

"Father?" I said, a void opening before me at the thought at leaving it like this, but he ushered me out the door with a hurried, "Thanks so much. Come again soon."

Passing out the door, I looked back over my shoulder. There was no mistaking the misery in his eyes.

Chapter 13 🦋

THE SUMMER WAS passing more quickly than I could have imagined. I was tormented with thoughts of Adam and Stanley's upcoming departure for Caltech. Mother had taken me to see M.S. 167, otherwise known as the Robert Wagner Middle School, and—since I was no longer subject to fits of screaming at a moment's notice—they had actually let her enroll me for the fall. I tried hard to keep that fact stuffed at the bottom of my mental cupboard of unwelcome prospects. While Adam had mentored me well enough in the rules of appropriate social behavior that a decent school was willing to accept me, I had absolutely no confidence that people my own age would find me any less strange than the ones who'd backed away from me all my life like a mound of runny cheese.

Besides, how was I going to survive without Adam and Stanley? I lived for my hours talking physics with them, particularly once Stanley H. Fiske painstakingly explained the cutting-edge challenge of quantizing chaotic motion, or predicting the seemingly random developments in chaotic systems based on their initial conditions.

But something else had been nagging at me for weeks. Adam knew I'd found the envelope from Father that revealed his address, but I still hadn't revealed to my friend that I'd actually been visiting him. So when Adam accompanied me home from a particularly exciting skip-fest at NYU, I realized it was now or never. Haltingly, I told him about making contact with Father. With some further hemming and hawing and a distinct feeling of disloyalty, I explained how

Father had caused the death of his only siblings by accidentally tripping his pregnant mother.

Adam looked appropriately shocked and distressed. As soon as he paid our cabbie and we ascended the see-through elevator, he rubbed my shoulder gently with his forefingers, asking in a soft voice, "Fleurie, does this mean you're changing your feelings about your father?"

As we entered the penthouse I was silent. Somewhere along the way, I'd concluded that we can't really change our feelings. Our feelings can change *us*, however, so I poked around inside to see if any such alteration had taken place. As I did, I could hear Stanley H. Fiske saying, "There is always something in your life that is insoluble; that is what makes us human—and if you have the astounding good luck to actually resolve it, you can count on the universe throwing you another insoluble bone almost immediately, if only to save you from becoming insufferably smug."

So this is how I ended up replying to Adam: "Father is my insoluble dilemma. When I think of how he treated Mother and Grandfather and our tree, I hate him, but when I think about his losses and his bum ticker and killing his unborn brother and sister without even meaning to, I feel sad for him."

Adam grinned at the phrase *insoluble dilemma,* muttering once I'd finished, "Oh, my shining Sire, what hath thee wrought?" (*Shakespeare?* I wondered. *Marlowe?* Were they the same person after all?) But then, in a disconcerting shift back to the twenty-first century, he added, "I take it he hasn't sprung his latest brilliant idea on you."

I didn't know what Adam was talking about. Father's mind was hardly in any shape to produce brilliant ideas for anyone. "What?" I said.

Adam replied calmly, "Stanley. Has he mentioned anything to you yet about living arrangements?"

This is just the kind of conversation that leads to wars, with one person thinking they're heading in one direction and another hurtling along a completely different road. I'm afraid I replied a little testily, "You *are* going to live in that dorm, aren't you? I've already written down 555 South Hill Avenue in three different address books, just in case Jillily chews through one of them, like she did the last ten pages of *The Age of Reason.*" The prospect of not having Adam around was only bearable with the knowledge of where he'd be. Worse come to worst, I could sneak out of the penthouse and use my saved-up allowance to take a bus to Pasadena. The detective in me had researched the cost of it and the spy had secreted the money behind my bottom bathroom drawer.

"Fleurie." Adam crossed the room and held me tightly, knowing how calmed I felt from a firm touch.

"Mmm?" I was too busy sniffing to utter a proper word. How reassuring: he still smelled of Campbell's Chicken Soup and B.O.

"Fleurie, I'm sorry I scared you. It's not me I'm talking about. It's you. Stanley wants to bring you out to Pasadena to live with him and his sister Gwen. She's moving in with him. He says he's hopeless managing a house without Doris. Anyway, he's researched it, and it all fits together perfectly. Walter Reed Middle School in North Hollywood has a program for the highly gifted. He's friends with the head of the program. It's not around the corner, but Gwen's retired and, like Stanley, she's never had kids of her own, and she's eager to pitch in with driving. That way, he can take up tutoring you in physics for real, in a way I never could. I'm surprised he hasn't mentioned it yet."

How was I supposed to wrap my brain around that? Pasadena? Living with Stanley H. Fiske? *Gifted?* No words wanted to come out, not even *ugga umph ugga*. Instead, I burst into tears.

I'm not exactly sure why I cried. After all, I'd done pretty well for myself all those years, learning to manage my boredom in a variety of ways and adjusting to an unthinkable amount of change, beginning with the sad lesson of the baby bird on the lawn and followed fast by my failure to apply sufficient water to Grandfather's balls. Lately, I'd been quite content to see myself as an odd duck who was at last beginning to learn to make herself understood. Adam had been a great success as a tutor, catching me up on common knowledge and helping me use words for feelings. Furthermore, by introducing me to his mentor Stanley H. Fiske, he'd bequeathed me an angel who seemed not just able, but actually eager, to engage with my circuitous processes of thought.

But gifted? The word suggested unusual talent. I don't know if you can imagine what that represented for a person whose utterances had for the better part of her life been treated as variants of *ugga umph ugga*. I'd learned to be careful about which thoughts I chose to express aloud, certainly to Mother and Nana and Sister Flatulencia and

Cook and Fayga and even Dhani and Ignacio, though Grandfather and Uncle Bob and Jillily could always be counted on to accept anything I cared to share (except that one dreadful pinch of Jillily's belly) without prejudice or judgment.

But my new scientist friends had loosened my inhibitions. First Adam, then Stanley H. Fiske and Amir Gupta and Katrina Kelly and Gunther Anderten and Tom Haggis, had shown nothing but curiosity about the contents of my mind—particularly my years' worth of observations of the void and its central place in the nature of things.

Now Adam was referring to those observations as gifted. Within seconds, I turned into an emotional wreck, but I still had to be convinced to let him wipe my face with the edge of his purple and white NYU sweatshirt. Looking pretty overwhelmed himself, he said, "I'm sorry, Fleur. I shouldn't have opened my big yap. Listen, let me take you over to Stanley's. He'll explain it better than I ever could."

It was the first time I'd been to Stanley H. Fiske's apartment. Adam and I walked through his wide-open front door to find the place crammed with boxes that Stanley H. Fiske was busy labeling with a felt-tip marker. If the lack of anxiety about personal safety said something about him, then so did the fact that the clothes and meager possessions he'd brought with him at the beginning of the summer were flung higgledy-piggledy into a couple of battered suitcases, while each and every one of the boxes containing his notebooks and texts was meticulously stacked and labeled, some with fairly complex descriptive annotations. Stanley H. Fiske, his salt-and-pepper hair streaked with dust, lowered himself onto a sealed rectangular box labeled Gravitational Wave Detection before motioning me to take a seat on Condensed Matter Theory.

Adam, always tactful, whispered into Stanley H. Fiske's ear, then left on a pizza run.

Stanley yelled after him, "Make it double pepperoni for me!" He grinned at me. "As soon as I get back, my sister's going to give me the business if I even try eating something made with processed meat. Or white flour. Why is it that everything that tastes good plays havoc with my cholesterol?" He reached forward to retrieve the obligatory quarter from the sewn-on label at the neck of my blouse. Handing it to me, he settled back onto Gravitational Wave Detection and crossed one olive green pant leg over the other, looking even more like a frog than usual. "I understand young Adam's let the cat out of the bag." I had a hard time facing him, but something in his voice made me look into his eyes. He said, "Do you know why I want you come out to California with us, Fleur?"

Not trusting myself to speak, I shook my head from side to side.

"I suppose you wouldn't buy the argument that it's because I've gotten pretty fond of our skipping. Which, by the way, is perfectly true."

I stayed silent. That one was already storing itself in my heart to be sorted out later.

"The fact is," Stanley continued, "you've got a mind that most of us would die for. Sure, your knowledge base is still fairly Swiss Cheesy, but you have a unique way of coming at things, and you're still young enough not to be bothered about orthodoxy and petty lines of demarcation between disciplines." His face becoming increasingly animated, he slid off the box and started pacing. I imagined this was exactly how he'd give one of his lectures, his vital body tracing the movements of his mind. "That's just what it takes to break through theoretical logjams. It's something that can't be taught, but it sure could get stamped out. I tremble at the thought of you going to the kind of school our current powers-that-be feel entitled to thrust on our unfortunate populace. It would be criminal to trap that imagination of yours in some limited way of thinking and deprive the world of what could be some significant discoveries." He came to a stop in front of me. "We just can't let that happen, now, can we, Fleur?"

When he put it like that, what could I say? I'd never even considered that my Lord-God-who-hates-a-void mind could be much use to anyone, let alone *the world*, but selfishness is something my first incarnation had taught me to abhor.

Then Stanley put a hand on my arm. I wasn't used to that. Holding hands, yes. Sometimes when we skipped, we'd lace our fingers together lightly, though I had to answer to Uncle Bob for it every time.

As if sensing my disquiet, Stanley gave my elbow a little squeeze and let go. "Now, I don't want you to think I'm trying to pull a fast one. You're a person in your own right. Would you like to come? Do you think you could handle leaving home and staying with my sister Gwen and me? Not to make this into too heavy-handed a pitch, but she's a good woman, our Gwennie, and a hell of a cook, despite what

I said a few minutes ago, especially when you get used to honey in your tea and nut burgers in your buns, and she's assured me she'd treat you as well as she treats my little Moggy."

Seeing my blank look, he said, "Oh, didn't I tell you? I've got a cat of my own. Used to have two, but Blackie died of old age a little less than a year ago. Ironic name, that. The cat was all white, but who would have countenanced a cat called Whitey? Anyway, Moggy's never been quite the same without her companion. I'll bet she'd come to life again with another puss around." Stanley H. Fiske shot me a sneaky look. Disavowals of heavy-handed pitches aside, he had to know that the suggestion that I could bring Jillily with me would be a significant scale-tilter.

I said nothing, but could feel Gravitational Wave nearly lifting me off Condensed Matter, pulling me toward Stanley H. Fiske's intentions. He pressed his advantage. "Adam tells me that one of the reasons your mother wants you to go to school is to make some friends. I do think you might have a better chance of making pals at Reed. I hate to be an intellectual snob, but frankly, I don't know what a bunch of average, everyday kids would make of you."

Nor did I. But, really, I didn't know what to say. Forget other children. Mother might still be pretty much of the absentee variety, but the thought of leaving Nana sucked me toward the most unthinkable of emptinesses. Yet there was this other simultaneous sensation I couldn't stop, like explosions in my tweeter, but much higher up, making my head tingle with the thought of a far bigger universe than I'd ever imagined.

Staring at me buggishly, Stanley seemed to be thinking out loud. "You could come home to visit, you know. Anytime you want. And you'd have Adam close by. *And* Amir. And Katrina and Gunther and Tom. And me, if that counts for anything." He grinned. "You just might need someone to bounce all those ideas about the void off of. You never know."

I was still perched nervously on Condensed Matter when Adam returned. I have to confess that, between too much Dunkin' Donuts and too much pepperoni pizza, I had to make our cabbie pull over more than once on our ride home to let me puke red jelly tide pools by the side of the street. I'm not much of a puker, so the experience gave me extra sympathy for Jillily.

After he'd gently dabbed my chin for the final time, Adam said, "You poor kid. Listen, if you want, I'll broach it to your mother. You shouldn't have to do it."

I realized afterwards that Adam wasn't a politician's son for nothing. He approached Mother first thing the next morning, catching her before she was able to arm herself with the first of many cups of black coffee that seemed obligatory for Bill W.'s friends. He started out by saying that his esteemed mentor had a novel proposal to put forth, one that would benefit my education enormously and offer an unusual opportunity for broadening my personal horizons. "Stanley would like to put it to you himself. Maybe we could talk about it this evening? I know you've got a meeting to go to before dinner, which works perfectly, since Stanley doesn't finish consulting till seven or so."

There's something about a skillfully executed preview of coming attractions that makes its recipient nearly pant for the real event. Mother was so anxious about what Stanley H. Fiske had to say that she insisted upon Nana and Cook joining her in our living room when Professor Fiske came to call. But it wasn't Mother who invited Sister Flatulencia and Fayga. Unbeknownst to me, Adam wasn't taking any chances. He knew about Mother's reliance on groups to help her know her own mind. She would not give her assent without some kind of consensus.

I found myself barely able to breathe the rest of the day. Adam was kind enough to let me take a long walk by myself after lunch. The weather was gloomy. It had sprinkled throughout my fifth lesson on *Remembrance of Things Past*, but I managed to shake some of my melancholy watching six young crows bounce in and out of a particularly ample puddle, making patterns that would boggle the best of minds.

I returned just in time for dinner. Mother was visibly tense throughout our meal. She picked at her mesclun salad and completely ignored her sole almandine, which, as you can imagine, did nothing for Cook's mood. As if to compensate for the strain, Nana tried telling a series of jokes she'd heard on the *Tonight Show*, but her delivery was so heavy-handed that Mother and Adam and Cook and I tuned her out long before she got to her punch lines. It was only when Sister Flatulencia and Fayga showed up that Mother seemed to recall herself. As if there could be any doubt—the scent of peanut butter and sugar permeating the apartment—she inquired several times how the home baked cookies were coming, nearly driving Cook mad, and she flitted around the living room, straightening pictures on the wall and tidying piles of books and magazines until even Fayga tired of her, insisting she sit down with the rest of us.

We were all more than a little relieved when our guest of honor finally arrived. I'm pleased to say, he did himself proud. Only with someone like Stanley H. Fiske would a serious debate over the guardianship of a minor start with a series of magic tricks. Sister Flatulencia was so distressed by her own enthusiasm for his cleverness—the Catholic Church doesn't exactly sanction the Dark Arts—that she laughed and farted at the same time, requiring an immediate group retirement to the dining room for tea.

As I munched my warm moon of a peanut butter cookie, I scanned the faces around the table. Mother seemed especially excited; she was the most intellectually inclined of the crew and could not get over having a Nobel Laureate at her table. Fayga was the least fazed. Instead, she fixated upon a gooey peanut butter chip on Stanley H. Fiske's chin until she simply could not stand it anymore. She passed him a napkin and rolled her eyes until he looked down at it cross-eyed and swiped his chin before resuming his story of accepting his prize to Mother. Adam looked nervous. Nothing had been said so far about my possible move to Pasadena. Then the doorbell rang and everyone looked confused. I rushed to the front door.

It was Father.

You'd have thought a mime had entered the room. Mother and Sister Flatulencia and Cook shot dirty looks at Fayga, who gave herself away with a sly grin. Later, Adam would explain to me the expression *brown-nosing*, which I found an inordinately crude way of describing the currying of favor, which in turn was quite an image and would work ever so much better for me, now that my belly had matured to the point where it could manage the spiciness of virtually any Indian sauce before it hit my butt.

Not surprisingly, Father was oblivious to the room's reaction. He strode toward the seated Stanley H. Fiske, where he positively loomed over him, ominously rubbing his hands like Nicolas Sarkozy contemplating a dish of frog's legs. "I understand you have something to propose regarding my daughter. I would have thought you would have had the respect to put it to me. The child has two parents, you know."

I stood behind Father, twisting my fingers and resisting the impulse to flap. Mother had known nothing of my visits to Father. Would she feel I'd betrayed her? She left the room and returned, lighting a Sherman. No one had the nerve to ask her to move onto the balcony.

Stanley H. Fiske considered Father with a serious expression, fetching a handkerchief from his pocket and honking into it several times. He removed his Coke bottle eyeglasses and wiped them with the edge of his green pullover. He settled them back over the bridge of his wide nose. He puffed out his cheeks, making me worry he was actually going to literally morph into a toad. Then he relieved me by sticking out a hand for Father to shake. "Stanley H. Fiske. Good to meet you. You're absolutely right, of course. No sense of propriety. Never did. Carried away by that amazing mind of hers. Selfish of me, of course. What do you think—she's something, isn't she? You must be shamelessly proud. Do forgive me."

I should have known by the slickness of his sleight of hand that Stanley H. Fiske could be a formidable salesman. Father was completely disarmed. He accepted Stanley H. Fiske's hand, shook it vigorously, and then pulled out a chair for himself. "Yes, of course. But what exactly are you proposing?"

I could see by their expressions that Mother and Nana and Cook were stunned to see him capitulate. Of course, they hadn't seen him circling the wagons with me in his latest living room, mounted on his trusty steed. But once Stanley H. Fiske outlined his plan, Mother didn't look so much surprised as outraged. "You can't be serious," she said. "She's twelve years old. You can't just whisk her away after all I've done to raise her."

Sister Flatulencia looked over at Nana, raising an eyebrow in an expression of exquisite irony.

But Father spared a look for neither of them. Instead he turned to me. "What do *you* want, Fleur?" The rest of them looked as if asking me what I wanted to do with my own life was a particularly novel concept.

I closed my eyes, aware of all theirs trying to pierce the unfathomable mystery of my mind. Opening them, I turned to Mother. "I don't want to be apart from you, and I don't want to be apart from

Stanley H. Fiske, either. But we can't be two places at once, at least not yet." Everyone else looked nonplussed, but Stanley and Adam exchanged a grin. "I have to do it backwards. If I go, I know what I will feel. I will miss you and Nana and Father and Sister Flatulencia and Cook and Fayga terribly. If I don't go, I will never know what I missed. I think that means I have to go."

Mother looked like she was a food processor, gagging on a load of dense carrots.

But Father had already gotten there. His eyes were wet and he had to clear his throat a few times. He shot me a sideways look. "Sorry, I'm just a little hoarse."

I felt like I'd swallowed a couple of golf balls and they were stuck just below my ears.

Nana rose abruptly and left the room, at which Father recovered himself enough to say to Stanley H. Fiske, "You realize, don't you, that if anything happens to her under your care, I will kill you."

Stanley nodded. "Sounds fair to me."

Father rose to give me a hug. It was stiff and awkward, but it was still a hug.

Looking back, it makes a certain kind of sense that it would take a Nobel scientist to help me make a decent connection with my father, first by giving me hints of how to go about pinpointing his whereabouts after he'd lost his mind, then by persuading Father to take the lead in letting me go. But who would have guessed, in the days of my first incarnation, that Father would actually shed tears at the thought of not having me under foot?

As it happened, if there's one phenomenon that stands out about the rest of that evening, it's tears. The second wave I had to contend with were Nana's. As Stanley H. Fiske and Adam and Father exited the penthouse, excitedly debating the mathematics of calling horse races, I went to find her.

When I did, she was doing something I'd never seen her do. Her body was spread across my bed like a broken bus and she hugged Jillily tightly to her chest. Her sobbing was louder than an over-full washing machine. I sat myself between the small space between the edge of the bed and her size nine shoe.

When she realized she'd soaked my cat sufficiently with her tears, she blew noisily into a tissue I'd been patiently holding out to her and said, "What will I do? Who will I care for?" It occurred to me that Nana missed the saved babies more than I ever imagined. I reached out to stroke her hair, but found myself soon enough in the vise of her embrace. I have to say it felt good.

It was Nana who suggested we look for Mother. We found her seated at her antique vanity table, staring into its gilt-framed mirror.

"I've botched it, haven't I? How else can you explain that she could leave me without another thought? That she would have made friends with HIM?" Of course, the *she* that Mother was talking about was *me*.

I was mortified. I'd seen Mother register my presence behind her by blinking several times, quickly. Evidently, she felt so betrayed that she couldn't even bring herself to address me directly.

What could I say? That forgiveness is another way of filling the void? That stubbornness pretends to fill it, but leaves you sickish and emptier than when you started, like too much popcorn at the Majestic? How could I say these things when I hadn't yet discovered them myself? Instead, I said something that shames me to this day. "Mother," I said, "I will never love Father as much as I love you. I will never love anyone, not Stanley H. Fiske or Adam or even Jillily as much as I love you." Mother looked shocked. Love was something we did not talk about in our family.

But she could not have been more shocked than I was. Because I was lying. Love is not about less and more. It is just what it is, and it varies in shape and scope and texture from one moment to the next and from person you love to person you love. I might have loved Grandfather best—meaning my love for him came from the purest part of me—but I couldn't say I loved him most.

It occurred to me then that this was not the time to be a soldier, or even a sneaky spy. "Mother, I have to take that back. You are one of the people I move in and out of the void with. My life would not be my life, I would not be me, without you."

Of course, once I mentioned the void, I had to explain myself. And not just to Mother. Nana was staring at me as if I hadn't even been as coherent as *ugga umph ugga*. I told them about the dizziness of standing on the precipice, about the everyday household terrors of being sucked down the toilet, through the bathtub drain, out the window, into the vacuum cleaner, toward the everlasting pit of eternal emptiness. Nana was silent but I could tell her mind was gnawing away at the concept. I knew she knew emptiness. Nobody needed to cuddle as many saved babies as she did without something pretty black hole-ish going on.

Mother was quiet. She knew quite a lot about the gaping pit, too. What were the booze, the cigarettes, the coffee, the Bill W.'s, if not void fillers of various varieties? The only one whom I doubted would begin to comprehend what I was talking about was Jillily, who'd followed me to Mother's room. She rolled onto her back, paws curled, inviting us to scratch her white apron of a belly. Mother and Nana and I reached for her at the same time. And as pleasurable as it was for Jillily, I was pretty sure it helped the three of us even more.

Little did I know that I would store that moment away in my Lord-God-who-hates-a-void mind. It would provide a pivotal clue when Amir, Katrina, Gunther, Tom, Adam, Stanley and I tackled the problem of re-materialization.

You see, imagining the feel of someone you love is one very big key to re-emerging from the void.

I'm pretty sure Michelangelo had a glimmer of that himself when he painted the image of God on the Sistine Chapel ceiling, reaching with His fingertip to animate the very first Adam, the one for whom my dear friend (and initiator of my third incarnation) was aptly named.

Chapter 14

SPEAKING OF GOD, flying in a plane feels a little like being one. Not Father's variety, perhaps—not Baby Jesus, nestled itchily against the straw in His manger, no crib for His bed. More like the Navajo Father Sky or the Hindu Indra or the Greek Zephyrus or the Aztec Ehacatl or the Lithuanian Dievas or the Polynesian Awha or the Aboriginal Ungud, all of whom are wind or storm or sky gods. Though I think Nana and Cook and Fayga and even Sister Flatulencia would agree that Ungud trumps them all, as the god of both rainbows and erections.

And speaking of erections, from the moment of our airplane's lift-off, I felt a surprising sense of power. Not just because the people and cars and buildings below became increasingly miniaturized, while I stayed the same size, but because I was being propelled directly into the unboundaried void and was living to tell the tale, rather foolishly describing every detail I saw out the moisture-streaked window to Jillily in her cat carrier, who no doubt was far more preoccupied by the dreams that were making her tail twitch than anything I had to say. Oh yes, I should have mentioned, Stanley H. Fiske had been kind enough to book the three of us onto an airline that allowed small pets in the cabin.

The trip to Pasadena took long enough for me to think about these things:

1. About my dead baby bird and whether his spirit was still in his shared grave with Anne Boleyn or if he'd

managed to find his way to the open sky, and if so, would he keep watch over me and Jillily and Stanley H. Fiske as we flew to Pasadena, but would Anne Boleyn feel lonely and resentful if he did?;

2. About Father and his far more interesting new mind;

3. About Mother, who had whispered in my ear at the airport that I needn't feel guilty for admitting that I loved her the most and that she wouldn't tell anyone;

4. About Nana and how she would fare fostering the little boy whom Mother had agreed to put up in the guest bedroom, and wondering whether that child would be a less thankless charge than I'd been;

5. About Cook and worrying a little that her doctor had insisted she go on a diet; I did so like her fleshy roundness;

6. About Sister Flatulencia and Fayga and whether they would keep Father's second incarnation of a mind sufficiently filled to hold his void at bay, perhaps by playing horsey with him, which, given Sister Flatulencia's talent for limbo, was something I was pretty convinced she'd do well at, if she tried;

7. About Dhani and Ignacio and Baby Angelina, who wasn't such a baby anymore and who had actually said, "Flewy," when they all waved me off at the airport;

8. About Jillily, ensconced under the empty seat to my right, who was tranquilized enough not to moan the whole trip the way she did on the way to the vet, but kept her back to me in her carrier so I would know that, woozy or not, she didn't appreciate being locked up;

9. About Stanley H. Fiske, who was quiet most of the trip, undoubtedly cooking up some more Nobel Prize-worthy ideas, and about Adam and how he was settling into his new digs, and about Gwennie and Moggy and all the features of Southern California that Stanley had described, like soft sandy beaches and a multitude of

amusement parks and no snow, only sun, and whether anyone would be like me or even like me at Reed.

I probably don't need to tell you that what I mostly thought about was Grandfather. Even though his spirit was stowed safely inside my heart, it bothered me to be traveling so far away from where his body was buried. I had memorized most parts of that body, from his thickly veined hands to the wrinkles on his face to his once bulbous balls, but having a grandfather in your heart and memory is never the same as having him sitting opposite you, stroking your hair and *ugga umph ugga*-ing. I found myself carrying on a silent conversation with him.

"Grandfather," I said, "I am flying. I'll bet you never imagined me flying higher than our favorite birds. Or maybe you did. Maybe that's why your eyes melted when they looked into mine, imagining me melting from one incarnation into another—from banger and pincher to bird call imitator, Jillily petter, diary keeper, weed waterer, Holi celebrator, baby bird killer, resurrection failer, tweeter exploder, *Remembrance of Things Past* studier, cat puke cleaner, paternal mind finder, Uncle Bob skipper, Stanley H. Fiske admirer, void fearer, void filler, void contemplator, continental traveler."

Grandfather didn't say anything himself. He just calmed my heartbeat with his moist eyes every time I remembered I was soaring through open space. I can't imagine how I would have managed my first plane ride without the knowledge that Grandfather was exerting every ounce of his invisible energy to keep us all in the air.

Stanley, meanwhile, had pilfered every extra peanut from what he called *the genus stewardi,* having charmed both of the women assigned to our cabin with disappearances and reappearances of coins, earrings, and even a can of Diet Pepsi. I would later learn that Stanley was what he liked to call "a nut for nuts," able to crack even the thickest of walnuts with one sharp snap of his wrist and to extract sunflower seeds from their shells with a deft little maneuver of his tongue.

But mostly what I did was stare out the windows, filling my stratospheric void with reflections on the big-bellied clouds above, tidy crop formations and toy cars below, and the cold of the window against my cheek as skeleton fingers of rain streaked by. I felt an unaccountable sadness. It occurred to me that, since God is so isolated

161

in His void that even when we fly up toward the ether we cannot touch Him back, rain is His tears reaching out to us. Like me with Grandfather—holding his spirit securely in my heart, but my skin lonely for his touch. I felt quite close to God right then.

But once we landed at the complex that Stanley H. Fiske insisted on calling LAX, thoughts of God went away. (As for *LAX*, why anyone would want to apply a word meaning *remiss* or *negligent* to a place where human cargo is shot into the air was way beyond me.)

At JFK, I'd been too preoccupied saying gallons of goodbyes to the family and friends of my first and second incarnations to notice the strangers surrounding us before we boarded our flight. It only occurred to me once we'd deplaned at the other end, me lugging Jillily's carrier in one hand and pulling my bright pink suitcase with the other, that airports are human versions of anthills. People were rushing everywhere, expressions of dour determination on their faces. Being humans rather than ants, they didn't all look alike. It wasn't just the variation of short, tall, fat, skinny, dark-haired, fair-haired, red-haired, no-haired, glasses, no glasses, hats, no hats, fancy clothes, wrinkled clothes, janitorial uniforms and pilots' suits, bad smells, good smells, blue eyes, brown eyes, green eyes and gray ones. The variety of suitcases, boxes, handbags, shopping bags, and odd-shaped containers they carried would fill a diary or two.

I felt confident that none of the suitcases was as perfect as mine. It was a lightweight rollered affair of neon-bright nylon, bought by a Father with a newly discovered concern that the nearly-bastard-child of his not get what he called "lost in the shuffle," as if I were an errant face card. The fact that Fayga had shined up the handle and that Cook had stuffed it with angel food cake and that Dhani had inserted a photo of Angelina and that Sister Flatulencia had blessed it with her favorite rosary and a couple of pungent farts and that Mother had purchased appliqué letters for Nana to stitch on it – B L A N C H E F L E U R R O B I N S – made me feel something I'd never felt before. When I tried to describe it to Stanley H. Fiske with a stumbling, "I don't know, kind of taller and safer and roomier but not particularly voidish," he summed it up simply as *pride*.

You can imagine how comforting it was when I saw Adam's face emerge from the sea of strangers as Stanley H. Fiske and I stood by a giant insect of a conveyer belt waiting for Stanley's boxes to tumble down. Well, at first it was just Adam, but then I saw Amir Gupta and

Katrina Kelly and Gunther Anderten and Tom Haggis. Adam had planned well. It was going to take all ten of their hands and more than one trip to haul Stanley H. Fiske's sixteen boxes out of the airport and into Tom's new Toyota van, but at that moment it wasn't their hands I was focused on, but their familiar grins.

I knelt to inform Jillily that the gang was all here, but she was too preoccupied realizing her tranquilizer had worn off to pay me much attention. Adam had the presence of mind to whisk her out to the van after the briefest of kisses on my forehead, freeing her from her cage just in time for her to vomit her guts out on the *L.A. Times Calendar* section. Needless to say, it took no end of coaxing to get her back in that carrier again. In the end, we had to stuff her in rather forcefully, butt first like a giant sausage, with Adam sporting a couple of ugly scratches to speak for his success. It simply wouldn't do to drive out to Pasadena with a terrified Jillily careening around.

It wasn't till we were all belted in and on our way, me in the front next to Tom, with Jillily on my right yowling and moaning, that I realized that Tom and Adam and Katrina and Gunther and Amir were all wearing T-shirts and shorts and sandals. It *was* rather warm, and when I struggled to pull off my sweater, Stanley H. Fiske lightly bopped me on the head with a rolled up *New Yorker* and said, "See? What did I tell you? So Cal's always warm."

So Cal wasn't the only thing that was warm. When we pulled up in front of Stanley H. Fiske's home on a street you might be pleased to learn was called Rose Villa, Gwennie Fiske was waving from the front lawn, rotund and smiley and sun burnt in a sleeveless white blouse and faded blue peasant skirt that was partially covered by an apron that read, "Physicists are Spacier," with the "a" purposely crossed out and replaced by an "i."

Stanley H. Fiske leapt out of the van, more froggish than ever, lifting his considerably shorter sister off her feet and swinging her round in a full circle, her plump legs kicking like exuberant scissors as Stanley shouted loud enough for several neighbors to step out their front doors. "Gwennie, you're a sight for sore eyes. Come meet our young Fleur." Only later did I learn that Gwen Fiske was somewhat hard of hearing, particularly on her left side.

Adam had to remove Jillily's carrier before I could get out of the van. He settled it on the sidewalk, and I emerged cautiously, forcing an outstretched hand toward Stanley H. Fiske's sister like a shy soldier. But Gwennie ignored my hand and pressed me to her body in a generous hug. As our two sets of bulbous breasts bounced against each other, I was pleased to discover she was pungent with scent—a rich mélange of cinnamon, garlic, and what I was later to discover was Jean Naté After Bath Splash. On the whole, not a bad combination.

Then she held me at arm's length, saying, "I hope I haven't overwhelmed you?" Before I could answer she pulled me to her yet again, this time smoothing my hair with a finesse that reminded me of Grandfather. In spite of myself, tears sprang to my eyes. As if sensing my distress, Gwennie let me go, making a kind of clucking noise and bending to Jillily's cage, exclaiming, "Who's a pretty puss, who's a pretty kitty?" while Jillily repaid her kindness by turning her back to her.

While Stanley and Adam and Amir and Tom and Katrina and Gunther lugged the cases in, Gwennie led me into the house, where we situated Jillily in the room that was to be my bedroom. It was nothing like the cream-carpeted affair back at the penthouse of my second incarnation, which had a queen-sized four-poster bed, pair of Picasso lithographs and arm chairs slip-covered in Liberty fabric Mother had ordered all the way from England. This room was much smaller, furnished simply with a white dresser and desk and a set of twin beds made up with matching quilts that Gwennie proudly told me had been sewn by her own dear departed mother, who, of course, had been Stanley H. Fiske's mother, too. While Gwennie explained that she thought I'd like to decorate the room myself, a part of me was distracted, wondering if the dead Mrs. Fiske was as froggish as her son, or more of a Butterball Turkey, like Gwennie. I interrupted Gwennie's inquiry about whether I leaned stylistically toward frill or iconoclasm with a question about where her mother was buried.

The way that Gwennie tilted her head to one side, narrowing her eyes as she studied me, made me worry that I'd reverted back to my *ugga umph uggas*, but then she laughed a big enough laugh to reveal a mouthful of silver-filled teeth and said, "Stanley told me to expect a unique sensibility. She's at Forest Lawn, m'dear, the Disneyland of Death, but what can you do? For a woman of her generation, being tossed out to sea the way I plan to exit this world just wasn't on. We can go there some time, if you like. It's actually quite a hoot, if you've got a taste for irony."

Well, you can imagine how confused I felt, wondering what the process of decomposition had in common with irony, but fortunately I was distracted from the whirliness of that particular pit by Gwennie's suggestion that, as she put it, "we let the literal cat out of the bag." It didn't seem such a bad idea. Jillily was pressing herself against the back of her cat carrier as if she were trying to merge with it, which was hardly going to help her acclimatize to her new digs.

While I struggled with the latch on the cat carrier, Gwennie had the good sense to sit very still on one of the beds, waiting patiently as Jillily oozed out. It took a lengthy exploration of the four corners of the room, me on my belly alongside her, before Jillily finally deigned to sniff Gwennie's toes, making that P.U. face of hers, with her mouth hanging open and her row of sharp little upper teeth exposed. Gwennie commented, "She smells Moggy, no doubt. If she gets used to the smell on me first, it might help."

Gwennie had already put down some dried food and water and a litter box in the small adjoining bathroom, which had no painted floral sinks, but did have a rubber duck mother with a line of imprinted ducklings lined up behind her along the side of the tub. The first thing Jillily did was pee in the litter box, crouching as shamefully as ever, then she ate, then she drank, then she pooped and had a pee again. Before she could cover her little brown poop bullets, the room filled with an effluvium resembling Sister Flatulencia's more sulfuric farts, and I felt my first serious pang of homesickness.

Gwennie emptied the poop into a paper sack, then insisted on showing me around. When we got to the kitchen, Gwen asked if I'd like to call home. I did, but of course I had to call several homes. Given what Mother had said at the airport I realized it was important to humor her delusion that I really did love her most by calling her first. The way she breathed made me suspect that she was smoking as we talked, and the sound of the patio door sliding open after she said she'd fetch Nana confirmed it. As for Nana, when she came on the line, she pretended she had a cold, but I knew she was teary. The fact was that I had to hold my non-phone-holding left hand in a fist to stop from crying myself.

It was a particularly odd kind of void that wanted to open inside me, knowing I was here with Gwen Fiske in a foreign kitchen, while an invisible Mother and Nana and home of my second incarnation kept right on existing thousands of miles away. Father wasn't home when I called, and I hoped he and Sister Flatulencia were riding their horsies round the neighborhood, but when I called Dhani and Ignacio's, Ignacio answered the phone right away. Before ringing off, I remembered to tell him the name of my new street. I guess Gwen heard me talking to him about roses, since the first thing she did after I hung up the phone was lead me out a pair of French doors to a narrow but long yard carpeted with mossy-looking grass and bordered by a hectic array of flowers.

I thought the garden was just perfect, especially once I discovered that Gwennie grew David Austins! These were the ones I recognized:

1. Abraham Darby;

2. Ambridge Rose;

3. Jude the Obscure;

4. The Dark Lady.

I was careful to take my time with each one. By now, you should be quite aware how easy it is for an Austin to take offense.

It was just as I was stroking Dark Lady's peony-like petals that a calico cat with a space ship for a head bumped up against me, giving voice to what had to be the world's most plaintive meow. I have to confess that I jumped back a bit at the sight of that head, nearly violating Dark Lady's personal space enough to be impaled on her thorns. Gwennie just laughed and came and scooped up her cat, craning her neck to the side to avoid being blinded by its bizarre headgear. "It's a protective cone. Haven't you seen them? No fleas where you come from? Poor Moggy's allergic. Look at this behind of hers." Gwen turned so I could have a front row view. "She's bitten herself so much she looks like a plucked chicken." Her butt *did* look something awful, fur-less and covered with zig-zaggy scabs in various stages of hardening. But her blue eyes were appealingly moist and actually looked right into mine as if she were wondering what I was thinking, so I hastily shifted my thoughts away from disgust toward appreciation for the silky coat that she wore everywhere but on her butt. I was gratified by the depth of the purr she let loose from her orange-triangled throat.

Of course, Jillily had no one to explain to her about the cone. When we brought Moggy into my bedroom later that evening to try to introduce the two of them, Jillily hissed and spat and retreated under the bed and refused to come out until Gwen swept Moggy out of the room and shut the door. We had better luck the next morning, when the two of them chanced to meet in the breakfast nook, Jillily finally having ventured forth to discover her new digs. Moggy had the good grace to hold still as Jillily judiciously sniffed and then licked her mangled butt.

As it happens, that was nearly the last time Moggy sat still when Jillily was around. Once she got de-coned, the two of them tended to spend most of their time chasing each other out of rooms, with Moggy holding her ground in Stanley's bedroom, Gwennie's bedroom, the living room and den and Jillily carving a slice of third incarnation home for herself out of the kitchen, the dining room, and my bedroom. They couldn't seem to come to terms over the backyard. If you listened to Stanley H. Fiske, they were a couple of feline Hitlers vying to occupy the Sudatenland. But I like Gwennie's analogy better. She said it was like having two only children. One thing that could be said of both Stanley and his sister: unlike Nana, neither one of them made a fetish of differentiating animals from people—which I suppose was one of the reasons I found myself feeling at home in So Cal in so short a time, the others being Adam (of course) and Amir and Katrina and Tom and Gunther.

As for animals, until my third incarnation, I'd only had the chance to acquaint myself with the feline and canine variety, and no doubt you can guess the species for which I felt fondest. As with so much else, it was Amir who broadened my horizons, in this case nothing to do with looped strings, but with a chimpanzee he'd rescued from a lab and was schooling to release into the wild.

Amir was becoming my second closest friend after Adam. Our earlier discussions regarding visibility and invisibility, matter and its voidish partner anti-matter, had been percolating inside me for ages, leading me to speculate about the dark night of a caterpillar's soul as it endures the dissolution of its cocoon. I felt fairly certain a caterpillar must believe it is dying, knowing nothing of its own wings until they spread of their own accord, lifting the onetime crawler away from the earth into flight.

How far can we trace back the genesis of a new idea? At the age of four, parsing out words from Sister Flatulencia's Bible, I'd read in *The Book of Genesis* that the world was "without form, and void," with darkness upon the face of the deep until the Spirit of God moved upon the face of the waters. Was it God moving across my waters now that led me to plumb the source of my greatest terror for some nugget that might be useful to science? God-prompted or not, the possibility of dematerialization arose inside me, brushing its wings against everything I thought was real.

It took me awhile to get up the courage to share my thoughts with Amir. The Fiske's were on a Costco run, and Amir and I were munching bagels and cream cheese in Stanley H. Fiske's pale yellow kitchen, a soft wind billowing Gwen's rather crookedly sewn nylon curtains so that they pleasantly stroked my shoulders. Amir didn't say much as I spoke, just tipped his chair back on its hind legs, scratching his arm languidly as he listened. His brown arms were a similar hue to Dhani's, and I felt a sudden urge for a Holi as he scratched away.

When I finally finished, Amir said, "Wow. Very cool. You know, it's the weirdest thing. I had a dream last night that I was swallowed up by a black hole and then spat out again with thermodynamic pro-pulsiveness. And guess what, you were right next to me, holding an enlarged looped string in your hand." He laughed, "Dude, my *dadi-ma*—sorry, my grandmother—would probably say it was a prophetic dream." His chair started to tip over, and he pulled himself back just in time. "I can see it now." His hands described a wide arc in front of him. "You're going to become the world's leading expert on demate-rialization." Seeing me shrink back, he said, "No, really. I'm pretty sure nobody's thought of this one before. No serious scientist, any-way."

I flushed at the appellation. The World's Leading Expert was such a huge leap from Sweetie Pie, Angel Face, Muchacha, That Creepy Child, You Poor Child, The Unluckiest Child, Sneaky Little Monster, and even Flurry and Fleurie. I felt embarrassed he would imagine me being the final expert on anything, especially anything to do with nothingness, given the previous claim to that territory by Sartre. But then again, Sartre probably lacked the advantage of an early household like mine, with so much time to kill. As I thought about it, it occurred to me that killing was probably a pretty apt metaphor for dematerialization. Killing time, anyway: finding a way to disappear into the darkest reaches of the void, only to come back out again, perhaps arriving in another country and perhaps, in a late-for-work-ish pinch, just a couple of blocks away.

I think he took pity on me for my obvious discomfort. He stood and moved toward the back door, "Want to come to my place? You can help me feed Lord Hanuman. He's probably starving."

Lord Hanuman was the chimp he'd rescued the previous spring, naming him after the Hindu monkey god. Amir seemed to alternate between respect for his Hindu background and what Tom liked to call "taking the piss." He practiced yoga regularly and cooked a chicken *tikka* second only to Dhani's, then he'd do something piss-takey like paint his forehead with a peace symbol *bindi* and perform Bollywood-style song-and-dance routines with Katrina.

Lord Hanuman was sufficiently comprised of equal parts charm and mischief to do justice to his Godly namesake. When I met him the first time, Katrina warned me to take it nice and slowly. She said Hanuman tended to run to jealousy of any of Amir's friends. So I sat back on Amir's second-hand black leather sofa and waited for the Lord's approach. In that way, I earned myself a kind of grudging acceptance.

By then, I knew plenty about jealousy myself. I was having to give Jillily extra chin scratchings and belly nuzzlings each night to re-assure her that Moggy didn't hold a candle to her. That wasn't too hard, because the mere fact of our having traveled through several incarnations together ensured that no other cat would install itself so completely in my heart. Unfortunately, though, while I stroked and Jillily motored, my mind often manifested its own brand of disloyalty that had nothing to do with cats, but everything to do with cattiness.

I suppose I could blame it all on the moon, since the moon controls not only the tides of oceans like the Pacific—in which Stanley and Gwennie and Adam and Amir and Tom and Katrina and Gun-ther and I swam with some frequency till we were goose-pimpled in-to quitting by So Cal's dismal version of winter—but also the cycles of a young girl's hormones. In my own case, that meant that the moon was responsible for red jelly blood spurting like clockwork from my tweeter, for stomach cramps that kept me writhing on my bed for hours at a time, for painful puss-filled eruptions, most typi-cally on the horizontal crease of my chin and at the outer perimeters of my nostrils, and for my sudden discovery that my old friend Adam had suddenly became a *male of the species,* someone whose face my wayward mind would summon whenever I was working toward one of those heavenly tweeter explosions that seemed to have become de rigueur as a prelude to sleep. You can imagine what confusion that cost me, let alone what hell I had to pay once Adam's new friend Stephanie began joining us at the beach, sporting nothing but a golden tan and a thong bathing suit and legs proportionally longer than a Barbie doll's.

Up until then, one of my favorite things about the beach was how democratic it was. Scads of people of all sizes, shapes, and colors shared the soft So Cal sand and screamed gleefully at incoming waves like one big, rambunctious family. Oh, sure, each little group marked off its own few feet of turf with beach towels and flip-flops and piles of magazines ineffectually held down against the pushy ocean breeze with Coke cans and straw carryalls and plastic bottles of Blue Lizard and Coppertone. But something about our generous hostess of an ocean seemed to bring out the friendliness in everyone: the four generations of Salvadorans sprawled across a couple of colorful Indian blankets who'd plied Tom and Amir and Adam and me with big, sloppy slices of watermelon; the white-haired toddler carefully placing her plastic shovel and bucket alongside my rugby stripe beach towel; the two ancient-looking Jewish men inviting Stanley to join them under their similarly ancient-looking umbrella after he'd expressed interest in their chess game.

The wind and waves swallowed our individual sounds and belched them right out again in merged bursts of song. Something in me relaxed so much in that moist, warm air that, as I bounced on my toes before diving into walls of foamy water, I'd pretend I'd actually come to the beach with the kids who lined up with equal excitement on either side of me. And sometimes one of them would crash into me as we twisted and tumbled under a particularly powerful wave, and we'd both come up gasping for air and rearranging our swimsuit tops and blowing our noses into our cupped hands before grinning at each other triumphantly that we'd survived a big one. It was moments like that when I forgot the void even existed.

But Stephanie Seidenfeld's undemocratically perfect body would change all that. If moving to So Cal was the beginning of my third incarnation, then she was to become the first of a series of a trials that would punctuate my pleasure as predictably as what Katrina Kelly liked to call Mr. Heavyflow.

As for Katrina, I'd learned by then that she wasn't exactly what you'd call sentimental. Especially about Lord Hanuman. Once I'd hesitantly described my ideas about dematerialization to Stanley H. Fiske and the rest of his crew and they'd all been working with me awhile to see how we could operationalize it, she told Amir flatly, "If you think you're going to have time for class work, taking care of that animal, *and* be part of the team working on Fleur's Theory of Dematerialization, you're nuts. You'll have to give him away. I'll bet the Goodall Institute would take him."

I was still astonished that my new friends were taking my idea seriously enough to want to work on it with me, but I knew what a sacrifice it would be for Amir to send Lord Hanuman away. He told me he'd fallen in love with the animal from the moment he'd seen him in a friend's lab in the Biology Department the previous spring.

As it happened, no one knew what to do with the chimp, whose blood, by a stroke of good fortune, lacked an enzyme the students were studying. Initially, Amir had the intention of adopting Lord Hanuman as a pet, but that particular fantasy was put paid when he returned from his summer fellowship at NYU, only to hear how poorly Lord Hanuman had reacted to being babysat by a series of attractive coeds who happened to be friends of Tom. I may not have mentioned that Tom had that beguiling Black Irish combination of fair skin, black hair, and green eyes that exploded women's tweeters with predictable regularity.

Anyway, Amir had returned to an apartment that bore baleful witness to Lord Hanuman's sense of betrayal. Upholstery had been shredded, books drowned in the toilet, and the ceiling of Amir's bedroom was covered with hardened chimpanzee boogers. Well, it took awhile to actually figure out what the latter actually were. It looked to Amir like some drunken art student had been practicing an amateurishly lumpy faux design, until Carina Despaccia, Tom's favorite female, described walking into the room just as Lord Hanuman was flicking a green and goopy booger upward with an evil glint in his eye.

During the early days of my third incarnation, when Stanley H. Fiske was still deluding himself that I was going to fit in at Reed, I spent many a Saturday with Amir at a series of rustic parks, debating how to prove the possibility of dematerialization while Lord Hanuman clung to Amir's hand, vocalizing as loudly as he could in an obvious attempt to reclaim Amir's attention. It wasn't so much that Lord Hanuman minded me personally—he liked to groom my hair, eating my dandruff like a delicacy, whenever Amir left the two of us for a Krispy Kreme run. But the chimp clearly saw himself as Amir's only child.

Amir had been slowly assimilating the reality that his method of introducing Lord Hanuman to freedom was simply not working, but the turning point came when we all least expected it, on a day when Stanley H. Fiske and Adam and Tom and Katrina and Gunther and I were waiting for Amir to join us at Stanley's classroom in the Caltech building called Lauritsen, named after the Danish-born physicist Charles Lauritsen, whose development of high voltage X-ray tubes was applied to the treatment of cancer patients and the advance of nuclear physics. Dr. Lauritsen was a contributor to the development of the atom bomb, which is pretty devilish when you think of it. I'm sad to say it was cancer that got him in the end.

Anyway, Katrina and I thought we actually might have discovered in a recent experiment a stunning anomaly in the theory of quantum electrodynamics, or the quantifiable interaction between light and matter, which had been a bedrock of our field for over seventy years. If we were right, the consequences could be huge, not only in shaking up a basic assumption of quantum physics, but also by providing a crucial clue in our pursuit of dematerialization.

But something was still missing from our attempts to quantify our discovery. Katrina was our expert on this turf, being a particular fan of the now deceased Richard Feynman, a major Nobel-winning contributor to quantum electrodynamics who'd once roused the Caltech campus with his loopy playfulness. Since Feynman was so famous for loving to shake things up, I imagined we had a guardian angel somewhere in the ether, rooting for us to prove him wrong.

Katrina was at the blackboard at the front of the room, mapping where our peregrinations had taken us, but when she turned around, she dropped her piece of chalk and let out a yelp of dismay. Stanley H. Fiske and Adam and Tom and Gunther and I turned in near-unison to see Amir entering the classroom with a guilty look in his eye and a chimpanzee on his arm.

Katrina's tone was acerbic. "How in the world do you think we're going to get anywhere with that *creature* around?"

As if to confirm her prediction, Lord Hanuman behaved as though an agent of Satan himself. As soon as Amir made the mistake of letting go of his hand, the chimp climbed onto one of the desks and leapt toward the lamp suspended above it, swinging from it with one long hairy arm, and with the other fetching poop-balls from his butt, flinging them at us like some mid-air bowler.

As if demonstrating the fight or flight reflex, more or less half of us—Adam, Katrina, and I—instinctively ducked under desks, while the larger half—Amir, Stanley, Tom, Gunther—went after Lord Hanuman, only to be felled by foul matter splattering their faces. From my perch beneath one of the desks, I watched Adam under the next one, frantically struggling to swab the poop from his eye with a corner of his shirt. Katrina shrieked as a rather stringy poop-missile hit the blackboard. Gunther let out a hysterical giggle, then shut his mouth tightly as Lord Hanuman looked to be aiming straight for it.

It was only when Security came to our rescue, alerted by Katrina's cries, that the possibility of order reasserted itself. Amir ran with them to fetch a cage from Kerckhoff Labs, then managed to coax a rather spent-looking Lord Hanuman into it. In spite of his mischief, it broke my heart to see Lord Hanuman locked up. After my own experience in a jail cell, I couldn't help but feel that was no place for any living creature, let alone a namesake of the Monkey God.

I don't refer to Lord Hanuman's godliness lightly. It was after he'd been tranquilized and while Katrina and Tom and Gunther and Adam and Amir and Stanley went to the Women's and Men's Restrooms to clean up that I finally emerged from under the desk, unscathed thanks to my soldierly survival skills. (You don't grow up in a household of projectile-vomiting babies without mastering the fine art of ducking.) I glanced over at the blackboard, then looked back again. The hairs rose on my arms.

Lord Hanuman's poop had appended a couple of stinky sevens and a well-placed wobbly zero to Katrina's white-chalked computations. Staring in disbelief, I realized a crucial piece of our puzzle had slotted into place! Like the Son of the Air and Servant of Rama Himself, Lord Hanuman had accomplished a miracle, potentially extending Feynman's findings on light and matter into new territory.

By extinguishing the clumps of light we call photons in a suitably graduated fashion, we might actually catalyze the dematerialization of the electrons interacting with them. For a moment, I seriously considered becoming a Hindu, until it occurred to me that it would give Father apoplexy, Sister Flatulencia another nervous breakdown, and might well make Anne Boleyn roll over in her grave. There are some things we have to sacrifice for the sake of relationship, and Hinduism was going to have to be one of them. Nonetheless, I decided on the spot to make a one-time contribution to the Indian Matrimonial Society. I figured it was the least I could do.

Chapter 15 🦋

WHILE LORD HANUMAN moved us one step closer to a Principle of Dematerialization, I'm afraid he wasn't qualified to share in our eventual recognition. But, perhaps even better from his point of view, the Goodall Institute succeeded in placing him at the Gombe National Park in Tanzania. Thanks to his orneriness, he was one of those fortunate once-captive chimps who manage the transition back to the wild, establishing a secure place for himself in a group of fifteen of his peers.

I'm afraid the same could not be said of me. So Cal's famous weather suited me just fine, but I found myself pining for the blare of New York cab horns, the wacky performance artists and street musicians of Washington Square, Central Park's aromatic blend of freshly-mown grass and horse poop. While I grew fonder and fonder of Stanley and Gwennie Fiske, I missed Nana's rough hugs, Dhani's delicious desserts, and the familiar scent of Chanel No. 5 permeating my room after Mother kissed each of my cheeks before leaving for one of her Bill W. meetings.

Plus, I was feeling pretty anxious about my upcoming first day of school. I'd had four weeks to prepare, which I did by reading Kip Thorne's *Black Holes and Time Warps*, working on dematerialization, accompanying my physics friends to the beach, learning the fine art of boogie boarding, mooning in misery over Adam, hating my pasty skin, hating my pimples, and hating Stephanie Siedenfeld. Oh, and decorating my bedroom with what Amir concluded was the most catholic collection of posters he'd ever seen. (And if you think that meant I'd plastered my walls with pictures that would satisfy the sensibilities of Sister Flatulencia's church, you're making the same mistake I did before consulting my dictionary.) What a difference a little capitalization makes. You might not be aware that *catholic* without a big "c" refers to breadth or liberality in scope or taste, whereas Catholic with the big "C" pretty much narrows the field to the preferences of one man, sometimes called the Pope and sometimes called—at least by Gwennie Fiske—That Misogynistic Sonofabitch.)

As for my own brand of catholicism, here's what you would have noticed upon entering my room:

1. A movie poster unearthed by Adam at a Hollywood Boulevard memorabilia store featuring the *I Dream of Jeannie* Jeannie starring in *The Harper Valley PTA*;

2. A fine pen-and-ink drawing of ten different Austins from England's Chelsea Garden Show;

3. A rare Ansel Adams photo of a fierce-looking coyote;

4. An old political poster of Father, emblazoned with the motto *Life—the ONLY choice!*, which, due to circumstances you will come to understand, had to be disposed of at the end of eighth grade, leaving a ghostly imprint of its shape on the wall;

5. An enlargement of a photograph of the 1927 Arsenal football team, sent rolled up in a cardboard tube by Dhani;

6. A shadowbox containing Stanley H. Fiske's collection of rare banknotes depicting famous physicists, including a melancholy Albert Einstein on a 5 Israeli Lirot and a 500 Danish Kroner featuring a pipe-smoking Niels Bohr.

I had managed to finish festooning my walls by the middle of September, which is just as well, since, once I began what felt like the most interminable episode of my life, my mind was otherwise occupied.

As you might imagine, my first day of school—given it was my first day of *any* school—was something of a shock. Gwennie and I had discussed it beforehand and agreed that she would leave me off at the curb. Anything else would have felt too babyish. But I hadn't reckoned on how crowded it would be, nor how trembly my legs would feel, making me worry that they might give way entirely. I had never ventured into the wider world quite so alone—the closest having been sneaking out for my assignation with the boy who called me Beautiful, and you know how that turned out.

Now here I was, swallowed amidst two thousand teenagers, who were making more noise than a clamor of crows on the tree of my first incarnation. I stifled the impulse to scream by focusing on placing one foot in front of the other and reminding myself to breathe.

The Independent Honors Program operated under the umbrella of an ordinary middle school, Walter Reed of North Hollywood, with its typical So Cal complement of students from every part of the globe. In Reed's case, a third of the kids were born outside the United States, mostly from El Salvador and Mexico, with more than twenty-six different languages spoken in their homes. I learned this, and not much more, during our first period assembly.

Getting to the assembly was a feat in itself. I bumbled my way through a maze of buildings to the auditorium, which I suppose I should have recognized sooner simply because of its size. Spying the familiar figure of IHP's math and science teacher waiting for me just outside the building, I nearly collapsed in relief. Mr. Harold Mayes-Hillman was an old friend of Stanley's and visited the Fiske home fairly frequently. He knew about the project that Adam and Amir and Katrina and Tom and Gunther and I were working on and would occasionally share a mangled Protein Bar from his jacket pocket while I used him as a sounding board for my latest thoughts on looped strings.

Right now he stood with glazed eyes, his back pressed hard against the wall. Clumps of students pushed past him, laughing and yattering in at least half of those twenty-six languages. I went up to him, and was greeted with a shy smile. He walked me inside. On a similar wavelength, we automatically aimed for the very last row.

Along with Ms. Peach and Mr. Phelps, Hilly would teach my core subjects for the coming year, although, along with the other IHPs, I'd still be required to join the broader population of students for language instruction and P.E. and music and drama.

Hilly was the archetypal absent-minded professor, which meant that his students treated him like prey. I was introduced to this sad

177

state of affairs during my first day of eighth grade algebra. It all happened when Hilly was busy scribbling a very basic, but nonetheless satisfying equation on the blackboard. I suppose I should have realized something was coming when I saw several of the students staring, not at the board, but at the oversized wall clock right above it. I heard a rustling right before it happened, and then, precisely at 1:45 p.m., all but two of the class dropped their algebra books onto their desks. I can't tell you what a jarring sound it made. I saw Hilly jump the second I did and was stunned that he didn't even bother to turn around.

As it happens, this dropping of the books on the first day of school in Hilly's algebra class was something of a tradition for IHP students, begun as far back as the late 1980's. I learned about it later from Amy Cowe, who—thanks in part to her unfortunate name and in further part to her unfortunate girth—became one of few IHP students I saw outside of school hours. Amy and I became allies of sorts right before the start of drama class the following day, when Steven Shlekt and Lashana Lake teased us for having failed to drop our books. I was so indignant on Hilly's behalf that I garbled my words badly and even flapped a few times while trying to persuade them that trying to scare our teacher was just plain mean.

It was amazing I was able to say anything at all. I'd been struck dumb by Lashana the moment I first saw her, slipping daintily into the desk immediately to my right in Ms. Peach's class. I couldn't seem to stop myself from sneaking quick peaks at her. She was so exotic looking, with her brightly beaded cornrows and sparkling green eyes, set like gems against her velvety dark-chocolate skin. I learned soon enough she was the queen bee of the eighth grade IHP, and the following week, as I rushed to my locker on my way to English, I was stung to overhear her say to the hive of girls surrounding her, "Have you tried talking to Fleur Robins? I swear, she's the weirdest kid to hit IHP since that guy two years ago who ended up shooting his stepfather."

Who knew when Gwennie had enrolled me at Reed that I'd have to endure not just the cruelty of Lashana Lake and her clique but hours of confining classes, the humiliation of being arguably the worst P.E. student who ever lived, speculations from strange boys in the hallways about my bra size, and solitary lunch hours nibbling the veggie sandwiches Gwennie packed for me once I realized Amy's relish in visiting my new home was more for Gwennie's cooking than the pleasure of my company? I'm ashamed to confess that, in my hurt, I found myself calling Amy *Big Dumb Amy* in my mind and drew on a cloak of assumed disinterest each morning as soon as Gwennie dropped me off for school. The fact was I was a lot sadder over my lack of friends when surrounded by thousands of my peers than I'd ever been in the relative isolation of my first and second incarnations.

I suppose I can't really blame Amy. Not many eighth graders would have wanted to skip up and down Rose Villa with a visiting Uncle Bob or count the inconsistencies in *Remembrance of Things Past*. Nor can I fault myself for being bored by a girl who wanted nothing more than to gorge on carrot cake while comparing what she called the *ass-worthiness* of the boys in our drama class. I suppose our IHP compatriots were too close for comfort for her. Most of the kids in Drama were far less intellectually inclined, so Amy found them safely enough off-limits to fantasize about. Sam Friedman was her favorite, with what she called "a butt worth dying for," with Hector Hernandez in serious contention. Hector I could understand. He was a whole year older—a ninth grade version of Benicio Del Toro. But the Sam bit was a mystery to me. I found it more than a little melancholic that Amy pined after a boy whose name for *her* was Fat Cowe. As for me, I was still obsessing over Adam each night while giving myself mini-explosions, which made the immature antics of boys my own age pale in comparison.

In my phone conversations with Mother—who typically called from her cell phone on her way to one meeting or another—I listened with a heavy heart to infinite variations on the theme of how thrilling her early teen years had been. And when I spoke (far more frequently) with Nana, I heard story after story about the young cheerleader she once was—though, frankly, Nana as a pom-pom wielder hardly bore thinking about. I was too embarrassed to tell either of them how my own middle school career had gotten off to such a pathetic start.

Any extracurricular pleasure was mostly contingent on the availability of Katrina or Amir. I spent the majority of my late afternoons in the Fiskes' back yard, alone with the Austins and a host of self-disparaging thoughts. Gwen would occasionally come out to check on me, but when she did I tended to greet her concern with sulky ingratitude.

Needless to say, my mood was hardly helped by my miserable monthly cramps. Gwennie took me to a gynecologist, but when Dr. Raker tried to put her clamp inside my tweeter, I went *fla fla fla* until she insisted Gwen take me home. I had come to take for granted how Gwennie took my odd quirks in stride, so I felt shocked and then guilty to hear the exasperation in her voice from the other side of my bedroom door after I refused to come out for the rest of the day.

Adam showed up fairly regularly for dinner at the Fiskes', and after appropriate praise for Gwennie's nut roast or vegetarian lasagna, I would share my latest speculations about dematerialization, with Stanley offering a pertinent question or two, while Adam demonstrated his divided attention by carrying on a simultaneous discussion with Gwennie on how things were going with Stephanie. By then, he was thoroughly bedazzled by his new girlfriend, who knew nothing of physics, but a lot about being beautiful.

Well, to be fair, Stephanie wasn't just about her looks. She was a Caltech student, after all, and as Gwennie liked to say, "Anyone attending the California Institute of Technology isn't exactly chopped liver." That phrase, by the way, is evidently derived from the fact that, in Jewish homes, chopped liver is typically served as a side dish. Stephanie Seidenfeld happened to be Jewish herself, at least on her paternal side, which I knew made her something less than a Jew by Israeli law, but just as vulnerable to being killed under the Third Reich.

But returning to where we were heading—which was my shameful envy of a woman whom Hitler's SS would have loved to get their hands on—Adam seemed to sense my reserve about Stephanie and tried more than once to convince me I should see her as a kindred soul, citing the research she was doing on the human predilection for thinking of ourselves as finite entities over time. Knowing something of love's blindness, I didn't bother to challenge him on the validity of the concept of finitude, which flew in the face of everything I'd learned of the universe's appetite for change and the human propensity for multiple incarnations. Nor would I ever reveal to him how devastating it felt to be losing any chance of something more with the only guy who would ever understand me.

That didn't stop me, though, from accepting his occasional invitations to join the two of them for dinner at Il Fornaio. I was a sucker for that restaurant's Angel Hair Pasta Diavolo. The presence of angels and devils in one dish seemed a fitting accompaniment to my vicarious ecstasy of watching Adam finger the edge of one of Stephanie's ubiquitous sleeveless blouses before tracing the length of her tanned and silken arm.

It was at one of those dinners that Stephanie began stoking the fires of my future ruination. It was after I'd slurped fifty-seven pieces of pasta and drunk enough iced tea refills to quell the heat of the chili peppers that she turned to me and said, "So, do you have a boyfriend yet?"

It was the *yet* that got to me. Without a beat I nodded. "Yes. His name's Hector Hernandez." As soon as the words flew from my mouth, I wished I could just suck them back again. I'd told what Nana would have called a bald-faced lie. I could just imagine Sister Flatulencia clutching her rosary beads in horror.

"Hector Her*nan*dez?" The way Stephanie said his name, drawing out the *nan* like it was some kind of sexy signal, snaked inside me before I knew it. That night, as my fingers found their way inside the folds of my tweeter, it wasn't Adam I imagined rubbing his member like the Antisocial Boy in the Garden of Eden. Instead I saw Hector's straining zipper, his muscular arms, his dark eyes with invisible puppet strings pulling my stiffened nipples toward him. As I wound my pubic hair around my little finger, I imagined tracing the circular tuft of black fuzz that Hector cultivated below his pillowy bottom lip.

The thing was, until my bald-faced lie to Stephanie, I hadn't even realized I'd noticed that *pillowy bottom lip*.

After that, things only got worse. The next time the three of us went out to dinner, I magnified my original sin by making things up about Hector. The fact that Stephanie couldn't seem to stop peppering me with questions didn't help. No, I said, he wasn't in the Independent Honors Program, but in the School for Advanced Studies, just one step down the gifted ladder. No, we didn't spend much time together outside of school, but ate our lunches together at gatherings of Walter's Read Café Book Club. In one sinful conversation, I enrolled the redoubtable Hector in the Chess Club, the Scrabble Club, and the Magic Card Club. I was glad Stanley wasn't there to hear me. Even though the Magic Card Club was about a game and had nothing to do with magic, he'd be ferreting out Hector at the next Back to School Night, and where would I be then with my bald-faced lies?

It was at one of those lie-telling dinners, this time at a French restaurant that Adam and Stephanie nicknamed Chez Doudoule after their favorite waiter, that Stephanie ordered pate foie gras. Even though my own name is French, I was just beginning to learn the language, so when her appetizer came, I had no clue to the source of the gooey loaf the waiter set down before her. It was only after I'd polished off a large-ish slab of tiramisu and half of Stephanie's pumpkin crème brulee that Adam started teasing her about having ordered the foie gras.

"I can't believe you made such a big deal about how fattening the crème brulee is," he said. "You wolfed down that foie gras like there was no tomorrow."

To which Stephanie replied, rather archly I thought, "Well, at least the foie gras's sugar-free."

Adam laughed loud enough for the couple at the next table to stare. "Yeah, and what about the fat content? Some poor goose had to endure weeks of force feeding through a metal rod jammed down its throat for your pleasure."

At which point, convinced I must have misheard, I said, "What?"

At which point Stephanie blushed, Adam explained, and I puked all over the table.

During our ride home, I couldn't help but notice that, for once, Stephanie was silent.
She was undoubtedly disgusted by what I'd done. She wasn't the only one. I wished I were a turtle with a handy hidey-hole of a shell. Once Adam dropped Stephanie off at her digs on Fair Oaks Avenue, I counted the seconds until we got to Rose Villa. Once there, I dashed to the front door, vaguely aware of Adam's footfalls behind me.

I emerged from the shower full of shame. Gwennie was waiting for me outside the bathroom door with a cup of chamomile tea, sweetened with two tablespoons of honey, just the way I liked it. She said softly, "How are you doing, lass? Do you feel up to talking to Adam? He feels terrible."

I'd had enough time in the shower to admit to myself I probably would have puked even without hearing about the geese. Lately my lies about Hector Hernandez were burning holes in my tummy, and I'd developed a penchant for purloining Gwennie's sample packets of

Pepcid, provided to her in copious quantities by her internist, probably thanks to all the grief I'd been causing her.

After winding a towel around my wet hair and tying my plush robe more tightly around me, I dragged myself into the living room, where I sat far enough away from Adam to prevent him from getting a whiff of any lingering puke smell.

Adam was hunched over his knees on Stanley H. Fiske's leather ottoman. The goose-neck floor lamp cast a small circle of light on his shoulder, its shape a reminder of what had gotten me puking in the first place. I burped and immediately regretted it.

Adam smiled sheepishly. "You poor thing. How are you feeling?" I noticed his own neck had gone a rather purplish shade of red.

"Okay."

"No, I mean it. I should have kept my trap shut. Especially after all that food. I'm really sorry, Fleur. That was totally insensitive. Foot in mouth disease."

I didn't say anything, studying instead the map of Florida on his neck, which was looking increasingly phallic, which did nothing for my policy of trying to ignore my tweeter before bedtime.

In the lingering silence, Adam got up and approached Stanley's overflowing bookshelf. Flopping into an Aeron chair and retrieving a copy of the *Journal of Magnetism and Magnetic Material*, he seemed to lose himself in it until he swiveled back toward me and asked, "You still hanging out with Amy?" Gwennie must have mentioned something, since I certainly hadn't.

"No."

He shoved the magazine back into the bookcase and came and sat next to me on the sofa. "How're your studies?"

"Oh, you know." Still anxious about smelling pukey, I tried inching away from him in unnoticeable increments, until I was backed so far against the sofa arm it hurt.

"Amir says you've been discussing the possibility of rematerialization."

I felt too glum to get going on that one, though just that morning I'd been dancing around Amir's apartment in excitement over where we seemed to be heading.

"You need to make friends, Fleur. You can't hang out with older people all the time."

"I'm not," I snapped. After all, I spent most of my time with Jillily, and she was younger than any of us.

"Well then, I hope you're not spending all your time with Hector. Boyfriends come and go, but friends last forever."

That felt pretty hypocritical, considering. Adam spent nearly all his free time with Stephanie.

I couldn't stop myself from blurting out, "You don't know what you're talking about. None of the girls want anything to do with me. They don't make sense. Why would they bother whispering about me, when they make their whispers loud enough for me to hear? Anyway, they think I'm weird."

Adam leaned over and pulled a wet curl away from my eye. "Oh, Fleur, you think I don't know how hard it is? You're definitely not weird, but you did have one of the world's weirdest childhoods. You may be intellectually way ahead of yourself—it's obvious you're going to be a giant in the quantum field—but your parents hardly prepared you for real life. You're still a little girl in many ways."

Having Adam fiddling with my hair was making my tummy hot and my tweeter even more fluttery. I tried to distract myself by speculating how someone could be little and gigantic at the same time. Could this be another key to the process of dematerialization? I'd learned by now one of life's little secrets: there was nothing more void-filling than speculating about the void. Frankly, though, I thought Adam was exaggerating about both ends of my behavioral spectrum. I wasn't nearly as little girlish as he liked to imagine (my moist tweeter a case in point) or nearly as gigantic in the mental department. If I were, other people would not be such an unfathomable mystery to me.

When I failed to respond, Adam gave me a sad smile and stood up, clearly prepared to go. My lips wanted to shout, "You don't understand anything anymore," while my tweeter wanted me to tell him, "No, please, don't go away," but instead I just shrunk away as he leaned over to kiss the top of my towel, then—realizing how rude I must seem—I tried to smooth things over with our ritual "Good night, sleep tight..."

To which he replied, grinning a wide, relieved grin, "Don't let the bed bugs bite." He told me he'd call tomorrow to see how I was feeling. I closed my eyes so I wouldn't see him walk out the door.

After Adam left, Gwennie tucked me into bed, but not before brushing my hair an extra hundred times. I've yet to understand why Gwennie brushing my hair produced the most heavenly of scalp sensations, while I could hardly be bothered brushing my own, it was such a chore. But this was one conundrum I didn't care to linger over. I just wanted her to keep on brushing.

Once she finally left the room, though, and I slid under the covers, my mind cycled back to Adam's advice. Maybe he was right. I could definitely make more of an effort, but so many of my classmates seemed like youthful versions of the people sticking metal pipes down the throats of geese, just to make fatty meals of them. As nasty as I could be, and as envious, I simply could not imagine doing such a thing. Nor could I grasp the kind of sensibility that would allow it. It was almost as if we belonged to different species.

Which got me fretting about Lord Hanuman. I knew that Gombe National Park was primarily a chimp reserve, but what would stop predators from wandering in? Lord Hanuman was the unsung hero of our work on dematerialization. He and I had been on rather intimate terms—I could still remember the feel of his fingers sifting through my hair for dandruff. It was a lot like Gwennie's brushing. Despite his inordinate possessiveness and a penchant for flinging distasteful body products around, Hanuman was essentially a sweet soul. I hoped to God he had the good sense to be careful about which creatures he stood next to at the watering hole.

There was no way I was going to be able to fall asleep on that note. I tried working on a mini-explosion, but every time I conjured up Adam's face, it offered itself in tandem with Stephanie's. There was no way that was going to work.

So I hauled out the by-now familiar face of the boy I'd never spoken to. And I'm ashamed to say it was Hector Hernandez's careless lack of anything resembling intelligence, doubt, or reflection that finally did the trick.

Chapter 16 🦋

MY ADOLESCENT MISERY only got worse, and I wouldn't be surprised if Gwennie and Adam, in particular, heaved a sigh of relief when I went home for Thanksgiving. The plane ride back felt far more precarious than the one that had brought me to So Cal, probably because I didn't have Jillily and her perfect fish breath to comfort me.

It was great to see Mother and Nana and Sister Flatulencia and Dhani and Ignacio and someone who I could no longer be justified in calling Baby Angelina waving and smiling as I emerged from my plane. But once I dumped my bright pink suitcase onto Nana's companion twin bed and came out to join the crowd in the living room, I felt at sixes and sevens, awkward with the little boy who kept a possessive hand on Nana's forearm, put off by the stranger I soon learned was the new man in Mother's life, and convinced everyone was staring at me solely because they couldn't believe the size of the bright red boil on my forehead. The only one who wasn't focused on me so intently was Angelina. If anything, she seemed frightened and shy when I knelt down to talk to her. It struck me then that she'd forgotten who I was. I missed Jillily terribly.

Mother only made things worse by turning to Nana and saying, "My God, she's the spitting image of my mother. Can you believe how beautiful she is?" At which point, everyone started nodding and clucking like a roomful of over-sized chickens: "She certainly is." "Que Linda!" "She's got a lovely figure." "Do you see those legs on her? She's nearly as tall as her father." I wished I could have melted all the way to the first floor.

Speaking of Father, I wanted to see him something awful. We'd only spoken on the phone once since I'd left for So Cal. Every time I'd called after that, I'd merely gotten his outgoing message, followed by a lengthy series of beeps and a mechanical voice saying his mailbox was full. Did he even know I'd arrived in New York? Had he managed to hold onto his mind?

But I learned soon enough that Father wasn't even in town. Sister Flatulencia told me he was touring the country publicizing his new book. I thought that was a good sign until Nana handed me a copy. Its cover featured a cherubic-looking baby floating across a pastel sky, a contrail of buttery letters spelling out behind it, "A Breath of New Life." Little droplets of dew below bore the subtitle, "The Glories of Foster Parenting." My heart sunk with the possibility that, in my absence, Father had traded in his new mind for his old one.

But I had no time to dwell on my disappointment. I had Thanksgiving dinner to navigate. Cook and Fayga hadn't been there to greet me at the airport only because they'd been busy preparing our feast. These were the dishes that Fayga had helped Cook cook, and I'm pleased to say Fayga must have rinsed her hands for days in lemon water, because not one forkful bore the slightest hint of Ye Olde English Furniture Paste:

1. Roast turkey with pomegranate gravy and porcini stuffing;

2. Cranberry and candied orange chutney;

3. Arugula salad with toasted pecans;

4. Spicy mashed sweet potatoes and carrots;

5. Eggplant and tomato tartlets;

6. Aunt Mary's best-ever pumpkin bread.

Aunt Mary, by the way, wasn't really anyone's auntie, but Cook's best friend from The Old Days. Cook was fond of saying that Aunt Mary made up in concocting delicious dishes what she failed to accomplish in her desire to marry and breed babies.

Anyway, the fullness of her tummy seemed to have crowded out Angelina's shyness. She and I shared a moment of wild delight, both of us nearly bursting from our seats when Dhani brought out the *rosogulla* she'd made for dessert. If you have ever tasted those sweet cardamommy balls of fried heaven, you will understand our riotous response. It came as no surprise when Dhani informed me they were the hit of last week's lesson at the Cookery School.

Prior to that, though, I did have a little trouble with the turkey. My episode with Stephanie's goose liver was still very much on my mind. When I told Cook I'd rather fill up on all the side dishes, Dhani assumed I'd become a vegetarian and explained to the rest of the table what a venerable Hindu tradition that was. I made a mental note not to ask for bacon for breakfast.

Dhani, by the way, had gotten decidedly rounder, just as Angelina had gotten taller and Ignacio a lot wrinklier, thanks, no doubt, to his days in the sun. Actually, everyone was showing signs of age. I had to admit that Mother's perfect white cheeks were a bit droopy. Fayga's silvery hair had thinned, especially in front, making her eyebrows stand out like angel's wings. Besides acquiring deep wrinkles, Ignacio had sprouted what he called a beer gut; he, at least, was no friend of Bill W. Cook, who'd fortunately failed on her diet, was decidedly fatter, her breasts like giant cushions resting on the vast divan of her belly. Nothing much, though, had changed about Sister Flatulencia, unless you counted the increased volubility of her farts, which I secretly thought should be entered in the *Guinness Book of Records*.

It didn't escape me that they were all heading toward the place where Grandfather had ended up. I didn't talk about it much, but he was always there, gracing the Grand Canyon of loss in my heart. While in the early days I had felt his presence as a comfort, my melancholic barreling toward adolescence made it seem more like an ache. If anything, being around Mother again—who was, after all, his daughter—was making the pain even more acute, as if those once bulbous balls of his were sitting on a nerve. For a brief moment, I couldn't help but hope that my work on dematerialization—well, actually, more to the point, its potential partner rematerialization—might be the forerunner to bringing spirits back from the dead.

But then, what form would those vanished souls take? Would it be the swollen-balled Grandfather returning to life, filling the house with the smell of ammonia, or the one with the wrinkled member? Or might it be a much younger version of him, too young and active to want to sit with me, watching our tree? And what of our tree, anyway? I suppose I'd have to rematerialize that, too. As you can see, the problems go on and on and frankly, even thinking of it now I get a headache.

Sandwiched between Mother and Nana at our long table and letting the last of a *rosogulla* ball melt on my tongue, I felt so close to being swallowed by the void that I nearly started pinching and banging. Adam later told me that everyone regresses around their families, and I have to admit that, at least in my case, he was right.

By the way, though Mother had insisted on sitting next to me, she spent most of the meal talking to her new man, needless to say one of the Bill W's. His name was Fred Forrest, and he bore a slight resemblance to Uncle Bob, which you'd think would have made him someone I'd get on with, and I tried, I really did, until I found out that he was a sleep researcher who experimented on cats. After that, I couldn't lean far enough away from the man—to the point where Nana began to fret aloud that I had some sort of nerve disease that was affecting my balance. I'm afraid I didn't feel free to comfort her with the truth, which was that all I wanted to do was go home.

The implications of that particular idea were not lost on me. With all its faults (no pun intended), So Cal had become my new home.

But I still had the rest of Thursday and all of Friday and Saturday to endure. I was much relieved when I discovered that the little boy Nana had adopted—his name was Cesar, actually Cesar Jesus de Maria Santo Domingo Marisco—was not going to sleep with me and Nana in her bedroom that night. There was already too much change to absorb.

I hadn't so far paid much attention to Cesar. Newcomers needed to take a back seat when I hadn't seen the rest of my first incarnation crew for so long. But once our guests had trailed out of the penthouse, with Mother making what I thought was overmuch of a fuss over the thoughtfulness of Fred Forrest in offering Sister Flatulencia and Fayga a shared cab-ride home, I was free to contemplate the child who'd been chosen to take my place.

Cesar was the same shade as Dhani, with a birthmark above the inside corner of his left eyebrow like an off-center bindi. The off-center bindi should have been a sign. Nothing was quite right about Cesar. He was forever climbing up on things, then proceeding to fall off them—except, that is, when he was busy clinging to Nana's arm.

He interrupted conversations all the time, especially conversations between me and Nana. When he wasn't jabbering in a combination of English and Spanish, he filled up every available blank moment with his odd little laugh. You could hear him coming from the next room, chattering nearly non-stop, pausing from time to time to giggle raggedly, as if struck by his own cleverness. Was this child having an even harder time with the void than I had had? More to the point, could what I was feeling be called jealousy?

After we'd bid everyone else goodnight, Nana having tucked Cesar into the same bed where Dhani's bun had burst from her oven, she pulled her own bed closer to mine and filled me in on Cesar's story, how his mother had been addicted to a drug called crack co-caine and how he was what she called ADHD. Nana lamented how much easier a baby I'd been, though there'd not been much she could do for me when I started my flapping. We talked until the city ceased its clamor. Nana fell asleep mid-sentence. I was comforted in my subsequent sleeplessness by the sound of her snores.

You might be interested to know that Nana was the only one to inquire how it was for me to live with Stanley H. and Gwennie Fiske. The denizens of my first and second incarnations tended to be more preoccupied by their own concerns, and their conversations were more *about* me then *with* me, centered on what I personally felt to be a misplaced nostalgia—as if our first and second incarnations were what Nana often observed that life was *not*: a bowl-full of cherries.

Over the next few days, I told Nana everything, save my current crisis concerning Adam and Hector Hernandez. Even though I'd come to discover that Nana's cave scent was at least a second cousin to the metallic aroma of my tweeter when I suffered the slings of Mr. Heavyflow, it didn't feel right to inquire whether she, too, conjured images of bulging male members to set off mini-explosions down below.

Pretty much everything else, though, I shared with her. About Stanley H. Fiske, his challenging questions and constant kindness. About Gwennie's near-deafness, her laughing spirit and salty tongue. About Moggy and Jillily and how much they seemed to enjoy hating each other. About my failures at P.E. and my infirmity at finding friends and the fact that our drama teacher was planning to do *Cats* in the spring. I tried to explain the project that Amir and Adam and Katrina and Tom and Gunther and I were working on. Needless to say, that part went way over her head, but otherwise, she managed to nod at all the right moments, even tearing up a few times, so I knew she was actually listening.

Of course, if I'd relied on her words to confirm that, I'd be in big trouble. After running the household of my first incarnation, Nana had gotten plenty of practice making Mack-truckishly clear what she wanted, but her capacity for commentary was still pretty spare. Helping me pack for my return to So Cal, she finally managed a terse, "You're not alone, girl. Nobody likes being a teenager. If the rest of us hadn't been through it ourselves, we'd fling the lot of you in the loony bin."

I'm afraid I've made Nana sound something of a Job's comforter. I'd learned in my early Bible study how four men named Eliphaz, Bildad, Zophar, and Elihu came to see Job after God made a bet with Satan that Job would remain a true believer even after God made him suffer a whole series of losses and physical agonies. As they watched Job sit on his void of a dung heap, those so-called comforters of his merely blamed him for his misery. What kind of friends were those? They were so mean that I bet no one since has ever been named Eliphaz, Bildad, Zophar, or Elihu. Come to think of it, I doubt there are too many Jobs out there, either.

Even though Nana's description of teenagers was pretty harsh, I knew at the time she was just trying to make me feel better. It was only later that I learned the wisdom of her words.

And speaking of wisdom, Mother decided she needed to offer me at least one educational outing during my visit. She woke up Saturday morning determined to take me to see a new Richard Serra exhibit at MoMA. When we slid into our cab an hour later, I couldn't help but notice that the card on the dashboard identified our cabbie as Korfa Bile. His name probably meant something quite different where he was born, but given the country he'd emigrated to, he might as well be called Job.

I don't know whether I've mentioned how sociable Mother had become since signing up as a Friend of Bill W. Within moments of the two of us belting up she'd engaged Mr. Bile in conversation, asking him where he came from (Somalia) and how long he'd been in the States (five years). It didn't take him long to launch into a vivid itemization of his worries over what might have happened to his sisters Aziza and Ayanna in his absence, which nauseated me in a way that even an overfed goose couldn't do. But I was all too aware that Korfa Bile had a lot more serious matters to contend with than a puking passenger, so I managed to hold myself together with some selective thigh pinching.

Once we arrived at our destination, Serra's exhibit didn't much help in the pukey tummy department. One of his massive sculptures was actually called "Torqued Torus Inversion," and though Mother said that it and its companion pieces "Band" and "Sequence" made her feel proud to be human, it occurred to me that being human seemed to include creating objects resembling giant rusty cans wrenched opened by a giant can opener, something guaranteed to send soft-fleshed, void-vulnerable girls into a bottomless gaping pit.

The good news was that, as the two of us wound in and out of the clumps of people dwarfed by looming, cold-walled spaces, Mother finally noticed my green face and rushed me to the ladies' just in time for my breakfast of scrambled eggs and waffles to blast into the toilet. The resultant splash managed to fashion a jaundiced-looking Etch-a-Sketch across my exposed knees, but Mother carefully cleaned me up afterwards and even offered me a swig of her travel-size Listerine to, as she put it, "put you right again." Actually, despite the fact that I knew Mother was committed to speak at a meeting as soon as she dropped me off at the penthouse, it was leaning against her body in the cab ride home—this time thanks to the services of a silent, if sour-faced, driver—that shored up my sagging spirits for my journey back to So Cal the next morning.

But the flight itself shook me up all over again. Have you ever flown through a lightning storm? Well, I did. Luckily, it came toward the end of our flight or I might have disappeared into the pit of eternal panic. With barely sixty seconds' worth of warning from the cockpit, the sky was transformed into a neon advertisement for human powerlessness. Our interior lighting flicked on and off like a strobe light, and the world outside looked decidedly surreal. But what was worst was our plane being buffeted by truly Jovian winds. If we were Roman, we might have blamed the storm on Jupiter Pluvius (the Rain God) or Jupiter in his Fulgurator (God of Lightning) incarnation. I didn't care who was to blame. I just wanted it to stop. It didn't help that, in between heart-stopping cracks of thunder, you could hear people up and down the aisle upchucking their Herbed Chicken Breast with Madeira Demi-glace.

It's amazing, though, how desire can trump fear. You'd think it would be the other way around. But I suppose it makes sense. The abundance of living species on our planet isn't due solely to the avoidance of predators. Tweeters and members also have something to do with it. Anyway, as I emerged from the arrival tunnel I saw Adam had been delegated to pick me up. His face looked so luminous I felt my own tweeter moisten, as if readying itself for the kinds of mini-explosions encouraged by Jupiter Summanus (Sender of Nocturnal Thunder). But the image of Stephanie in Adam's arms forced my mind off my own body, or at least gave it a proverbial cold shower instead. "Why do you like Stephanie so much?" I asked, as we sped through the terminal.

Adam shot me a surprised look. We were approaching the crowded Baggage Claim area. He held up a "wait a minute" finger and pulled me and my pink carry-on towards the luggage chute. Stationing us securely at a good suitcase-grabbing spot, he turned to face me. The conveyor belt wasn't moving yet. Perhaps LAX wasn't just an acronym.

Adam said, "Okay, now we can talk. What was that about?"

"What?"

"About me liking Stephanie."

"Oh, I just wondered."

He stared at me as if I'd uttered some variant on *ugga umph ugga*. "Now that was a hell of a non sequitur. Did you have a good trip?"

"Pretty good. Is it because she wears those sleeveless blouses?"

Adam laughed. "Fleur, has anyone told you what a nut you are?" I could feel my face turned red, and he added quickly, "Okay, okay. I'll humor you. Let's see. The blouses? Sure, I suppose the fact that she's in such great shape doesn't hurt. I mean, Stephanie's a great person. You know how she is—funny, smart. But she *is* gorgeous. I still can't believe a girl like her is into a crip like me."

I couldn't believe my ears. Adam loved Stephanie because he thought she was doing him a *favor*?

And who would have guessed Adam thought of himself as crippled? According to Webster, a cripple is disabled, but Adam? With his penetrating intellect, perfect brown eyes, capacious compassion, and Campbell's Chicken Soup B.O., he was more than able on many counts. Not the least of which involved his ability to loosen at long-distance a lava-flow of feeling from the tip of my tweeter to the top of my scalp and the bottoms of my size six feet.

Nevertheless, his comment about Stephanie's beauty explained why he paid her more attention than me. I was getting freckles on my face, and pimples were popping up with increasing frequency. Gwennie said I was pretty, but I knew she was lying. And, even if I were, it would only make the girls at school hate me more. The more I thought about *them*, the more depressed I got, erasing any positive effect of having been away.

Things got even worse at the onset of winter vacation, just before my thirteenth birthday. I was coming out of the kitchen when I saw Moggy chase Jillily out of the den, through the living room (which that day necessitated a detour around a not-yet-decorated Christmas tree), and down the hallway. Running after the two of them to prevent the possibility of all-out warfare, I saw Moggy stop suddenly, then begin to stagger helplessly from wall to wall.

A rush to the vet produced the news that she'd gone blind. With Gwennie and me huddling together bleakly in a waiting room filled with sighted animals, Dr. Bharati performed a series of tests to confirm the cause of Moggy's blindness, returning to the pee-puddled waiting area to inform us it was kidney failure. I could not help but stare at Dr. Bharati's long beak of a nose, which looked like a lighthouse in a thick mist until I realized I was crying and wiped my eyes. The vet offered us two options: put Moggy down or see if subcutaneous fluid injections might at least temporarily revive her kidney function and restore her eyesight. That particular pair of choices was what Adam would have called a *no brainer*.

I ended up giving Moggy her fluids every other day, rolling out the tall metal stand with its suspended pouch of saline fluid and a trailing plastic tube, to which I would carefully attach a fresh needle. I had to tap the needle first to release any lurking air bubbles before grabbing a decent palmful of loose fat on Moggy's back so I could insert the needle just under her skin. I was the only one in the household who could tolerate doing this. I had a pretty good idea why. I'd learned from my shameful episode of Jillily-pinching that causing pain to one's own cat dictates descent to the deepest layer of hell. Needless to say, the discovery that liquid could be injected intravenously to arrest the processes of nature caused me no end of grief in the Grandfather department, but I had learned by then to live with self-recrimination as a kind of subliminal musical score to what Adam, in his more depressed pre-Caltech days, used to call *This B-Movie Called Life*.

If Moggy's current incarnation was a B-Movie, then she was handling it like an A-list star, with Jillily proving a worthy supporting role at the foot of the bed, watching with what seemed like real compassion. As for Moggy, as I struggled with her infusions, she leaned patiently against me, radiating a body-heat worthy of the Egyptian solar goddess Bastet. Once I got the needle in, my own heartbeat relaxing into alignment with her rhythmic motoring, I watched with wonder as she swelled like a lumpy pillow.

My commitment to Moggy helped fill the bleak hours of winter break. Oh, sure, my physics pals threw a yummy five-million-calorie party at the Rose Tree Cottage tearoom celebrating my thirteenth birthday, and Gwennie enticed me out of the house for trips to movies and Borders, as well as a major shopping splurge at the Gap. But our outings only reinforced my awareness of my situation, as I observed kids more or less my own age out with other kids my age, walking in pairs or mini-tribes, laughing shrilly into their cell phones, using their bodies as exclamation points as they intoned innumerable "Oh my Gahhds" and "She didn'ts!" and "Can you believe its?!" For all their "Oh my Gods," you'd think they were extremely religious, but the number of "fucks" and "assholes" that punctuated their conversations tended to disprove it.

Aware of Gwennie's eyes traveling from gaggles of girls back to me, I tried to put a brave face on it, but I knew that she knew how crummy it felt to be me.

The good news was that the life-saving liquid injections restored Moggy's eyesight. By the time the new year arrived, she was thoroughly enjoying her latest incarnation. Since cats reputedly have nine lives, I didn't even want to conjecture which one she was living. It was sufficient to see her kittenishly bat the bottom-most layer of bubble lights on our fabulously festooned Christmas tree and chase Jillily around the house again. But something new was occurring even in that department. Every once in awhile I caught the two of them licking each other in a shaft of sunlight, though they immediately arose when I entered the room and pretended not to know each other, as if they had their reputation as enemies to uphold.

Little did I know that one of my own new lives was about to begin.

The second semester started off much the same as the first, with me sitting singly at the most secluded of Reed's lunch benches, weary of watching the other kids acting like life was one long, unbelievably hysterical joke. I was convinced I'd missed out on some crucial humor gene; life for me was becoming, if anything, increasingly UN-funny.

Walking into Edna Roderick's second semester drama class wasn't any easier. My breasts had grown another bra size during winter break, and I'd heard nothing but beastly comments about my body from non-IHP boys all morning.

On top of it all, I'd just gotten my period and ended up arriving in class a full five minutes late, due to having to rub my jeans with cold water in the girl's bathroom to vanquish Mr. Heavyflow's traditional calling card from the crotch area. My badge of shame was sufficiently close to the thick Levi's seam to be barely visible, but I wasn't taking any chances.

To my horror, the only desk available was right beside Hector Hernandez. I couldn't help but notice that he had a small-ish mole at the corner of his left nostril, and that he was wearing his dark hair slicked-back from his forehead, which was exercising a magnetism on me that rivaled the strongest of gravitational waves. I was going to die on the spot if I didn't keep my eyes averted from Hector, so I gave Ms. Roderick the half of my full attention that wasn't devoted to mentally monitoring the bloody seepage from my tweeter and images of that same part of my body exploding at the thought of Hector Hernandez's bulging biceps.

Our teacher wasn't wasting any time. We'd read the play *Cats* together during our first semester, and she'd evidently been assessing us the whole time. With a show of self-importance, she waved her cast list. As she barked out our names, my classmates alternately giggled, groaned, or clapped at the feline incarnations they were soon to assume. "Macavity!" Who would play the villain? "Steven Shlekt." Well, that certainly fit. "Demeter!—Amy Cowe."

Someone nearby whispered, "The Cowster? Better not have her dancing around. The stage'll fall in." I saw Amy's face turn red.

"Munkustrap!—Hector Hernandez." Several of his friends called out, "Dude!" Then, "Jennanaydots!—Fleur Robins."

As if stricken by Moggy's blindness, I had to sense rather than see Hector's body lean toward me, feeling the warmth of his breath tickling my ear. "Cool. You're my love interest. Are you up for that?" Although he whispered, several boys in the class snickered, as if getting the message from some invisible adolescent sound wave. By the time the bell finally rang, the void had swallowed me and spat me out again several times over.

I barely recovered enough to sit still through the rest of my classes. Even Hilly noticed something was amiss and stopped me at the end of Algebra to ask if things were going poorly with my project. I had no idea what he was talking about, replying abstractedly, "Jennanydots," leaving him standing open-mouthed as I floated out the door.

Hector turned out to be a far faster mover than I was. After a few weeks of initially awkward but increasingly exhilarating rehearsals together, he caught up with me one Friday as I rushed off for nutrition break. Pushing his shiny black hair back from his forehead, he asked if I wanted to rehearse after school sometime, throwing in—almost as an afterthought—"Hey, you wanna go to a party at my friend Sylvia's next Saturday? Her mom and dad are gonna be in Piedros Negras for her cousin's Quinceneria."

In quick succession, I thought, Piedros Negras! A party! With Hector! What's a Quinceneria?

My first inclination was to say no; the whole thing was far too overwhelming. You might recall that Piedros Negras was where Ignacio had learnt of Joseph Smith's epiphanies, reportedly delivered by an angel from outer space named Maroni. I'm afraid the story became a bit of a joke in the home of my first incarnation, with Nana converting Maroni into the noodle and cheese dish Cook liked to prepare with the first lofting leaves of autumn. So when Hector mentioned Piedros Negras, all I could think of was that erstwhile angel Maroni, covered in cheese.

To my dismay a treacherous wave of giggling escaped my throat. I knew from witnessing my IHP peers that nothing more betrays one's lack of social grace than nervous laughter. But Hector was laughing, too, saying, "Yeah, I know. Perfect, huh? We can pick you up. My homie Arthur just got his license. Here, write down where you live." He proffered a pen and a left arm bearing a tattoo of the Madonna and Child, whose cosmology—when you consider the conceit of the Annunciation—wasn't all that different from Joseph Smith and his astronomical angel. Once I realized Hector wanted me to write down my address on his body, I obliged him with a wobbly *1399 Rose Villa* (skin is not nearly as stable a substance as paper), taking care not to interfere with Baby Jesus and his immaculate mother.

Of course, as soon as I got home, I realized I'd constellated a crisis of major proportions. Not knowing what else to do, I called Adam, who, as you might imagine, was more than happy to give me Stephanie's number.

She might be my archrival, but someone had to teach me how to make myself beautiful. I felt more than a little guilty when she greeted my request with obvious enthusiasm.

That Saturday, our first stop was a mall in Century City. It wasn't that Pasadena didn't have its own clothing stores, many of them located in a charming cluster of old Spanish-style buildings in a part of the city called Old Town. But Stephanie said she'd grown up a Westside girl, and Century City was evidently—from the vantage point of commerce, anyway—the heart, if not the navel, of the Westside.

Speaking of navels, the first feminine ritual that my mentor made me undergo was the installation of a silver ring at the outer rim of my belly button. It happened while we were heading for our first stop, a shoe store, since Stephanie insisted a wardrobe should be constructed like a building, from the ground up. She skidded to a stop in front of a shop window glittering with shiny rings. "Wait. I've always wanted a navel ring, and you, my sweet, are going to be my excuse to get one. Adam will get off on mine, and the kids will think you're cooler than cool because of yours."

I wasn't sure I wanted to be cool, or how a ring could be attached to a navel, at least one that didn't protrude like my mother's (which I'd caught sight of in my first incarnation, the same time I saw her wild puff of pubic hair). But I certainly wanted to be beautiful, and if wearing a decorative piece of jewelry on my belly would win Hector Hernandez's heart, how could I say no?

What I hadn't really thought much about was that navel rings are attached by piercing, which jumped to the front of my mind once Stephanie and I walked inside, setting off a buzzer and causing a girl with wall-to-wall tattoos on her arms and rings creeping up and down her ears to emerge from the back of the shop, saying, "Sisters? Up for some bonding with body candy?"

To which Stephanie responded, "I wish" (to the former, which shocked me), "You bet," (to the latter, which confused me), then scared me by bending down and whispering, "You don't have an aversion to needles, do you?"

What came to mind in that instant was how I'd felt having my blood sucked out by the pediatric nurse before the dog who should have been put down made a lunge at me. But that was then, I reminded myself, and this was now. I was, after all, the moral equivalent of that nurse these days, at least as far as Moggy was concerned. And even though I was putting life-saving fluids *in* to Moggy's body, while the blood-drawing nurse had been taking essential fluids *out* of mine, if having blood drawn would somehow make me appealing to Hector Hernandez, I calculated I could tolerate a little fear. But that was before it dawned on me that it wasn't just a needle I was facing, but a silver ring perpetually penetrating my person.

In spite of myself, I started to flap, which made Stephanie stiffen with surprise, but had little effect on the girl with tattoos, who looked perfectly unfazed and said, "I know what you mean. Pain is a total drag, but I promise you, I've got to be the world's expert. See? I did my own." She opened her mouth to reveal a tongueful of silver balls and rings. "After the first little pinch, you don't even know they're there." The view of that tongue mesmerized me like Stanley H. Fiske's magic.

I watched with fascination as she grabbed her gear, lifted my blouse, swabbed me with alcohol, clamped a little flap of my skin—such a familiar pinchy feeling that a wave of nostalgia washed over me—then zipped a needle through one end and out the other before I could even say, "Ouch." She threaded a little ball-tipped ring through the opening, slapped a gauze pad slathered with Neosporin on top as Mack-truckishly as Nana on a particularly hectic saved-babies day, then concluded the whole operation by holding out her hand for a high five. I responded, feeling like a one-armed conjoined twin trying to clap with my one-armed partner.

Once she'd gotten her own navel pierced, I let Stephanie lead me in and out of shops and in and out of dressing rooms in an uncomprehending daze. How she was able to conclude that one outfit looked "like shit" but another was "just perfect" was utterly mystifying, but by the time we'd both had our faces made up in Bloomingdale's cosmetics department, I felt so overwhelmed that I was rendered literally speechless. The pointy-shoed woman who'd turned my face into a Holi-esque mask held up her mirror at various angles, asking earnestly, "How do you like it?" but I couldn't even muster a pleased *ugga umph ugga*. Stephanie shot me a look that suggested I just might be the rudest person in the world.

She drove us home with a set jaw and me sitting silently beside her, tears streaking my make-up so that I must have looked like the world's weariest clown. Well, actually, she drove us almost all the way home before pulling to the curb on Colorado Blvd., crying herself now in jerky bursts. "Okay, I have just worked my ass off for six straight hours to get you the most fantastic wardrobe any normal thirteen-year old would kiss the fucking ground to wear," she said. "Adam keeps telling me how fucking brilliant you are." Mimicking Adam, her tone became increasingly acrid. "'Fleur's breaking totally new ground in physics.' 'Stanley says she's a scientific genius.' 'Did I tell you what Fleur discovered today?'" She put her face so close to mine that I saw individual grains of powder on her forehead. "Is that the problem here? Was this whole exercise just a little too fucking SHALLOW for you?"

I am not nearly as bright as some people think I am. It took all that wrenching effort on Stephanie's part for it finally to dawn on me that *she* was jealous of *me*! In a flash of insight, I felt a surge of compassion for Cesar Jesus de Maria Santa Domingo Marisco. How awful for him, to be cast aside by his drug-addicted mother, suffer the non-stop voidishness of ADHD, and be adopted by a Mack-trucker who actually cared about him, only to have some older child with a full set of biological parents treat him like some kind of unforgivable usurper.

As for Stephanie, how could I explain to her that I wasn't ungrateful, only suffering from the shock of knowing that, with my piercing, I now had a permanent hole in my body through which the void could sneak in any time it pleased?

I wanted to apologize, but all that came out was, "I didn't...I wish I could ...it's not that I don't..." Stephanie stopped crying. She glared at me with racoonishly mascara-ringed eyes. I felt like such a bumbler. Why couldn't I just say, "I'm sorry?"

I tried again. "Please don't hate me. I know I'm weird. It's just that...I can't seem to help it."

Stephanie drew back as if I'd struck her. We sat there, staring at each other, raccoon eyes to raccoon eyes.

Then something odd happened. Stephanie's head tilted ever so slightly, as if she were trying to get a better view, and then I saw the hard set to her features soften like melting wax. "What was I thinking? Dragging you around like a puppy dog." She leaned forward, then undid her seatbelt so she could come closer. She wrapped me in her arms. I caught a faint whiff of coconut. "Poor little genius," she murmured into my hair. "It really isn't easy for you, is it?" I shook my head, careful not to move so much that she'd loosen me from her sweet-smelling grip. She continued in a contrite voice, "I don't know what got into me. I was really crude just now, wasn't I?"

To which I could only reply, "Yes."

She responded with a flood of laughter, dribbling just a little and not even noticing it.

I laughed, too, but with considerably more reserve, taking advantage of the general hilarity to finger the edge of her sleeveless blouse and run a hand down her tanned and silken arm, confirming the wisdom of Adam's ardor. She pushed me away slightly, shooting me a questioning look, then just shook her head and gave me a quick chicken peck on each cheek, French style, reminding me a little of Nana and a little of Mother. She slid back to her side, belted herself in, and turned on her CD player. We listened to Liz Phair the rest of the way home.

By the time we got back, Stanley and Gwennie were already having what they liked to call their pre-prandial drink. Stephanie and I set down our bags, blanketing every available inch of the already cluttered living room floor. Gwennie Fiske wasn't exactly the world's champion housekeeper, though she hated the mess her brother made with sunflower seeds, and Stanley, of course, had a rather intense attachment to books, which he tended to strew about absentmindedly as soon as he'd digested what he needed from them. Most of the current assemblage had to do with entangled states.

My make-up was mostly gone by now. Stephanie had cleaned the snotty scarification from my face in the car, reminding me of Nana when she fetched a Kleenex from her purse and moistened it with spit, swabbing me first and herself second. I saw that Gwennie didn't need an ounce of makeup herself. Her cheeks were flushed with cooking and a glass or two of red wine. She scanned the evidence of our shopping trip. "So, what'd you get?"

Never one for the tactful intro, I blurted out, "a pierced navel."

Gwennie's response was pretty predictable. She said, "Good Lord!"

Stanley, on the other hand, shot me a conspiratorial wink. "Joining the natives, eh? Good, good. Now tell me how you and Amir are getting on with looped strings."

All three of us stared at him. Maybe his genius had somehow propelled him straight from childhood to Nobel prize-hood, because he sure could learn a thing or two about being thirteen.

Chapter 17 🦋

IT WAS ONLY thanks to Amir that I made it through the subsequent week. As far as science went, Stanley had been no fool in asking how we were doing with looped strings. We all sensed they might play a significant role in moving us forward. In the days before Sylvia Nava's party I spent countless hours at Amir's chimpanzee-booger-ceilinged digs, trying to wrap my mind around the still tenuous connection between strings, gravity, and the possibility of dematerialization.

Of course, such a possibility remained to be proved. Dematerialization was still just an idea spun from a moment's meditation on the dissolution of a caterpillar preceding its transmutation into a butterfly. In order to scratch that particular itch, I was having to acquaint myself with not just quantum mechanics, but also the vast realm of human biology, in particular the properties of our bodies' basic component, the multi-talented (and, I hoped to prove, at least five-dimensional) cell.

Between my consultations with Amir and the state of my aggravated belly button, I barely slept all week. Once I did drop off, with Jillily spooned inside the quarter moon of my body, I suffered a series of difficult dreams—one with Stephanie preferring to smooch with me over Adam and me not objecting—that made me wake in the middle of the night, aching to have someone to talk to about something more than the interface of physics and biology.

There are times when nothing but a black cat with white tuxedo markings and a question mark tail will do. I found myself mumbling my anxieties about the upcoming party into Jillily's motoring belly. She repaid the confidence by cleaning my face from nose to chin. Since a cat's tongue is far raspier than our own, I ultimately had to dissuade her, rolling her onto her back and tickling her belly to let her know that my disinclination to be licked wasn't personal.

Which, I supposed, leads me to my evening with Hector Hernandez. It was at Sylvia Nava's party that I discovered Jillily wasn't the only Fleur-licker in town.

The evening started uneventfully enough. At Gwennie's insistence, Stanley had already vetted Hector by phoning his mother. Delighted at the opportunity to practice his Spanish, he'd found her a soft-spoken widow who worked at Caltech's Avery House cafeteria, which, in Stanley's book anyway, made her one of the family. Hector arrived at the door promptly at seven thirty, the running motor of his friend Arthur Ramos' car hacking and coughing at the curb so loudly that Stanley went out and conferred with Arthur under the opened hood while Gwennie gave Hector what she later said she wished had been more of the third degree. To his credit, Hector was suitably well-spoken and presentably dressed—no "crap in the pants" oversized jeans that Gwennie and Stanley detested, but razor-pressed chinos and, mercifully, a starched long-sleeved white shirt obscuring baby Jesus and his mother Mary.

He offered Gwennie his cell phone number and Sylvia's address and his assurance that he'd have me home by midnight. Nevertheless, I thought I detected lines of worry on both Stanley and Gwennie's foreheads as they waved us off. As for me, I was only halfway present, the rest of me floating somewhere above my head.

Sylvia's home was located in a modest, but well-tended part of Pasadena, where most of the faces we passed on the street were various shades of brown. Despite Hector's praise of my prettiness—I was wearing the flowery slip-dress Stephanie had selected for me and at least some of the make-up we'd purchased at the Bloomingdale's cosmetics counter—I felt like a white-masked ghost gliding amongst the living.

By the time we'd parked, Hector had rolled up his sleeves (revealing a dove on his right wrist, a companion piece, I supposed, to Mary and Jesus on his left), slicked back his hair, and whispered a few times in my ear, which, as you can imagine, was doing nothing to help me forget my trembly tweeter. This whisper-in-ear-tweeter-get-wet drill was getting to be a habit.

There was already quite a crowd filling the modest stucco house when we arrived. Pulling me by the hand, Hector led me through several noisy rooms to a rather neglected looking backyard that Ignacio would have loved to get his hands on. I was introduced to Sylvia, Sylvia's cousins Delores and Jennifer and Adolfo and Ruben, about twenty other brown and black-eyed boys, and a like number of brown and black-eyed, red-lipsticked girls, most of whom teetered on daddy longleg heels that I marveled anyone could walk on.

Unlike my IHP classmates, they all had big smiles for me and acted like having me there with them was the most natural thing in the world. I myself felt about as natural as a rabbit in a litter of cats and couldn't figure out what to do with my hands, so I was more than relieved when Hector stuck a glass of frothy liquid into one of them. I took a sip and humiliated myself by spitting it right out again, spraying a surprised Hector in the face. Ruben said to Hector, who was rubbing his eyes, "Vato, did you ever consider the girl never had a beer before? I mean, shit, man, didn't you say she was one of those geniuses at your school?"

He made a spiral motion over his head and everyone within hearing distance laughed. "Those people don't need to get high, their heads are already up there." Even though they kept smiling at me to let me know it was all in good fun, I felt unspeakably voidish, which led me to take a long draught of the drink, forcing myself not to gag and capping it off with a burp that I managed to swallow back into my throat, giving me a momentary pang of nausea.

I was smart enough during the rest of the party not to eat any of Sylvia's homemade burritos. After that episode with Adam and Stephanie, I didn't want another puke disaster. But Hector, in between holding me so tightly as we slow danced that I could feel his bulging member, kept plying me with plantain chips and pineapple wedges, saying I needed to have something in my belly to balance off my second Corona. He whispered into my ear again. "Can't let you get drunk, little Fleur. Your parents'd kill me. Besides, I've got other things in mind for you."

He swiped his Jesus and Mary hand gently across my breast. I wasn't sure whether he did it on purpose, but my tweeter felt as tickly as a cat's belly. I wondered whether Mary had felt something similar when her dove came to announce the coming of Baby Jesus. I considered as well, then rejected, correcting Hector's assumption that Gwennie and Stanley were my parents, shelving until later my guilt that I rather fancied the notion.

I realized then that the beer had gotten the best of me. If I didn't urinate soon, I was going to burst. I excused myself and found my way through a prettily wallpapered bedroom which might have been Sylvia's to a bathroom on whose toilet tank stood a skinny vase containing one wilting red rose. I conveyed my condolences and sat there for what felt like ages, beer and noise and nervous excitation having loosened a fascinating flood of pee. Even with the dying rose behind me, I felt unaccountably ecstatic. Someone had turned up the music even louder to compete with shouted conversation and intermittent bursts of laughter. If I could only think straight, I was sure I could graph the party's aural patterns. Instead, I inspected my face as I lathered my hands with a sculpted sweep of soap aptly named Dove, deciding I looked rather beautiful. Stephanie Siedenfeld had known what she was doing. I needed only to touch up my Shu Uemura Lolishine Rouge lipstick to perfect the picture.

When I opened the door to Sylvia's bedroom, its bed piled with purses and shawls and a couple of leather jackets, Hector was standing there waiting for me. I remember smiling rather loftily at him as I prepared to exit the room, but then he whispered in my ear, "Wait a minute. There's something I want to show you." The next thing I knew he'd swept everything off Sylvia's bed and me and him onto it.

I'm sorry to say the rest of it gets pretty fuzzy. Two things stand out, though: Hector discovering my navel ring and licking my still somewhat sore belly button, producing a simultaneous pain and pleasure, and Hector fitting a penis that looked larger than both of Grandfather's bulging balls into what felt like the world's tiniest tweeter (mine), all the while whispering *"linda paloma, linda paloma"* into my ear, which, thank Mary and Jesus and a whole parade of gods, made my entryway just slick enough to stop me from passing out with pain.

Why in the world, you might ask—as did Gwennie and Mother and Nana and Sister Flatulencia much later—didn't I stop him?

I have contemplated that question more times than I can count and can only conclude that it had something to do with my aforesaid fluttery tweeter, the indescribable heaviness of Hector's body, and the fateful intersection of the scent of Dove soap and his murmured mantra *linda paloma, linda paloma,* which you might recall from Ignacio's early pining for Dhani means *beautiful dove, beautiful dove.*

In the weeks following the party, nothing was comfortable, least of all my tweeter—which felt so tender to the touch that I didn't dare try bringing on a mini-explosion, even if I'd wanted to. Which I didn't. All that wetness over Adam and Hector had evaporated like morning dew on a sizzling So Cal day. I was actually glad that Adam was on a Cheap Hawaiian Getaway with Stephanie; I couldn't have borne having to look him in the eye during that time.

As for Hector, he and I avoided each other like the plague. I thanked the Lord we were still memorizing lines for our roles in *Cats* and not having to rehearse together. I wasn't certain what was going on in his mind, but was fairly sure it included disgust over the panoply of pimples that had sprouted on my face the minute we left the party. Stephanie later speculated that my breakout was a reaction to the Estee Lauder liquid foundation, but I felt it had more to do with the fact that my face had not been immune to the sweat that blanketed my body by the time Hector pulled his penis away, his now-shrunken member worrying me that I'd killed him until I was distracted by the sticky goo he'd left on my tweeter and thighs.

As to what had actually occurred at the party, especially the bit at the end before he urged me to pull up my panties and get up or he'd have me home late and be murdered by my parents, I preferred not to think of it, and thanks to the old cupboard in my mind for unwanted thoughts, I pretty much didn't.

It wasn't until nearly six weeks later, when I heard Amy Cowe squealing in the girls' bathroom stall next to mine, "Oh, shit, I got my period," that I realized I hadn't gotten mine. After a few days of puzzlement, I ended up asking Gwennie if she'd ever had to wait for Mr. Heavyflow. I'd taken to marking my moon cycles on a whimsical little calendar she'd given me for the purpose, having had one too many accidents at school with no sanitary napkin on hand to spare a visit to the nurse's office. Our school nurse was a taciturn woman named Wanda Haite, of all things, and she inevitably delivered an interminable lecture on being prepared, along with an embarrassingly bulky Always Maxi-pad.

As for my question about the misbehavior of my menses, Gwennie responded in a surprisingly sharp voice, "How late are you?" and when I said, "Almost a month," she said, "Have you ever been late like this before?" and when I said, "No," she said, "You haven't been fooling around, have you?"

Which was how I ended up spending half the next morning in my gynecologist's office, where both the temperature and Dr. Raker's face felt far too cold for a girl awaiting what some might call her fate and some the Hand of God. Having my blood taken felt bad enough, but when Dr. Raker called Gwennie and me back into her consulting room several hours later to brusquely announce, "You, my dear child, are pregnant," all I could think was that I might have been born with a curious mind, but I was hopelessly backward in every other way. Taking refuge in science like a weed aiming for the sun, I'd cultivated my imagination, but neglected the practicalities.

It was only much later that it occurred to me that one of the consequences of Sylvia Nava's parents' attendance at a Quinceneria in Piedros Negros was what would become my most miserable memory. Who knew that the Butterfly Effect could produce such unbeautiful results?

When we returned to Rose Villa and Gwennie informed Stanley H. Fiske that I was pregnant, he cried out, "What! Good Christ, how could this have happened? The child's only thirteen years old!" But before either Gwennie or I could respond, he reached for me with an expression of infinite sadness, his thick glasses fogging over with tears. "Oh, my dear Fleur. I fear we've failed you miserably." I felt my face grow hot as I began to realize what a terrible ripple effect a few moments of stupidity could create. Holding onto me so tightly I wasn't sure which of us was holding the other up, he turned toward Gwen, groaning, "Her father will never forgive me. I'll have to take her home."

I was humiliated. I'd let Stanley H. Fiske down after he'd gone to such trouble to bring about my third incarnation. I'd let Adam and Amir and Katrina and Tom and Gunther down on the brink of busting some standard assumptions in quantum physics. I'd let Moggy down. Who was going to give him his saline injections? I'd let Gwennie down by not confiding in her about Adam and Hector and my trouble-making tweeter. They all disagreed with me. Well, all but Moggy, who couldn't speak, but Amir assured me he'd take over the task of caring for him, giving me the impression it would fill a little of the void left by the departure of Lord Hanuman.

As for Father, I didn't even want to think of what he would say. *I* certainly didn't want to be the one to tell him.

But there are some people you have to be straight with. When Adam returned from his vacation with Stephanie looking tanned and happy, I hated to break the news, but I did. He exploded. "For Christ's sake! You're only thirteen years old! What happened?"

Humiliated, I started to explain, but when I got to the beer drinking, Adam blew up all over again. "Son of a bitch! Little bastard actually planned it! And didn't even bother to use a condom!"

By then, it was taking almost all my resources to resist the urge to flap and scream. I forcibly propelled my mind in another direction. "I think I'm suffering my first existential crisis," I confided. "I can't sleep. I keep thinking how Sartre said we *are* our choices, and now I've made a choice that's ruined everything."

But Adam wouldn't have any of it. "Oh, come on, give yourself a break. You didn't do anything wrong." He lowered his voice confidingly. "Hey, Stephanie told me she was thirteen *her* first time. *And* knew what she was getting into. You were out of your league. Hector's older than you, isn't he?" I nodded glumly. Adam expelled a frustrated breath. "Old enough to know it's the guy who's supposed to take responsibility. Especially if he's got a clue you're a virgin."

He grabbed me in a tight hug then, tucking his chin over the top of my head and filling my nostrils with my favorite scents of Campbell's Chicken Soup and B.O. "Forget about Sartre," he said slowly, as if something had just occurred to him. "I'd say his pal Camus might have more to say about your situation. Especially the irony of you getting knocked up the first time you have sex."

Intrigued, I wriggled out of Adam's grasp and waited expectantly.

He raised an eyebrow. "Didn't I ever tell you how Camus was overheard saying when he was young that the most absurd way to die was in a car accident, then sure enough, just three years after accepting his Nobel Prize, that's exactly what happened to him?" I shook my head. Adam continued. "He was discovered with an unused rail ticket in his pocket."

I smiled at the time, but I'm ashamed to admit that, as I considered my own situation later that evening. I imagined it was worse than Camus'. The way I saw it, no one consciously chooses an accident, but few are forced by other than what my father always called "the weak excuse of 'circumstances'" to consider having an abortion—which was what everyone I knew in So Cal was advising, except, of course, Jillily and Moggy, whose blank stares when I posed the question made the most sense of all.

Kill a baby? Everything in me objected. Mine, as you well know, had been a home filled with saved babies, and if I'd been ordered to avoid that wing of our house, the sound of their screaming and laughing and *ugga umph uggas* was still the musical score to my first incarnation. I'd watched Baby Angelina pop from Dhani's oven and had fought to keep alive one Grandfather, one baby bird, and one very determined weed. I should have seen it as a sign when I pridefully pronounced myself beautiful at Sylvia Nava's party in a bathroom shared with a dying rose.

On the night before returning to the town of my second incarnation, I dreamt one long dream of intercourse and medical instruments, heartache and heavy water, a piteousness of doves. I awoke in a sweat, only to find Jillily crouching at the foot of the bed, eyeing me in horror, as if I might be considering putting *her* down, too.

It was an exhausted version of myself who boarded a flight at LAX with Stanley H. Fiske by my side. Stanley had confessed to me that he'd been thrown out of his own depth, too, and had even found himself retrieving an old childhood ritual—prayer—in hopes I would recover from this debacle with what he called my good and decent heart intact. He allowed, as well, that he'd offered a Hail Mary Full of Grace or two in the delusory fantasy that my mother and father would not look too unkindly upon him.

At that moment, I myself was not too concerned about the state of my heart. I was more concerned with my body—which seemed far too young to bear a child—and my good sense, which seemed far too lacking to raise one.

No, if there was anyone's heart I was worried about, it wasn't my own but Father's and what the effect of my news on his ailing ticker would be.

Chapter 18 🦋

LOSING SOMEONE TO death is one thing. You can fold them into the hole in your heart and feel something of them inside you. But how do you deal with losing the living?

Before confronting the problem of how to tell Father, I had to run the gauntlet of Nana and Mother and Sister Flatulencia and Fayga and Cook and Dhani and Ignacio and Baby Angelina and Cesar Jesus de Maria Santo Domingo Marisco. Mother came first, a weeping willow at our JFK arrival gate, every line in her lovely face pulling downward as if she'd fallen victim to heavy gravity.

Stanley H. Fiske had the grace to pry my fingers from my pink roll-on suitcase and step to the side just as Mother enclosed me in a hug worthy of Nana's fiercest Mack truck maulings. Neither of us said a word, but we did sway a bit and ended up scooting to the side like a four-footed beast when a tired traveler bumped against the bundle we'd become, saying, "Do you think you might you might have the decency to make room for a few other people? Some of us actually want to get out of here."

When we finally pulled apart, mostly because Mother's snot was matting the top of my head and making it itchier than a case of hives, I saw that her tears had intersected her wrinkles to trace a Tic-Tac-Toe format on her face. Resisting the temptation to pull out a pencil, I wiped the wetness away, seeing her sadness replaced by surprise.

"Oh, sweetheart, don't worry about me," she said. "It's you we're all worried about. You do need to know how much everyone loves you."

Those were dangerous words. As I believe I've mentioned, I'd been making as much use as possible of my drawer for unwanted thoughts, and words like *worry* and *love* were likely to spill everything out simultaneously. I started to flap, then Mother took my hands and cupped them in her own. "Fleur, we've failed you. *I've* failed you. But I'm not going to let you down this time. I know it's not easy, honey, but we'll work this out. I promise."

This was a new Mother, and while she seemed considerably more engaging than the old one, I didn't really know what to do with the change. I wanted to insert her words of care and concern somewhere safe inside me, but there was no existing outlet to plug them into. So, instead, I secretly pinched the fascia of my left palm and found comfort in the familiarity of self-inflicted pain.

What Mother meant by working things out remained to be seen. The ride to the home of my second incarnation was punctuated by variations of Stanley H. Fiske's abject apologies and Mother's mantra, "No, please, it's not your fault." Which, of course, it wasn't. That prerogative was mine, and each time they repeated their ritual, what Stephanie Seidenfeld had once referred to as my Venus Mound grew pinker and pinker with pinching. Stephanie, by the way, was a particular fan of palmistry, much to Adam's disgust. She'd told me I had an unusually long lifeline, which at this moment in time I seriously regretted. Why hadn't my own absurd fate followed the course of Camus'?

Our arrival at the penthouse made things all the more confusing. If Mother had acted out of character at the airport, Nana bested her by placing a gentle hand on my head when I walked in the door and suggesting I might like to rest awhile by myself in her bedroom. "You've had a long trip," she said to no one in particular, which I'm sure everyone realized was a euphemism for "Your life is falling apart and you've been captured by the void."

Nonetheless, I was happy to take her up on her offer and relieved to note that Cesar Jesus de Maria Santo Domingo Marisco was nowhere in sight. All I needed was a saved child rubbing my sinfulness in my face.

He did arrive later, though, accompanied back from his ice skating outing by Sister Flatulencia, who had no doubt demonstrated her agility on ice, which I remembered quite well, along with her legendary skills at limbo. By the time they returned, I had happily been plied with enough of Cook's angel food cake to momentarily lose my mind to the excitations of sugar and was listening with unaccustomed interest to the rest of the crew's small talk, most of it concerning the striking difference between the biting weather here and So Cal's unusually humid heat wave.

Dhani and Ignacio and No-Longer-a-Baby Angelina arrived promptly at six, and I said a silent thanks that the gathering seemed not to include Fred Forrest. While a baby killer trumps a cat killer in the monstrosity department, I knew I was never going to take kindly to the man. I did wonder, though, and suppose I still do, why Mother had to meet every crisis by committee, which might be fine when replacing an alcohol addiction with the company of Bill W.'s, but lacked a certain subtlety when it came to tiny tweeters and bulging members and wanted-but-unwanted babies.

I guess I had to learn the hard way—which Nana crudely described as "flat on your ass"—that babies cannot always be readily counted as wanted or unwanted. Just as I had both wanted and not wanted Hector Hernandez to peel off my pants and place his tongue on my belly button, I found that I both wanted this sad little burp of the meal he had made of me and wished the whole thing had never happened.

And while I would like to say that the not wanting was based on hard thinking and philosophical reflection, when push came to shove I could not imagine swelling up like Alice in Wonderland after her biscuit and propelling a watermelon-sized object out of my too-tiny-for-a-member tweeter. I couldn't wrest from my mind memories of Dhani collapsing into any available chair, claiming she was going to burst in half from the pressure of her ever-burgeoning bun. Nor could I bear the thought of childbirth postponing my search for the key to dematerialization. As for returning to Reed, my breasts were already busting through my C-cup; Lord knew what the boys in middle school would make of bigger boobs and an even bigger belly.

And yet, and yet, there was Once-a-Baby Angelina sitting across from me at the dining room table, her eyes shiny black pearls as she asked Dhani and Ignacio "Wha dis? Wha dis?" about everything in sight. I couldn't help but wonder if the bunlet in my belly might have eyes as dark and luminous as hers. Hector was, after all, quite a compelling looking boy. Besides, what if my baby's hint of a mind contained within it the capacity to create the cure for cancer? Spinal injuries? Diabetes?

What if he—or she—were the second coming of Christ? A creature at least as lovable as Jillily?

What if the soul of my bun was the re-incarnation of Grandfather himself?

Either way I went, the resolution of my dilemma was guaranteed to send me straight into the abyss. But one thing I knew for sure, I would not remain in the home of my second incarnation, sealing my fate to one of standstill. Baby-murderer-to-be or not, I was determined to pursue my own separate destiny. At least then I might justify the fact that Mother had not aborted *me*.

All these things I thought at the dining room table, not knowing that tears were making a sodden mess of my portion of Cook's delicious Quiche Lorraine. It was Cesar's small hand on my shoulder that jolted me back to the moment, his silly giggles stilled for once as he stared up at me. "You gotta boo-boo?" He ran around the table to Nana and butted her chest anxiously. "She gotta boo-boo. She gotta boo-boo."

But it wasn't Nana, or even Mother, who escorted me from the table, but Sister Flatulencia. She took me into Nana's room, sat me down beside Nana's comforting cave-ish robe on the extra twin bed, and had me tell her the whole story of how I'd gotten my bun. And if you think it was hard to tell the tale to an ex-Nun, you haven't reckoned on the power of Sister Flatulencia's flatulence. Her belly was rumbling so noisily as we sat there that I figured I'd better get the facts out fast, or I'd be drowned in the effluvium.

So this is what I said—I don't know if I took a breath the whole time: "I was trying to figure out how to bridge the molecular paradigm and string theory—especially the undoubted existence of multiple dimensions and its implications, you know, for the possibility of dematerialization—but Adam's eyes and Hector's bulging biceps kept getting in the way. I thought Stephanie was making fun of me, and that's when I made everything up about Hector. But then I realized he could help me make my mini-explosions just as easily as Adam. But I was too ashamed to tell anybody about that, and that's what I get for being such a private person. I should have listened to Adam and developed my social skills. And then there were these breasts and nobody at school liking me, so when I went to the party and everyone kept smiling and then the beer made me feel like Jillily having her belly rubbed. But not licked. First it was my ears and then my navel. I got so wet I worried I'd peed in my pants, but I had just gone to the bathroom. The red rose was dying. I should have known. The ring still hurts. Do you think I should take it out?"

Sister Flatulencia looked very perplexed. So much so that I guessed she'd forgotten to fart, because all I could smell was Chanel No. 5—which prompted me to look around and, sure enough, I saw that Mother and Nana had slipped into the room while I was talking. Of course, Nana had to lead me through the whole thing again, but this time I made a little more sense. And when I came to the pain of Hector's bulging member busting into my tiny tweeter, all three said, nearly in unison, "Why didn't you stop him?"

So I repeated about him whispering in my ear and how melty that made my body and how it was a relief to stop thinking that way about Adam. I continued, "When I tried to explain to Gwennie about the entanglement of Dove Soap, Hector's Jesus and Mary left hand, his Holy Spirit right one, and all those *linda palomas*, she said it was all just a coincidence and what did that have to do with unprotected sex, anyway?"

Nana broke in protectively, "She said that? What would she know? A typical old maid remark if I ever heard one."

But Mother, looking thoughtful, murmured, "Not coincidence. Synchronicity."

Nonplussed, Nana and Sister Flatulencia stared at her.

But I was intrigued. "What's synchronicity?" I asked.

Mother waved a hand as if she were erasing a blackboard. "Oh, don't ask me to explain it, Fleur. I'll get it all muddled up. I just know it has something to do with those times when everything comes together in one giant coincidence, but it isn't." She flushed. "A coincidence, I mean. You see what I mean?"

She was right about the muddling. I could see why Mother hadn't tried tutoring me herself. But she'd gotten me interested. As soon as I could, I looked up the word, which was quite gratifying, since synchronicity was right in line with Stanley H. Fiske's contention that life is pure paradox. The idea was developed by the Swiss psychiatrist Carl Jung in collaboration with his patient Wolfgang Pauli, the Nobel physicist whose concept of exclusion is foundational to all of chemistry. The two of them used the term synchronicity for the acausal connective principle relating to meaningfully coincidental events. Like a bar of soap, Annunciatory arms, and the sweet sound of *linda paloma*.

As it happens, Pauli's final days were marked by a meaningful coincidence of its own. Throughout his life, he had vexed himself with the question of why the fine structure constant, a kind of proportional fingerprint of the energy levels of any given element, has a value nearly equal to $1/137$. As the dying Pauli pointed out to his assistant, the number of his hospital room just happened to be 137.

Who knew that my remarks to Mother and Nana and Sister Flatulencia about the effect of all those doves on my tweeter would lead me to Pauli, whose stunning notion of nonrelativistic spin stimulated in turn a whole new slant on my pursuit of dematerialization? I felt fairly certain the synchronicity of it would undoubtedly have pleased both him and Jung, especially when you consider that the word vulva derives from the Latin root *volvere*, which means "to turn over in the mind."

But I hadn't come back to the home of my second incarnation for reflection. It was Sister Flatulencia who again proved her properties as one of the angels of my life by offering to accompany Stanley H. Fiske and me to Father's digs to present him with my predicament. Dressed less casually than usual in pressed black slacks and a tailored black jacket buttoned over a predictably froggish olive green shirt, Stanley was shaking as visibly as I felt, so I secretly thanked Jesus and Mary and multiple saints and sinners that Sister Flatulencia was with us. Of all the crew of my first incarnation, she was least intimidated by Father.

Father opened the door himself, an expression of shock overtaking his disturbingly thin face when he saw us. As if suddenly shy, he failed to ask why we were there, but informed us that Carmelita was busy in the kitchen and would undoubtedly want to include us in her latest attempt at the perfect flan.

As I watched him rush from the room, his old flannel trousers sagging where they used to be snug, my heart dove into my belly. He definitely did not look like a well man. How could I risk straining his already overworked ticker? But harsh reality is an equally demanding taskmaster. I knew there was no way to avoid delivering my news.

When Father returned to the living room, finally asking to what he owed the pleasure of our company—a rather formal greeting, I thought, for one who'd played horsies with me in that very same room only last spring—I found myself looking to Sister Flatulencia to break the ice. That wasn't exactly what she broke, but it had the same effect. Father rose again, saying it sure was cold outside and perhaps he should see if Carmelita might offer us hot tea along with our flan.

If I hadn't felt so impatient I would have flapped. Instead, I tried recalling how many circuits of the room Father's fine steed and my own pony had traveled, until Stanley piped up bleakly, "I guess it's really up to me."

Neither Sister Flatulencia nor I offered much of an argument, so when Father reappeared with his tea tray, Carmelita fast behind him to set down four appetizing looking flan cups, Stanley H. Fiske began coughing and hacking like Arthur Ramos's old clunker, as if priming an engine that barely had an ounce of go. Sister Flatulencia tactfully took Carmelita's arm and steered her out of the room.

Father sat beside me, smiling awkwardly, still in what is curiously called blissful ignorance. Stanley H. Fiske cleared his throat all over again, worrying me that he might actually mutate into a frog, and then where would I be? Instead, he managed to compose himself for an arguably apt introduction. "Actually, we've got a bit of bad news for you."

Father said, "Is it Margaret?" in a worried tone that was a bit of a shock itself.

Stanley, his jump-started car struggling to pick up steam, said, "No, no. Nothing like that." Cough. "It's my fault, of course. Not a proper amount of supervision. I had no idea, out of the modern loop, so to speak, and I don't mean vibrating strings. Or that thingamajig in her navel, for that matter." Cough, cough. "For which I should also probably take responsibility. Dumb, when you think of it. Forgot she's only thirteen. It's her mind, you see. It fools you." Cough, hack, bring handkerchief out of pocket and pass it across the mouth just in time. Croakily now: "I'd hate me myself if I were you. Simply unforgivable."

Father looked at him blankly.

"Yes, well anyway, the long and short of it is that our Fleur's gotten into a bit of a situation. Way over her head. And, needless to say, way too young. I feel awful."

I had to give Father some credit. He said what any rational person would. "For God's sake man, can't you get on with it? What has the child done?"

"Well, it's not exactly what she's done as what's come of it." His face matching his shirt now, Stanley forced out the words, "I'm afraid she's pregnant."

Father's face was a mask of disbelief. "Pregnant?" he said wonderingly, as if he couldn't quite fathom it. Then his voice shifted to something decidedly Darth Vader-ish. "What have you been playing at? Taking my daughter out to California and letting someone molest her? I hope to God it wasn't you." Somehow both men were standing now, Father barely restraining his fists at his sides.

Stanley stepped back, waving his hands in front of him. "No, no, not me, man. What do you think I am? No, it was a boy not much older than Fleur. Not a bad kid, really, just a little fast for the likes of our Fleur."

"Our Fleur? Our Fleur? Since when is my daughter your Fleur?"

At last the moment had come. Father looked down at me as if I were something small and squashable, a toddler underfoot. "How could you do this to me?" The venom in his gaze nearly took my breath away. "Didn't you learn anything from your own beginnings? Look what a wreck it made of your mother. Who's going to bail you out of this mess and support the two of you?" He struck a finger-wagging pose reminiscent of one of his old campaign posters, the one with the slogan *Thou Shalt Not Murder* from the Ten Commandments. Actually, some scholars think there were more than ten and some claim there was an earlier set of commandments, a document called *The Ritual Decalogue*, its final prohibition being *Do Not Cook a Goat in Its Mother's Milk*, which I'd have thought was only decent under the circumstances. As, of course, is the prohibition against murder—which is why it was hard to argue with Father.

But I did. "Father, what if there won't be a two of me? Just me. I don't think I should have this baby."

His eyebrows flew up. "You've got to be joking."

"No, Father. I am very sorry and very upset, so this is definitely not a joke. Not unless you are Camus. But I doubt he laughed much, anyway."

I saw a purplish vein in Father's neck begin to beat ominously. "Camus! Is that the boy's name? If the little sonofabitch were here,

I'd wring his goddamned neck. Creeps like that ought to be hung." As I may have mentioned, despite his habit of citing the Bible's prohibition against killing, Father seemed to have no problem with capital punishment. Nor much of a memory of having proffered the seed for my teenaged Mother's only bun.

Without warning, Father stepped forward and caught the side of Stanley H. Fiske's face with his fist. I was relieved to see that Stanley seemed unfazed, if suddenly somewhat sunburned looking, or at the least the kind of sunburn where you fall asleep at the beach with the umbrella only covering half of you. Thank God, he showed no wish to retaliate, though that seemed to even further infuriate Father, who looked around for who else was handy.

Before I knew it, my face was stinging bitterly, and the void descended on me until I heard, as if from a long distance, "My, God, man, you hit your own child," then Sister Flatulencia's "How could you?" followed quickly by Father's "Why not? She's a slut! Get her out of here." And suddenly, as close to my throbbing ear as Hector's world-changing whispers, Father let loose a flow of verbiage along with gobs of sticky spittle. "Don't come running to me when you realize the damage you've done. You're not my daughter, do you hear me? Don't you ever come here again."

There is an expression Sister Flatulencia used to utter when we'd walk home from watching an old time western at Classic Movie Night at the Majestic. It was *Saved by the cavalry*.

This time, though, it wasn't the cavalry, but Mother, who later said she hadn't been able to sit at home a second longer. I guess she knew firsthand how Father was likely to react. Coiled now on the couch, I heard a banging on the front door and peeked from behind my elbow to see an adrenalinated Father leap across the room to fling it open.

The Mother who came into the room was a force of nature. Taking in my face, which, quite frankly, felt less like a face than meat personally tenderized by Cook's wooden pounder, Mother visibly grew a foot or two. I made a mental note to reflect on this at some later date—so to speak, *vulvistically*. Right then, though, was certainly not the time. Mother's voice was deep and loud enough to bring a quaking Carmelita out of the kitchen. "Don't you ever, EVER lay a hand on her again." She stood up on tippy toes to face Father eyeball to eyeball. "If you do, Frank, I swear I will kill you."

Altogether, this was way too much talk of killing. No one could stop my flapping now, not Mother, not Stanley, not Sister Flatulencia. Father did manage to deliver his parting shot, however, as they hustled me out the door.

"I meant what I said. I never want to see your brat again."

Into my bottomless pit of loss fell two quite dissimilar objects: Father's horse and Father's ticker. I could not help but reflect that—despite their disparate weights, and thanks to the unique properties of gravity—should there actually be a bottom, they would both land in hell at the very same time.

I let my mother stroke my hair all the way home. For once, I did not mind that she was crying. If anything, it was rather cathartic, since I could not cry myself.

Instead, I was preoccupied with what I was planning to do to my bun. The truth was, for all my bravado with Father, I was not so confident about the conclusion I'd come to. Ever since Mother and Nana had said the decision was up to me, I'd thought I'd pretty much known what I needed to do, but now I wasn't so sure.

My hesitancy revealed a further flaw in the abortion debate. If Father and his pro-life friends tended to single out fetuses for their more tender feelings, the pro-abortion contingent certainly didn't advertise the agonies of making the little spark of new life in one's own belly die.

Over the next few days, the mood in Mother's penthouse mimicked the weather. Manhattan was encapsulated in a dismal mist, and reports from So Cal of a persisting heat wave seemed as Martian as Leland Du Ray's footless baby clothes. Things were sufficiently somber that Nana elected to send Cesar for a sleepover at a schoolmate's, but it was clear that she was missing him. I knew that Stanley H. Fiske was chomping at the bit to get back, though he kindly kept his presence to a minimum, spending hours debating the finer points of particle accelerators with his old colleagues at NYU. Though I could see no outer signs of my pregnancy but burgeoning breasts and an exaggeration of my already overdeveloped sense of smell, I knew my bun wasn't getting any smaller.

On the third morning, I woke to ask if anyone had time to drive me to the Cookery School. Something told me I might benefit from returning to my roots. When Nana said, "They're closed on Sundays," I replied, "I know," to which she responded, "Well, you might bump into Dhani. I know for a fact she's rehearsing a lesson on Indian cooking." I looked at Mother, who was busy pushing scrambled eggs around her plate.

Avoiding eye contact, she claimed she was committed to speaking at a meeting of Bill W.'s that day. I suspect she dreaded setting foot on Father's old grounds. Mother looked at Nana. Nana looked at Sister Flatulencia, who'd been camping at our penthouse ever since Father's fit. Sister Flatulencia said, "I'll take you." I was pleasantly surprised. I had been worrying she might detest me for contemplating contravening the Pope's command. But just to make sure, as she drove us out of the parking garage, I asked, "Do you hate me?"

Flashing me the quickest of looks—Sister Flatulencia was a cautious driver and tended to be rather religious about keeping her eyes on the road—she said, "Hate you? Why would I hate you?"

"For...you know." I placed a hand on my still-flat belly and slid a few feet into the void before she responded with a heavy sigh.

"Oh, that. Maybe in the past I would have been angry, but I'm certainly not now. Everything seemed so much simpler then, but, frankly, I always found the old black and white a little cold." She laughed without humor. "So many don'ts. Of course, it went without saying that sex was unmentionable. Outside of marriage it was unthinkable, and abortion was pure abomination. Despite all the pieties about hating the sin but loving the sinner, I witnessed enough hate to populate hell several times over." She reached up to scratch her head, absentmindedly tucking a tendril of kinky hair back inside her bandana. "Frankly, Fleur, I can't see anything you've done as a sin. Foolish, yes. No, not foolish. Naïve. Young. But you're in a rather wide company there." Sister Flatulencia braked rather suddenly as the light ahead went from yellow to red. Turning to face me, she put a hand on my cheek. "No," she said wonderingly, as if she'd just discovered it, "I'm just sad. Very, very sad."

Even though we both ended up crying a little, her comments were a great help. Evidently, I wasn't the only one who'd gone through several incarnations. I was never quite sure how much of a singular duck I really was.

Once we got to the grounds, I thought I'd made a mistake in coming. The Austins were drooped over their invisible beds with an excess of melancholic moisture. Anne Boleyn, whose namesake's miscarried baby boy may well have contributed to her beheading, and the baby bird I'd buried beside her did nothing to enliven my mood.

Baby Eros and his erupting little member only reminded me of my moments with Hector Hernandez, and the glowering fish in the first fountain still glowered. Further along the path, I realized someone must have had a field day with herbicides—I couldn't find even one descendent of my original hardy weed. Shielding my eyes from what was fast becoming a steady drizzle, I hurried past the spot where the tree beloved to me and Grandfather had once hosted innumerable flocks of birds. I was overcome with the urge to return to the penthouse. How foolish I'd been to think I'd find anything but loss here.

I went looking for Sister Flatulencia inside the school, finding Dhani instead, sweating over a pot of something that smelled Masala-ish at one of the vast kitchen's Viking stoves. No-Longer-a-Baby Angelina sat on a stool beside her, licking honey from her delicate fingers.

Dhani exclaimed, "Oh, my gull!" as soon as she saw me, rushing over to give me a one-armed hug as she held aloft a dripping ladle. "I've just been thinking of you," she said. "Sweet child, I couldn't believe it when your nana told me. What a dreadful boy—I simply can't imagine…how are you doing?"

What could I say? I couldn't take my eyes off Angelina. Light shone from her mischievous eyes like two bright moons. Dhani flung her ladle with a loud clank into the sink. She grabbed hold of my hand and, yanking it with emphasis with every word, decreed, "Better days will come again, my love. I swear it. Tell me what I can do. Anything. Anything at all." I shook my head, warmed too much by her kindness to feel safe to speak. I watched her pad in her stockinged feet to the fridge to retrieve a big stainless steel bowl, from which she spoon-fed me a few swallows of some nearly-set rice pudding while Angelina laughed as if it were the funniest thing in the world.

After I chicken-pecked a giggling Angelina all over the top of her honey-sticky head, Dhani and I said a series of lingering goodbyes. Dhani extracted a promise from me to call her any time I wanted, day or night. A part of me could have stayed in that kitchen forever.

Not sure whether I felt lighter or heavier, I went looking for Sister Flatulencia in the saved babies' wing. There were no hints of its previous incarnation as a refuge for that peripatetic population, save the faint scent of sour milk somehow surviving remodeling and multiple coats of new paint. Returning to the private wing, I paused for a pee in my old bathroom, watching my urine swirl down the hole I'd once feared would swallow me, and washed my hands with—what else?—Dove soap in the sink bedecked with hand painted flowers. I stared at my face in the mirror. My features were more elongated than when I last stood here but somehow a little fuzzy looking, as if they hadn't quite settled into what they were aiming for. At that moment, it occurred to me that, really, I had no choice at all. I was not finished with my own childhood, odd thing that it was. It wasn't much, but it *was* mine.

Father's rage gurgled from the black hole inside me, saying how could I be so selfish? Why couldn't I give birth to my baby and let some one else save it? He was right, of course, but the thought of having the child and giving it away sounded crippling. But wouldn't killing the child do the same, or worse?

Someone knocked on the door, and I opened it. "There you are." Sister Flatulencia's green face told its own story. I quickly traded places with her, hearing a trumpet of ominous wet farts echoing from the bathroom the moment she locked the door.

We were silent as we drove away, both of us presumably preoccupied by thoughts of the silent third presence in my belly. No one was home when we got back to the penthouse. Sister Flatulencia distractedly said she was going to take a walk, which in this weather struck me as more of an excuse for flight than pleasurable excursion.

On my side, I was only too relieved to be left in peace to ferret out Mother's etymological dictionary. It seemed suddenly essential to see what the scholars had to say. What they added to my inner debate was more nuance than news, but their ambulation around the word *abortion* managed to move things forward in my mind. I learned that the word referred to something not arising, and that the words *abortion* and *miscarriage* were once used interchangeably. Only later was the distinction made between spontaneous abortion, typically caused by fetal defects, and the planned variety, which arose, I supposed, from defective mothers.

I thought and thought about my baby not arising. About whether that would leave her subject to suffocation by a kind of compressed void. I realized I was already thinking of her as a *she*. Was I right? I suppose I'll never know. But sometimes, as Stanley H. Fiske liked to say, "you've just gotta go with your hunches." I had a hunch, all right. It was that the soul of my child would be in danger if I didn't find a roomy enough place for her, so when Grandfather's hands reached forward, his eyes all soft and melty, how could I possibly say, "No?"

The inside of my heart was getting crowded. I did not want to suffer any more loss. I suppose that was why I tried visiting Father a couple of times before returning to So Cal. The first attempt was the day after he hit me, and the second on the way to airport. Mother was kind enough to have our limo wait at the curb. On neither of those occasions would Father come to the door. I knew he was standing there, right on the other side of it. I don't know how I knew it, but I did.

Mother had offered to come back to So Cal with me. I knew she cared about me, but I couldn't imagine having her perfect Chanel Infrarouge lips anywhere near my face at a time when my upper lip was likely to become a pool of runny snot at the foot of a teary waterfall. We simply didn't have that kind of physical connection. I fancied she was a little relieved when I said no. Nana, I might have said yes to. But—possibly out of deference to Mother—she hadn't offered, and somewhere inside me I knew that Gwennie Fiske's kindness and practicality would carry me through.

Mother and Nana were joined by Sister Flatulencia and Cook and Fayga and Dhani and Ignacio and Angelina (but not Cesar, who was in school) when they came to the airport to send me off. They all kept brave smiles on their faces, but I knew they wanted me to know they shared the heaviness of my heart as I struggled to prepare myself for what I'd decided to do.

Alas, their hope was contravened by another lesson I was learning in what Nana called The School of Hard Knocks. As much as we may have angels in our lives, we face our most difficult moments alone. My mind was a movie projector in a darkened theater, picturing various permutations of my bun being dismembered. I wished she could dissolve decently, with a soft little pop like a Dove soap bubble, but I knew her demise would be messy and violent. Were Father and his friends right? Were her nerves and brain sufficiently developed to signal pain?

There are moments when even the void looks good.

Chapter 19 🦋

FOREVER A FAN OF CLICHÉS, Nana had whispered to me before I'd boarded my plane, "Hang in there, kid. When things feel this bad, they can only get better."

Whoever had first coined that phrase hadn't been living my life.

Gwennie was waiting for Stanley and me at a prearranged point in front of one of LAX's maze of parking structures. As soon as we stuffed out bags into the back of her Prius and belted ourselves in, Gwennie locked eyes with me in the rearview mirror. Heaving a great sigh, she said, "I might as well tell you now. Things took a turn for the worse for our dear Moggy while you were gone." She bit her lower lip. "There's no other way to say it. She's gone."

I saw Stanley take off his glasses to wipe his eyes. As for me, I kept my own hands busy roughly pinching my thigh as Gwennie sought to reassure me that Amir had followed my infusion instructions to the letter, but that nature had won out in the end. She shook her head. "What it comes down to is that it was *Moggy's time to go.*" The silence that followed her little speech spoke volumes. It would soon be time for my bun to go, but nature had nothing to do with it.

Once we got to Rose Villa, Jillily eloquently expressed her own sentiments about my desertion by keeping her back to me the whole time I unpacked, tail twitching furiously until I circled the room several times on hands and feet, sniffing my way toward her crossed white paws in abject apology. From then on, though, she proved to be a great comfort, doing an especially thorough clean-up job of my salty face as I lay on my bed, having mental arguments with Father in anticipation of what Stanley and Gwennie had taken to calling "your procedure." It was a battle I couldn't win.

Euphemisms, of course, are useless in certain circumstances. I myself was sticking with the term abortion, especially as it pertained to deformity, which I figured said all there was to say about the state of my mortal soul.

I'm sorry to say I was at least a little tempted to cut my veins and join my baby in the ether, so I was actually relieved when, on the morning that Gwennie went to Whole Foods to stock up for Easter break, I found myself cutting off most of my hair instead.

When Gwennie came home a few hours later to find a snarly nest of hair on the bathroom floor, she gave a giant gasp and cried because she couldn't brush my long locks before bedtime anymore. She blurted out that I looked like a boy now, then apologized, but I thought it made a certain sense, since what had being a female brought me, anyway?

But when Adam came to visit that night he said he thought I looked chic, like Jean Seberg in *Breathless*. As if I'd stabbed my hair out of vanity.

Mostly though, he kept trying to interest me in Tom and Gunther's recent attendance at a lecture by biophysicist Misuo Hiramatsu, who'd discovered that human hands, foreheads, and foot bottoms emit a measurable glow. The rest of our team was hoping that we might harness that light in propelling people into the void for purposes of dematerialization. In the mood I was in, I wanted to say we needn't go to all that trouble to accomplish the task.

Amir knocked on my bedroom door a few nights after that, wondering if there was anything he could do to bolster my spirits. It was the night before my operation, and, thanks to Father's voice squeaking away inside me, I couldn't think of anything but my bun's upcoming capital punishment for the crime of being born to an abortion of a mother. I turned my head to the wall and refused to respond.

Stanley tiptoed into my room a little while later and sat on the edge of my bed, pulling Jillily onto his lap and making her motor while he mentioned to me a few things he thought I should know. "My dear girl, you will get past this," he said. "I know this is the most awful moment of your life, but you are as strong as they come. I learned a thing or two about your past from your nanny, Fleur. I had no idea. Listen to me…" He gently pried me away from the wall and rolled me over. I was ashamed to be seen with my face as bloated and red as a Valentine's balloon. I'd read a few months before in Manchester's *A World Lit Only by Fire* that we celebrate the obscure Saint Valentine solely as a Catholic replacement for the pagan holiday Lupercalia, when girls were whipped with thongs of sacrificed flesh to ensure fertility and ease the pains of childbirth.

I doubted they had any handy rituals to ease the pains of abortion.

"You are not doing anything wrong." Stanley said.

Who did he think he was kidding? Stanley H. Fiske might be a magician, but he could hardly erase the sin from my heart.

"I know you're blaming yourself, Fleur, but I think you're old enough now to understand that sometimes life is simply unfair. Well, maybe not simply, but certainly without meaning or reason."

When it became clear I wasn't going to respond, he stood and said, pretty pathetically I thought, "Well, at least you'll have all of Easter vacation to recover."

That one, at least, mobilized speech. I flung a feeble, "Well I certainly won't be dyeing any Easter eggs" at the door as he left the room.

As soon as Gwennie and I arrived next morning at the deceptively tidy facility where Dr. Raker would do her dirty work, I was ushered away by a nurse with a wart on her cheek shaped like a miniature steamship. She had me undress in an Eau-de-Lysol bathroom. I emerged in a cotton gown that barely covered my rear end, which, along with my arms, was covered in goose bumps. Captain Nurse had me slide onto a gurney. It was while she struggled with the curtain around my bed that I caught a glimpse of the dark-haired girl in the bed next to me, who, even without her black mascara and red, red lipstick, bore a distinct resemblance to Sylvia Nava.

I couldn't help it. As soon as the nurse had inserted my saline drip—a lot more ruggedly, I thought, than how I'd managed Moggy's—I stretched the fingertips of my other arm to push aside the curtain. Yup. It was Sylvia. She looked at me uncomprehendingly for a second or two, then her eyes widened in horror. "Oh, shit," she said. "Dude, don't tell Hector. If this gets around…You've got to promise me, kid. If my dad finds out, he'll kill me."

I nearly laughed at the irony. Instead, letting the curtain slip from my hand, I found myself fighting panic, wanting to shout, "No! Stop! I don't want to do this!" But the drip had done its work. I couldn't seem to find the breath to move my lips, and my eyelids felt heavier and heavier. They simply would not stay open.

The next thing I knew, Gwennie was holding a plastic pan under my chin as I puked and puked until I was heaving a whole lot of nothing. I didn't even think about Sylvia again until I returned to school the following week.

That particular Monday began poorly, with Hector accosting me before I could even cross the threshold of our drama classroom. "Wait," he hissed. "Sylvia said she saw you at the clinic." So much for Sylvia's consistency. "It wasn't mine, was it? I hope you're not gonna go around saying I raped you or something. You know you wanted it as much as I did." Then, in a stunning shift of topic, "Hey, your hair looks cute like that."

I don't know that I have ever felt so confused. But I couldn't be bothered anymore with Hector Hernandez. I was too preoccupied with my dead baby and my Father. The former was at least cradled in the arms of Grandfather. The latter had become a haunting presence, throwing accusatory epithets into every spare room of my mind.

Chapter 20 🦋

THE ENSUING SIX weeks were marked by what Gwennie took to calling a Class A Case of the Doldrums. You might have thought that Stanley making arrangements for me to take my high school equivalency exams and enter Caltech in September would have lifted my spirits, that the prospect of being able to focus nearly fulltime on the problem of dematerialization would have galvanized a better mood. But I was pretty much mired in the conviction that nothing I might accomplish scientifically would hold a candle to all I'd managed to destroy. Oh, I continued to work with Adam and Amir and Katrina and Tom and Gunther on our project, and we actually made some progress during that time, but my heart had gone missing and I wasn't particularly moved to go looking for it. I knew any chance of future happiness was gone.

As it happens, I was wrong. For all its lasting impact, the turning point—otherwise known as *vertex* and etymologically rooted in the images of whirling columns and whirlpools—snuck in rather prosaically on an unusually sticky So Cal June day. The latest heat wave hadn't cracked an inch, confirming our melancholy conviction that global warming was all too real. Even the Fiskes' normally efficient central air was losing the battle against the devilish humidity.

I was sprawled across the living room sofa in my gym shorts and a sports bra, leafing rather dispiritedly through a copy of Rilke's *Duino Elegies* propped atop my bulbous breasts. In my post-non-partum depression, not even David Oswold's elegant translation could excite me. On the contrary, the book kept slipping down my sweaty stomach to my navel ring, which I'd kept to remind me of my villainy.

Gwennie was draped equally lethargically across the living room's oversized armchair—a dog-eared Dorothy Sayers in one hand, a Diet Coke in the other—when something sounding like a smallish bomb gave me a start, causing my falling book to nearly decapitate a sleeping Jillily, who shot out of the room with remarkable alacrity for someone previously committed to all-out torpor. Gwennie frowned after the cat and looked back at me. "What was that about?"

"The noise."

"What noise?"

Gwennie's hearing was definitely not improving. But now I was sufficiently curious to force myself up from the couch, pulling my damp shorts out of their Murphy before I reached the front window. A Starving Students moving van in the driveway of the house opposite ours was the main event, the opening of its rear doors clearly the source of the sound. A whining motor signaled the lowering of a ramp from the back of the van. A bandanna-headed man looking nothing short of miserable came down it, bearing a pair of matching table lamps with pink paisley shades.

Simultaneously, a girl about my age with a shiny black ponytail emerged from the rear of a seriously dented burgundy Volvo station wagon parked unevenly in front of the house. She lugged a plastic cat carrier through the front door as if it weighed a hundred pounds. When she came back out again, she turned to look in my direction as if some sixth sense had alerted her to my gaze. Without a moment's hesitation, she waved. My hand rose in response before she disappeared into the house again.

Despite Gwennie clamoring, "What is it? Who's out there?" I stood rooted to the spot, making up a little tune under my breath to Lewis Carroll's *ugga-umphic* "*Oh, frabjous day! Callou! Callay!*"

The rest of the day passed uneventfully, and, when Stanley came home, I went about setting the table just as I did every night. But, a half hour later, a knock at the door interrupted Stanley and me just as we were trying to fit the last of our rather underdone peas into a couple of straws. Stanley was bent on proving to Gwennie that her peas were more suited to shooting than human digestion. "That'll be

Amir and Adam. Better get it," Stanley sighed. Despite his age, he did so like to tease his sister. I saw Gwennie's relief as I ran to the door.

But it wasn't my physics pals but the girl from that morning, smiling as confidently as she had earlier. "Hell-o," she said, in an accent reminiscent of Dhani's. She stuck out a hand. "I'm your new neighbor. My mum said, 'For heaven's sake, you can't be wanting to intrude on strangers at the dinner hour; for all we know they're private people,' but I told her, 'No, Mum, the girl waved at me. She's clearly the friendly sort.' Honestly, between you and me, I've been aching to pop over ever since I saw you."

The girl was talking quite quickly, but if anything it made her seem more interesting. Catching a quick breath, she went on. "Two months in Boston and another in Costa Mesa with not a moment's conversation with anyone under thirty. My mum and dad's parents are loves and the blokes and birds at M.I.T were terribly sweet, but, really, a girl could go batty with all that infinite dimensional control systems tra-la. I'm Sammie, by the bye. Must be more chuffed than I thought to be so rude."

Sammie she was. Or to put it more accurately, Lakshmie Samara Rachael Schwartz. But I learned soon enough that, except for her mother—who usually referred to her as Flake, after Cadbury's melty chocolate stick—she liked people to call her Sammie.

As soon as Sammie said her name, I told her mine. Her response took me aback. "Fleur? Now isn't that brilliant? Dad said my very first word was *flower*, after seeing an arrangement of roses on my first birthday. Pretty prophetic, given the garden we inherited when we moved to Primrose Hill. Our dining table was eternally awash in petals. Alas, they usually ended up coming out with the rest of Midget's regurgitated grub. Thank goodness you don't have a quarantine. The UK is simply over the top where rabies are concerned."

I wanted to invite her in, but was afraid I'd be rude if I interrupted her. So I slowly backed into the living room, and fortunately she seemed to get the message and followed me.

All the while, she continued her lilting patter. The frothy quality of her voice set my favorite kind of goose bumps in motion across my scalp.

She gave an emphatic little shake of her hair, which—free now from its ponytail—fell across her forehead in graceful waves. "Mum is convinced that roses are the only flowers worth cultivating. That was one of her primary reservations about moving to the States. She had this picture in her mind of nothing but kitschy palm trees, until one of her friends reminded her that Pasadena is hardly a backwater, and besides, thanks to a bloke called David Austin, the old fashioned ones have made a rather spectacular comeback here. And so they should. They're dazzling." She stopped a moment and cocked her head. "You're quite a stunner yourself, you know. I wish I could wear my hair like that, but with these ears I'd look like a pot with oversized handles. I'm not surprised you're called Fleur."

While she caught a breath, I had a moment to reflect on Sammie's rather florid forwardness, but of course, once she confessed her fondness for my favorite flowers, she could have announced she was a mass murderer and I still would have been disposed to like her.

As I backed my way into the dining room, Sammie managed to introduce herself equally effortlessly to Stanley and Gwennie, earning a seat at the table, from which Gwennie speedily swept all evidence of her brother's folly. Accepting a glass of milk with a grateful "cheers" and munching appreciatively on Gwennie's four star carrot cake, Sammie proceeded to regale the three of us with a hair-raising story of a flight across the Atlantic climaxed by an alarming five hour detention at Logan Airport, her mother evidently sharing the name of a suspected terrorist.

She explained how they'd spent two months in Boston fruitlessly awaiting the return of some of their supposedly lost luggage. The two of them had been staying with Sammie's paternal grandparents in Orange County ever since, as Sammie put it, "to re-gather our wits and kit ourselves up with some new clothes to replace the ones pilfered by the FBI or CIA or whoever thinks a five foot tall woman who literally would not kill a fly and her frightfully jet-lagged daughter are a threat to your national security."

I couldn't help but notice that, as Sammie sat with one leg crossed over the other, her foot jiggled even faster than she talked. She gave an apologetic little smile. "Please don't think I'm insensitive to what happened at the Trade Center. We didn't have a telly and Mum and Dad were trying to keep the day special—horrid luck, as it turned out, having been born on September 11—but I saw enough of what was in the *Guardian* the day afterwards to fall sick for a week, and believe me it wasn't the birthday cake. Mum called it 'unimaginable evil.'"

She stopped for a moment, as if to make room for all of us to say a little silent prayer, but—like a force of nature—she couldn't seem to stop herself for long. "But I suppose some did, didn't they?" she said. "Imagine it, I mean."

Stanley gave a grim grunt of acknowledgement.

Sammie frowned. "I've heard some people say they're worse than dogs, but what dog in his right mind would do such a thing? When we paid our respects last month—we couldn't exactly be that close and not visit the site, could we?—Mum swore she could still hear the screams. But what followed, well, it's just that many of us tend to have a rather different perspective in Europe." She stopped, looking around the table guiltily. "But I forget. Mum keeps reminding me we're in a whole new world now and until I get acclimatized to what the natives do and don't believe—they say that your President might well have stolen the election. I hate to think that's true—it *is* supposed to be a democracy. I know I should keep *shtum* about things like Iraq and torture and Mr. Bush, but still. Anyway, where was I? Oh yes, back in Costa Mesa. Just as well, really, since Mum *did* have to learn how to drive a car four times the size of our old Mini on what we still can't help but see as the wrong side of the road, and my gran was probably the only person who had sufficient patience, thank God, to stay pat in the passenger seat while Mum put more than a few dings in that lovely Volvo estate."

Within half an hour, Sammie had made it clear she shared my love of David Austins, Gwennie's politics, and Stanley's fondness for the value of doubt. But, ultimately, it was her disarming openness that won all three of us over. After we finished our dessert, Gwennie excused Sammie and me with a beaming, "I know you girls will have a lot to talk about."

Sammie followed me eagerly down the hall, and before I knew it, she had inspected every inch of my room, admiring my assorted posters and complimenting me on my taste in literature. At my invitation, she installed herself comfortably cross-legged on my bed, where she continued to gab a mile a minute, stroking an obviously smitten Jillily's tummy.

Amongst other things I learned that evening was the fact that, though her vocabulary was that of a highly literate adult, Sammie wasn't even thirteen. The fact that she'd been born on September 11 was to be one of the many bonds between us. Growing up, my own birthday was never been celebrated with much fanfare, coming only four days before Christmas—a fate I share with Josef Stalin. It isn't exactly something I like to advertise.

Anyway, I was disappointed to learn that Sammie wasn't particularly interested in physics, but despite that flaw she was clearly what Gwennie called *bright as a button* (which only works as an image if you're not wearing, as I was when Gwennie first employed the figure of speech, a blouse with decidedly dull wooden buttons). I found it quite entertaining that she was such a non-stop talker, and I was more than a little thrilled to discover that, like me, she was a non-stop reader, keeping several books going at a time. Plus, she was a certified lover of cats. She said her own cat was called Midget, which she allowed was a misnomer, since Midget weighed a good twenty pounds and liked nothing more than to lumber onto his hind legs at the dinner table and lay an upended paw on your lap. Which was why the cat's second name was *Beggar.*

As we sat on my bed that first night, we compared notes on our backgrounds. After I explained that the Fiskes weren't actually my parents, Sammie wanted to know how I could stand being so far from Mother and Father and how they could stand being apart from me.

It felt like way too long a story, so I merely replied, assuming an airy tone, "Oh, it's not like we were some happy little family. My parents are divorced." When I saw Sammie's face fall with genuine sympathy, I felt awful for pretending to be so cavalier. "Oh, it's really not that bad," I hastened to add. "Better, really. He was horrible to her. Now he's free to travel all time, giving his big spiel against abortion. He used to be a Republican senator. You may have heard of him. He's one of the darlings of the religious right." I took some satisfaction in Sammie's expression of disapproval, pushing down my own disgust for killing my bun with a secretive little pinch of the outside of my thigh.

I forced myself to continue. "Believe me, my mother's hardly pining away with loneliness. She goes to meetings a lot—she's in AA—and she has tons of people around the house all the time. Actually, it's a regular United Nations back there. I've got a nanny whose family was from Ireland; she's adopted a boy whose mother came from El Salvador; then there's Dhani and Ignacio, who used to be our cook and our gardener. Ignacio's from Mexico, and Dhani comes from Islington...well, really, she was born in Delhi."

Sammie perked up immediately. "That's brilliant!" she cried. "I was born in Jaipur myself." She added with some pride, stoking Jillily with extra zeal, "I'm a bit of a mongrel, actually. My Indian mum and Jewish father met while they were both working for Amnesty International. We moved to England when I was just a few months old." That explained her complexion, which was a coffee color just a teaspoon of cream lighter than Dhani's, and which—when I complimented her on it—prompted her to confide in me that some of her Orange County neighbors had asked her which part of Africa she came from and one idiot at the South Coast Plaza actually referred to her as "nigger."

Given how much of a talker Sammie was, I was surprised at her silence when I asked about *her* family. The overlong pause explained itself soon enough. "I'm an *only*, too," she finally said, "so nobody to fight for the best bedroom or the last slice of Yorkshire pud. My mum's been hired to teach at Caltech, which she never would have accepted if my dad hadn't died last year in a rather remote part of Indonesia for want of a simple tetanus shot." The flatness of her tone spoke volumes about the hole in her heart. But then she shrugged and said, "Mum's name's Aadita, by the way. She says she and my dad and I were meant to be a threesome from the beginning of time and we'll be connecting again down the cosmic road, so I might as well stop dwelling on the past. That's one thing about Mum. She's a lot more broad-minded than her interest in boring maths might suggest."

I forgave Sammie soon enough for her dismissal of math and science as boring, especially once she listened with what looked like genuine interest to my explanation of our team's pursuit of dematerialization, commenting with a cocked head, "You've got a mind like a composer, don't you? It works in layers, like a symphony." That, plus the way she threw her arms around me at the end of the evening, declaring, "I believe I've found my best ever best friend," left me breathless with joy.

When Stanley insisted on walking her back across the street, I heard her shout as they stepped onto the sidewalk, "I can't wait for you to meet my mum." I thought at the time, *if her mum's anything like Sammie, I can't wait, myself.*

I paid my first visit to Sammie's new digs the very next afternoon. She flung open the door, revealing a beamed entry hall and a living room bulging with boxes. Jasmine incense stole into my nostrils. As soon as she saw it was me, Sammie said a hearty "Oh, goody," then grabbed my hand and led me down a long hallway, lit from above by a series of skylights. "Mum's dying to meet you. When I told her about the Austins she nearly fell over. I'm sure Midget's around here somewhere. Do you think he and Jillily might get on?"

But, before I could answer, I was being tugged into a room so jam-packed with containers that I could barely see the diminutive woman fussing with a computer in the far corner. "Blast and damn," she muttered. The truly obese cat on her desk jumped down with a thud, causing the woman to look up. I couldn't tell where the cat disappeared to, probably somewhere behind a row of boxes. The woman ran a hand through her silken gray hair. "Bloody hell," she grumbled. Then, "Sorry. Flake, maybe you can do something with this thing. The man from the cable company promised it was ready to go." Then she put her head to one side, released the wrinkles from her face, smiled crookedly, and, brushing crumbs from her lap, stood up and angled through a narrow aisle toward us. "And you are Fleur. How perfect that Flake found you on our very first day."

Remembering Nana's admonitions about meeting adults, I said, "Pleased to meet you, Mrs. Schwartz."

At which she snorted, "Oh, heavens not. The gray hair's bad enough. I'd much prefer it if you called me Aadita." Before I knew it, two graceful brown arms swept around me and cinnamon-scented lips touched each of my cheeks. For some reason my own eyes watered as her luminous black ones stared into them. "Let me put the kettle on. I'm afraid I've jumped the gun on our scones. I've got a rather pathetic sweet tooth." That crooked smile again. She led the way out of the room, Sammie humming happily behind me.

"You must tell me how such a young girl has gotten herself admitted to one of the premier physics programs in the country," Aadita threw back over her shoulder as she rounded a corner. "You must be frightfully brilliant."

To my surprise, the kitchen was all in order, granite counters gleaming, mismatched but pretty cups and saucers lined up neatly on open shelving. I wondered if Aadita was a mind reader when she said, "I know, but one simply cannot greet the day without a proper kitchen to make tea in. Flake helped, of course. We stayed up half the night, which is how I got to know so much about you. I feel quite certain we'll all be fast friends, don't you?"

Was she kidding? With all that warmth, I was a goner.

By our second cup of Earl Grey, I'd learned that Aadita had trained in the social sciences, but, with a strong background in mathematics, she'd slid down what she called *the slippery slope of quantum theory* after she took a course taught by Fred Alan Wolf at the University of London. She confided that she was also a practicing Buddhist, feeling something had been lacking in her unusual-for-India secular home, and had in fact come to the attention of Caltech with an article she'd published investigating the links between contemporary currents in physics and mathematics and age-old concepts of Hinduism and Buddhism. At my request, she offered a neat summation of her particular take on the natural incidence of fractals, or self-similar objects—the most common example being the frond of a fir, which is a similar, if not necessarily identical, replication of the whole. I found myself wondering whether fractals might be a helpful clue in unlocking the portal to dematerialization.

As I managed to thoroughly litter my place setting with scone crumbs, Aadita pried all the details of my own project from me, commenting in the end, "But that's simply extraordinary. You, my girl, are on the brink of changing our world." She turned to Sammie and tussled her shiny locks affectionately. "And we thought the *internet* was speeding everything up. You *are* a clever girl to have found such a friend." I must confess that the look the two of them exchanged filled me with a bleak envy.

Just as I was trying to talk myself into a little more generosity of spirit, Sammie jumped up, and I nearly spilled my tea onto my third helping of scones. "Midge!" she cried, wrapping her arms around the bulbously-dimensioned animal who'd waddled into the room. He jumped onto my lap with a grunt, and I felt his weight. Fortunately, he was one of those felines who instinctively know when to keep their claws in. As if to counterbalance his obesity, he had one of the most beautiful cat faces I'd ever seen—not, of course, as aristocratic as Jillily's, nor as King-of-the-Jungle-ish as Moggy's, but sweet-eyed and soft, as if he'd been crafted out of butter. Lord knew, he looked as though he'd been eating it.

He stared at me soulfully, then, with great precision, extended a paw toward my half-eaten scone. I threw Sammie and Aadita an inquisitive look. Aadita said with a guilty laugh, "Oh, go ahead. No use pretending he got that way with us refusing him scraps."

The fact was, Midget was so fat that, after a few months in multicultural So Cal, he would acquire a third name, the Spanish diminutive for Fatty. I thought it suited him so well that I thereafter thought of him solely as *Gordito*. As a matter of fact, Sammie and her mother tended to assign everyone multiple names, which, given my own family's penchant for changing nicknames, was quite comforting.

In no time at all, the two of them managed to add several to my own rather voluminous list, including Fleur Beurre (since I liked to slather my dinner rolls with what anyone else might deem an excess of butter) and Flappy, which thank goodness referred not to my habit of flapping when distressed but how I walked when I wore my favorite sparkly flip-flops.

But all of that would come later. At this moment, Sammie beamed at me as I patted Midget's thick fur while he relished every last crumb of my scone, until Aadita rose with a sigh. "No rest for the wicked and all that. Flake, I'll give you an hour, then I'm afraid I really must claim your computer expertise. I should be able to find at least a few of my textbooks while you play."

Sammie kindly hefted Midget off my lap and led me to her bedroom, where the first things that jumped out at me were the painted canvases in various stages of completion leaning against every wall. Sammie dismissed my exclamation of surprise with a brisk, "Just a bit of a hobby to pass the time," but it didn't take much persuasion for her to tell me about her art. She showed me what she called her *Portfolio of Possibilities*, a collection of preliminary drawings of vast circles that were crammed with anything that struck her fancy—words, faces, studies of Midget and Aadita, a perfectly enlarged peach pit. They were beautiful and unusual, and I told her so, watching a grin spread across her face as wide and pink as a So Cal sunset.

I wasn't kidding. Sammie's dynamism wasn't only expressed in her quick speech. So much tended to catch her artistic attention that her subjects frequently spilled outside of their circles, which gave her finished canvases what Aadita liked to call "an air of pure chaos." Since Aadita was a quantum mathematician well versed in chaos theory, I knew she meant the comment as a compliment. Chaos, as you might recall, is the theory associated with the Butterfly Effect, otherwise known as *sensitive dependence on initial conditions.*

As we talked, it occurred to me that Sammie knew all about the void. She called it loneliness and referred to it specifically in relation to her father. I, in turn, knew what it was to mourn a beloved relative and listened with fellow-feeling to her stories of him taking her to museums in London—the Tate, the Tate Modern, the V and A, the National Gallery—and of her dancing with him, her smaller feet planted on his larger ones while he whirled her round their Lambolle Road flat.

"It was heavenly when he was home. He should have stayed. I'm never going to let my work take me away when I grow up. It's too hard on the family." That was one of the few times I heard Sammie betray her bitterness.

Sensing her distress, I asked her, "Did he you call Flake, or one of your other names?" She stared at me blankly. "You know." I added quickly, "Lakshmie? Or Samara? Rachael? Or Sammie?"

I saw her travel inside herself before answering, "Mostly Samara, since it was where my gran was born. But when my dad stroked my forehead to help me get to sleep, he called me his *gutina shuma.*"

Curious and more than a little envious, I had to clear my throat before asking, "What does that mean?"

"It's Yiddish. It means 'good soul.'"

Which was exactly what Sammie proved to be. Gwennie liked to say she had "a wonderful attitude," which I sensed from her tone was something she thought I could learn from. And she was right.

Once I had Sammie in my life, nearly everything became more possible, though the murder of my bun wasn't going to leave my mind anytime soon. I certainly wasn't disposed to mention it. During the first months of our friendship, we spent virtually every waking hour together, eager to cram in every inch of our likes and dislikes before being rudely interrupted by the new school year. We celebrated Sammie's birthday by renting all the Harry Potter videos out so far, with me teasing Sammie that we'd only be the same age for three months, and then I'd leap ahead of her again.

On September 15, Sammie nervously trudged off to Charles W. Eliot Middle School. Despite her gift for sociability, she was understandably anxious about fitting in at an American school. A lot more anxious than I was about beginning classes at Caltech.

Luckily, my transition to college at thirteen didn't end up being nearly as traumatic as you might imagine. Since I'd been coming onto campus ever since moving to So Cal, Stanley's classroom had become a second home, and most of the physics faculty and students were already familiar with me. I wasn't any younger than the school's previous youngest freshman and was following in my father's footsteps in the height department (five foot six and counting), so it wasn't as if anyone took much notice of me on my first day. That didn't mean it was easy. As soon as school started, I had a full docket of homework for my courses in Electricity and Magnetism, Multivariable Calculus, and Introduction to Supersymmetry and String Theory.

But the hours before dinner were Sammie's. Our games ran the gamut from chess to jump rope and pleased Gwennie no end. She'd been lobbying me all along to lead more of what she called a balanced life, which I had mentally dismissed as akin to a balanced diet, which in Gwennie's world meant no French fries, no lamb *masala*, and no Caramel Kreme Crunch Krispy Kremes.

But Sammie and I didn't just play. We read side by side, sometimes the same book, which we ended up discussing along with our studies. Sammie was more of what Stanley H. Fiske would have called "a sentimentalist." Having had a couple of fairly normal parents had given her a pretty positive view of things, so our discussions about the stories we read usually went something like this:

Sammie: "Wasn't that the most brilliant book ever?"

Me: "Oh, I don't know. I wasn't too keen on the bit about her nearly drowning in the ripe tide, not knowing which way was up or down."

Sammie: "But that's the point. Her whole life was like that, and then her father came back into her life and helped orient her."

Me: "We - ll, if you can trust that he doesn't decide he hates her after all."

Sammie: "Why in the world would he do that?"

I hadn't yet filled Sammie in on the more daunting vicissitudes of my previous incarnations, only sharing in the most general way that I'd led a rather strange and sheltered life before Adam and Stanley discovered my aptitude for science. As another only child, and one who'd moved around a bit herself, Sammie took my outsiderishness for granted and commented when I told her that Stanley and Gwennie and Adam and Amir and Tom and Katrina and Gunther and Jillily were my only So Cal friends, "I know what you mean. I never got on with most of the Sloanies I went to school with."

"Sloanies?" I asked.

Sammie knocked her forehead with the heel of her hand, muttering, "Silly me. No wonder the kids at school find me a bit obscure." Then she grinned. "Okay, we'll make you a fluent Brit-speaker yet." She explained that *Sloanies* is slang for Sloane Rangers, which she called, "Pretty much the types I went to school with in South-West London. They're sort of like your preppies. Mum and Dad really stretched to send me to the best public school they could. I didn't have the heart to tell them that budding Sloanies don't exactly fall over themselves to make friends with a *Jewdist* colored girl."

Odd ducks or not, Sammie and I were still teenagers, so we spent a fair amount of time gossiping about our peers. I confided in her about Amy Cowe's system of *ass-worthy* ratings and my math classmates' habit of torturing poor Hilty by dropping their books. Once school started, she shared her frustration about the precious few girls she could relate to at Eliot Middle School. Really, there were only three: a sweet girl named Mi-sook, who attended Korean-language classes after school each day and every Sunday, and identical twins Sophie and Tamara Cabanchip, whose orthodox Jewish-Argentinian parents wouldn't let them play outside of school with anyone outside their own religious community.

You would think that now that she was enrolled in our version of public school, with its typical So Cal population of what Gwennie liked to call mixed nuts, Sammie would be a shoo-in for a popular social life. But—perhaps even more so because of her savvy in the social grace department—she was appalled by her all-American classmates' rudeness to their teachers and overwhelmed by their sexual forwardness. Unlike me, her body was slow to mature, shaped, indeed, more like a Cadbury's Flake than my own top-heavy hourglass, and I was pretty sure she hadn't discovered the world of mini-explosions, nor the kind of obsessions that had led to my own undoing.

In fact, Sammie found the flirtatious forays of the boys in her grade laughable, which didn't exactly encourage me to broach the topic of my own sexual fallibility and which automatically deleted from our dialogue any mention of the boy in the Garden of Eden,

Adam's attractiveness, anything regarding Hector Hernandez, or my banishment from the kingdom of my Father's love.

But while I skirted those particular departments, Sammie and I still had plenty to talk about. We had an ongoing debate over our favorite fictional protagonist, which, since we were both avid readers, went through multiple permutations, from Harry Potter's highly verbal pal Hermione Granger to sweet young Rufus in Agee's *A Death in the Family* (Sammie's), with my own preferences wavering between *A Wrinkle in Time*'s telepathic Charles Wallace, John Irving's solemn *Son of the Circus*, Dr. Daruwalla, and that abused "Bastard out of Carolina" called alternately Ruth Anne and Bone.

Since we admitted we were both flummoxed about how to be female, we indulged in endless comparisons of Aadita's flair and foibles with Gwennie's and Mother's and Nana's and Sister Flatulencia's and Fayga's and Cook's and Dhani's. Sammie rolled on the floor laughing when she realized we really did call Sister Flatulencia Sister Flatulencia (though I did hasten to assure her that we used only the Sister part of her name to her face, reserving the more descriptive appellation to ourselves).

Sammie was more than a little interested in my description of celebrating Holi with Dhani, inspiring Aadita to comment during our heavenly cream tea the next day, "Flake tells me you know something about our Indian customs and even celebrated Holi. Myself, I just loved Holi. Everyone did. It was virtually the only time when those abominable caste and gender discriminations didn't apply. It's infinitely disappointing that such things continue in this day and age." Actually, I would have wanted to witness a bit more discrimination on Dhani's part when Father interrupted our Holi by nibbling her lip and thanked the Lord that Baby Angelina was resembling Ignacio more and more as time wore on.

I spent a fair amount of time lying on Sammie's bedroom carpet with my eyes closed, moved to reverie by her descriptions of the plentiful royal parks of London, which sounded like expanded versions of Father's grounds, except they were publicly owned, guaranteeing that no one could chop down a perfectly good tree out of sheer spite nor decree who could and who could not walk there. Because my first playground was particularly large and verdant and Sammie's earliest pleasures were kite flying with her father on Primrose Hill and counting as many of Regent's Park's 30,000 roses with her mum as they could before tea time, we both had a hunger for things green.

Sammie knew all sorts of interesting London park facts, such as Kensington Gardens hosting tributes to both Peter Pan and Princess Diana—which seemed somehow fitting as neither would ever age—and the chilling news that Hyde Park was acquired by Henry VIII in 1536, just four years before the beheading of Anne Boleyn. I had already learned how a man interested in acquiring beautiful expanses of land could be callous toward those closest to him, but still.

All those British parks made me wonder why Dhani didn't just stop at Islington on her way from Delhi, rather than come all the way to the U.S., but I was glad she hadn't or I wouldn't have known that a woman could walk with such grace, nor what it was like to see a live baby come into the world. Of course, the latter train of thought made me melancholy all over again. But it wasn't the same hopelessness I'd felt right after my abortion. Thanks in great part to the enlivening companionship of Sammie, my feelings about my aborted bun—whom I'd begun to think of as Baby X—were transforming into something Sister Flatulencia had alluded to: simple sadness.

Well, in truth, not so simple, but at least I was being moved by some invisible force around dams of shame and guilt into true and watery grief. I couldn't recall having cried so much since Adam held me B.O.-close at Grandfather's fiasco of a funeral. As for shame, did you know it can make you sick? I had been suffering non-stop tweeter pain since sex with Hector, with Gwennie plying me with one antibiotic after another until Dr. Raker swore it was psychosomatic and suggested we consult a therapist. Instead, I got Sammie.

Sammie and I were becoming increasingly intimate friends, to the point that, when she finally got her first period in October, it was right in sync with mine. We joked about our twin bloated bellies so much that one of us—I'm afraid I can't remember which one—decided we were *belly sisters*, which over time permutated into *bellasistas*, body sisters, and *bodysatvas*. But still, it was months before I could even think of telling Sammie about the more voidish elements of my own body's life, particularly the perverse events preceding her appearance on the scene. It took a visit to the grounds of my first incarnation to spur me on.

I had invited Sammie to spend Thanksgiving with me at Mother's. Aadita was only too happy to let her join me, having umpteen exams to correct and no tradition of celebrating what she called *the European rape of the Americas*. Once I'd given her twelve reassuring hugs and extracted a promise that Jillily could share her bed while I was away, Gwen stood sniffling on the front lawn till Adam loaded my bags and then Sammie's into his battered old Camry. Gwennie was heartbroken that she'd be celebrating the holiday without me. I evidently wasn't the only one who imagined the Fiskes were my actual family.

We arrived at the penthouse on the eve of Thanksgiving. After her ill-fated flight to the U.S., Sammie had something of an allergy to flying, so I'd kept her distracted with endless games of Hangman, Ghost, and Rock, Paper, Scissors. The two of us were greeted by the whole household, and I couldn't help but notice Sammie biting her lip when Sister Flatulencia reached out to shake her hand. I dug my fingernails into my palm praying she wouldn't burst into laughter.

Nana put me through a series of tearful chicken peckings of my head and cheeks before Sammie and I were allowed to fall onto her twin beds. Nana had volunteered to sleep with Cesar Jesus de Maria Santo Domingo Marisco on the living room sofa bed. She'd clearly softened since the old days. I knew how fond she was of sleeping on her own pillow on her own bed. It was hardly lost on me that last Thanksgiving I'd been pre-Hector, pre-baby-murder, and pre-Sammie. Was it possible that so much could change in a year's time? And then I had to laugh. I was working on a project that might one day help human beings dematerialize and reappear again and here I was moaning about change.

As the French say, *"Plus ça change, plus c'est la même chose."* When I woke the next morning, the whole penthouse smelled of turkey. Cook, as usual, was going all out for the occasion. Though the non-linearity of physics had been slowly weaning me from my habit of list making, I couldn't resist itemizing Cook's dishes in my diary:

1. Raw artichoke and avocado salad;

2. Minty carrot soup;

3. Herbed roast turkey with baked chestnut dressing;

4. Green beans and sliced almonds;

5. Mashed potatoes and parsley parsnips;

6. Pumpkin cheesecake.

Seated in the place of honor at the head of the table, Sammie announced that the meal was enough to persuade her to give up her British passport, which caused Cook to turn so red I worried she'd have a heart attack. Sister Flatulencia lifted her wine glass in a rousing, "Here, here!," while Fayga, having watched me gorge myself on my third helping of turkey, noted rather waspishly that I seemed to have given up my stint as a vegetarian. In one fell swoop I was back in the restaurant where Adam had described the forced feeding of geese, but my forkful of yet another piece of moist turkey breast won out in the end.

Thanks to Cook's cooking and Sammie's stories, it was a jolly evening, though I did miss Dhani and Ignacio and young Angelina. As it happened, Thanksgiving coincided with the final day of Dhani's mother's visit from Islington, and the Hertado family had begged off with the assurance that Dhani would host a proper Indian meal for Sammie and me at the Cookery School on Saturday.

Fred Forrest was absent from our Thanksgiving dinner, too, but, if anything, him being out of the picture provided something extra to be thankful for. Who needed a cat killer at the table to remind me of my own crime? Mother had prepared me for his absence with a mysterious, "He went off the wagon and it fell off the cliff." The three lines bisecting her forehead forbade me to pry.

But she wasn't too sad to giggle when Sammie ended the evening by raising her glass of milk and clicking it with Mother's Perrier tumbler, crying out gaily, "Cheers to the cook for the lovely grub!" Needless to say, the whole table followed suit, with Cook not knowing where to look and Cesar knocking his own plastic juice cup against Nana's wine goblet so enthusiastically that we had to quickly remove everything from the tablecloth and lift it away from the burled wood dining table to prevent orange juice from staining the table.

That night, the two of us curled together into one of the twin beds so we could gossip about the evening, Sammie ventured in an unusually halting way, "Fleur, you haven't spent a second alone with your mum." She was twisting a lock of her hair nervously, the sound of her fingernail grazing her pillow case becoming a little annoying. "If my mum hadn't seen me for months, I wouldn't be able to get out of her clutches for ages and ages."

I sat up then, pulling one of Nana's throw cushions to my belly. She was right, of course. How could I explain that, since I'd had to make do with mother's absenteeism for so long, I barely thought about it anymore? If anything, since she'd left Father and stopped drinking and had a world of Bill W.'s to fill her void, I was mostly relieved to not have to think of her much at all. I had to admit to myself that the living person from my first incarnation I missed the most was Nana—though, needless to say, if we included the dead, Grandfather headed the list by a mile. But time had shifted even my connection to Nana and her cave scent, with Gwennie and Stanley seeming more and more like the mother and father I'd been meant to have before some mixed-up angel sent my spirit into my teenaged mother's unwilling womb.

The only clue that I hadn't securely sealed up my longing for Mother forever was the butterflyishness I felt in my belly whenever I watched Sammie and Aadita in one of their easy embraces. But I couldn't tell my friend that—she'd only feel guilty—so I said with some finality, "My mother's kind of a group person. Not much for one-on-ones. That's why AA's so perfect for her. Besides, we know we love each other, and that's what counts, you know?" To which Sammie responded by opening her mouth as if to say something, then closing it again, two pink patches springing up on her olive cheeks.

I yawned ostentatiously and said, "God, I can't believe how much I ate. I've got to go to sleep," before I slid out from under the covers and got into the other bed.

I guess I managed to convey that I really didn't want to talk about it. Sammie didn't say another word about Mother. Besides, I hadn't been kidding about being stuffed to the gills. If anything, we both spent most of Friday in a state of bilious oblivion. But by Saturday we felt fit enough to consume yet another gourmet meal. Sister Flatulencia was kind enough to drop us off at the Cookery School before her shift began at her new part-time job at Borders. Thank God, after all those years, she'd finally broken down and begun to experiment with that over-the-counter Manna from Heaven, Bean-O, or we would have had a full-scale crisis on our hands.

I could tell that Dhani was prepared for us as soon as we opened the door of the home of my first incarnation. Sammie sensed it, too. She visibly sniffed, then grinned one of those broad Sammie grins that made everyone around her glad to be alive. As you might imagine, Sammie and Dhani got on like a house afire, Sammie yattering away a mile a minute and Dhani plying us with enough Rogan Josh to turn our poop red for days. Thank heavens Dhani had the good sense to soothe our insides with Jhajaruja—a yummy confection made from corn and milk and ghee and sugar, with heaps of raisins and nuts on top—or I doubt we would have made it safely onto our plane the next day.

Dhani's background was considerably more conservative than Aadita's, the latter having come from a home run by two communist members of India's Parliament—though all of Aadita's childhood friends had been Hindus, so she'd steeped Sammie in the richness of Hindu lore. By a series of conversational skips, punctuated by moans of pleasure emitted by Sammie and me as we scooped up the last of Dhani's Rogan Josh with Naan, the three of us ended up debating the moral of the *Ramayana,* the signature story of the primate hero for whom Amir's Lord Hanuman had been named.

Dhani described to me in vivid detail Hanuman's rescue of Rama's abducted wife Sita, capping it off with an abrupt, "Of course, once Sita was returned to him, Rama ended up banishing Sita for the shame of having been raped by the demon king of Ravana."

Sammie, making a face, offered the editorial comment, "My mum says it's so Indian—punish the woman for the crime of the man."

To which Dhani retorted, "But no. Rama repented. In the end, he asked Sita to come back."

Which elicited from Sammie, "Yes, but Mum says that by then Sita knew what a piece of work he was, so she chose to live with the Earth Goddess instead."

At which point I, sensing a conflict coming, interjected: "Does any of this have anything to do with Holi?"

Which shifted Dhani's expression from doubtful to delighted. She looked the two of us over, taking in our jeans and T-shirts, and held up a finger before grabbing a stepstool and sliding it towards one of the tall cupboards. She had her back to us now, revealing how cooking Ignacio's corn flour-based favorites had widened her once-pert behind, and I could tell she was rummaging behind a mass of spice bottles on one of the higher shelves. Triumphant, she stepped down, in each plump hand a couple of bottles of colored confection-er's sugar. "Shall we?" she asked.

Without another thought for Rama or Sita or the Monkey God, we flew out the back door into what was now a vast herb garden.

I got the first innings. Dhani and Sammie screamed and giggled as I flung handfuls of pink sugar at them. Dhani got me back with some turquoise, and then Sammie saturated both of us with sunflow-er yellow. Dhani ran to get the hose while Dhani and I smeared each other's faces with gritty streaks of red. But Dhani and I both jumped when we heard the back door creak open.

A man's face peered around. I gasped.

"Ai, *querida mia*, what are you doing?"

Ignacio's thick black eyebrows lifted in laughter. I breathed again. By what trick of black magic had I imagined it was Father?

He disappeared, then Once-Baby Angelina burst out the door, screeching in a near-panic at the prospect of being left out, "Wait! Wait fo' me!"

Angelina was several inches taller than the last time I'd seen her, and her features had gained definition. Her skin was cocoa-colored, smooth as satin. Her lips made a heart-shape, and her dark eyes took up half her face. She was the most beautiful child I'd ever seen. I burst into tears.

It took awhile to calm me down, the calming consisting of me refusing to let anyone touch me, Ignacio sweeping Not-a-Baby Ange-lina away, Sammie helping Dhani re-coil the hose, and me forcing myself not to flap or pinch. I saw Dhani give Sammie a little nod in the direction of the grounds, and Sammie suggested we take a walk.

"You did promise me a turn around these extraordinary gardens. Mum won't forgive me if I can't describe every single one of your mum's Austins to her."

I didn't say a thing, simply started walking. Fast. Even the ener-getic Sammie had to struggle to keep up with me.

I came to a stop at the first fountain. The sight of Baby Eros' peeing member brought all my sinfulness back to me. That mossy member of his bore little resemblance to Hector's throbbing red one, and the child god's apricot-sized balls were hardly reminiscent of Grandfather's more grapefruity sacks, but the whole ensemble still suggested the essence of masculinity. I stood awhile, revisiting scenes at some distance on the space-time continuum that still registered quite viscerally.

It felt like only a few weeks ago that I'd rushed Grandfather to the bathroom with his pajama trousers hindering his feet, only days since I'd watched the flower water around his zipper sadly fade as he lay in his coffin. As for Hector pushing his penis at my inflamed belly button before forcing it toward my tweeter as if he were taming a beast, I nearly cried out with the pain of my bursting hymen.

I had to hand it to Sammie. She stood beside me silently before settling herself onto the grass, legs crossed yogini-style. As if from a great distance, I heard her sing, "*Raa Maa Daa Saa, Saa Say So Hung*," in her singularly sweet soprano. I recognized the tune. Aadita called it the Sushmuna Mantra and had taken to intoning it every evening, right after dinner.

As you may have gathered from her iconoclastic career trajectory, Aadita was never one to get stuck in orthodoxy. She'd recently added Kundalini meditation to her Buddhist sitting practice and was taking Sammie with her on Saturdays to a class at Golden Bridge Yoga led by a Sikh with an impressive white turban, which was a double bonus for me. It gave me time not to be torn between playing with Sammie and working on my project and offered food for thought concerning the resonance between yogic journeying between the boundaried and the infinite and our team's efforts to catalyze materialization and dematerialization.

And just in case *Raa Maa Daa Saa, Saa Say So Hung* sounds like *ugga umph ugga* to you, you might like to know that it roughly translates into *Sun, Moon, Earth, Infinity, Infinity, Experience, Identity, the Vibrating Infinite Reality*. The way Sammie had once explained it, singing the mantra took your breath up your spine from your belly center, through your heart, your throat, and your brow to your crown point, and then back down again. Since we were avowed belly sisters, she thought I should know.

One thing was certain. Hearing her singing soothed me. I sat down beside her and did my best to join in. Before I knew it, a friend from the past appeared out of nowhere. Uncle Bob plopped down on my lap, making up in enthusiasm what he lacked in pure pitch. I snuck a quick, grateful glance at him just in time to see his black walrus moustache jiggle like a pair of dancing worms to that final emphatic *Hung*.

Sensing my barely-suppressed laughter, Sammie opened her eyes and smiled beatifically. Wise old friend that he was, Uncle Bob made a quick dive for my pocket.

Sammie held out a hand and without a nanosecond's hesitation. I took it. A moist wind had picked up around us, presaging rain, but I didn't care. As we sang together, I couldn't help but notice the willow's tender caress of Baby Eros' tiny member.

It was time.

"Sammie," I said, "There's a lot I haven't told you."

I took a deep breath and began, starting with sneaking out of the home of my second incarnation with Uncle Bob, who blushed in my pocket as I revealed his existence. I had to give it to Sammie. She barely batted an eye.

"So there I was. Sammie, I swear, it was just like I'd always imagined, right out of the Bible—the Garden of Eden. But when the boy sat so still, watching me pull down my panties, I knew something was wrong. His face just didn't look right. And taking my clothes and pulling them against his body like a teddy bear. Who does that? It was as if his void was located in his crotch. I thought everybody's void was like mine—alternating between my head and heart."

But Sammie wasn't about to get lost down that particular side-alley. "Wait a minute. The bastard sits and watches you while you're freezing your arse? Fleur, he wasn't just hugging your clothes. He was wanking off."

"Wanking off?"

"Playing pocket pool. Spanking the monkey. Pulling the pud."

You can imagine my confusion, until Sammie finally found a word I knew. "He was masturbating, Fleur. Did you really think he was snuggling your clothes like a teddy?"

Sammie's tone was so exasperated that I began to pull into myself like a tortoise. But she seemed to sense where I was heading. Turning beet-red, she clapped a hand to her forehead. "Oh hell, talk about wankers. Listen to me. You're telling me about the most awful moment in your life and I'm rattling on about sex ed."

I hated seeing Sammie looking so guilt-stricken, and, besides, she was getting it all wrong. So I explained how that was hardly the worst moment of my life (having a dead bird, a dead grandfather and dead baby in my heart to prove it). Especially since it had led to mini-explosions, which just went to prove that some bad things can actually lead to good.

"But then, the mini-explosions only wanted to come when I thought about Adam, instead of the Boy who Called Me Beautiful, especially after I saw him stroke Stephanie's arms, so you can imagine how relieved I was when they shifted again, this time in response to thinking about Hector." I started to hyperventilate as I approached my reluctant enrollment in the ranks of the Pro-Choice, but Sammie stopped me and led me through a few slow *Raa Maa Daa Saa*'s. Which made sense. If it took all the king's horses and all the king's men to put together Humpty Dumpty, I could definitely use the sun and the moon and the earth and infinity to help me speak of my own fall from grace. "There I was," I added bleakly, "trying to save a twenty-year-old blind cat and the next thing I knew I had killed my own baby."

"Oh, Fleur," Sammie murmured, in a tone of infinite sadness.

But kindness wasn't currently on my menu. I cried, "Who would have thought I would join forces with the devil abortionists?"

Sammie, who up until now had been cultivating a Zen-ishly neutral air, pulled back and frowned. "Devils?" she asked. "Whatever do you mean?"

When I explained, she replied with some shock, "What's the use of believing in that?"

To my own surprise, I couldn't come up with an answer—which was the moment when I finally appreciated the value of doubt.

I'd been needing a healthy dose of doubt all along. As it happens, once I got certainty out of the way, the world would become a new place, wobbly and wet and open, previous assumptions sloshing around inside me, with many of them going under forever.

Which is where Stanley and Niels Bohr came in. When Sammie and I deplaned at LAX the next day, Stanley gave my friend a big hug and me a welcome home gift. Always a sucker for something wrapped, I tore off the paper to see it was a biography of Bohr. That night, I read it from start to finish, particularly piqued when I read that the famous physicist had once been a goalkeeper for the Danish professional football club Akademisk Boldklub, formed in 1889 by a group of multitalented academics. I phoned Dhani with that tidbit the very next morning, but I wasn't her friend for nothing. I assured her that, while the Boldklub were evidently pretty good in their time, I was willing to lay a wager they wouldn't have bested Arsenal.

But, more to the point, Bohr's less athletic contributions to the world included the Theory of Complementarity, the notion that items can be separately analyzed as having several contradictory properties. A common example is that light is both a wave and a particle. It was thanks to Niels Bohr that I started looking at the dismemberment of Baby X from a different angle.

Before Niels Bohr, I had thought of Baby X's demise as the end of two lives—hers and mine. But the truth was that, for me anyway, my bun's demise was both an end and a beginning. As Bohr once said, "How wonderful that we have met with a paradox. Now we have some hope of making progress."

It occurred to me that, with the help of Stanley H. Fiske, crossing the bleak desert of choice had liberated me from the distractions of middle school math, musicals, and the Hector Hernandezes of this world, though nothing was going to save me from the devilish duo of envy and longing that sidled into my heart whenever I observed noisy groups of presumably bunless kids my own age on the street. At such times, I forced myself to set my sights firmly on my project, more determined than ever to crack the puzzle of dematerialization once and for all.

With Bohr in mind, I was banking on the idea that, in the not-too-distant-future, it would all come together. I would come to see Baby X as the sacrificial offering for the advance of science and the potential simplification of travel and hope she herself could appreciate her place in history from inside the hole in my heart.

And just in case you think that particular perception left me feeling sanguine about what I'd done, let me set the record straight right now. An aborted child is like a phantom limb, invisible to the world, but a source of constant, aching regret—which is, as I've come to learn, the true nature of sacrifice, whose etymological root is the pairing of *holy* and *accursed*. I carry my limb sometimes as a heaviness, sometimes as the lightness of unalterable purity. No matter what else is going on, some subterranean part of me is swaying, as if in time to a melancholy piece of music, say, the central adagio of Rodrigo's *Concierto de Aranjuez* or The Beatles' *Eleanor Rigby*. Baby X, my unbaked bun, my severed limb—she is my secret sorrow and my secret spring. I can't help but believe that Niels Bohr, son of Christian Bohr and a

Sephardic Jewess, and himself a prince of paradox, would know just what I mean.

Chapter 21 🦋

AS THE DAYS of my fourth incarnation began to regularize, Sammie and I saw less of each other. She was being pulled into the inexorable vortex of middle school madness—too much homework, after school clubs, silly social dilemmas, being regularly harassed by a couple of ridiculously immature boys. As for me, I was setting my sights with a single-minded intensity on forging a bridge between the material and immaterial worlds.

I was all too aware that my goal would hardly be attainable without accessing the achievements of innumerable others. As Sir Isaac Newton wrote to Robert Hooke in 1676, "If I have seen further it is by standing on ye shoulders of Giants." Newton proved to be one of my own personal giants, a second cousin to a flat-out angel in my book, with his intuitive affinity for the infinite. Consider the question he put forth just a few years later: "Are not gross bodies and light convertible into one another, and may not bodies receive much of their activity from the particles of light which enter into their composition?"

Newton was prescient. A mere three hundred and eighty years later, a team headed by Eugene Polzik at Copenhagen University managed to teleport two different objects over a short distance from one spot to another in a split second, with light as the carrier of entanglement, entwining two particles without physical contact. I studied the reports of their work with mounting enthusiasm, for it confirmed some of the central assumptions of our own project. During the same week, Aadita lent me a couple of current articles on relativistic and nonrelativistic quantum mechanics, also known as Schrodinger operators, that proved quite helpful in regard to the condensed matter component of our model.

During my first few months at Caltech, I had wrestled with the question of how we might harness that illuminating challenge offered by physics to nineteenth century rationalism that the very act of observation alters the objects observed and can actually cause things to disappear. I grappled with what sorts of tools might allow the process of observation to be exponentially magnified to catalyze the process of dematerialization. How could that process be brought full circle to facilitate re-materialization? The one was hardly going to be useful without the other. We would be fools indeed if we pioneered a means by which people and objects could be made to fall into the abyss without being able to bring them back again. If dematerialization were our sole object, a mere variant of the neutron bomb would settle the whole affair.

So engrossed was I with my work that I was stunned to wake up one morning to a beaming Gwennie wishing me a happy fourteenth birthday. I'd been too busy to even speak with Sammie on the phone for nearly a week, and Gwennie had to remind me that Sammie and Aadita expected the three of us for dinner that night.

Aadita's Tandoori Chicken was so moist it rivaled the yummiest dishes of Dhani's, and Sammie's animated imitations of some of her more clueless classmates were hilarious, but I have to admit I was distracted during most of the meal. All-too-aware that I had to get up at the crack of dawn the next morning for a conference call with a physics grad student in New Haven, I gave Sammie the most perfunctory of hugs at the end of the evening, actually relieved to walk out the door.

I had been just as hasty the previous weekend on a last-minute Christmas shopping trip to Old Town with Gwennie, purchasing a button-lapel black turtleneck for Sammie and items small enough to ship affordably to Maine—where Mother and Nana and Cesar had spontaneously decamped to Mother's new boyfriend's digs for the holidays. In my fever to finish shopping, I was forced to do a rather deft sidestep of the void as I recognized the features of one of my old Reed classmates in the face of our clerk at Silver Me.

She gave me a blank look when I reminded her we'd sat next to each other in drama class, her palpable disinterest yanking open the cupboard in my mind reserved for tightly folded longings to be like other girls my age, with their casual self-involvement, their easy flirtatiousness with boys, their even easier comfort in their own skins. I foolishly told myself that, even if we barely saw each other lately— she cramming for exams, me obsessed with dematerialization—I still had Sammie.

As the New Year approached, Adam and Amir and Tom and Katrina and Gunther and I preoccupied ourselves with reading, reflecting, debating, and consuming enough Krispy Kremes to gain us an aggregate twenty-five pounds, but still the final pieces of the puzzle eluded us. Later, Stanley H. Fiske would call my attention to a wonderful little book written by the late Harold Rugg called *Imagination*, in which the progressive educator reviewed the creative and scientific breakthroughs of a number of individuals and identified a common process of chewing at a problem until giving up in frustration, then being rewarded shortly afterwards by a stroke of intuition with the sought-for solution. As it turned out, that could pretty well sum up what happened with my solution to the problem of dematerialization, though credit must be given to my learning about the Jeweled Net of Indra at the Fiskes' Christmas Eve dinner just three days after my birthday.

It was an extraordinary night in many ways. Most of the faces around the Fiske dining table were familiar—Stanley, Gwennie, Adam, Amir, Katrina, Tom, Gunther, Sammie, Aadita—but a primatologist named Serena McKenna had joined us, too, in what ended up being a synchronistic stroke of luck. Jane Goodall's heir apparent in the anthropological world, Serena had met Stanley H. Fiske the previous year at a New York gathering honoring Kofi Annan.

The two of them had gotten on famously, so much so that when Amir finally managed to place Lord Hanuman with the Goodall Institute in Tanzania's Gombe Stream National Park, using Stanley as his reference, she got in touch with him again—Stanley, that is, not Lord Hanuman, who was still doing quite nicely in the home of his third incarnation. And when Stanley learned she was going to be in So Cal over the holidays to speak at a fundraiser for one of Dr. Goodall's pet projects (no pun intended), he'd lost no time inviting her to Gwennie's vegetarian Christmas Eve dinner.

The fact that she recalled Stanley at all was something of a miracle. Like Dame Goodall herself, Serena McKenna suffered from

Prospagnosia, which I witnessed firsthand when I opened the front door at seven p.m. on Christmas Eve to a diminutive black-haired woman, who looked me right in the eye and said, "How good to see you again, Stanley."

Prospagnosia, also known as *face blindness*, is a disorder of perception that impairs one's ability to recognize faces and often, therefore, remember them. I couldn't begin to think how Goodall and McKenna managed at all, let alone with one another. Did they mistake each other for chimps half the time? And how did they tell one chimp from another? I wasn't about to ask.

Fortunately, Stanley materialized right behind me. "Serena!" he cried, with a little hop of excitement. "The gang's all here and they're dying to meet you. Come in, come in!"

It didn't surprise me that Serena and Stanley had hit it off well. If anything, the connection unsettled me. No insult intended, but Stanley was wearing one of his favorite olive green suits that evening, and the slim-limbed Serena McKenna, clad in a black and iridescent green tunic top over black velvet leggings and sporting a pair of black-framed spectacles, had the air of an attractive but nonetheless buggish giant fly. Watching Stanley cast those froglike eyes of his down upon the petite primatologist, I had the horrid fantasy of him flicking her up with his tongue.

It wasn't until our pre-prandial discussion of the smallness of our world—prompted by Katrina marveling at the few degrees of separation between Jane Goodall, Kofi Annan, Stanley, Amir, Lord Hanuman, and Serena McKenna—that Aadita shared with us the image of Indra's Net. We were seated around a fire that Tom and Gunther had constructed to perfection with a placement of logs designed to maximize the updraft. The illuminated Christmas tree in the corner added vibrancy to the living room's glow.

Hogging the heat in front of the fire, Jillily was licking her hindquarters with rather embarrassing enthusiasm, and Aadita had the good grace to segue into a sufficiently distracting topic. She'd been sitting with her arm around Sammie's shoulder, gently stroking her daughter's hair. She pulled away now and sat forward. Gesturing with her dark head in the direction of the tree, she delicately dispatched a stuffed Calamata olive before commenting, "Your tree is simply beautiful, Gwen. You make me wish I'd gotten one myself. It calls to mind Indra's heaven."

Gwennie, her face and *Physicists are Spicier* apron covered in flour, said, "What's that when it's home?"

Aadita nodded earnestly, her dangling silver earrings reflecting the firelight. "Actually, home is an apt image—home for me being, of course, India. If you asked one of my Hindu friends, they would tell you that the heaven of the god Indra is composed of a wondrous net of silk strands stretching infinitely in all directions, every intersection suspending a shining jewel whose surface mirrors every other jewel and the net as a whole."

As if aware she was no longer the center of attention, Jillily sauntered sulkily from the room, followed by Gwennie, who muttered something about her nut roast. I half-heartedly asked if I could help. More than a little relieved when she said, "No," I savored the elegance of Aadita's image along with my third jalapeno and garlic stuffed olive.

Serena McKenna leaned forward from her rather precarious perch on the edge of Stanley's leather hassock and commented enthusiastically, "What a wonderful metaphor for the earth's ecosystem. Would you mind awfully if I lifted that image for an article I'm working on?"

Grinning with the delight of one scientist inspiring another, Aadita shook her head, but I couldn't strop myself from interjecting, "Yes, but don't forget, the Indra of the *Rig Veda* is also a god of war"—which got everyone going on the inevitable Iraq rant for a while, until Gwennie called us to dinner, begging everyone to shift the topic in aid of digestion.

I managed to sit next to Serena McKenna. Bug-eyed and brilliant, she fascinated me. Adam pulled out a chair to my right. Aadita, at the other end of the table, patted the chair next to her, and Sammie glanced across at me, her face closing itself slightly before she sat down beside her mother. Everyone else found their places. The next few minutes were filled with enthused raves over the lavish spread. Gwennie had done herself proud, setting out her best Deruta dishes and three bottles of a particularly fine wine. Feasting my eyes on the table, I counted myself blessed and wished only that Mother and Nana and Cook and Fayga and Sister Flatulencia and Dhani and Ignacio and Not-Such-a-Baby Angelina and even Caesar were with us. Fighting what threatened to become a fit of melancholy, I sent a silent prayer toward the hole in my heart where Grandfather and Baby X dwelled.

I watched Aadita help Stanley to a generous dollop of caramelized shallot mashed potatoes. As he proceeded to dig in, she offered the still-mountainous bowl to Serena McKenna. As if there'd been no interruption to their previous conversation, Aadita turned to the anthropologist. "You're right, of course. Indra's net can be analogized to everything from self-similarity, or fractals, to computer networks and neural networks of the brain."

While everyone went at the spicy vegan roast as if this were their last supper, something about what Aadita had just said teased at me from a dim corner of my mind. I sensed the solution to our puzzle tantalizingly perched in my blind spot. Science and religion were joined at the cusp of the eminent and immanent, but how to operationalize the site of that crucial intersection?

I couldn't wait to share this particular mental itch with my Caltech crew, which I did as soon we came together again the day after Christmas. It threw them into something of a mass intellectual meltdown. The quandaries of science were one thing; trying to reconcile them with philosophy and spirit were quite another. They tried accompanying me down that path, they really did, but as much as we turned and twisted the topic, not one of us could get hold of an Ariadne thread to pull a working model from the chaos. If anything, our joint frustration made things increasingly tense between us, which, over the next few days, infected Stanley and Gwennie, as well.

As usual, they took it out on each other. Stanley had become increasingly peevish at being deprived of meat, and Gwennie nagged Stanley non-stop about being such a slob, feeling bound to make a fuss whenever she found a pile of sunflower seed shells on the carpet. I had to admit the shells *were* an inconvenience. Twice, Jillily got one stuck in her throat, and, the second time, it was only after a lot of false starts and a two inch worm of Laxatone that she finally puked the pesky thing onto the living room rug, along with a surprising collection of other contraband ingestants, including a nose ring Stephanie had lost during a sneezing fit nearly a year ago.

Things weren't much better between me and my own sibling, though mine was of course the belly, rather than genetic, variety. I'd been woefully oblivious during our Christmas Eve dinner of Sammie's boredom over all the talk of neural networks and fractals.

Sammie was no slouch in the intellect department, but her mind tended to work in a liberal arts-ish sort of way. Looking back, I realize I effectively ignored her the whole night, letting her languish at the opposite end of the table while I lofted in the heady climes of science.

And it wasn't just that night. Sammie phoned a few days later to see if I wanted to make plans for New Year's Eve just as I was trying to wrap my mind around a particularly pesky mathematical detail. I said, "Make it fast, will you? I'm getting stuck on something perfectly simple and if I don't call Katrina soon I'm going to blow my brains out."

In an unusual fit of pique, Sammie said, "I don't know if you've noticed, but you're always ringing off for some reason or other." She went on to accuse me of taking our friendship for granted.

Still in a hurry to get off the phone, I murmured, "Don't be silly. It's just that I know I'm on the brink of something and I can't quite see it. If I let myself get distracted, I'll lose the whole thread."

To which she replied, "Is that all I am—a distraction? Thanks very much. I can't believe what a selfish prat you've become." I realized later it was a difficult time of the year for her, as holidays tend to be on the heels of personal loss. I'm sure it didn't help that Aadita was buried in grading final exams.

But I couldn't see my way through to Sammie's side of things and dismissed her objections as simple envy, throwing in, "I'm sure you've got other things you can do. If you could only understand what I'm working on, you'd be a lot more patient." She hung up on me. A part of me wanted to call her back, but I dialed Katrina's number instead.

As soon as Aadita got wind of our feud, she intervened, persuading both Sammie and me to join her the next day in a new yoga class she'd discovered that was taught by Siri Sajan, a young woman she claimed was one of this earth's angels. Needless to say, I couldn't possibly say no to that kind of build-up, angels having saved my life innumerable times. As for Sammie, she couldn't say no because her mother hadn't given her the option.

The next morning, Sammie let me into her house wordlessly, and we stood awkwardly in the hall waiting for her mother. The two of us followed Aadita to the car with some reluctance, our bodies stiff with attitude. I'm ashamed to say that it occurred to neither of us to offer to help the diminutive Aadita load our three heavy rubber yoga mats—one purple, one orange, and one blue—into the back of the Volvo.

As you may have noticed, anger is the kind of emotion that likes to crowd other feelings out. But something else managed to squeeze in when Sammie and I spied a small group of neighborhood children bent intently over some object on the sidewalk. I suppose you might call it a kind of instinctual curiosity, for it was our feet rather than our minds that decreed we simultaneously cross the street to investigate further. Naively, I imagined the children studying a hardy weed breaking free through a crack in the cement, but when we got closer I saw they were burning ants with a magnifying glass.

I began to flap violently, while Sammie—crying "Shame, for shame!"—chased them off. Only when they'd disappeared around the corner did Sammie return, her face the color of burnt sienna. The two of us stood side by side, watching the remaining ants carrying their fallen comrades back to the nest. Our hands sought out one another's like magnets. Linked in that fashion, we crossed back over the road.

The dark spell had been broken, but, all during our yoga class, the image of the gratuitous burning of ants lodged in my mind like a constipated turd. What was it that took people like Jane Goodall and Serena McKenna off to Africa to champion the rights of chimpanzees, while others delighted in torturing ants that weren't even raiding their sugar canisters?

My mind ineluctably strayed to pinching Jillily's belly all those years ago, which—while considerably less of a crime than murdering a bun for the sake of convenience—seemed to bear a sorry similarity to the vicious appetite for ant burning. What kind of monster took pleasure in causing others pain? But then it occurred to me that Jillily wasn't just the victim of such an impulse but also a perpetrator. Hadn't she proudly leapt to my bed with a mangled hummingbird in her mouth just a week ago?

I knew that Dhani and Aadita would have been far more at home with this problem than I. The gods and goddesses of the Indian sub-continent spoke to a kinship between birth and destruction, kindness and killing. The war god Indra of the Heavenly Net was a far cry from the saccharine version of Christ my Father had touted on TV.

Unfortunately, once my mind retrieved my father from the invisible cupboard I thought I had securely stuffed him in, I went spinning down a powerfully pit-ish chute, falling straight into the Child's Pose when I should have stayed upright with the rest of the class, my hands aloft in the Guyan Mudra and breathing the Breath of Fire. Siri Sajan lived up to her reputation and, without an ounce of judgment, floated over to gently re-position me.

But my bleak mood persisted, gathering into a thick thundercloud by the time I slid under the covers that night. Even Jillily's paw caressing my cheek proved little comfort. For a few brief moments, I'd seen my father in his best, most playful, light. But I wasn't a saint. Those brief moments had hardly been enough to balance all his rage and rejection.

Had he disliked me because *I* hadn't been enough? I tried telling myself that it was his delusion of having some direct channel to God that had come between us. I had little doubt that the ancient Greeks—as Stanley liked to say, "No slouches, civilization-wise"—would have accused Father's fight against abortion as a kind of theomania, or "crazed enthusiasm," but I couldn't help but wish he'd been half as crazy about me.

I was distressed enough that I even raised the topic with Mother during one of our weekly phone conversations. Fresh from a continuing ed class in feminism at NYU, she replied in an acid tone, "Oh, don't be silly. That's so typical of us females. No, I think it's all down to his fear of women. Did you know that, thousands of years ago, everyone worshipped goddesses and not gods? They thought women had the power to make babies on their own. Once men figured out they were a necessary part of the process, they decided their children belonged more to them and they could dictate what women did with their own bodies. Like most men, your father can't stand anyone of the opposite sex who shows signs of being anything but subservient."

I worried about Mother's new zeal to make up for her lack of a college degree. I rarely heard her speak with such venom. As for her theory about Father's fanatical anti-abortionism, I thought it probably had more to do with the tragic consequents of an energetic little boy squirming at the confinement of a church pew and inadvertently tripping his pregnant mother, something Jesus would no doubt have had something to say about. Which Father, for all his messianic fervor, might have realized if he'd actually *listened* to that particular god's penchant for forgiveness.

It dawned on me that listening might just be a disappearing art. But then Serena McKenna came to mind. She'd done an especially fine job at listening to *me* as the two of us had carefully hand-washed and dried Gwennie's beautifully-wrought but decidedly chip-able dishes after our Christmas Eve dinner. Her encouragement of my project had been equaled by her appreciation of my feelings for Jillily, particularly once I regaled her with the story of two creatures, one human and one feline, sniffing their way around a penthouse in order to help one of them feel at home. Before she'd left that night, she'd shaken my hand and said in a tone of great seriousness, "Never betray that creature love of yours, Fleur. The scientist must always take second place to that." I couldn't help but notice that, thanks to my cat, I'd metamorphosed in a few short hours into becoming myself in Serena McKenna's Prospagnosic eyes. Despite my great respect for the man, I really hadn't been comfortable being Stanley.

I wondered whether Serena McKenna's struggle with sight had given her a greater gift for taking others in.

Twisting fitfully in my bed, I accidentally leaned my elbow on Jillily's tail, and she responded with a fierceness that reminded me of the hummingbird she'd so recently murdered. But if a dead bird or two was the price of Jillily's continued existence, I was willing to bear the sacrifice. Which, of course, was not to say that the hummingbird would have agreed. I supposed Indra might have appreciated the irony of the same person striving to save birds and feeding the cat who lived to kill them, which gave me a thread of hope that the neighborhood kids who'd burned the ants might not all turn out to be mass murderers.

I had an intimation then that, for all our strivings for progress, it was probably never going to get any better. People would die, we would still struggle with aggression and terror, the void would swallow us up over and over and spit us out again. At least for that moment, a blanket of humility spilled over me. Even if I succeeded at finding the formula for dematerialization and re-materialization, I would never crack the code for what St. Augustine called the circular God whose center was everywhere and circumference nowhere. Whatever we humans cooked up would be but a pale imitation.

I'm sorry to say my humility lasted the equivalent of a cosmic nanosecond. During that window, Sammie and I made up sufficiently to spend New Year's Eve together, watching a couple of our favorite DVD's—my pick *Moulin Rouge*, Sammie's *The Dead Poets Society*, over which we both sobbed while consuming far too many pieces of Zelo's deep dish pizza and a carton apiece of Ben and Jerry's Cherry Garcia and Chunky Monkey ice cream. The next morning I woke from a far-too-brief sleep, glad that I'd had the sense sometime in the middle of the night to set the alarm clock to 9 a.m. I hadn't told Sammie what I had planned for this morning, and I shuddered to think what she would say if she saw me rushing to shower, dress, and grab one of Gwen's homemade blueberry muffins before dashing out the door for Caltech. I knew Sammie would have a hard time understanding the kind of scientific obsession that would lead me and Adam and Amir and Katrina and Tom and Gunther to actually schedule a meeting on the day the whole rest of the world was sleeping in.

I needn't have hurried. Our efforts that day proved thankless. Amir had caught a cold, Gunther was mooning over a pre-med student who'd jilted him, Tom was hung over, and Katrina was suffering what she called the Mother of All Menstrual Cramps.

As for Adam, he seemed fairly distracted over some miscommunication with his new girlfriend Jessica. He hadn't seemed the same since Stephanie had thrown him over the previous month, and now Jessica was threatening to do the same, claiming she was nothing to him but a rebound girl. I'd had a surprisingly hard time myself coming to terms with Stephanie taking herself out of the picture.

The pain of getting pregnant had pretty much dissolved any mini-explosion-y feelings I'd had for anyone, turning my attitude toward Stephanie from envious rivalry to gratitude for the personal interest she'd taken in me. Though I hated the pain she'd caused Adam, some part of me couldn't forget the amount of time she'd taken to try to make me beautiful. Playing pretty was something I'd always wanted to share with Mother when I was little—having to make do with sneaking little dots of Infrarouge on my lips and spritzes of Chanel. No. 5 behind my ears, instead.

Since no one but I seemed to want to focus on our project, I left Caltech for home around five, more than a little disheartened. There was a note from Gwennie on the kitchen counter. She had finally managed to drag Stanley to the after-Christmas sales, and they hadn't gotten back yet. I knew Stanley would be hopping mad (no pun intended) by the time they got home.

Jillily was there, though. She'd evidently felt badly for not reciprocating her Christmas gift of three catnip-filled felt mice, for she'd placed a real one on my pillow. Its eyes were glazed over and a dried drop of blood punctuated the dour line of its mouth. I disposed of the carcass next to the dead hummingbird beneath the Dark Lady's invisible bed. As I wiped moist earth from my hands, my mind, which had felt like cotton candy all day, turned back with dead-mouse clarity to the problem of evil, which perversely worked up my appetite. I realized I hadn't eaten since my breakfast muffin.

The kitchen was tidy and the refrigerator full. But a full refrigerator in Gwennie's kitchen was a far cry from the confections filling the fridge in the home of my first two incarnations, especially when Cook was cook. I made a desultory attempt at a leftover slab of vegetarian lasagna before wandering back to my room with the last of the carrot cake, by far the better of the two options. Dropping crumbs all over the keyboard, I composed an e-mail to Serena McKenna, starting off with my frustration over trying to sort out the relation of black holes to heavy gravity and ending with a description of the ant burning episode.

To my surprise, she responded almost immediately. "I can well appreciate your anguish, but you mustn't be too hard on us humans," came her response. "We're barely out of the swamp, evolution-wise. Do you know we at the Institute are having to mount a campaign against the traffic in what is euphemistically called bushmeat—actually chimpanzee flesh—when there are only 150,000 of our closest living relatives left on the planet? But then again, you physicists are like the advance guard of a new species. I remember first reading about black holes in space and marveling at the existence of minds imaginative enough to conceive of them. Of course, it gave me the chills thinking about those invisible cavities swallowing everything in sight. As for your ant burners—alas, I suppose each of us has a moral black hole somewhere."

Time stopped for me right then. Why hadn't I seen it before? The Jeweled Net of Indra. Fractals. Everything reflecting everything else. Dark matter existed—*had* to exist—not only outside us, in the vast heavens, **but underneath our own skin in the form of *cellular black holes.*** Prove their existence, find their points of entry and their correct calibration, and the formula for dematerialization wouldn't be far behind.

In a fever, I tore apart my room looking for the copy of Misuo Hiramatsu's paper I'd been given months ago. We'd been looking at his work from the wrong angle. I knew now that the glowing emanations he'd detected on the human body were the footprints of cellular black holes, dying flares of infinitesimal bits of material on the surface of the skin being sucked into the void, a cosmic trade for the new cells constantly generated by a living being: light for dark, dark for light, anti-matter balancing matter. Hiramatsu loomed large in my mind as I saw myself standing on his giant shoulders, the two of us tracking our prey: the foreheads, hands, fingernails, foot bottoms he'd photographed as our guides to the infinite play of dematerialization and return.

I finally found the article. It was under my bed, smeared with Krispy Kreme raspberry jelly that brought back a frisson of fear from the days of red jelly candies and falling asleep pinching the folds of my tweeter. If anything, that little reminder of my first incarnation packed my labors with even more intensity. I spent the rest of the night reading and re-reading Dr. Hiramatsu, googling more than two hundred of the 22,500 links inspired by his research, getting under the covers and writing in my journal once I was too tired to sit at the computer.

I had to fight off Jillily as my exhausted scribbling became increasingly illegible. At the best of times, she treated the process of handwriting as something sacred and mysterious. She liked to watch my pen scratch across the page with round, mesmerized eyes, until she couldn't stand it anymore and tried reaching for the pen herself, as if she could clasp it with those curled white paws of hers and be magically transformed into a more powerful creature who could open cupboards, Friskie's food tins, and the window any time a bird teased from outside with fluttering wings.

I know I finally fell asleep, since I woke to Stanley shaking my shoulder. I discovered later that Gwennie had fetched him in a panic when she couldn't wake me—that's how dead to the world I was. "You're lucky Gwennie's so worried about you," he said when I finally opened my eyes, "or she'd give you hell about the state of this room." Digging dried sleeps from the corners of my eyes, I looked around. The place looked like a bomb had hit it. But then I remembered. I leapt out of bed and handed Stanley my notes. He sat on the edge of the bed while I saw to Jillily's food. Cats are no respecters of events beyond their own needs. When I popped back into the room from the bathroom, a metal scooper in one hand and a full paper bag's worth of poopy litter in the other, I saw Stanley tugging a handkerchief from his pocket and removing his glasses to wipe them.

"You've done it," he croaked.

He was right. I had.

Stanley grabbed my hand and hopped me around the room with him, undeterred by the fact that I still clutched a bag full of cat poop. The poop smelled suspicious. I wondered whether Jillily had been at the sunflower seed shells again.

Stanley may have gloated and Gwennie, once she was sure I hadn't died, may have cheered, but there was still a huge amount of work to do. I would need my team to challenge every one of my assumptions and then, if my idea held up, help me document each stage of my mental journey. I must say that the final version that came from our efforts was elegant, thanks especially to Adam's affinity for the English language, Amir's growing expertise in molecular biology, Tom's patience over the more tedious particulars, Katrina's knack for seeing the holes in my logic, and Gunther's gift for addressing them.

Our work on the paper ended up taking us two months, and, in that time, the Supreme Court had agreed to consider another case regarding the legality of late-term abortions, which made me no end of anxious, for I couldn't decide whether I was pro or anti until it occurred to me that neither position was necessary if you factored in that precious mental commodity: doubt. After we sent the paper off, I had class work to keep up with, Mr. Heavyflow to torture me, Jillily-vomit to clean up, and—now that I was no longer consumed with dematerialization—Sammie to listen to, as she struggled to sort her way through the perils of a normal adolescence. There is something quite wonderful about the rituals of everyday life. They sort out the prickly bits left over from troubling tension. I was happy enough to turn in my assignments on time, coach Sammie in her crush on a sweet-sounding red-haired eighth-grader—providing us with no end of discussion over whether she should let him anywhere near her newly burgeoning breasts—and actually have time to curl up with a series of good books, the concave curve beneath my own breasts warmed by Jillily's reliably motoring belly.

So it came as a bit of shock when our published article arrived in the mail just before Easter break. Adam and Amir and Gunther and Tom and Katrina and I sat together with Stanley in his crowded Caltech office and silently read our copies of the *American Journal of Physics*. By the time I looked up, Gunther was clumsily scrambling onto Stanley's desk, scattering papers everywhere. He leaned out the window and cried exultantly to the stunned students below, "Vi av Gud!"—which, in case you don't speak Swedish, translates as "We are God." One couldn't work with Gunther for as long as I had without picking up a few words here and there. In spite of myself, I made the sign of the cross. I wasn't my father's daughter and Sister Flatulencia's goddaughter for nothing. Gunther had joined Icarus in the solar god's dangerous realm.

Hubris. As the days wore on, I wish I'd been as cognizant of my own.

Stanley was so excited to see our results in print that he insisted on taking me out for a skip at the Huntington Gardens, while the rest of the crew went to a local pub and got what Adam later called *shit-faced*. Adam, by the way, had been selected as a research fellow by Harvard, to begin in the summer, and was prepared to carry on a long distance relationship with Jessica. While I still thought he was handsome, my tweeter seemed to have gone on sabbatical, taking a backseat to my mind as a source of pleasure. I later learned that Sigmund Freud was well familiar with the phenomenon and had dubbed it *sublimation*, a phrase first coined by the alchemists, referring to the process of purifying a substance by heating it into a vapor, and rooted in the Latin *sublimis*, meaning *lofty*.

My disinterest in making mini explosions didn't feel particularly lofty, nor did I—at least not yet. As Stanley and I skipped in and out of Henry Huntington's invisible rose beds, he prattled on and on about what a genius I was. He said he'd already gotten calls inviting me to a couple of back-to-back physics conferences in Europe—one in Paris, the other in Florence. But all I could think was that even the most world-shaking discoveries were hardly a fair exchange for an unresurrected Grandfather and the phantom limb of an unborn bun. But then I imagined Siri Sajan interjecting, "Perhaps they could be a beginning. Excessive humility is inappropriate when serving something larger than yourself."

I put more zip into my skip, allowing the infectiousness of Stanley's enthusiasm to wash over me, and even Uncle Bob, hiding in my jeans pocket, twirled the ends of his handlebar moustache as we bumped along.

Chapter 22 🦋

THE EVER-PRACTICAL Gwennie came up with the idea of a press conference at the celebratory three-course vegetarian bonanza she hosted following the publication of our paper. The meal included a soy-based macaroni and cheese concoction that Cook would have died to claim as her own, and the wine and (in my case) Hansen's Key Lime Soda were flowing like water. I suppose it was inevitable that the discussion veered into the kind of nauseatingly self-congratulatory back-slapping you might imagine, with Aadita and Sammie and Gwennie and Stanley the patient audience for our innumerable toasts to what advances C-Void might presage. (And in case you're wondering, *C-Voids* had quickly become our shorthand for cellular black holes.)

Gwennie began to pile up our dirty dinner dishes just as Amir lifted his third glass of Merlot. "Here's to the disappearance of garbage." Gunther, his face red with a surfeit of wine and undiminished hubris, shouted, "Garbage, hell. Dematerialization will revolutionize travel. Bye bye cars and outrageous gas prices. For that matter, hassling luggage at the airport." Skipping a perfectly-timed beat, Katrina added dryly, "Being cornered in a bar by some loser."

Into the ensuing laughter, it was Aadita who introduced the possibility that our discovery would not be met with unmitigated approval. Aadita and Gwennie were the most political of our company, and, once Aadita broached the topic, Gwennie went galloping right after her, looking as if she might fling the soiled macaroni and cheese platter over our heads like a Frisbee.

The tittering began to die down as Aadita related a story she'd heard the previous weekend on Ira Flatow's *Science Friday*. "I could hardly believe what I was hearing. Some of your country's top drug companies are actually patenting the genetic determinants of drug reactions, not to help people know ahead of time whether or not they would benefit from a particular medication or would have an adverse drug reaction, but to actually prevent that information from becoming available." She stacked her salad plate neatly atop her dinner dish, adding, "They're evidently worried their sales will plummet if only those people likely to respond well end up buying one of their constipation aids or cancer drugs."

Into the ensuing shower of indignation, Gwennie threw in a prediction that sent goose bumps marching up my arms. "If Big Pharma is willing to throw thousands of people off a cliff by failing to prevent avoidable side effects, what do you think Big Oil is going to do with a discovery that might one day make automobiles obsolete?"

Gwennie's solution was a simple one. "You should hold a major press conference before the powers-that-be have a chance to squelch your news. At least then, when the shitstorm hits, you'll have some of the world on your side to battle the Neanderthals."

Gwennie's language might be coarse, but she wasn't stupid. But even she couldn't have predicted one of the more damaging angles our adversaries would be shooting from. Just a few days after our announcement was reported in the *Science Section* (barely a single column) of the *Los Angeles Times*, the front page contained an article (nearly a quarter of a page) headed, "Pro-Life Crusader says Potentially World-Changing Discovery Worse Than Human Cloning," with the sub-heading, "Senator Robins cites daughter's autism as excuse for moral lapse."

I learned right then that loss is not the only catalyst for a broken heart.

Needless to say, my friends were incensed. Even the opinionless Cook called to comment on Father's new Campaign America to Crush C-Voids, otherwise known as CACC—his detractors were already calling his group *Cacklers*. She said his recent actions cemented her conviction that he was "one vindictive S.O.B."

Stanley hastened to put in motion Gwennie's suggestion, but the trouble with press conferences is that they tend to activate some button inside people that generates phony granny grins. My own trouble was that, with the memory of innumerable press conferences in front of one particular sycamore on Father's old grounds, I wasn't grinning at all. As I stood with my physics team on the front steps of Caltech's Beckman Auditorium, the lusterless sky reminded me all too much of those afternoons Grandfather and I liked best—the two of us sitting side by side, matching Canadian blankets on our laps, with me counting aloud the species of birds on the branches of our winter-bare tree.

Katrina had to jab me in the ribs and Adam to roll his eyes multiple times in the direction of Stanley H. Fiske's head, towering over rest of the small gathering, before I woke from what Sammie liked to call a personal pity party. But once I registered Stanley's presence, grinning wasn't much of an effort. He was literally hopping from foot to foot. Didn't anyone else notice his resemblance to a toad?

Once the assorted Caltech luminaries, three members of the press, and a TV camera crew had themselves situated, Stanley leapt up several steps to the microphone to introduce us. It was his public clout, after all, that had gotten the media out in the first place. Compared with plane crashes, child abductions, and major corporate chicanery, scientific announcements were generally non-starters when it came to paying for commercials and selling papers.

"When future generations look back to this moment," he began, "they will marvel there weren't more of your media colleagues here to record the scientific breakthrough my young friends are announcing. Today, humanity leaps forward, not one small step, but a thousand light years. Today, all our assumptions of what is real—and really possible—collapse like one of my sister Gwendolyn's vegetarian soufflés." Okay, so nobody laughed, especially not Gwennie. But, excepting the latter, they all smiled politely in tacit acknowledgement that exceptions had to be made for people a hundred times cleverer than themselves.

But things got a lot squirmier, for me at least, when he introduced the team. I'd known ahead of time that I would be the one to read the abstract of our paper and to field the inevitable disbelieving questions, but I'd foolishly discounted what Adam warned me would be the reporters' intense interest in my age. After all, it was hardly the relevant topic when we were proposing a significant shift to our paradigm of reality.

But I suppose they had a point. My sole peer and best friend couldn't even be there, since most thirteen-year-olds are required to be at school at eleven o'clock on a Friday morning. As a matter of fact, Sammie was taking a dreaded American history exam at the very moment I spoke into the microphone. As she had pointed out innumerable times over the past few days, she'd be considerably more confident if she were being tested on the monarchs of Great Britain, but, belly sister that she was, she had taken time from her anxious cramming to unearth a dried four leaf clover for me that she had found with her father while kite flying on Primrose Hill. I clutched it in my trembling hand, the microphone squealing intermittently as I spoke.

That night, Sammie and I exchanged war stories. Her exam had been computer-graded, so she already knew she'd passed with flying colors. As for me and my first press conference—well, I'd survived. We decided to celebrate the next day by going shopping. Sammie had been asked on a proper first date by the red-haired boy (whose name, by the way, was, Jack Green), and what girl going on a first date doesn't instantly get thrown into the land of "I've got nothing to wear?"

Aadita was only too pleased to drop us off on Colorado Boulevard. Pasadena's Old Town was our favorite place to shop. Unfortunately, it was nearly everyone else's favorite place, too. It was an unseasonably hot April day, and the sidewalks were wall-to-wall noisy, sweaty humanity. It was when we were trying to squeeze our way from H & M to the Gap that I saw a familiar face coming toward us.

I did an about face and ran across the street just as the light shifted from yellow to red. I was barely aware of Sammie running behind me, shouting, "Fleur, have a care! Are you mad? You're going to get yourself killed!"

Seven honking cars later, I anxiously scanned the crowd across the street, muttering through my panting breath, "I'm so sorry, but I can't believe it. I know I shouldn't mind, but God..."

Sammie impatiently banged her H & M bag against her leg, looking as if she didn't know whether to be angry or curious. "What in the world is it?"

"It was Hector. Hector Hernandez. I saw him coming in our direction. He looked just the same, only a little taller, I guess." Breathing heavily, I leaned against a stoplight, causing a Hispanic woman pushing a triplet stroller's worth of Anglo toddlers to nearly crash into us.

Sammie grabbed my arm. "Right. We've got to get away from this lot. Here." Before I knew it, she'd veered us inside the cool interior of Il Fornaio. Great. This was turning out to be a regular Old Home Week.

But the fact was that my old favorite Angel Hair Diavolo turned out to be just the ticket. Sammie tried cheering me up by speculating what Hector Hernandez had been up to since the last time I'd seen him. Her contributions escalated from "having to re-take eighth grade algebra" to "banging his English teacher."

I snorted just as I was swallowing my iced tea, which promptly shot out of my nostrils. "Ow," I protested. Who knew how badly peach-flavored iced tea could sting the insides of your nose?

Even as we laughed, the place in my heart where Baby X lived ached terribly, and I couldn't help but wish I hadn't seen her father's still-handsome face standing out like neon in the crowd.

But, that night, CNN started playing and re-playing dueling footage of our press conference and Father picketing with a bunch of Cacklers in front of the offices of the American Association of Physics Teachers in Maryland. It occurred to me that, now that the mainstream media had gotten hold of my discovery of C-voids, Hector Hernandez would become the least of my worries.

I was right. Within days, Adam and Amir and Tom and Gunther and Katrina and I became fodder for everything from acrimonious exchanges on the floor of Congress to the "List of Top Ten Ideas Guaranteed to Piss off People Who Think Children Should be Seen and Not Heard" on David Letterman, who continued for several weeks to make corny dematerialization jokes about me being heard but not seen. I know because Adam TiVo'd it for me. He actually thought it was funny.

It was shortly afterwards that I had an unusual phone conversation with Mother. She and Nana were long time Letterman fans, and she was worried I'd be upset. Frankly, I was touched she'd thought to ask. But my relations with Mother had been awkward for so many years that I merely said, "If he only understood Schrödinger Operators, he'd take the whole thing a lot more seriously."

Mother went silent for a moment, then said, "Yes, well...how's your friend Sammie?"

"Oh, she's quite good. She got an A on her American History exam, and she's finally cracked open *A Wizard of Earthsea*. I've been trying to get her to read it for ages."

"Mmm," Mother replied, sounding distracted. "Do you have other friends, Fleur?"

I didn't answer. I had no idea what Mother was getting at. But before I could ask her, here's what she of the hundreds of mutual friends of Bill W. said: "Oh well, sometimes just one person who knows your heart does the trick."

I was so taken aback by Mother's comment that I actually felt a little excitement when she proposed coming out for a visit. "The truth is, I've been invited to speak at a convention in Las Vegas," she confessed, "but I can't come all that way without seeing my girl, can I?"

Needless to say, it hardly felt terrific to be the side dish for her main meal. Nevertheless, it was a novel experience seeing her walking through the rooms of my current incarnation a few weeks later, trailing competing scents of Chanel No. 5 and Sherman cigarettes through the Fiske home. Mother had pulled up in her rented Lexus earlier than we'd expected, and when she kissed me on each of my cheeks I was actually glad that Gwen was still at Trader Joe's, picking up what Sammie liked to call "some odds and sods" for tomorrow's breakfast.

I led Mother anxiously to my room, where she neatly installed her suitcase in the corner before proceeding to carefully examine how I'd festooned my walls. You can imagine my relief when she pronounced, "It's lovely, Fleur. You've certainly developed your own sense of style." I was gratified, as well, to see her take her time petting Jillily, who deigned to purr in recognition.

It wasn't until Mother went into the bathroom to have a pee that it occurred to me that I had something more to show her. As soon as she emerged—her wrinkled nose reminding me I hadn't yet emptied Jillily's litter box—I beckoned Mother to follow me, calling over my shoulder, "Wait till you see the backyard!" You can imagine how tickled I was to introduce her to Gwennie's Dark Lady, Abraham Darby, Ambridge Rose and Jude the Obscure. To her credit, she took her time, appreciatively sniffing each and every one.

Just as she was paying her respects to a twin-blooming Dark Lady, a hearty "There you are!" boomed out from the back door. We looked up to see Gwennie barreling toward us, taking a shortcut off the cobblestone-paved pathway and hastily tucking her faded red blouse into her stretchy-waistband jeans. Like a dancer, Mother extended her hand with a graceful flourish and elegantly tiptoed in Gwennie's direction, careful not to dig her three-inch Manolos into the rye grass.

Gwennie had never met Mother before, and I was apprehensive about whether the two of them would get on, especially after hearing Gwen comment to Stanley one night, "Funny, AA having that conference in one of the four bellies of the alcoholic beast."

Laughing, Stanley had asked her what the other three were, and she'd promptly replied, "Capitol Hill, old New Orleans, and the entire United Kingdom. Do you think she's still sober?"

To which, Stanley had merely commented, "Watch it, girl. She *is* the child's mother."

But there the two women were, shaking hands like amiable diplomats. Gwennie turned her good ear toward Mother so she could hear her say, "I want to thank you for making my daughter feel so at home; you and your brother have been very generous, given her opportunities I never could. I wasn't exactly the most maternal sort of mother, if you know what I mean."

I had to hand it to Mother. If Gwennie had been primed to resent her intrusion, Mother's disarming candor won her over on the spot. And to Gwennie's credit, once she'd treated the two of us to a yummy wood-fired pizza binge at Avanti, she insisted we spend the greater part of Mother's time in So Cal on our own—which we mostly did, except for inhaling a full English breakfast prepared by Aadita and going on several excursions that included Sammie. I have to say Mother was the most childlike of the three of us at Disneyland, where she insisted on buying each of us Mickey Mouse ears at Main Street's Mad Hatter, bursting into tears later on when hers fell off on the Matterhorn.

But Gwennie took us both by surprise when she suggested that Sammie and Aadita and I fly out to Las Vegas, too, telling Mother, "That way, you'll get more time together, Aadita will get a much-needed break from grading papers, and Fleur will be able to have fun with her friend while you're conferencing."

Aadita proclaimed it "a brilliant idea" and was so quick to go along with the plan that I secretly speculated that she and Gwen had cooked it all up ahead of time. It was a superb arrangement. While Mother and her Bill W.'s consumed enough coffee and smoked enough cigarettes to stain half the teeth of the western world, Aadita and Sammie and I got to thrill to the artistry of Cirque de Soleil, laugh ourselves silly at the Orleans Hotel as we tried to land at least one bowling ball anywhere but in the gutter, ride to the top of a fake Eiffel Tower, and debate the morality of keeping God's creatures captive but well fed at Siegfried and Roy's Dolphin Habitat. My favorite part of the trip, though, was getting to share a room with Sammie, where we played an aggregate of five games of Scrabble, three games of Chess, a couple sets of Hang-Man and innumerable bursts of Rock, Paper, Scissors. We vied with each other over how long we could maintain the mindset of Shunia, the yogic state of nothingness, and jointly completed the *New York Times* Sunday Crossword in a record twenty minutes; best of all, we whispered secrets into the wee hours under the humped duvet of our shared double bed.

While I might not have had much bonding time in Las Vegas with Mother, she'd given me the gift of several unusually precious days with my bellasista. In aid of fitting into her new world, Sammie might have shed some of her charming British accent, but her garrulousness and wit were still intact. She managed to take the piss out of all the blue-haired, over-lipsticked matrons at the slot machines, all the fake-breasted, over-lipsticked younger women at the gambling tables, and all the freckled, over-lipsticked pre-teens at the pool. It was a wonderful relief from the fuss over C-Voids to indulge in catty comments. I even debated whether I ought to stay at Caltech or return to public school. Of course, once I shared my dilemma with Sammie, she took the piss out of *that*.

"Right. 'Let's go slumming with the normals.' It's so much more fun studying the dead white men of early American history than coming up with ideas to change the world. And, by the way, aren't those middle school girls friendly? They'll just love some hottie genius coming to school to steal their boyfriends."

The hottie part was our joke. It was actually how one of the letters to the editor of *People Magazine* had described me. What it said exactly was, "I was excited to read about Fleur Robins' new theory, but when I turned the page I couldn't believe what a hottie she is. I hope you print a lot more articles about her." The fact that the letter writer described himself as a twelve-year-old physics nerd from Wichita, Kansas put something of a dent in his credibility.

All things considered, though, better a hottie than a dog.

I had no idea what to do with my sudden celebrity. Seeing my own photo staring back at me from the pages of a magazine was like encountering some stranger who, for some unfathomable reason, was pretending to be me. I mean, it wasn't actually me whom people recognized on the street, was it? Not one of them knew about Jillily and Grandfather and our tree and red jelly candies and Baby X and Sammie and Sister Flatulencia's doozies and Nana's cave scent...well, I think you get the gist. Instead, all they seemed to see was either a brainiac or a mental case, a Cackler-fighter or someone who "should go back where you came from," which—from the nasty tones of their voices—was presumably the tenth circle of hell. Since so many of the people who suddenly thought they knew me tended to sneak looks at me with their mouths hanging open, I began categorizing them as dogs, which, I might not need to tell you, helped no end in mitigating what Sammie came to call "the aggro."

But eventually, despite the controversy swirling around C-Voids and P.D. (or the Principle of Dematerialization), there was a period when my personal life returned to something recognizably normal. David Letterman stopped putting me on his top ten lists, and magazines gave up trying to persuade Gwennie and Stanley to have me pose for their covers—I'm afraid the amount of fan mail generated by the piece in *People Magazine* had made an enemy of me forever of Caltech's mailroom staff.

But, in case you haven't noticed, our notion of normal tends to be rather fluid, its parameters defined by whatever we grow accustomed to. Because it all occurred incrementally, I barely noticed that Sammie's tree of life and mine were bending away from each other again. Her flirtation with Jack Green mushroomed into the obsessiveness of first love. She discovered in drama class at Eliot Middle School something the rest of us had known all along, that she had a decided dramatic bent, and was rushing off to private acting lessons every Saturday afternoon following our weekly hour of yoga with Siri Sajan. Still, she managed to make as much time for me as I managed to make for her in between working on potential applications of P.D., and attending a series of good will appearances at conferences around the globe—typically with some permutation of Adam, and

Katrina, and Amir, and Tom, and Gunther—on behalf of the monster we'd unleashed.

I'm afraid the latter series of activities went a long way in stretching that head of mine into something resembling a giant balloon. I actually began to think of myself as the genius I was touted to be, conveniently forgetting the direction that pride proverbially goeth. After returning from a conference in Rome, I actually flaked on movie plans with Sammie three times in a row. Once we finally managed to sync up, devouring popcorn like there was no tomorrow as we sat in our favorite fifth row seats watching *The Chronicles of Narnia*, I blithely assumed my presence served as a satisfactory amends.

It was Gwennie who blew the bugle announcing the coming battle. She can't be blamed though. All she did was break the news.

It all started on one of those smoggy So Cal October days. Sammie and I were sitting on my bed, sweating like pigs despite our shorts and T-shirts, with Jillily sandwiched between us, when Gwennie knocked on my bedroom door. Jillily was fast asleep, oblivious to our snickers over her somnolent gas attack. That was another thing about feline aging—it stirred up a state in a cat's intestines that rivaled Sister Flatulencia in her pre-Beano days.

But when we saw Gwennie's face, Sammie and I sobered up fast enough. Gwen was wearing her *Physicists are Spicier* apron and had a smear of flour across her cheek. She knelt at the foot of the bed and took my hand, stroking it repetitively in a way that I found unaccountably annoying. I forced back the temptation to shrug her off. "Fleur, dear, I've just gotten a call from your Nana. I'm afraid I have some bad news."

My heartbeat accelerated as my mind rifled through the possible scenarios. *Nana? Has the cave scent gotten to her? But she was in good enough shape to make the call. Please God, not Mother. I should have nagged her more about the smoking. Could it be Sister Flatulencia? She's a clean liver, but not such a great driver. Cook? She was pretty obese again. They say cholesterol is a killer. Fayga? Furniture paste poisoning? Dhani? Not possible—too young. Ignacio? Strong as the earth. Baby Angelina? Children are always having accidents.*

As if reading my mind, Gwennie shook her head. "It's your father. He's in intensive care."

I suppose I might have had some sort of reaction if Sammie hadn't at that very moment fallen off the bed. It was quite a phenomenon, actually. One moment she was waiting, as I was, for Gwennie to cut to the chase, the next her eyes went shuttered as if she were practicing the meditative state of *Shunia* and then, in exquisitely slow motion, she slid eelishly onto the floor. Only later did it occur to me that she owed the grace of her movement to the fact that she was unconscious at the time.

Gwennie had to slap her face to bring her to, and in my ensuing dash to phone Aadita to come over right away, I quite forgot about Father. Well, not really, but I'd recalled my sly soldier back to active duty and was using Sammie's fainting fit to put off facing my feelings. Needless to say, Sammie hadn't been able to put her feelings off at all. The combination of the words *father* and *intensive care* had brought her own loss in the father department right back to her.

It was only when Aadita had arrived to shepherd Sammie back home and Gwennie had phoned Stanley at school to let him know what was going on and I'd taken refuge in my bathroom, claiming a tummy ache, that I could fully contemplate the additional information about Father that Gwennie had spat out to me as she was dialing Stanley's cell number. I stared at myself in the bathroom mirror, only the slightest bit bothered by the noxious fumes from Jillily's litter box. At least, in that regard, I had my priorities straight, despite what Sammie claimed later.

It was Father's ticker, of course. The same ticker that had humbled him enough to let me into his good graces for a while. The ticker that evidently hadn't been humbled enough to keep me there. Even with him lying in the void of some hospital ICU, I was still terribly angry with Father. Staring at my expressionless face in the bathroom mirror, I was beginning to notice it myself.

Which was when Gwennie knocked on the door and said, "Fleurie, dear, it's Sammie. She wants to talk to you." Gwennie scanned my face as I emerged from the bathroom. She looked a bit perplexed by the dryness of my eyes. She handed me the phone.

"God, Fleur, I am so sorry. That was the last thing you needed. What a selfish pig I am. Have you talked to your mum yet?"

How could I tell her that I couldn't imagine my mother reacting any differently than I had? That all I wanted to do was get some Laxatone for Jillily and some ginger snaps for myself, shut the door on everyone, turn off the lights, and bury myself under the covers, maybe even indulge in a pinch or two.

Instead, I said, "Yeah, well, I haven't had a chance yet, have I? We've just sorted *you* out, haven't we?"

Gwennie shot me a sharp look and, I'm ashamed to say, Sammie sounded guilty. "What a prat I am. Right. I'll get off the phone so you can call home." Before hanging up, she whispered, "Ring me if you need me."

The fact was, I wasn't of a mind to be needing anyone. More to the point, I wasn't of any mind at all.

Gwennie had the good sense to leave me to my own devices, letting the void swallow me for a while. But not long enough. Within the hour, she was knocking on my door again. It was Mother on the phone and she *was* crying. So much for making assumptions about other people's emotional lives.

"Fleur, Fleur."

Mother, Mother. I dug my nails more deeply into the palms of my hands. "Yes, it's me."

"Fleur, I don't know how to tell you this. Sister Flatulencia just called. I'm afraid he's gone, Sweetie Pie. We're both fatherless daughters now. Except in your case, well, I know it's got to be hard, him going before making amends." Oh, Lord. The Bill W. *spiel.* "Do you want to come home?"

I rolled her question around my mind. Home? As Stephanie Seidenfeld might have said, "What planet was *she* on?" It hadn't been home for ages. "I don't think so, Mother. I've got a lot to do. Stanley's set some conference at Caltech next week, then, before you know it, it'll be finals."

Mother went silent for so long that I nearly asked her if she was still there, but then she allowed rather hesitantly, "Yes, well, I suppose that's best. Sometimes distraction's the best remedy. Keeping on with your routine."

Only it wasn't. Routine, I mean. Things would proceed to get even more chaotic in the days to come.

For one thing, the press seemed to have decided in some secret society meeting that millions of people would not get to sleep at night if they didn't know my precise reaction to the death of the father who'd been vigorously campaigning to protect the world from the contents of my mind. Even if I'd been tempted to share my most personal feelings with a host of strangers, how could I? Father's death had pretty much emptied me out.

Which made me even more vulnerable to the phone call I received three days after Father died and one day before his burial. It came at six in the morning. I know because I was already awake, having been debating since three o'clock what to do about Father. I knew I wasn't going to his funeral, but I didn't want him haunting my mind, an angry ghost with a decidedly unfriendly agenda.

I flicked a look at my bedside clock in response to the simultaneous sounds of the telephone ringing, Stanley swearing, Gwennie's slippers slapping up the hall, and Jillily leaping from the curve of my belly onto my cluttered desk in one neat move.

Just as Jillily unloaded last night's dinner down the side of the desk, Stanley burst into my room with Gwennie right behind him. He thrust the phone into my hand. I didn't want to take it. One more call from Mother asking if I wanted to talk about Father's death would simply be one call too many. But Stanley, who looked like he was going to jump right out of his skin, insisted.

I said a wary, "Hello?" and heard a thickly-accented and rather breathless voice say, "Miss Robins? This is Lars Isaksson. I am calling as Chairman of the Royal Swedish Academy of Sciences to personally congratulate you. The Academy is so impressed by your discovery of C-Voids and your Theory of the Principle of Dematerialization that we have voted to award you this year's Prize in Physics." I heard whispering in the background, then Professor Isaksson added, "We know the award will be controversial—among other things, you will be the youngest recipient ever—but the implications of your work for the advance of science are tremendous. We are very much looking forward to discussing it with you in Stockholm."

Only the fact that Stanley was hopping around my room like a frog on fire persuaded me that this wasn't some practical joke. I didn't know what to think or say but couldn't help be aware that my fingers were trembling and I couldn't stop blinking. Gwennie gestured frantically, and I realized that the man on the other end of the line was waiting for me to respond.

I managed to squeak out a paltry, "Thank you" before I burst into tears. Stanley liberated the phone from me and took it into the hall. I couldn't be bothered trying to make out what he was saying.

My mind was already filled to capacity. Where was I going to fit this unimaginable piece of information? For the first time in my life, I could have used a little more void.

Chapter 23 🦋

I SUPPOSE FOR any normal human being, winning the Nobel Prize would pretty much trump everything else. But, in the following few days, I couldn't stop obsessing over the fact that Sammie could no—would not—understand why I refused to go back to New York for Father's funeral. What did she know? She'd had a father who'd read to her, listened to her, babysat for her when her mum went to sitting practice. In short, a miss-able kind of father.

I realized later that she saw my refusal to attend my own father's internment as a reflection of Nobel-winning egotism rather than dread of returning to the place where I'd failed to resurrect Grandfather and been pincered by you-know-who for trying. But she didn't give me a chance to explain. Calling excitedly to tell me she and Aadita had just heard the news about my Nobel on KPCC, she segued rather abruptly to asking when Father's funeral was. When I responded, "I don't know. It doesn't matter, anyway. I'm not going," she actually hung up on me.

I couldn't help but notice it was beginning to become a habit.

Oh, I know, I could have called her back. But just the thought of it brought up memories of banging at Mother's closed door as a child. Since Sammie had been the one to hang up on me, not just once, but two times now, I told myself it was up to *her* to call *me*.

My belly roiled with disquiet, but I was already in a state of overwhelm, given the intersection of my father's death with learning about the prize. I felt I'd been chopped into pieces, each of which was going about its tasks remarkably unconcerned about the others.

It wasn't exactly Multiple Personality Disorder—all the *me*'s were pretty much the same age, with the same voice, clothing, and personal quirks—and it certainly wasn't multi-tasking, which requires a juggler keeping all the balls in play. My own juggler was desperately trying to find her way out of a bottomless black hole.

Which, oddly enough, didn't stop the other Fleurs from continuing to function. I guess the closest analogy would be the proverbial headless chicken, one of whom, by the way, is reputed to have survived for eighteen months before realizing it was unseemly to be anything but dead. In my case, death was not an option. That was thanks to a newly emergent part of me who was only too pleased to mask her misery behind fame. Father's death had dissolved from the front page, which, for a day or so anyway, became my own dominion. Whatever the media had made of my age until now, I became for a time the miracle child of the western world. Never mind that other kids knew how to have a proper boyfriend, dance without looking like a cat with fleas, and inhabit a body without everything going wrong at the same time.

One of the sorrier consequences of having no shopkeeper to mind the store was that my body went on strike. My bowels couldn't decide whether to flow like beef broth or congeal into sharp-edged pellets devilishly designed to defy my rectal muscles' superhuman efforts to release them. I developed a fungal rash on my legs, was plagued with a persistent parade of bladder infections, and my periods came and went as inconsistently as our cable connection. In between press conferences and photo shoots, Gwennie hauled me to every kind of doctor known to mankind, including an allergist improbably called Dr. Aitchly, who tested me for cat allergies, to which I gratefully tested negative.

It was an odd thing to have my many selves diverge so decidedly from the path of my body. Despite my sensory wallow in the Slough of Despond, most everyone said they never saw me look better, and, if I do say so myself, my photograph in *People* magazine—on the cover, this time—looked gratifyingly glamorous. When I say *everyone*, though, I am excluding the one with whom I would most wish to share my joy. (Well, except Grandfather, whom I could sense grinning inside me with a sincerity that would put to shame every one of the world's phony grannies.)

The missing fan in my fan club was Sammie. Despite my rupture with her daughter, I managed to keep in touch with the even-handed Aadita, who was thrilled for my good fortune and pleased that her knowledge of Indra's Net had been put to such good use. It was from Sammie's mother that I learned my bellasista had broken up with her boyfriend, was at sixes and sevens with the group of friends she'd made at middle school, and had even quit her acting lessons.

It was nearly impossible to fall asleep at night, knowing that a mere forty odd yards of asphalt separated the two of us. In truth, it felt more like forty incarnations. The problem was we were both impossibly stubborn.

In the few months following the announcement, I grew my hair out, cut it again, had a stylist repair the damage and persuaded her to dye a few of the front locks bright red—which Gwennie reversed after a quick trip to the cosmetics department of Rite Aid. What she didn't take care of, because she never knew about it, was my sneaking out to Old Town one night to have a tattoo inked onto my lower back. What *I* hadn't anticipated was that my chosen emblem, *Nobelist*, would be misheard by Riku of Riku's Righteous Tattoos as *No Bull-shit*—which just goes to show you the wisdom of writing things down when your tattoo artist has a dubious grasp of the English language. That was the bad news. The good news was that the sensation of needles spitting at my sacrum saved me no end of pinching and banging. Remember, these were tense times.

It didn't help that it was only myself whom the Nobel Committee had chosen to honor, when I knew for a fact I would have gotten nowhere without my team. But Adam and Amir and Katrina and Tom and Gunther kept reminding me that the idea had been mine from the get-go. As Tom put it, "Hey, every Nobel has a backup group singing the *doo-wops*. They add some flavor, but they're not the main dish." If anything, all five seemed absurdly grateful that I sang their praises to anyone who'd listen. It goes with saying that I insisted they be my guests at the awards.

But not even the support of my backup singers could combat the nastiness and controversy swirling around me in the period between *The Call* and *The Ceremonies*. Much is made in the media of where people were and what they felt when they received their call from the Nobel Committee. In retrospect, I felt the most affinity with Elfriede Jelinek, who refused to accept her award in person because of a social phobia and who told an interviewer that getting *The Call* felt like having a black hole in her head. I personally had the black hole in my head years *before* my call, but I can't see that it makes much of a difference.

If Father's death had taken some of the cack out of the Cacklers, it did nothing to halt the efforts of Big Oil to bring me down. Never mind that the additional publicity afforded by the Prize set the field of physics even more flagrantly on fire, stimulating scads of research projects devoted to applying my theory. You might not be aware that scientists can be motivated by more than the sheer love of discovery. Ambition is a word not unknown in academic circles. But the already gaping rift between science and religion's more literal proponents was being cannily exploited by the oil lobby, with me typecast via a vicious letter-writing campaign to every major American newspaper as something akin to the poet Yeats' "rough beast slouching toward Bethlehem to be born." I don't know about you, but I have never heard of anyone slouching toward birth, not even an aborted one. Struggling, yes. Screaming? Definitely. But slouching? Perhaps there are some things even a prophet can't be expected to understand.

And please don't think for a moment that I use the word prophet lightly. Even before I'd been dragged into the midst of a national furor over the morality of our breakthrough, Gwennie had wakened me to the fragile state of our world's sanity. The vacillations of various leaders on global warming and stem cell research smacked a little too much of a useless mother staring down at her sobbing infant. The center was definitely not holding.

I'm sorry to say that the intensified turmoil over C-Voids put a damper on my desire to expand the concept. Instead, I read cheesy romances, obsessed about my appearance, and paid a visit to the home of my second incarnation. I was shocked by how much change had occurred. Nana and the increasingly hyperkinetic Cesar Jesus de Maria Santo Domingo Marisco had gone from inseparability to civil war.

Mother had found herself a considerably younger Bill W. boyfriend. Cook had stunned everyone by running off to the Bahamas with a retired sous-chef, leaving Dhani to run herself ragged at the Cookery School. Sister Flatulencia was wearing a new set of ill-fitting dentures, which clicked like castanets whenever she opened her mouth. As for Baby Angelina, she'd grown taller than Cesar and had already out-classed him in the language department. Thanks to her attendance at a mid-city nursery school, she was now fluent in English, Spanish, and Hip Hop, greeting my belated birthday gift of a delicate gold charm bracelet with an enthusiastic, "Ooh, Auntie Fleurie! *Phat bling!*"

On my first night back in New York, I confessed to Mother that I was fretting about what to wear on December tenth. The Nobel Awards Banquet was what they called White Tie and Tails, which Adam said meant he and Amir and Tom and Gunther were going to have to humiliate themselves in penguin suits, while we females would have the pleasure of wearing evening gowns or our national costume as an alternative. Since the current national costume for girls my age required showing several inches of butt crack, I knew I had to opt for the former. It wasn't so much my crack I was worried about as the words etched above it. *No Bullshit* might be apt in its own way, but under the circumstances it might be construed as a crudely worded plug for our side of the dematerialization debate.

Of course, I said nothing to Mother about *that* and made sure she stayed out of the dressing rooms of the myriad shops she took me to in our search for the perfect Nobel dress. It was when we were on our way to Barney's that Mother started elbowing me every minute or so. I finally stopped in the middle of West 17th Street and demanded to know what she thought she was doing.

She laughed. "I'm just letting you know when I see a cute guy checking you out."

"That's just because of the *People* magazine cover," I replied dismissively.

"No, it's not, and you know it."

And I suppose I did. I'd had a small waist and bulbous breasts for what seemed like forever, but now that I'd learned to style my hair and care for my teenage skin, I felt a little like a butterfly discovering she was no longer a caterpillar. It hadn't exactly escaped me that something had come together in my face over the past few months. Everything was somehow, well, *proportional*, as if I'd gotten blessed by the Golden Mean. Only an indefinable intensity to my expression offered the clue that behind my blue eyes sat a strange sort of mind.

After exhausting what felt like every high-fashion boutique in Manhattan, Mother had the bright idea of heading for the Meatpacking District. We made a pit-stop at Washington Square, and it was there, attracted by a particularly enthusiastic looking weed, that I actually found a four leaf clover—which immediately reminded me of Sammie. The next thing I knew, I was crying like a baby while Mother held me close to her Chanel No. 5 breasts. As I listened to the evenness of her heartbeat, I had to admit she'd come a long way, and I hope you don't think I mean miles. For the first time in my life, I ended up voluntarily confiding in Mother. I explained what had happened between Sammie and me. "But it's not my fault," I added hastily. "I mean, hanging up on me twice, leaving me just dangling on the other end. That's not exactly how you treat somebody you care about."

Mother opened her mouth a few times, then closed it again. She probably wanted to tell me to stop being such an idiot and just make up with Sammie. Instead, she took my arm and held me tightly to her side, making sympathetic sounds before confiding in me, "You know, the closest I got to having a real friend before I got sober was when your father hired Sister Flatulencia as my companion to help me through my pregnancy."

I felt a stab of guilt for ruining my mother's young life, but I was too shy to say so. Instead, I offered a jokey, "What a stinky way to learn about friendship." Mother snorted. As if taking her cue from me, she kept her conversation light for the rest of the day, and we actually ended up having a good time. I ended up choosing a breathtaking peony and chrysanthemum embroidered gown in Alexander McQueen's modern cave of a showroom, with Mother insisting I take the dress back with me to So Cal to have the waistline taken in.

Back in So Cal, I tried my new gown on for the Fiskes. Stanley said he thought it made me look like a million bucks. I didn't dream of telling him what it *had* cost. I was dying to show Sammie my dress, but I'm ashamed to say I couldn't bring myself to phone her. If I called to ask her over now, I was afraid she'd accuse me of simply showing off.

I ended up flying to Stockholm without her blessings. I had my Caltech team and Stanley and Gwennie accompanying me on the journey, which should have helped, and I suppose it would have if I weren't so aware of being the odd and lonely duck I was obviously fated to be.

Chapter 24 🦋

MOTHER AND NANA had flown to Stockholm ahead of us and were waiting at Arlanda Airport when our flight landed. After cordial greetings were exchanged and the team headed for a taxi to their guest digs at Stockholm University, Mother gave me a satisfyingly long hug until Nana grabbed hold of me, showering my head with what must have been a hundred chicken peck kisses. Our plane trip had been nearly terminally boring, so I was only too relieved to let Mother and Nana fill my void with their fussing and was particularly grateful for the cashmere throw they competed to tuck tightly around me. I thought I knew winter, but this was ridiculous. Even without the severe snow that was being forecast for the following week, I couldn't stop my teeth from chattering. I noticed that Mother's and Nana and Gwennie's hands had a slight blue tinge and that our stretch Mercedes limo's heater seemed to be struggling.

Stanley H. Fiske alone seemed impervious to the cold. Sliding from window to window, he provided a running commentary on the scenery. "Look at these colors—peach, yellow, baby blue—they're just like the Easter eggs I used to dye as a kid." I couldn't help but reflect that Stanley was still a lot like that little kid. But he was right—the best word for the architecture was *sweet*. I learned later that one of the city's predominant styles was called Swedish Grace and speculated that the pastel colors and fanciful touches on the buildings were designed to mitigate months of dismal polar night.

I felt frozen *and* pitish when we dropped the Fiskes off at the home of one of Stanley's physics friends from the Swedish Academy.

I was beginning to feel anxious about being separated from my fourth incarnation family. After all, they were the ones who'd hiked the long hike with me to this particular pinnacle, and I felt exposed without them. I was terrified in particular that some Swedish reporter was going to materialize out of nowhere to stick a microphone in my face and ask about my stand on the politics of P.D.

But Mother was determined to make my trip magical. She had booked us into a sumptuous suite at the Grand Hotel, right at the edge of a harbor parked with pretty multi-colored boats. As I stumbled into the lobby, a surreal sensation swept over me. This place was straight out of a fairy tale. I must confess I felt a certain disquiet. My first years had been spent in grand digs and were made up mostly of misery. This five star hotel was even grander, and I couldn't help but crane my neck looking for the thirteenth fairy—the one who shows up uninvited at a fabulous banquet and puts a curse on all the guests and everyone ends up frozen in their seats with their forks halted halfway to their lips. As Mother signed us in at the front desk, I uttered a silent prayer to Zeus in his role as Friend of the Stranger to see me through the coming week.

When we got up to our room, we discovered that the staff had a sweet-scented bath awaiting us, actually sprinkled with rose petals. Mother and Nana insisted it was mine, and, given the steam rising from the oversized tub, I wasn't about to object. I let my body sink into the deliciously warm bath, while Bach's *Jesu, Joy of Man's Desiring* played from a speaker on the wall. Pushing petals across the water, I pretended they were little boats ferrying miniature versions of Grandfather and Sammie and Jillily to visit me, with Uncle Bob bringing up the rear, until my eyelids grew heavy and my fingers resembled pale prunes.

Thank goodness I remembered to cover my *No Bullshit* butt with a thick white bath towel before coming out of the bathroom. The last thing I needed was hysterics over what I'd done to myself.

I don't know about you, but I've decided that jetlag was sent by the devil to punish us for leaving too heavy a carbon footprint. I spent the next twenty hours fitfully trying to sleep mine off, coming up for air just in time for Mother and Nana to rush me into my new purple Anna Sui suit for the American Laureates' luncheon at the U.S. Embassy. I barely had time to dot some Chanel Infrarouge lipstick onto my lips before we had to go.

Nana impatiently flung open the door of our hotel suite, ready to hustle me out, but, before I could exit, Mother held up a hand and looked me up and down. Nodding with obvious satisfaction, she turned to Nana. "What did I ever do to deserve such a beautiful and talented daughter?"

Nana managed to wipe the smile from Mother's face with a brusque, "Not much. But then I've never met a parent yet who didn't try to hitch a ride on their kids' achievements."

Needless to say, our ride to the luncheon was marred by just a little tension. I had to do my imitation of George Bush calling to congratulate me for my award—"Yer a credit to yer country; you make all our wings take dream"—to get the two of them loosened up again.

The American Embassy turned out to be large and modern and impersonal, not exactly an example of grace, let alone the Swedish variety. We had to go through a purse and passport inspection by two unsmiling American security officers wearing earpieces and suits that failed to disguise their ample chests and bulky biceps. Nana said, "This one here's the physics winner," but neither of them batted an eyelash. If anything, they looked disappointed they hadn't found bombs in our handbags. The darker haired one said to the other, "Okay, they're good to go," and curtly directed us to the room where the luncheon would take place. "If you leave, get stamped, or you'll have to go through security again." No "Congratulations," or "Really? But you're so young," or even a polite "Welcome." I heard Nana curse them both under her breath with a loser-at-Hearts vehemence as she marched ahead of me. "Act like they belong here more than we do." In all fairness, I thought they probably did.

This particular disoriented Stranger was in desperate need of a Friend, so you can imagine how relieved I was to have Stanley stride toward us when we entered the room, his already-wide face split into a huge grin. He actually picked me up and swirled me in a full circle, croaking into my ear, "My dear, you are the sensation of the science world. I am so proud of you." For a moment, everything went blurry. Stanley's palpable pleasure was something a certain sort of father—a father, for instance, like Sammie's—might have shown for his child. Fortunately for me, Stanley turned me loose into Gwennie's welcoming arms. She had just enough nervous B.O. emanating from her pits to calm me down.

Before I knew it, someone was calling my name. Gwennie pointed me toward our table, and I saw Adam gesturing madly for me to join him. I felt more than a little self-conscious as I approached him and the rest of the team, all of whom huddled close to one another. It was hard not to notice how people were shooting curious looks at us from every corner of the room.

Adam pulled me close to his chest, reassuringly radiating a Campbell's Chicken Soup scent even here in Stockholm, until Amir said, "Hey, you can't monopolize the boss," and gave my shoulder a nice squeeze before offering me a tenuous hug of his own. His predominant odor was Vademecum, the zippy-tasting local toothpaste I'd sampled myself before leaving the hotel.

After two hugs in as many minutes, I was sure my face matched my dress, and I gave an apologetic little smile as I managed to step back a bit to compose myself. But, if anything, my discomfort increased. I was used to my team wearing jeans and T-shirts. Seeing them in their best clothes, they looked older, more mature. I felt as though a chasm had opened up between us, and I hung onto the back of a cream-skirted folding chair to keep myself from falling in.

Fortunately for all of us, someone sounded a gong and the Ambassador made a little speech, fussing with patriotic fervor over the number of Americans awarded this year and inviting us to take our seats and chow down. Our oglers turned their attention to the company at their own tables, and my friends and I breathed a collective sigh of relief. Stanley rushed over and took his place at our table, but not before holding out a seat for Katrina.

Until that moment, it had never dawned on me that Katrina was a real beauty. Her shiny chestnut hair stylishly pulled into a tendrilly knot and her slip lip dress showing the kind of figure men mini-explode over, she smiled up at Stanley with a grace that gave me goose bumps. She appeared to be having a similar effect on Tom, who couldn't seem to keep his arm off the back of her chair. Gunther, however, had gone all Eeyore-ish on us, showing none of the manic enthusiasm he'd been exhibiting ever since we'd finalized our formula. Gwennie said later she thought he'd been thrown into shyness in anticipation of meeting his king, but Stanley thought it was more likely that his Scandinavian tendency toward depression had reasserted itself.

Stanley, by the way, had prepared a surprise for me, having pre-vailed upon the Ambassador to invite one more guest to the luncheon. I embarrassed Nana by squealing with delight when Serena McKenna showed up at our table. It didn't help when I introduced the two of them and Serena responded, "I'm sorry, I didn't catch the gentle-man's name." But they discovered soon enough they had something in common. As we all settled in for our four-course extravaganza, Serena reached into her purse and brought out a few photos of Lord Hanuman in a state of pure bliss, being nit-picked enthusiastically by two female chimps. Nana, with a gleam in her eye, trumped her by hauling out of her own handbag a whole album of baby and toddler photos of me—many of them bald, replete with bumps and indenta-tions, which made me wish I could bury myself under Nana's old cave-scented robe. To her credit, Serena McKenna did a great job of pretending she knew who she was looking at.

While the rest of us overstuffed ourselves on caviar and herring fillets and prawns and smoked dinner sausage and ham and cured pork leg and brown cheese and white cheese and dessert pancakes with blueberry, lingonberry, and strawberry jam, Mother kept running outside to smoke Shermans with the Ambassador. I couldn't help but wonder what her new beau would say if he knew.

I wished I'd inherited some of her poise—even more so a few days later, when, after a tour of special sites in the city, including a turn at ice skating in Kungstradgarden and a taste of arguably the best hot chocolate in the world at a nearby café, I gave my formal lecture to the Swedish Academy. As soon as I stood up, I realized I should have listened to Nana and peed ahead of time. So much for asserting myself against a woman who knew me better than I knew myself.

Fortunately, I had a podium in front of me to hide the tapping right foot that kept my bulging bladder in check. I was okay once I began, though I barely looked up at my audience as Adam had coached me to do. After I finished—and following a blissfully linger-ing pee—he told me my talk had been very clever, and we both laughed, since he'd had as much of a hand in writing it as I had. Speech writing wasn't exactly my forté.

The actual awards ceremony took place in the Stockholm Con-cert Hall on December 10, the anniversary of Alfred Nobel's death. The whole Nobel extravaganza is yet another instance of the Butterfly

Effect, in this case the result of a premature obituary of Alfred Nobel that was published in a French newspaper, headlined, "The Merchant of Death is Dead." The man who invented dynamite had evidently felt so ashamed of how he was going to be remembered that he wrote a new will setting aside most of his estate to fund the Prizes.

Nobel might have died a humbler man than when he started, but the fanfare attending the awards ceremony was enough to further enlarge *my* head. A huge crowd of people stood behind red velvet ropes to watch us arrive, and His Majesty the King of Sweden himself presented us with our diplomas and medals after a flourish of fancy trumpets.

Giddy and flush-faced, I let myself be led out of the bright blue art deco building for the journey to our awards banquet at Stockholm's City Hall. But somewhere between the Concert Hall and City Hall we passed a Gothic church replete with gargoyles and a giant graveyard. I fell into a deep funk. Back home were one Grandfather, one Father, and one Baby X, none of whom would be resurrected even a breath's-worth by any of these festivities. I missed Jillily. I missed Aadita. And I most decidedly missed Sammie. I knew how much she'd have loved this beautiful old city. I knew how hard we'd have giggled together when the trumpets blared. And I knew how much she'd have taken the piss out of all the pomposity.

Mother and Nana were too busy comparing notes on the Fantasyland feeling of meeting an actual king to notice the downturn in my mood. It was just as well. There was nothing more depressing than having people point out how out of sync I was with the rest of the world.

Fortunately, I managed to muster a phony granny grin by the time we arrived at Stockholm City Hall. Again, we entered the building to shouts and applause. I shivered. Inside, I would have to give another talk. A podium had been provided, and the guests stared up at me from elegant china and crystal place settings. The banquet table seemed about a mile long, and everyone looked like idealized versions of themselves, Mother especially in her iridescent green satin gown. Stanley, thank God, was literally up to his old tricks, fishing what I assumed was a krona from behind Nana's ear.

Nana, by the way, cut a quite unusual figure. She wore a brown and black linen shawl over a brown and black knee-length gown, which, thanks to her full-bellied, full-bosomed girth, contributed to a sort of square-shaped effect. But, never mind, she was sending me the kind of smile that put me in mind of certain chicken peck kisses, so who cared that she looked like a UPS delivery box?

This time, I'd had much of my speech written by Mother. This is how I was going to begin: "It is astonishing to be included in such distinguished company, a fourteen-year-old Alice in a most exquisite Wonderland." But as those well-honed words prepared to exit my lips, something rose up in me, Mack-truckishly shoving them aside. Wouldn't I be succumbing to my own version of opinionlessness if I merely followed Mother's formula? Hadn't the gods intervened in the form of Riku the Righteous Tattoo Artist to specifically mark me a No Bullshitter?

Wrestling with my inner intruder, I feared I was seriously at risk of blurting out my own version of *ugga umph ugga*. But the pull was too strong.

The first words tumbled right out of my mouth as it they'd been waiting forever, "Maybe it all would have happened differently if the baby bird on the lawn hadn't given me my idea about my grandfather's balls." The audience gave a collective gasp and rustled ominously. I should have stopped right there.

But I didn't. It was as if my thoughts couldn't fly from my mouth fast enough. "All my life I've suffered from a terrible fear of the void. So when the gods brought me together with Stanley H. Fiske, I had a chance to investigate the thing that scared me the most. I guess you could call it a kind of homeopathy for intolerable dread. Stanley wasn't my only scientific angel. My discovery of C-Voids rests on the shoulders of many others—Adam Manus, Amir Gupta, Katrina Kelly, Tom Haggis, and Gunther Anderten should be standing up here, too. But, really, this whole thing started with my failure to resurrect my grandfather and ended up benefitting from aborting my baby, as well as the loss of my best friend. You have to be pretty single-minded to make any kind of scientific breakthrough, and all kinds of things suffer. The thing is—after all that, I still don't even know if the possibilities of P.D. will ever see the light of day, thanks to honorary members of the Flat Earth Society like my own dead father and greedy men who care so much about profit they're willing to risk global catastrophe."

Something in me was shouting, "No! You can't do this!" But, evidently, I could. I asked, "What's the point of sacrificing almost everything for scientific discovery if a bunch of Neanderthals are going to sabotage it in the end? Isn't the birth of something new and unknown worth more than that?"

I stopped then. For a few brief moments I had been a channel for a river, but then the river moved on. I imagined death feeling a little like it.

Looking back, I am surprised I was allowed to finish. I suppose it says something for the Nobel Committee's tolerance of strange birds that I was.

Before stepping away from the microphone, I let myself take a long look at my audience. The thirteenth fairy had arrived, after all. She was *me*. There were too many open mouths to count. Frowns, too. I noticed Stanley staring at Gwennie, who was staring at Mother, who stared at Nana. No one, actually, was looking at me, and for a moment I thought I had actually dematerialized. Had I accomplished the cellular exchange on the strength of sheer shame? If so, I was going to need to rethink our formula.

But then I sensed a pair of eyes upon me and sought them out. It was the King of Sweden. He wasn't exactly smiling, but the tips of his lips curled up slightly and I was almost certain I saw a glimmer of humor in his diamantine eyes. But then a series of photo flashes blinded me and I knew I had to get away or something botttomly pitish was going to happen. I ran out the door, finding my way through a maze of streets to a dead-end alley, where I flapped and flapped, freezing to the bone, until Adam found me. It was a miracle, really. He was like some cosmic homing pigeon, drawn to me in my moments of direst free-fall. I gave my wrists a break once I saw him coming, dragging his leg in an uneven pattern.

His limp had gotten worse. I knew it was my fault, and I knew he would deny it.

"Fleur, it's okay," he said, flinging his jacket over my shoulders. "Come on back. We can't eat that great grub without you."

His casual tone was so kindly faked, I would have cried if I hadn't been so cold. Through my chattering teeth, I managed to get out, "No. You go on without me. They should have given you guys the award, not me. I'm too weird."

"Are you kidding? We're only the extras. You *are* C-Voids. *And* P.D. Your beautiful brain was the kitchen that cooked all this up. We just cleaned up after you." He looked at me hopefully, but saw I wasn't buying. "Come on. It's freezing out here."

I realized with a guilty pang that his whole body was shaking. I let him lead me back to the City Hall. At my insistence, he left me outside the banquet room and slipped inside to persuade Mother to make my excuses—which is how she and Nana and I ended up eating an intimate dinner in our hotel suite, seated around a glistening teak table that was faintly redolent of Ye Olde English Furniture Paste. Under the circumstances, the smell was quite comforting.

I was still in a state of shock, and, to their credit, Mother and Nana acted as though nothing untoward had happened. The meal delivered by room service was an elegant version of our local Pasadena smorgasbord, and it was substantial enough to help land me back in my body. I was actually starting to enjoy myself a little until a sudden blast of ABBA from a wedding reception downstairs made me spill strawberry sherbet on my Alexander McQueen gown. Mother ran to the bathroom and returned with a washcloth. She carefully rubbed my dress until my pink splotch blended—rather nicely, I thought—into the floral pattern. Flinging the washcloth onto a blue-rimmed dish bearing the last remaining sweet and sour meatball, she inspected her handiwork, saying with some satisfaction, "There. Nearly dematerialized."

I gave her attempt at humor a grateful smile. She squeezed my arm so Mack-truckishly I wondered if Nana had been giving her lessons. But then she planted such a tender kiss on my forehead that tears stung my eyes. She pulled back and looked at me and brushed a strand of hair from my cheek, saying, "You know, it's ridiculous wasting this extraordinary dress of yours on Nana and me. I think we're in good enough shape to successfully crash a wedding, don't you?"

We both turned to Nana, who merely crossed her thick arms across her chest and said, "Don't look at me. If you want to risk getting arrested in a foreign country, it's your lookout. I'm going to bed." (I think Nana was a little hurt that I hadn't mentioned my loss of living with her and Mother in my list of sacrifices.) So Mother and I slipped downstairs, holding hands for courage, and shouldered our way into a now-deafening wedding party. I thought we did a pretty good imitation of invited guests. We certainly managed to make free with the amenities.

Well, to be honest, Mother ended up smoking in the lobby most of the evening with—who else?—a Scandinavian Bill W., while I, drinking my first ever glass or three of champagne, danced more gracefully than I'd ever thought possible with a series of nearly-white-haired, impossibly good looking young Swedes, one of whom simply could not be convinced I wasn't a slumming princess.

Of course, Stefan Carlsson would discover soon enough who I really was. The morning papers were covered with it, headlines screaming variations on one simple theme: "Shame! For shame!" Studying *The Local*, Stockholm's one English language newspaper, with eyes that had pins sticking in them didn't help. Who knew what a pincer of a headache a little champagne could bring on? I suppose it was folly to read the paper, but I'd been nothing if not curious since the day I was born.

Mother bought me a hat to wear on the plane trip home.

I didn't know which was worse: humiliating myself or making my dead grandfather and Baby X subject to public scrutiny. How was I ever going to live it down?

Fortunately, we bumped into Serena McKenna at the airport. I'm proud to report that, even with my hat, she recognized me. "Good girl," she said. "I haven't seen such moxie since my father told the nuns at my Catholic school to stuff it. Fleur, my sweet, you told the true story of human achievement. Wrong turns, rotten luck, success from suffering, human frailty. The gold from the slime. I can't wait to tell Jane Goodall. She'll love it."

On the flight back, I fretted over whether I'd spoiled the success of P.D. forever. Big Oil was going to have a field day with the Big Idiot who'd chosen the Nobel Awards Ceremony to describe her grandfather's gargantuan testicles. I'd let down Adam and Amir and Katrina and Gunther and Tom and Stanley, but also the world. It was going to take a miracle to repair my destructiveness.

But maybe a miracle was precisely what it would take for us humans. Some Cassandras were predicting it was already too late to counter the fossil fuel contribution to global warming, and we were all goners, anyway. I wasn't so sure, myself. When it came down to it, it would probably be the butterflies who'd decide.

But I still had my own small life to live. How was I going to cope with the isolation I knew was coming? For one brief moment,

I'd succumbed to the delusion I was a superstar, when in fact I'd been a supernova on its way to becoming a giant black hole.

My train of thought was interrupted by a commotion down the aisle. One of the genus stewardi was objecting in a tone of considerable affront, "No, ma'am, I am *not* the man who promised to bring you a cup of tea, but I'll be happy to get some for you." Serena McKenna was staring up at the statuesque stewardess as if she were some kind of Martian.

In spite of myself, I laughed. The world might condemn me as a fool and a fraud, but at least I'd have the Prosopagnosiac primate women on my side.

Chapter 25

ONE THING YOU can say about public humiliation: it's a tremendous tonic for thick-headedness. As much as I wanted to hide from the world, I couldn't hide from *me*.

I suppose you could say that losing my self-respect was one loss too many. The hole in my heart was starting to get crowded. There had to be something between a gaping void and an overstuffed sofa like the ones you see dumped on the side of the freeway with their springs sticking out.

Maybe it was shock or perhaps simply shame, but, whatever the cause, my missing center managed to kick her way out of her casket and was conducting a thorough review of everything I'd done wrong. Oddly enough, my relentless emotional reckoning seemed to be giving me some physical relief, as if I were a reverse image of those Catholic predecessors of Sister Flatulencia who scourged their bodies to heal their souls. The bumps on my calves started softening, the mildest of cramps announced the coming of Mr. Heavyflow, and well-formed poops plopped at nearly the same time each morning into what Adam liked to call the john.

As the congregation of Fleurs reassembled, they ended up concluding there were a few upsides to my social catastrophe. For one thing, I was at considerably less risk of prostituting my soul to celebrity. Adam thought I was being paranoid, but I couldn't shake the feeling when I went out that people I passed were thinking ill of me, so I spent a fair amount of time in omphaloskepsis, otherwise known as contemplation of one's navel.

Other favorite vacuum fillers were listening to music on my bed and writing in my diary in Gwennie's back garden, which, p.s., gave me the opportunity to renew my relationship with Abraham Darby, Ambridge Rose, Jude the Obscure, and the Dark Lady. When I touched my lips to the latter's soft surface, she let fall a single peony-like petal to show me how badly she'd suffered my absence.

Perhaps you would like some comic relief learning which songs I listened to while stretched out on my bed, you-know-who motoring like crazy beside me. Here are a few of them:

1. Nirvana's *All Apologies*;

2. *The Hardest Part* by Coldplay;

3. *Karma Police*, Radiohead;

4. *Wake Up Alone*, Amy Winehouse;

5. U-2's *I Still Haven't Found What I'm Looking For*.

Oh dear. Not so comic reliefy after all.

You'd think my scientific curiosity would have fled in the face of such misery, but it didn't. I began to pick at the problem of rematerialization. Or, more accurately, it began to pick at me until I knew I had to do something.

My forgiving team was only too happy to come together again—but first they had to circle the territory with side issues, much as a dog walks round and round his lumpy bed before settling into it. As soon as we piled into Stanley's chaotic office, jostling for space amidst its teetering towers of books, physics journals, and giant boxes of contraband Cocoa Puffs, Amir began rhapsodizing over Serena's photos of Lord Hanuman, Adam filled us in on more than we ever wanted to know about his nightly phone conversations with Jessica, Tom and Katrina kept smooching in the corner, and Gunther, who'd made a stopover in his hometown of Malmo before returning to So Cal, cycled depressively over how lukewarm his parents had been about his contribution to P.D. I sympathized with Amir, wondered whether Adam's new girlfriend's arms were as silky as Stephanie's, tried to avoid staring at Tom and Katrina, and wondered if Gunther, who'd flown Icarus-ishly high just a few months ago, might be just a bit bipolar.

I also thought it was more than a little strange that we were working toward the possibility of rematerialization, yet all my team could talk about was relationships.

I still had so much to learn.

Have you ever considered that, while you are busying fighting off boredom with your own personal dramas, the world keeps on spinning out its infinitely larger ones? As I struggled with the problem of reversing cellular implosions, I was all-too-aware of the efforts to bury P.D. You probably won't be surprised when I tell you that, within days of our return, the Cacklers had come scurrying out like roaches from behind a toilet, joining a regular anthill of anti-abortionists as they crawled toward the Big Rock Candy Mountain of Big Oil. And please don't blame me for the mixed metaphor. It was Gwennie's, not mine.

While I couldn't get it out of my head that I'd handed the oil companies their golden opportunity to link C-Voids and P.D. with immorality on a Smorgasbord-sized platter, Gwennie saw it differently, claiming, "Fleur, love, you've simply got to stop the self-flagellation. Personally, I find the opportunity to fight several of my favorite foes in one fell swoop even more fun."

My own objection to the Cacklers wasn't that they thought C-Voids and P.D. spelled the end of civilization, but that they seemed untroubled by doubt. For all I knew, dematerialization would create a host of unwelcome consequences—maybe people would lose track of objects they'd made disappear, or perhaps our species would jump ship and overpopulate some other dimension. But how could we outlaw the human imagination? It was the most powerful factor in our continued residence on a rugged planet and, second only to mini-explosions, the chief consolation prize for our awareness of the inevitability of death. What if the outcome of our living experiment turned on fluidity and openness and the willingness to step back and say, "Oops, I was wrong. Time for a little course correction?" Which was exactly what Gwennie was trying to foster when she came home to So Cal and immediately founded *C The Big Picture*, an organization devoted to supporting scientific contributions to ecological consciousness and species survival, its centerpiece being the advocacy of continuing research in the area of C-Voids.

Having whetted her appetite for conquest by foisting a diet of nut roasts and spinach and mushroom quiches onto a couple of

hopeless carnivores (me and Stanley), Gwennie pursued her new pas-
sion with as much of a vengeance as her campaign to convince me
I'd done nothing especially untoward in Stockholm. I should have
known something was afoot the first morning after our return to So
Cal, when I found a copy of the resumé of a fellow Nobel winner
waiting for me to the right of my cereal spoon. His name was Phillip
Lenard, the 1905 Physics Prize Laureate, who'd evidently attacked
Einstein as "the Jewish fraud" and became an adviser to Adolf Hitler.
The next morning, it was Cordell Hull, winner of the 1945 Peace
Prize, who was instrumental in blocking entry to the United States of
a shipload of desperate Jewish refugees from Nazi Germany, many of
whom, when forced to return, died in concentration camps.

Gwennie was indefatigable. Along with my delectably crunchy
Grape Nuts, I ingested the details of 1976 recipient Daniel Carleton
Gajdusek's incarceration for child molestation, Boris Pasternak's
forced refusal of his 1958 Literature Prize by sadistic Soviet party-
poopers, as well as Jean-Paul Sartre voluntarily declining his own in
1964 for fear he'd turn himself into an institution—which I personally thought couldn't be half as bad as Elfriede Jelinket's situation; I'd
rather turn into an institution any day than have my head turn into a
black hole.

Harold Pinter, who did accept his Literature Prize in 2005, had
done so by videotape, since he was suffering from a rare mouth infection—which didn't prevent him from saying, amongst other
things, "The crimes of the United States have been systematic,
constant, vicious, remorseless, but very few people have actually
talked about them. You have to hand it to America. It has exercised a
quite clinical manipulation of power worldwide while masquerading
as a force for universal good. It's a brilliant, even witty, highly
successful act of hypnosis."

Was it possible that my own confession of abortion, disloyalty
and failure wasn't the most flagrant flaunting of Nobel custom? That,
with all its pomp and ritual, the Nobel Prize was as pitted as its recip-
ients' personalities?

But getting back to Gwennie, all this Nobel trivia was merely a
revving of her motor. As she put it, "You, at least, had the guts to say
what was on your mind outside your own small circle. I've been
shooting off my mouth about the importance of talking truth to

power for so long I've even bored myself. Now's my chance to actually do something."

I was hardly in a place to object to anyone else's efforts to conquer boredom, but I did worry over the immensity of the task Gwennie had set for herself. Grandfather had suffered his stroke at the age of fifty. Father had fallen at sixty-four. I couldn't help but notice that, with her hearing worsening by the day and the bags under her eyes turning into checked luggage, Gwennie wasn't getting any younger.

Nor was Stanley. He'd seen me all the way to the finish line, but I'd made such a hash of things in the end. Anyone else in his position would have been angry, or at least a little annoyed. But then again, Stanley was hardly your garden-variety mentor.

The extent of his kindness became abundantly clear during our first time alone together after returning to So Cal. Gwennie had gone for a major fridge-restocking run to Whole Foods, and I was sharing a regular sniff-a-thon in the backyard with Jillily, both of us enjoying the last of the Austins' late winter bloom. I was nearly knee deep in fallen petals when it occurred to me that my feline friend was not going to live forever. Thankfully, Stanley appeared at the back door to save me from the darkest reaches of the void. Smacking his lips froggishly, he proposed an illicit snack fest. We sat side by side on the living room sofa, taking advantage of the windfall of Gwennie's absence to crack sunflower seeds a mile a minute in between bites of a couple of Mars Bars Stanley had managed to sneak past his sister's eagle eyes at Arlanda Airport. We were both big fans of alternating sweet and salty tastes.

When he'd consumed every morsel of his candy bar, Stanley heaved a satisfied sigh and slouched back against the sofa, his legs stretched out like a couple of cast away stilts, his lap littered with sunflower seed shells, and his head placed perfectly against the spot on the sofa already darkened with his somewhat greasy hair. The spot was something Gwennie liked to throw at him when they were having one of what, in saner moments, they laughingly called their "sibling spats." She would admonish him, "Can't you wash that prizewinning head of yours a little more frequently?" And he would shout back, "How many times do I have to tell you? It's the grease that keeps me from going bald."

Anyway, getting back to our blissful sweet and salty moment, Stanley leaned forward to wipe a smudge of caramel from my chin and said, "So, how'd you like Stockholm?"

I nearly choked on my Mars. "It was okay."

"Just okay, was it?"

"Well, you know…"

"What do I know?"

"What a dumb speech I made."

"Fleur." Big frown. "What I know is that you won some well-deserved recognition. What I know is that my colleagues at the Swedish Academy can't stop talking about your theory." He cracked a couple of seeds absent-mindedly, spitting the shells onto the carpet. Gwen was going to kill us. "Fleur, have you forgotten all the work you put into P.D.? C-Voids are something that aren't just going to impact physics or even, potentially, our reliance on fossil fuels. I've been getting calls from biologists all over the globe. Can you imagine the potential applications to the field of medicine?"

"What about the Cacklers? They're trying to ban all future research."

"Hell with the Cacklers. They may put up an annoying obstacle or two, but you'll see. This political baloney will calm down, a new administration will get voted in, and saner heads will prevail."

"Saner heads! *I'm* the one who lost her marbles." Betraying tears started sidling down my cheeks. "I don't know why I said all those things. Something weird came over me."

He gathered me into his arms, and my heart soared as I smelled the bitterness of his pits. "Fleur. Fleur. What came over you was being young and innocent and subjected to far too much public scrutiny. Sweetheart, it's not as if you hurt anyone. You were a good scientist. Everything you said was true."

It was hard to take in his words when my mind was occupied with having been called *Sweetheart*. The name was a second cousin to Sweetie Pie, but infinitely less dangerous. I forced myself to focus. "But I did hurt someone. I hurt a couple of people. Father and Grandfather and Baby X. What are they going to think of me?"

"Who's Baby X?"

"My unbaked bun."

I could see him working on that one. "I get it." He gently pushed me back and held me at arms' distance, enunciating carefully. "Fleur, they're dead. Nobody can hurt them."

"How do you know that? You can't know that."

"Honey, I know."

He might think I'd ceded him the point by my silence, but I wasn't going to quibble. I was still wondering how anyone could think I had a sweet heart. We sat in silence until the words snuck out, "Stanley, even though I've been working all this time on the void, it still scares me."

He gave me a shrewd look, nodding. "Of course it does. You think being scientists stops us from being human? Do you know that, besides the sucking reflex, the fear of falling is one of only two instincts we exhibit from birth? It's called the startle reflex. We need to feel securely held and not alone, despite the reality that, in fact, we're born alone and die alone. Maybe even because of it."

It occurred to me that Stanley had more in common with Sartre than I'd realized. I thought I knew what he meant. I was, after all, quite familiar with the land of Alone. But I couldn't help but wonder what Aadita or Siri Sajan or even Pauli might have to say about the matter. Was there a way to reconcile the substance of Stanley's words with the equally indelible wisdom of Indra's Net, fractals, the Butterfly Effect, synchronicity?

One of Stanley's favorite mottos was that we needed to know ourselves as simultaneously very ordinary and very special. Might alone and not alone be some kind of corollary?

As for me, I'd been flip-flopping for ages between seeing myself as a saint and worrying I was a worm. I took another bite of Mars to give me courage. "Stanley, things have gotten an awful lot better lately, but I still can't understand... Why do you think Mother didn't put up more of a fuss about me coming to So Cal?"

"What do you mean?"

"Well, I can't imagine Aadita letting someone she didn't know take Sammie off to some other part of the country. Not even with the assurances of a mutual friend."

Stanley stared at me, licking the salt from his lips. "It's a good question, Fleur. I'm not sure I have the answer." He stood abruptly, and I couldn't help but notice that a few shells still adhered to his pants. "Why don't we go for a bit of a skip and work on it together?"

We ended up at our favorite skipping spot, the Huntington Gardens, but only after dust-busting the mess we'd made. We cleaned up the sunflower seed shells for two reasons, one of which was Gwennie's fastidiousness and the other Jillily's belly. As you might recall, shells tended to serve an emetic function when it came to my cat.

I didn't mind people looking at me as I skipped with Stanley. And look they did. After all, you don't often see one twenty-first-century teenager and one exceedingly tall and froggish man skipping hand in hand amid roses and herbs, crossing quaint little bridges in a Japanese garden. I can't begin to fathom what they'd have said if they'd seen my invisible Uncle Bob, his moustaches wiggling as he struggled to keep up with us. When your legs are short it takes many more steps to cover the same distance.

As it happens, Stanley didn't have any answers. But he listened. As we stood on the moon bridge, facing the temple bell that had been inexplicably strapped down sometime in the past year so that no one could ring it, he listened to me explain how spending time with Mother in Sweden had made me wonder why it had taken us so long to make anything like a real connection. Looking back, I couldn't help but compare Mother's air of hesitancy with Nana's matter-of-fact competence. "At least with Nana," I continued, "I knew where I stood. But Mother was so delicate I mostly worried about *her*. Honestly, after Grandfather died, I don't think I could have survived but for Jillily." I fought back tears. "And that's another thing. I've known Jillily ever since she was born. I must have been about two years old. I'll never forget how her mother had to lick her out of a little sac, and how her eyes were squinched shut as if everything was too bright. I don't know what I'll do when she goes, except maybe jump into the grave with her." I watched Stanley closely. He didn't even blink, so I went on. "And I worry about Gwennie, too. She's working so hard. Do you think it's a sin I've been pretending she's my real mother?"

Stanley was the smartest man I knew, but all he had to say in response was, "You women! The way you dissect your feelings about relationships leaves us poor men in the dust. Speaking of which, we haven't seen your friend Sammie around for some time. Everything okay?"

I avoided his question by pointing out the beauty of the koi in the pond below us. They *were* extraordinary, especially the Goshiki, their black skins accented with red, white, and brown.

I grinned. "Do you know what a group of goldfish is called?" He made the face of a strangled toad and I knew I had him. "A *troubling*."

"God dammit!"

I did a little victory dance. "That's twelve to eleven, my advantage."

"Do you think I can't count?"

Stanley and I had a running contest over who could stump the other with the more esoteric of group names. Among the previous point-winners were a bike of bees, a clutter of cats, a rabble of butterflies, a congregation of alligators, and a coalition of cheetahs.

But getting back to troubling, I couldn't seem to get away from the fact that everyone I knew was concerned about the absence of Sammie.

Including, remarkably, Gunther Anderten. The occasion for his comments was a trip we took over the hill to his favorite haunt, an out-of-the-way teashop called Elixir. Gunther had phoned me at around two o-clock on December twenty-first, saying he'd overheard Adam telling Stanley it was a damned shame I was refusing to celebrate my fifteenth birthday. Given Gunther's general air of awkward abstraction, when he managed to hem and haw his way toward a stuttery, "Listen, there is nothing better for the blues than a cup of Mango Mate Energizer Tea," it felt rude to refuse.

Gunther drank his Mango Mate and I sipped my Shanghai Spice in Elixir's bamboo-enclosed garden, which we shared with only two other customers, a pony-tailed man having his Tarot cards read and his fortune teller, who crossed her eyes and ostentatiously yawned, patting her mouth in some sort of strange ritual every time she turned up another card. Gunther's tea seemed to be working. He became increasingly animated, culminating in standing up to do a little jig in imitation of Stanley on the Nobel dinner dance floor. The Tarot reader shot us a look of intense annoyance, then went back to her yawning and patting.

I don't know if I've mentioned that Gunther has a wandering eye. I don't mean a proverbial one, but a real physical impairment called Strabismus. Adam told me that, if his parents had had the condition treated before Gunther turned six, all would have been well. As it was, his body had suppressed the vision in his unstable eye in order to prevent him from going mad from double vision. It never fails to amaze me how the body has its own wisdom.

Actually, though, it drove *me* a little mad looking Gunther full in the face, not knowing whether to make contact with his stationary eye or try to keep up with his wandering one. Opting for the former, I joined him in laughter over his demonstration of Stanley's version of dancing.

Which is when he confirmed my concern about manic depression by pulling a face, scraping his chair back from the table to sit down again, and putting his head in his hands. "I can't believe my family showed so little interest in our work."

I couldn't believe they hadn't had his eye fixed, but I wasn't about to say so. Instead, I said, "*Tell* me about it."

But then he shifted gears on me so suddenly he nearly took my breath away. "And what about your Sammie? What kind of a friend is she, anyway? I would have thought she would be making a party for you today. I would have thought she would have wanted to come to Sweden to see you receive your award. I mean, even that woman was there. You know, the one who can't see faces."

He should talk. His left eye was rolling around in its socket like a shiny blue marble.

But I had to admit, hearing him judging Sammie like that made me uncomfortable. As if, somewhere in that dense head of mine, I suspected our rupture might have been a teensy bit my own fault.

In contrast with Gunther, Adam turned out to be an equal-opportunity evaluator, but it wasn't until the day he came to say goodbye that Sammie became a topic of conversation between us. Before then, my sly soldier had done an excellent job keeping the souring of our friendship under wraps, capitalizing on Adam's twin obsessions of keeping the fire lit in his long distance relationship with Jessica and closing up shop in So Cal.

Since returning from Stockholm, I'd been spending the kind of time with Adam that I had in those early days of mastering math, studying Sartre, and lapping up literature. And while we might not be discussing Proust anymore, we did engage in a fair amount of remembrance of things past. It was as if I was trying to inhale his very essence so I wouldn't be devastated by his departure. Fat chance. I should have learned by then that the anticipation of loss is useless as a protection against the pain and shock of the actual blow.

But our time together did have the advantage of providing another opportunity for learning. Both Adam and I had known the bite of abandonment—in his case, by a mother whose vanity was stronger than mother love, in mine, by one who, in all fairness, had probably been too much of a child herself to be expected to take on responsibility for a new life. Each of us had had fathers who'd forsaken us for a cause.

To compensate, I'd had Grandfather—*oh, Grandfather!*—and Jillily and Nana and Fayga and Cook and Dhani and Ignacio and even Uncle Bob. He'd had his grandparents to take care of him, his corkscrewed leg to make him kind, and Stanley H. Fiske to notice his capacity for clever thinking.

But neither of us knew how to say goodbye to each other. In that regard, we were equally ignorant and would be simultaneously one another's student and teacher.

On one of our last afternoons together, Adam ended up ferrying me to the vet, which had to be some secret tenth circle of hell. Jillily had been peeing on the carpet, a possible sign, I knew, of cystitis, so I gritted my teeth and stuffed her into her cat carrier, which Adam set carefully onto my lap once I strapped myself into his car. Actually, I was in such a state that it took me three tries to fasten the shoulder harness, not so easy when your cat is sending out *Get me out of here, can't you tell I'm dying?* signals from her glorified cage.

As was her wont, the same Jillily who literally fought tooth and nail to keep out of her carrier as I struggled to slip her inside it couldn't wait to get back into it after Dr. Bharati had examined her. It made sense to me. Who wouldn't prefer the prison of a cat carrier to the voidishness of an icy examining table where people inserted tubes into your butt, needles into your back, and massaged pee out of your already painful tweeter?

When we returned home, with Jillily tail-curlingly relieved to be on familiar turf again and me relieved that she had no infection and merely needed to be switched to wet cat food, Adam reminded me that I'd once used my old yellow potty stool as a piggy bank.

Smirking, he added, "Only in a filthy rich household would a cat be allowed to play with five dollar bills as toy mice."

"Yes," I shot back, "And you made fun of me about it *then*, too."

He actually stepped back a few paces, banging the back of his head against my bookshelf. "Shit!" Rubbing his head, he said, "You're right. I'm sorry. It's just that I've never gotten over how eccentric your household was. Full of women and a cast of thousands

315

coming in and out all the time. Your mom has to be the least anony-mous member of AA who's ever lived. And that Sister....what's her real name, anyway?...You've got to admit, a farting nun is something of a novelty."

I nearly said, "What about your Campbell's Chicken Soup B.O.?" But I didn't. I knew Adam was trying to spare himself the pain of anticipated loss.

Instead, I said, "You don't know how important that potty stool was to me. I used to stand on it so I could see myself in the mirror. It gave me evidence I actually existed."

He stared at me. "That bad?"

"Well, not all the time."

But he'd read my diaries.

He pushed aside a pile of CDs to sit on my bed. Shuffling through them, he raised an eyebrow. "Elton John? Isn't that a little before your time?"

Giggling, I grabbed it from him and inserted it into my comput-er, clicking forward to one of our favorite karaoke songs. Adam jumped off the bed and, grabbing a pencil, held it to his lips. I grabbed a pen and joined Adam in an enthusiastic, if slightly out of tune back-up to *Rocket Man*.

We collapsed onto the bed, laughing. Adam pushed his hair back from his forehead and looked around the room. "Hey, Fleur. Do you still have all those diaries?"

"Some."

"The first ones were something. All those lists!"

"I know. But they kept me busy." I took a deep breath. "It meant a lot to me that you thought they were interesting."

"Interesting? Give me a break. They were what convinced me I had to introduce you to Stanley."

As we talked, it quickly became apparent that we each had dif-ferent recollections of him introducing me to Stanley. I remembered it being at the university. Adam thought it was a donut shop. We transcended the conflict by getting into Adam's car in pursuit of Krispy Kremes.

The drive back was one of those seemingly inconsequential moments you never forget. Adam said, "Hey, check this out," and selected a CD, fast-forwarding until he got what he wanted. "Kate Bush. It's called *Hello Earth*."

Her voice, describing the night sky, was haunting.

We listened in silence, me savoring my Caramel Kreme Crunch as if it were my first and not my thousandth, Adam driving slowly, claiming his steering wheel was sticky with Apple Fritter. I thought it more likely he wanted to prolong our time together.

Before he went home that evening, I told Adam he was the next best thing to having a big brother. What I didn't mention was having made mini-explosions while imagining his bulging member. Why bother, when I could barely recall the feeling anymore?

The fact was no one would ever replace Adam. He had been my one human constant for three of my four incarnations. And if he had seen my naïveté become, well, a little less naïve, I had seen him change, too. He certainly wasn't the shy young boy with a limp anymore. According to Katrina, Adam had become King Shit on Campus, and even Stanley had commented that he had to beat the women off to get a few moments alone with him.

On the day he came to say goodbye, he brought me a potted Perdita rose.

I had to fight not to break down entirely. Adam kept rubbing his eyes. I saw our sadness leaking out of us in the form of bubbles floating skywards and watched them pop in a variety of interesting patterns.

Adam said, "Fleur?" and I landed back on earth again. He took me in his arms and said rather huskily. "God, I love you."

Getting a whiff of his perfect B.O., I mumbled, "Me, too. How am I going to survive without you?" I pulled away from his hug. "What about rematerialization? We're going to need the whole team to come up with the solution."

"Whoa, Nelly. We've already talked about this. I'll be working on my part of the puzzle in Boston. And we're going to be teleconferencing once a week. It'll be virtually the same as being there."

"No, it won't. It won't be the same at all. Not to talk to about—you know, personal things. I won't have anybody."

"But you will, Fleur. You've got the guys and Stanley and Gwen and Sammie."

"No, I don't."

"What do you mean?"

"I don't have Sammie. She isn't speaking to me. Well, anyway, we aren't speaking to each other."

He looked baffled.

"She actually expected me to go to Father's funeral. Got mad at me when I didn't. Just because she had a father who made her kites and found her four leaf clovers and knew what she liked and didn't like and made her chicken soup when she was sick and listened to her when she was sad and took her to museums and pantomimes and *Starlight Express*."

Adam burst into laughter. "Jesus, Fleur, don't tell me you're letting the Green Eyed Monster get the best of you over *Starlight Express*. That has got to be the worst musical in human history."

"Isn't."

"Is."

I knew what he meant, of course. Not about the musical, but the monster. Adam was the one who'd forced me to read Othello in the first place. Shakespeare must have been a dog man. I hated his characterizations of cats, though I had to admit I myself was disturbed by Jillily's predilection for playing with mice and birds before she killed them.

And now to use the image in relation to *me*? "That's not fair. I'm not a Green Eyed Monster. I'm not mocking Sammie, and I'm not feeding off her. I just don't like being hung up on all the time."

Adam's eyes took on that I'm-sorry-I-hurt-you-but-just-listen-to-yourself look. "Fleur, don't you think she might still be pretty raw from losing her own father? Can't you give her a little latitude here? You've told me yourself she's the first best girlfriend you've ever had."

Adam had offered me many new perspectives over the years, including the possibility of compassion for myself. He added in a tone of considerable kindness, "I know you're in pain. It's awful when you can't tell which is worse, having your father alive or losing him. Sounds like Sammie's dad was so good she might have a hard time getting what that's like for you. But she's only human and she's smart and you can explain it to her. Come on, why don't you give her a call?"

Before he left, before we went through a final, nose-runny clingfest, I promised him I'd think about it. And I did think about it. But that's all I did. I suppose I resembled my father more than I realized, because my mind was stuck on the insistence that it was her turn.

The fact was Sammie and I were both stubborn, and, unlike the action in Rock, Paper, Scissors, there was nothing to break our stalemate. Two rocks rubbing against each other create nothing but friction, or at best fire. But as you might be aware, our old friend Jacob, he of angel-wrestling fame, used a rock as his pillow and chose the same rock to mark the site of his vision of heaven's ladder. So maybe there was hope the gods would send something out of the ordinary to break the spell.

As it happened, it was in the most prosaic of settings, in point of fact a local Coffee Bean and Tea Leaf, that the gods chose to intervene. Gwennie had left the house earlier to run off some brochures, and I decided to venture out myself around midday, determined to see if Riku might recommend a tattoo removal service. I figured the odds were increasing that one of these days I'd forget to hide my butt from Gwennie and activate an episode of all hell breaking loose.

That was one reason. The other was so superstitious I was barely able to admit it to myself. What if having *No Bullshit* etched over my bum crack was somehow sealing my fate as the feminine equivalent of the boy who said the emperor had no clothes? He wasn't exactly the most popular of people, was he? Besides, Ignacio used to swear that bull shit made the best fertilizer. (Though I must admit I thought at the time that a little goes a very long way.)

At any rate, as I rattled along toward Riku's, I saw ahead of me one of those ubiquitous So Cal trios of Gap, Borders, and Coffee Bean and Tea Leaf. As Nana would say, "In for a penny, in for a pound." I figured I might just manage to make a side trip for a scone without being noticed. After all, I had on my Greta Garbo hat from Mother, didn't I?

As soon as I entered the Coffee Bean, I spotted a familiar silvery head bent over a book by the window. Oh, Lord. But I would hate myself if I didn't approach her.

"Aadita."

She looked up from her reading and frowned. Before I knew it, she'd struggled up from her seat, knocking over her half-empty coffee cup. "Bloody hell. Look what I've done." As I swept her book and bag off the table, wiping both with the bottom of my Caltech *Weapon of Math Destruction* T-shirt, she murmured, "Ta, love," before wrapping her arms around me, knocking my hat slightly askew.

"What a surprise. And what an extraordinary hat. How wonderful it is to see you."

Her obvious delight shamed me.

The blond-braided barista who'd literally leapt over the counter moments before asked anxiously, "Are you okay? Didju get burned?"

Aadita assured her she was fine. As for me, the place was filling up, and all I could think was that I needed to get the focus off our table. I persuaded the barista to let me mop up. "Can you get her another...?" I looked over at Aadita.

"Viennese Blend."

"Viennese Blend and a chamomile tea for me and..." My eyes darted to the display case. "A blueberry scone. Aadita, do you want one, too?" She shook her head.

I exchanged the wet rag and some dollars for two cups and a scone. I brought everything over in two trips and sat down. Thankfully, everyone seemed intent on their own orders, their own books, and their own laptops. Aadita blew on her coffee cup. I forced myself to eat. Neither of us seemed in a hurry to speak.

Finally, brushing crumbs from my lips, I gave her an attempt at a smile. "This scone doesn't hold a candle to yours."

"Do you think? I wonder if I should experiment with blueberries. Flake's father used to speak so fondly of all the flavors in the U.S. Blueberries, cranberries, and—can you imagine?—chocolate chips. Of course, at home they wouldn't consider such a thing."

I sensed a subtle shift in her mood and began to speak, far too quickly I'm afraid, about the challenges of rematerialization. I went on and on about the ideas I'd been kicking around with Adam and Amir and Tom and Katrina and Gunther, until I realized by her expression I'd lost her. I ended lamely, "It's not as easy as you'd think to bring something back to life again."

She gave me a long look and then began gathering her books from the floor. "I'd love to stay and chat, my sweet, but I've got Schrödinger Operators at two." She zipped her laptop bag, adding almost—but not quite—as an afterthought, "Perhaps you would consider asking Gwen to bring you to Siri Sajan's class tomorrow." She paused a beat. "Flake has decided to resume her yoga practice."

Did I detect the slightest note of reproof in her voice?

After Aadita left, looking particularly tiny as she lugged one laptop, one bulging purse, and a couple of heavy math books, I made my pensive way not to Riku's Righteous Tattoo Parlor but to the Huntington. It was too far to walk, so I had to take a bus full of Mexican and Guatemalan and El Salvadoran nannies to get there.

Finding a patch of fairly dry grass, I sank down opposite a magnificent Metasequoia. At its feet, a murder of crows was hounding a solitary squirrel. I counted thirteen birds in all. Actually, the counting took more than a few seconds, as they kept hopping around, taking off, and re-landing. All of it accompanied, as you might imagine, by a drunken brawl of sound.

While crows are reputed to have the highest IQ of all avian species, I found them seriously lacking in the charm department. Frankly, it amazed me that, with their hinky hopping and oily-looking wings, they could actually fly at all. As for their birdsong, who doesn't prefer the multiple melodies of the mockingbird or the toy-like whirr of a hummingbird's wings to the crow's predilection for cacophony? It has been said that their group name is called a *murder* because of a propensity to feed off human corpses, but, not having witnessed such a thing, I felt they merited their moniker based solely on what I felt like doing to them when they penetrated my peace with their racket. I was pleased to see the squirrel was managing to stand his ground.

Which is, of course, something of a side alley. My main thrust of thought concerned Sammie.

Have I mentioned that it is a cornerstone of quantum physics that each moment is filled with infinite possibility—albeit often with vanishingly small probability? Meditating on my estrangement from Sammie was like looking through a kaleidoscope. One spin of the circle and everything changed.

With the dial set in one position, my thoughts went something like this: "What does *she* know? She got to dance on her father's feet," and "Isn't she the one who preferred the company of a pimply-faced boy and his gaggle of middle school minions to *mine?*" I suppose I don't need to spell how unsatisfying that little slice of self-righteousness was.

I knew my resentment wasn't totally unfounded. Certainly, she'd been wrong in expecting me to attend Father's funeral. Hadn't she been listening when I'd explained about him barring me from Grandfather's burial? Had she forgotten the pincers and the punching, my banishment for having an abortion, Father's below-the-belt *my-daughter's-autistic* Cackler campaign?

Just thinking along those lines riled me up all over again, feeding a renewed sense of superiority. Despite my calamitous Nobel speech, I was still a celebrity. Hadn't Terry Gross' people called? Even *60 Minutes* had contacted my publicist. And yes, don't laugh, I actually had one. Like it or not, as Gwennie had recently reminded me, I was still the poster girl for dematerialization, and how I was perceived could well have an effect on whether our work got shut down or not. You can imagine how *that* felt in my current state of mind, but I had to concede that Gwen could hardly be expected to mount a national campaign countering Big Oil's attack on P.D. *and* try to help rectify my public image by arranging a series of interviews designed to demonstrate I wasn't a total nutcase—which was just what my poor publicist was attempting to do.

But then an invisible hand swooped down and tweaked the dial. The thought of appearing on *60 Minutes* made me shudder. Did I really want to humiliate myself in yet another public forum? And speaking of murderous crows, wasn't part of the reason for killing Baby X my single-minded ambition to make things disappear and reappear again?

I had dismissed Sammie's quarrel with me as sheer envy. But even a fool would have recognized it as the simple longing of a friend for her friend.

Sammie was right. Somewhere along the way, I'd become a self-deluding, self-centered prat. Or perhaps I'd always been one. The crows chose that moment to lift off en masse, blotting out the sun with funereal wings.

I found my way home, feeling nothing if not humbled, and, as soon as I found her, I hugged Jillily tightly to my breast, as if I could stuff her vibrating body into my abyss. Thank God for Jillily. I pulled her even closer, which didn't stop my eyes from traveling to the opposite wall, where just six months ago I'd hung a framed needlepoint Sammie had found for me in an Old Town antique shop. It was a silhouette of two girls sitting together under the arch of a graceful willow. At the very bottom, in carefully-sewn crimson letters, it read, "Friendship is like a sheltering tree."

I thought about Aadita's suggestion. The last time Sammie and I had made up from a spat, we'd been on our way to Siri Sajan's. Was it possible some Kundalini magic might fix our broken friendship?

There *was* something special about Siri Sajan's studio, which wasn't technically a studio at all, but a converted house, cozy with Persian rugs placed higgledy-piggledy over wall-to-wall cream carpet and permeated by the scents of jasmine incense and wheat grass candles. Everywhere you looked there were statues of the Buddha, the elephant god Ganesh, the goddess of compassion Kuan Yin. As for Siri Sajan herself, she was one of the angels of this world. Her hair twisted into a light brown topknot over her Fra Angelica face and her pristine yoga garb putting my cat-hair covered sweat suit to shame, she managed to correct my poses without the slightest hint of judgment. I had to be the clumsiest yoga student who had ever lived.

My breathing was shallow, and I had to concentrate like crazy to even approximate the process of yogic respiration, my air tending to get trapped at the Muladhara chakra, propelling gas from my butt like an earlier incarnation of Sister Flatulencia. Siri Sajan never laughed at my body's crude rebellion, just commented, "Don't worry. Happens all the time. Try taking it a little slower on the inhale, letting your stomach really stick out before breathing up to your diaphragm."

Sure enough, even when I arrived at yoga class a good fifteen minutes late the next morning, Siri Sajan threw me a warm smile. As six pairs of eyes shot up at me from the carpet, I hurried to a corner, hastily removing my shoes and unrolling my purple mat. I'm afraid I was a worse student than usual that day, going through the motions on automatic pilot and breathing in all the wrong places. All I could think was: *Sammie's here.* We'd locked eyes for one millisecond when I'd entered the room.

Which didn't prevent me from feeling surprised when, after we'd finished our closing song, she came right over to me. "Sorry they're giving you such a hard time about your speech," she said, as I scrambled to my feet. "I read it in the paper. Quite interesting, actually. Not nearly as much of a cock-up as everyone's calling it."

I could have kissed her for that. Serena McKenna had been far more effusive in my defense, as had Nana, in her own way, with a churlish, "What do they know? Let *them* try and invent C-Voids" (which I hadn't, of course—only discovered them). But despite their kind efforts, it was Sammie's rather abbreviated comment that meant the most to me, for it signaled I hadn't been cast by her mind into some bottom-most pit of eternal nothingness.

Unfortunately, she slipped from the room before I could thank her. I did, however, manage to overhear another student ask my yoga teacher what the name *Siri Sajan* meant. My yoga teacher responded simply, "Great Friend."

The phone was ringing when I got back home. Throwing my yoga mat onto the floor, I snatched up the phone before the call went to voicemail. It was Dhani, her voice sounding unusually frothy, as if she were on the verge of giggling. I could hear Ignacio's favorite mariachi song, El Nino Perdido, blaring in the background. When I commented on it, she shouted away from the phone, "She can't hear me! You've got to turn it down." Speaking into the mouthpiece again, she said, "Sorry. It *is* bad, isn't it? Like a street full of crows."

Struck by the synchronicity, I jumped in with my recent experience at the Huntington Gardens. She replied with surprising eagerness, "Aren't they in San Marino?"

"What—crows?"

"No, the Huntington Gardens."

"Ye-sss," I said, puzzled by the non sequitur. "Why do you ask?"

Now she really *was* giggling. "Hang on a moment. I've got someone here who wants to speak with you."

Another voice came on. "Fleur?" It was Mother.

Disoriented, I asked, "What's going on? Are you guys having a party?"

Mother was laughing herself. "Well, I suppose you could say that. Certainly a celebration." Her voice grew more serious. "Listen, Fleur. Ever since Stockholm, I... well, frankly, I miss you terribly. It's ridiculous having you live so far away."

My body stiffened. If she thought I was going to leave So Cal...

But she must have read my mind. "Don't worry. I'm not asking you to move back. You've made too much of a life for yourself at Caltech. No, I'm coming out. *Moving* out. I've already got an AA contact working on it—an agent with Coldwell Banker. She's got a property that sounds perfect. It's on Courtland Avenue. She says San Marino is heavenly."

My knees threatened to buckle. It was lucky there was a chair behind me to catch me. My heart couldn't decide whether to beat unbearably quickly or simply stop.

It was Stanley, of course. He must have phoned Mother after our conversation and laid a royal guilt trip on her.

But now Mother was saying, "The terrific thing is that we're all coming out together. It'll be just like old times. Well, sort of. Nana, Cesar, Sister Flatulencia, Fayga. And—I'm so pleased—Dhani and Ignacio have just agreed to make the move, too. It'll be perfect. But listen, love. I've got to dash. I'm speaking at a meeting in twenty minutes. We've got so much to figure out—let's talk soon, shall we?"

I suppose I must have mumbled some sort of goodbye, because Dhani was back on the phone, her voice pitched high with excitement. "Your mother is such a generous woman, Fleur, bringing us all with her. What an adventure! I hear the weather's a lot like Delhi."

As she went on, a gob of bile welled up into my throat. Mother's little fiefdom. No wonder she'd decided she needed one of San Marino's famously huge homes. That crowd would hardly fit into a nice little Pasadena bungalow. And speaking of nice little bungalows, what about Gwennie and Stanley? Did Mother assume I'd simply jump at the chance to leave my adoptive family and move in with her? Had it occurred to her that trying to make amends in this way might just be a wee bit selfish, as in comet-crashing-into-my-current-life selfish?

But then I stopped myself. I'd gotten in the habit of closing the door on Mother, just as she'd once closed the door on me. The truth was something had been changing ever since Father died—as if the death of our mutual tyrant had loosened something in Mother. The question was, could it loosen something in *me*?

Dhani was busy rhapsodizing about what she'd heard about Southern California. It dawned on me that the crew of my first incarnation had been *her* adoptive family—of course, she'd want to come, too. As for me, I certainly wouldn't mind witnessing the growing up antics of Little Miss Phat Bling herself. What a great instance of the *sensitive dependence on initial conditions* it would be if my ignominious Nobel speech proved to be the catalyst to subsequent generations of Hindu-Catholic Hertados spreading their genes amongst the moguls and movie stars of Hollywood.

But Dhani had shifted gears. "I've had it with teaching cooking. I wouldn't half mind opening a little restaurant. Your mother's AA friend told her there's a sophisticated palate for fine Indian cooking where you are." I forced myself to focus on her complaints about the Cookery School. "You would not believe it," she moaned. "This is a dessert week. We have one a month, and guests stand in line to get in. My students worked very hard to create the most delicious sweets.

This time I chose some that are prepared especially for Holi: Besan Ke Ladoo—you will be happy to know made with real rose essence—Malai Peda, Sweet Puris. But what did they want seconds of? Kheer. Kheer, I tell you. Simple rice pudding."

Suddenly, I was filled with such profound nostalgia that I nearly fainted. Instead, I said, "Dhani, will you tell me how to make it?"

"It? What is the *it?*"

"Rice pudding."

I pictured Dhani pounding her forehead in frustration. But that wasn't about to stop me. I ran to fetch a pencil to write down my shopping list. Who knew what heaven could be made of milk, sweetened condensed milk, cardamom, sugar, Basmati rice, slivered almonds, raisins, and saffron?

When she returned home, Gwennie—who was always looking for ways to cheer me up—was only too pleased to drive me to Whole Foods. As I waited for her to pull her Prius out of the driveway, I saw a lone crow, suspended less than a foot from the ground, do a breathtakingly graceful glide, like a slow-pitched ball, from one side of the street to the other. I made a silent amends to the murder family.

As soon as I slid into the car, I told her the news. She sucked in her breath and nearly ran a stop sign.

"I'm not leaving you guys!" I cried.

She crossed the intersection and pulled over to the curb. Turning to face me, she said, "Okay, kiddo, you definitely took me by surprise. But listen; let's be smart about this. Your mom coming out here has to be a good thing, and I think at the bottom of your heart you'll agree. It's about time you had more of the pleasures of a normal life." She added emphatically, "If there's one thing I have no intention of doing, it's getting in between you and your mother." Then her eyes went all melty. "If there's another, it's stopping loving you. Wasn't it you who told me about the Big Pie Principle?"

I shook my head stubbornly. "That was Adam's idea."

"Well, fine. But it still applies. We're just going to have to learn to stretch a little more. Don't look so sad." Then she shot me a sly smile. "Besides, Rose Villa's a damned sight more convenient to Caltech than Courtland Avenue."

As usual, Whole Foods was thick with shoppers, elbowing one another and butting in line to get first dibs at the ripe mangoes and rice-cheese-and-spelt quesadilla samples. But we managed to get out of there in one piece. When we arrived home, we donned our matching *Physicists are Spicier* aprons. Gwennie helped me blanch the almonds without getting them soggy. Our very last step was to pour our preparation into pretty lotus-shaped bowls handcrafted in Delhi that Dhani had given me last Christmas.

I went to bed that night feeling slightly less voidish, even breaking into a little song as Jillily ritualistically licked my cheeks and chin. It was our Kundalini closing mantra: "May the longtime sun shine upon you, All love surround you, And the pu-ure ligh-ight within you, Guide your way on." I was well aware my voice was not nearly as mellifluous as Siri Sajan's, but it was evidently good enough to get Jillily's motor going on its strongest setting.

As I was dropping off, a television newscaster's voice infiltrated my bedroom from the den. Gwennie's hearing sure wasn't getting any better. The TV was so loud I could hear one of those excessively hearty weathermen forecasting tropical-type weather for tomorrow: "Time to break out the leis and hula skirts, folks. You're gonna get some bang for your buck. Expect some serious lightning storms along with that rain." Just before succumbing to the cocoon of sleep, it occurred to me how ironic it was that Zeus the Thunder God was also the Friend of Strangers.

The dream I had that night was devastating. In it I saw a young boy—barefoot, freckled, exuberant, his arms outstretched like angels' wings—sprinting across an open field until he disappeared into the horizon. Somehow I knew in my dream it was Grandfather, heading for his next incarnation. I woke to my own moaning. *Oh, Grandfather, I am going to have to let you go.* Then sleep wrapped me tight again.

When I emerged from my covers the next morning, my body was sticky with sweat. The weatherman had been right. The day had dawned hot and humid, teetering on the edge of rain—the kind of day that filled your very bones with lassitude and lethargy. Certainly not the sort of day you'd expect to see someone jumping rope at some speed, up and down the sidewalk. Now, I don't know about you, but I rarely see a fourteen-year-old skipping rope at all, let alone under a sky that looked like someone's heavily smudged mascara. I thought I discerned in that repetitive motion of hers—she could have gone around the block, after all—a kind of smoke signal.

I watched for a while, noting how much the hue of her blouse approximated the perfect pink of an Anne Boleyn. I decided she looked somewhat peckish. I wasn't surprised. With all that skipping, she'd undoubtedly worked up an appetite.

I ran to the fridge. The rice puddings had set perfectly. I felt pleased I'd taken the trouble to hydrate the raisins before adding them. They were the fattest I'd ever seen. I placed two of the bowls onto one of Gwennie's aquamarine trays, poured a little milk into each bowl, and carried the tray to the front door. Undoubtedly drawn by the sound of the milk carton being opened, Jillily nearly tripped me as I walked, rubbing in and out of my tread with her question mark tail as I tenuously transferred the tray to one hand to open the door. "Not now, my love. I promise I'll give you some later." She skittered away speedily enough as I opened the door to a dramatic drum roll in the sky. The clouds had burst and thick drops were beginning to fall.

Sammie looked up as I stepped outside, her expression somewhat impatient, as if we'd made a date to meet and I'd kept her waiting. I suppose I had. Her jump rope a sinuous snake at her feet, she simply stood there, getting wetter and wetter. Her black hair was curling into squiggles. Her Anne Boleyn blouse clung to her chest, a colorful contrast to her burnt sienna face. I thought she made quite a picture.

The pink and brownness of her reminded me I had a tweeter. Not that I was drawn to her as what Gwennie had once called *a sexual object* after we had witnessed two women kissing passionately on a shopping trip to Old Town. It was more that Sammie's budding breasts stirred a memory in me of my ambivalent adventure with the boy who'd named me Beautiful and all the subsequent chaos of sensation before I had a police pistol shoved in my face. For a brief moment, arrows of energy made me aware of my second chakra.

That was the thing about being fifteen. One moment you were a little green nub, itching with innocent playfulness, the next thing you knew you were a flowering reed, twisting and pulsing to an ageless rhythm. It was all so confusing.

There were a couple of noisy crackles, and the sky lit up like the Fourth of July. The rain was coming down hard now. The wind moved it in sheets, first in one direction, then another, criss-crossing random splotches of gum and bird poop and crazy-quilt cracks in the sidewalk. Everything smelled steamy, ripe, brand new.

I ran to Sammie's front porch right behind her, my tray an increasingly heavy pond with twin floating lotuses of pudding. Without a word, she took one of the bowls. I set down my tray. We sat side by side on the bottom step, our heads shielded by the overhang but our shoes too wet to even bother about. Our bodies touched at the shoulders and hips as we slurped our watery desserts, which made up in sweetness what they now lacked in bulk.

Sammie stuck out her tongue at me. It was a polka dot affair— moist pink skin coated with milky pudding and spotted in nice little patterns of almond slivers and raisin bits. I stuck my own tongue back at her, creamy drool spilling from the corner of my mouth. She said dryly, "Okay, you win the rank disgusting contest."

The two of us started tittering, which steamrolled soon enough into barely controlled hysteria. I think we both knew we had a lot of tough talking ahead of us. A drought of many months is hardly cured by one soaking. But for now it didn't matter. For now, the sky was alive with light and sound. The world was being washed, and we were being washed with it. We laughed as if we'd never laughed before.

I grabbed my tweeter. "Stop," I cried, "you're going to make me wet my pants." I snorted and rice pudding shot out my nose. You can imagine the impact of that one. The pee situation was becoming quite serious. I tried standing up, but that merely served to give gravity the upper hand.

I gave in then, gave up all the holding of a lifetime, peed in my pants in front of Sammie and Aadita's house. All the heaviness of the past fifteen years passed right through me—unbearable loss, confusion, and solitude spreading in a puddle that would soon enough be washed away by the rain.

Sammie saw the yellowish water pooling at my feet and howled. "Fleur Beurre," she cried, "you are the craziest bird I know." I didn't doubt for a millisecond that she meant it as a compliment.

"Takes one to know one," I managed to get out, sounding less like a human than a hyena.

I sensed the Lord looking down on us, His void bursting with wetness and curiosity and no small pride at what He and His butterflies had engineered this time. Watching me and my belly sister together again—laughing at nothing, laughing at everything. Savoring the sheer relief of it.

Seeing that it *was* good.

Acknowledgments

Many hands assisted in the birthing of this novel. Its emergence would not have been possible without discerning commentary on various drafts and extraordinary transfusions of practical and emotional support from my keen-eyed, luminous-souled offspring Claire Noble and Chris Heath, as well as "friends of Fleur" Harriet Friedman, Constance Crosby, Judie Harte, Robin Palmer, Jessica Trupin, Elizabeth Trupin-Pulli, Molly Jordan and Hawk Koch, the late Elizabeth Strahan, Deborah Howell, Sharon Weiner, Susan Bredhoff, and Bill Hornaday. I am indebted, as well, to the helpful advice and generous encouragement of Gilda Frantz, Michael Gellert, Naomi Lowinsky, Patricia Damery, Jeremiah Abrams, Deena Metzger, Jennifer Karson Engum, Tom Karson, Gene and Linda Karson, Barbara Horton, Siri Simran Khalsa, Judy Altman, Daniel House and Patty Micciche, Nancy Mozur, Cydny Rothe, Robin Wynslow, Jeanine Roose, JoAnn Culbert-Koehn, Kathie Clarke, Carolyn Raffensperger, Deborah Jiang Stein and the rest of my social media tribe, the stellar students of my Creative Daimon seminar, and the Women Analysts' Meeting of the C.G. Jung Institute of Los Angeles. And since I've played so fast and loose with science in this work of fiction (for which I should be held solely and personally responsible), my gratitude is great to Ara Chutjian, who tried to ensure that I didn't entirely butcher the kaleidoscopic worldview of quantum physicists, those masterful riders of the waves of cosmic reality and human possibility of whom I stand in absolute awe.